Til Death Do Us Bard

ROSE BLACK

Til Death Do Us Bard

HODDERSCAPE

First published in Great Britain in 2023 by Hodderscape
An imprint of Hodder & Stoughton
An Hachette UK company

1

A CIP catalogue record for this title is available from the British Library

Hardback ISBN 978 1 399 72468 5
Trade Paperback ISBN 978 1 399 72469 2
ebook ISBN 978 1 399 72470 8

Typeset in Plantin by Manipal Technologies Limited

Printed and bound in Great Britain by Clays Ltd, Elcograf S.p.A.

Hodder & Stoughton policy is to use papers that are natural, renewable and recyclable products and made from wood grown in sustainable forests. The logging and manufacturing processes are expected to conform to the environmental regulations of the country of origin.

Hodder & Stoughton Ltd
Carmelite House
50 Victoria Embankment
London EC4Y 0DZ

www.hodderscape.co.uk

To anyone who has ever felt unworthy of love.
I hope you learn to see yourself as those who love you do.

Content warning: mentions of domestic violence (not from the protagonist).

Chapter One

For the fourth time today, Logan regretted leaving his axe at home. Bodies pressed in around him. Shouts and cheers battered his ears. No chance then of hearing anything coming up behind him. A tightness in his chest stifled his breathing.

Long fingers closed around his own.

'We can go home if you like,' Pie whispered beside him.

Logan glanced at his husband – and by gods, that was still a strange-tasting word – and shook his head. A fluttering settled in his stomach, and his feet felt lighter. They'd been married six months, but Logan fell in love with Pie all over again every time he looked at him. The bard was tall and slender, with a jawline cut from marble and a smile like a summer's day, soft and warm.

Logan took a breath, forcing his swooping stomach to settle, and let his surroundings wash over him again. Not a battlefield, a festival. No monsters in sight. No one likely to creep up on him but a peddler or fortune-teller plying their wares.

And his expression alone was usually enough to keep them at bay.

'Don't fuss,' he said, as Pie paused to allow a group of children to pass. They carried pieces of a wooden ship, ready to put together on top of the bonfire at sundown.

'But fussing with you is my second favourite pastime,' Pie replied, his lip protruding into an adorable pout that made Logan want to bite it.

'No, it isn't. Your second favourite pastime is spinning elaborate tales to anyone who'll listen, and your third favourite is drinking,' Logan quipped back.

'You know me so well.' Pie grinned, and there was a note of satisfaction in his voice. Pie saw him, and Logan found that he liked being seen. 'Though I'd argue that those are work for a bard, not pastimes.' He held up a finger. 'Even the drinking. Especially the drinking. So, I redirect you back to my original point.'

Logan sighed. 'No fussing.'

Pie narrowed his eyes, scrutinising Logan for a moment before yanking on his hand and pulling him toward a couple of wooden benches near the makeshift bar. He pushed Logan onto a seat and returned a moment later with two tankards.

'Is your leg hurting?' He handed over one of the tankards, full of a dark and frothy ale. 'And before you say anything, that's not fussing. That's just asking a question.'

Logan shook his head. The serpentine scar on his calf never stopped aching, but the pain was easy to dismiss currently. He took a sip from his tankard, watching the strips of coloured cloth that were stretched across the streets flap lazily in the breeze. In the centre of the town square, children danced to a pair of pipers, and off to another side, a roast hog was turning on a spit over an open fire. The rich, meaty scent made Logan's mouth water.

He hadn't expected to retire – an uncommon outcome amongst adventurers. Logan had imagined his end in the form of slavering jaws in some gods-forsaken corner of nowhere. Now he had a cottage and a husband, and there was nothing to do today but drink and relax and anticipate eating roast pork.

If only it didn't make him feel uneasy.

'I saw you trying to reach for a weapon. Would you rather be out there' – he waved at the distant horizon – 'off fighting monsters?'

Logan took a long sip of ale and leaned against Pie. The uneasiness retreated. 'Out in the mud and rain, battling something slimy, poisonous, or both? What makes you think I'd give up a warm cottage and having my socks darned for that?

Besides,' he added with a growl in his voice, 'I can still be Logan the Bear for you whenever you like.' He pressed his teeth against Pie's ear.

Pie laughed. 'I'll take you up on that later. But I mean it. If you're not happy, we can just go home. We don't have to stay. I know you're not fond of music . . . or crowds.'

'I like music plenty,' Logan replied with a snort. 'Just not keen on bards.'

'Yet here you are, married to one.'

Logan rested his head against Pie's shoulder. 'This one's special.'

Part of him did want to go home. They didn't need the rest of the world when they had each other, and there was always more work to be done around the cottage. But he also knew how much Pie enjoyed playing with other musicians, and if it made his husband happy, then that was enough for Logan.

One of the pipers in the square called to Pie. Logan plucked the tankard out of Pie's hand and pushed him to his feet.

'Go on. I'm quite happy here.'

Pie picked up his lute and gave Logan a kiss. 'Don't drink too much, it makes you gassy. I love you.'

'*Cheek*.' Logan kissed him back. 'I love you too.'

The group of musicians struck up a lively jig, and more people poured into the square. A pair of women, gazes locked together, whirled around in perfect harmony, their quiet smiles mirrored on each other's faces.

Logan finished his beer, then Pie's, and set the tankards down on the bench with a thud. This time he'd do it right. This time he'd be a good husband. He headed over to the peddler's stalls on the far side of the square, fingering the coins in his pocket. A gift. That was a good start.

Children scattered as he passed, pointing and whispering in not-quite-hushed tones about his scars. He snorted. There were many more hidden under his clothing, along with the tattoos that told of monsters killed and battles won. Forty-two years marked out in ink on his skin. Little brats like that might think him scary, but he was not nearly as scary as the creatures that met their end at the blade of his axe.

Most of them had probably never seen an adventurer. The growing population had driven the monsters back to the wilder areas of the island, and there was little need for them in quiet towns like this one.

He felt the old twitch in his guts, the one that sometimes woke him in the darkest hours. The one that said he still had an obligation, that retiring was selfish. He told it to fuck off, as he always did, but remembering his past made it loud, bold. He could be an adventurer, out there protecting people, or he could be retired, settled down with Pie.

Bitter experience had taught him that he couldn't have both.

He forced his attention back to the sellers and their wares: pewter amulets of various patron gods, festival ribbons in red and yellow, and rings carved from hematite, but he settled on a soft woollen scarf that matched the green in Pie's eyes.

'Happy Founding Day,' the woman said, a note of wariness in her voice, as if she expected Logan to run off with her goods rather than offer her coin.

He grunted an acknowledgement. The anniversary of the country's birth meant little to him. 'How much?'

'Half a sovereign.'

Logan laughed. 'You're joking, right?'

'Not at all,' she replied with a dismissive sniff. 'Without magic, prices are on the rise. Do you want it or not?'

He haggled half-heartedly, then handed over the coins. He'd heard the king had forbidden magic use a year ago, but the consequences hadn't reached their tiny village yet. Magic wasn't a common skill, tending to run in certain families. Few of them tended to be adventurers. There was more money to be made in assisting trade; the country was known for a particularly fine spellcaster-produced glass.

The ban left him conflicted. On the one hand, magic had little direct influence on his life. But magic was as much a part of the country as adventuring was. Spellcasters had been amongst the early settlers who took on the job of taming the wild and abandoned island. And banning something simply because it was dangerous rankled him. Axes were dangerous. *He* was dangerous.

Would the king one day decide to ban adventurers?

Someone placed a hand on his shoulder, and Logan spun around, his hand instinctively reaching for his missing axe.

'Sorry to trouble you.' A barrel-chested man faced him down. Logan might have taken him for a fellow adventurer, but the black under his nails and the small burn marks on his shirt suggested blacksmith instead. 'We could use another strong pair of hands to help carry the wood over to the bonfire.'

Music drifted across the air and Logan shrugged. He shoved the scarf into his pocket. 'Lead on then.'

When he turned back to the square and the dancing, the two pipers and an enthusiastic tambor player remained playing, but Pie was nowhere in sight. Logan gazed around the revellers. Pie was tall, lanky, with auburn hair past his shoulders. He should have been easy to spot, even in a crowd.

Logan's stomach dropped and he started for the square at a run. People stared at him, and he forced himself to slow down. This was silly. Pie could be fetching more beer, or pissing, or talking to someone. The bard knew everyone in Stowatt it seemed, so it wouldn't be unusual for someone to pull him into a discussion.

After confirming that no one had seen Pie at the bar, or by the roasting hog, Logan moved away from the festivities. The town was small enough that it didn't have a gods-square, just a series of small shrines running down one street. Each of them was decked out in red and yellow flowers and ribbons, apart from the shrine to the death goddess, which had several sheep ribs arranged in a criss-cross pattern.

Footsteps ahead made him tense and reach once more for the axe that wasn't on his back. A man in a fox fur-lined cloak walked down the street towards him, head down. As he passed Logan, he raised his head and gave him a grin. Younger than Logan by some ten years, he had a narrow face with a small, scrawny goatee. Logan watched him walk away, an itch to fight scratching in the back of his mind.

The man's clothes, posture and expression screamed adventurer, but Logan didn't recognise him. Of course, he'd been out of the business for six months now. The bigger question was what an adventurer was doing here. Stowatt wasn't on any of the major roads, so it was unlikely any of the gentry needed escorting through the forests. No battles or wars. It could only mean a monster was on the loose.

He tensed, thinking of the children dancing in the square. Thinking of Pie. No axe, so he'd have to improvise. Or maybe the stranger had a spare weapon. Logan started to call to the man, but he'd disappeared. He was about to try and find him, when Pie suddenly called his name. Logan turned back to see his husband emerge from the same direction as the stranger.

'Logan . . . what are you doing?'

'I wasn't sure where you'd gone.' The words came out awkward, oppressive, controlling. He didn't mean Pie belonged under his thumb. He turned away to hide the heat creeping up his neck, but Pie caught his hand.

'Can we go home, please?' Pie glanced over his shoulder, then down at the ground. Anywhere but at Logan. He worried at his lower lip.

'Of course,' Logan replied instinctively, but . . . If Pie was safe at home, Logan could take his axe and go hunt. Been a while since he'd tracked anything, but the man had probably been staying at the tavern and he'd pick up the details there. Logan pulled Pie close. There was a sour scent to Pie's breath. 'Are you sick?'

'Think I ate something I shouldn't,' Pie replied. 'I'm fine. I just want to go home.' The words came out in a tumble.

But they'd eaten the same breakfast and Logan felt fine. He put a hand on Pie's forehead. His skin was a little clammy, but not hot. 'Did you see the adventurer?' he asked as they turned away from the main square and started back toward their cottage. 'Fox-fur cloak, crossbow, bastard sword, pair of daggers. Had a beard like a goat and a face that wasn't far off one either. There must be something wrong. Let me get you home and I'll come back and see what's up.'

'He's not an adventurer.' Pie shook his head. *Unlikely*, Logan thought to himself. 'He's just . . . just a messenger. He had an invitation to a gig, that's all.'

'I *see*,' Logan replied, catching the way Pie's eyes darted to every door and window. It was good there was no monster, of course it was. But for a moment, the call, the thrill of his old life had been loud in his ears. Now, a different feeling all together was settling into Logan. Pie was lying to him. Logan had never met a messenger with that many weapons. And the look he'd given Logan – that was one professional to another.

It was a short walk from the town to the village where they lived – the last vestige of civilisation pressed up against the moors, little more than a sprinkle of houses around an inn. If the little village had ever had a name, no one knew it anymore.

The cottage sat on a little rise away from the main cluster of homes, a single-storey building of whitewashed stone with a neat, thatched roof, surrounded by a bed of vibrant flowers. Such a simple, unassuming structure, but for Logan, who'd lived on the road for two decades, the sight of it often brought deep warmth to his heart.

Home.

Pie let himself in to start on supper, while Logan fed their pig and the pair of goats. He stomped past the little apple sapling he'd planted this spring, the leaves fluttering in the breeze. In a few years, the tree would bear fruit and then they'd plant more, maybe even have a whole orchard.

The itch he felt earlier had settled into a heavy knot at the base of his spine. Pie was prone to exaggeration, as all bards were, but he'd never lied.

Not to Logan.

He stamped the mud off his boots and paused, fingers not quite touching the front door. The idea of confronting Pie tied his stomach in knots. Besides, he was probably reading too much into things. Letting his own private fears cloud his judgement. If Pie said the stranger was a messenger, he was a messenger.

Inside, Pie spooned soup into two bowls and set them on the table. A fire burned in the hearth, bathing the walls in a warm light. Logan's axe on the wall reflected the glow from the fire. More ornament than weapon now.

Logan took a seat on the bench as Pie slid up against him, his hip pressing comfortably against Logan's. A bottle of whisky sat open in the centre of the table, some of the contents clearly missing. The sharp scent cut across the smell of warm broth and fresh vegetables.

'Where did you get that?' Logan asked. It hadn't been in the house this morning, and he hadn't seen Pie take it.

Pie shifted his gaze from the bottle to the floor in a swift motion. 'I, er, borrowed it. I'll pay them back. I thought we could have our own celebration.' He carefully poured measures into two wooden cups and offered one to Logan. 'Here's to Captain Miranda and the storm that blew her ship off course. And here's to our forgotten island full of monsters and dead necromancers. What a place to call home.'

Pie pushed the cup of whisky toward Logan, who accepted it without a word. Pie's tone was light, but the humour didn't reach his eyes.

'What's wrong?' Logan asked as Pie downed his cup in one and poured himself another drink. 'Did something happen earlier?'

'No. It's nothing,' Pie responded, knocking back his drink and reaching for the bottle again.

Logan nudged it out of his reach.

'It's nothing.' Pie sighed. 'I'd just rather spend the evening reminiscing with you. Do you remember last winter, when we got snowed in? Stuck in that inn, nothing to eat but that blood sausage that made everyone fart? If the snow hadn't melted when it did, I'm pretty sure we would have all suffocated!'

'The Prancing Foal,' said Logan. 'Only you called it the Farting Foul and the name stuck.'

'Innkeeper hated me,' Pie agreed. 'Not sure why. I happen to know he's done a roaring trade since I publicised that little adventure.'

Logan settled down to eat, some of his tension melting away. They shared more memories as the contents of the bottle slowly disappeared, and the sun gradually followed. By the time the stars were out, Pie was swaying on the bench.

'Bed,' Logan said firmly, smiling down at his husband. As Logan stood, something fell from his pocket. The green scarf. He picked up the delicately wrapped parcel and held it out to Pie. 'Here, I got you this today.'

Pie stared at the brown wrapping for a moment before snatching it out of Logan's hands and pressing it to his face. He failed to stifle a sob, which made Logan chuckle.

'Definitely time for bed.' Logan slung his husband's arm over his shoulder. 'It's only a scarf.'

'It's the best scarf,' Pie replied, his words slurred.

Logan manoeuvred him away from the table and hearth and over to the big bed that occupied much of the other half of the room. He eased his husband onto the big bear pelt, helped him out of his shirt, and untied the leather thong that bound his hair. Pie curled up, and Logan pulled the patchwork quilt Pie had made last winter over his shoulders.

'Gonna be with you shortly.' He kissed Pie's forehead. 'Just going to check on the pig.'

'Logan, I . . .' Pie caught his wrist. ' . . . I need to go to the city tomorrow. I broke a string.'

Logan glanced past the wooden clothes chest, Pie's discarded peacock-feather hat, and a collection of daggers with chipped blades he hadn't mended yet, until his gaze reached the lute perched against the wall.

The lute with all six strings intact.

The next day, Logan was regretting his life choices.

Well, not all of them. He'd never regret pushing Pie out of the way of that axe, and he didn't regret putting his foot down about walking to the city together. The ache in his leg was making him tire of other things, like people with axes and grudges. And having a husband who ducked and evaded all his questions.

The rain didn't help.

The region was notorious for it: a fine, consistent spray that didn't so much fall as smear itself across the air. There was no way to avoid it, no material that could keep you completely dry. No matter how high or tight your collar, the rain always found its way down your neck.

Pie, hungover and sullen, had spent the journey in silence once it became clear he wouldn't be able to prevent Logan from coming along. Logan had wanted to say something to explain that whatever Pie really needed in the city, he wouldn't judge him for it, but he couldn't find a way to start that didn't open with 'You lied to me.'

So, he pushed on through the rain despite the pain in his leg. He'd desperately avoided showing any weakness, setting the pace hard as he had done in his prime. Years ago, he could walk twenty-five miles in a day and still have the energy to kill any creature that crossed his path. But it was no longer years ago. The journey had taken most of the day, and there was no disguising the limp. The pain that came with every step brought waves of nausea. He stumbled, and Pie caught his arm.

'For a man nicknamed the Bear, you are as stubborn as a goat,' Pie said, breaking his silence. 'Put your arm around me, you great idiot.'

Logan gratefully put his arm around Pie's shoulder, taking some of the weight off his injured leg.

'I don't need a bodyguard, Logan. I don't need you to injure yourself because you think I'm weak.'

'I don't think you're weak.' Logan stared out across the moorland. The city was still about an hour's walk from here. 'I think you're precious.'

Pie sucked in a breath, his face flooding red. 'Dammit, you're not helping. You can't watch out for me every second of every day. You must trust me to take care of myself.'

'I *do* trust you.' Logan tightened his grip around Pie's shoulder, though the knot in his gut tightened. *You lied to me.* 'It's everyone else I don't trust.'

The road turned, and the city of Tallywell came into view below. Logan hadn't been back here since they passed through six months ago, looking for somewhere to settle down. High walls of pale grey stone jutted out of the ground, nestled in a bend in the river, standing taller than anything for miles around. The bulky barriers, ugly and functional, wrapped around the densely packed buildings inside, keeping them safe.

'Well, you're going to have to,' Pie muttered. 'Come on. It'll soon get dark, and they'll shut the gates on us.'

They passed through the wide city gates with plenty of time before dusk. As night settled in, the doors would swing closed, trapping those already here inside and keeping out anything creeping through the darkness. Things were better than they had been when Logan was a child – there hadn't been a monster attack in the area for seven or eight years now – but not enough that people would willingly give up the comfort of fortifications and closed doors.

At the gates, armed guards checked carts and wagons and compared faces against a series of sketches pinned up in the gatehouse. Their names were noted in a logbook before they were allowed to pass.

'Never used to be like this,' Logan muttered, and Pie shook his head.

Inside the walls, wooden houses crowded close together, facing off across muddy streets. Not only larger than Stowatt, it was also denser and darker, with no open spaces for dancing and bonfires. Beggars squatted at crossroads, and rats scuttled between alleys. The last time Logan passed through, it had been crowded but thriving. Now, the place had a pervading scent of dampness and dejection, as if folks here were waiting for the break in the clouds covering their lives.

The inn stood on the main thoroughfare, close to the gate. The open door spilled out warm firelight and snippets of conversation. Logan, cold, hungry and in pain, had never seen a more beautiful sight. Pie helped him to a table near the fire, and Logan sank into the chair with a contented sigh.

'Stay there,' Pie said. 'I'll go get us some supper.'

Logan waved him off, unable to help even if he wanted to. He let the heat of the roaring fire caress his aching body, washing away the throbbing pain and leaving behind a deep, simmering exhaustion.

The inn was busy tonight. Many of those gathered in the common room had the appearance of travellers. Their clothes were functional and worn, and that wary look in the eye gave them away. Now that magic was illegal, there were more travellers on the road, many carrying messages between towns. One more thing that had to be done by hand once again.

Pie returned with two tankards and a room key. He pushed one of the pewter vessels towards Logan. Not a dent or scratch on it. The ones at the local inn near their home all bore the marks of friendly and not-so-friendly arguments. In a small community, grievances didn't wander, and the inn gave them a beer-fuelled outlet.

'You know I love you, right?' Pie said, reaching for Logan. The tips of his fingers, calloused by lute strings, stroked the back of Logan's hand.

'Of course.' It had taken him a long time to believe it, believe he was worthy of it, but looking at Pie's earnest expression, he could never doubt it.

'I'm sorry about yesterday. But it's nothing, really.'

You're lying. Logan shook his head. He didn't want to push Pie. The middle of the common room wasn't the place for a fight. 'If you say so.'

A barmaid with a plait down to her waist and cheeks that dimpled when she smiled brought over two bowls of dark stew. Dumplings floated in the broth like clouds, and Logan's mouth watered at the rich scent. She said something quietly to Pie, who gave her a smile and a nod in return.

'They've agreed to let me sing,' he said as she wandered off again. 'Been a while since I've done it unaccompanied.' His fingers twitched as if missing the lute.

'You'll be fine.' Logan gave Pie's hand a squeeze.

Pie returned a small smile, looking down at the bowl in front of him. 'Thank you. I . . . I love you, and I want to be with you forever.'

They'd never been shy about saying it – *words never wore out, they just got more polished*, or so Pie said. But this was twice in short succession, and the words hit Logan like a blow. Especially as he'd had little more than a grunt or a nod out of Pie since they'd set out that morning. It didn't feel insincere. In fact, the opposite. Perhaps Pie was feeling more open now. If he could keep his husband talking, he'd get some answers.

'Forever,' Logan repeated, pointing his spoon to the knot tattoo on Pie's bicep. Such a small symbol to carry so much weight. His gaze dropped to his own matching mark, following the interlocking lines around and around. They'd married under the auspices of Hawkint, god of roots and hedgerows, mostly because they'd come across the stone shrine on the moor on their search for a place to settle down, and the moment had felt right.

Neither had any affiliation to the deity, but still, they'd said their oaths under the oak tree, sealing their promises with blood and ink. Marriage, the priest of the hedgerows said, was about roots growing together, twisting into one another.

Pie went back to staring into the bowl, his spoon trembling in his hand, and Logan reflected on how little he really knew about Pie's roots. He never spoke of his family, except once, earlier in the year, after his brother died. He was educated, but his accent was carefully cultivated to sound like everywhere and nowhere all at once. The first time they'd met, he'd worn a signet ring, but Logan had never seen him wear it again.

'Enough of this, Pie. You're in trouble, aren't you?' The words tumbled out before Logan could stop them. Pie's eyes went wide. He looked away.

'It's nothing. I just need to take care of a couple of things.'

'Why won't you talk to me about it?' Logan thumped a fist on the table. Pie flinched. The conversation in the room lulled as several people turned to stare. 'Whatever it is, I can help,' Logan whispered.

'No, you can't,' Pie said softly. His expression was haunted, a tear forming in the corner of his eye.

The barmaid hollered, pointing to the raised platform in the corner of the room.

'I need to go,' Pie said. 'They're ready for me.'

Logan grabbed his wrist.

'Tell me everything when you're done. Whatever it is, we can fix it together.'

Pie paused, his gaze fixed on something behind Logan. His lips moved, and then he nodded to himself. He leaned over and kissed Logan's cheek. 'I'll tell you everything. I promise.'

Logan settled back in his chair, calmer now. Any problem that existed could be defeated as long they could see it. Problems that floated in the shadows like wraiths, unacknowledged – those were harder to put down. Tonight, he'd get to the bottom of this, and tomorrow they'd start on the path to sorting it. He downed the rest of his drink, feeling the alcohol warm his insides, and signalled for another.

Pie's voice floated across the tavern, quelling the conversation. He sang of a mermaid who gave comfort to the lost and lonely. It was magic the way a bard could dominate the room with their voice, as if the music made them greater than their physical form. Even without his lute, each note carried echoes and images, emotions that bypassed the mind and buried themselves in the heart.

The barmaid brought Logan another tankard but refused his coin. He shrugged as she walked off, her braid swaying hypnotically behind her. It wasn't unusual to be drinking on the bard's tab. The warmth, ale and Pie's soothing voice wrapped around him all lulled Logan into a comfortable stupor. He hoped the neighbours were feeding the pig well and that it was receiving its customary scratch behind the ears..

Whatever Pie's problem, they could fix it, tomorrow. Together.

Midway through Pie's set, Logan's head began to droop. Pie finished his song and announced he was taking a break and would be back shortly. He walked back to the table and put an arm around Logan's shoulder.

'No falling asleep here, you,' he said, his expression soft and loving. 'Come on, let's get you to bed.'

Logan finished his drink, something gritty irritating the back of his mouth. He staggered to his feet, the heat of the room making his vision swim. He put his arm around Pie's shoulder, letting the bard lead him upstairs.

He hadn't noticed himself getting this drunk.

'I'm sorry,' he said, leaning against the wall as Pie unlocked the door to their room. 'Don't know what's come over me.'

'It's probably the consequences of your stubborn arse marching at full speed for ten miles today,' Pie replied, his face pinched into a frown.

Logan staggered into their room and slumped onto the bed, sinking into the straw mattress. His back would hate him in the morning, but he didn't have the energy to care. Pie pushed Logan's shoulders down so he was staring up at the wooden beams of the ceiling as they swam in and out of focus. A moment later, he took off Logan's boots and sat on the bed next to him. He whispered something in the darkness that might have been 'I love you' or maybe 'sorry', or maybe it had just been Pie's breath against Logan's skin.

Logan closed his eyes.

When he woke again, the sun had risen, and the room was empty.

Pie was gone.

Chapter Two

The sensible, more rational part of Logan's mind guided him out of bed and into his boots before he started assessing the situation. Pie was just downstairs fetching breakfast, or perhaps he'd slipped out early to pick up catgut. The less rational part of him was worried he'd never see his husband again. A deeper, quieter, part of him wanted to point out that his head hurt and the grip he had on last night's meal was getting more tenuous by the minute.

The room was bare, apart from the bed, with no obvious signs of Pie. No clothes, not even a stray hair. Just Logan's own bag, sitting at the end of the bed. He grabbed it and slung the axe on his back. Logan could remember Pie here last night. He remembered the soft brush of his breath on Logan's cheek, but the rest of the evening blurred into a mess of warmth and beer. He'd only had a tankard, maybe two. He probed his tongue around his teeth, noting the same grittiness he had the night before. His vision faded, the room spinning, forcing him to reach out and grip the wall.

Had Pie drugged him? His heart hammered in his chest. Logan closed his hand into a fist as a wave of fear and pain surged through him. The idea turned his stomach. No, impossible. Pie wouldn't do that to him. Wouldn't run knowing that Logan would go mad with worry. Logan recalled Pie's words last night: *I'll tell you everything. I promise*. He'd been willing to open up, had admitted he was in trouble. But if it was not Pie who had drugged him, then who else? And if they'd done this to him, what had they done to Pie?

Rational Logan lost control.

He burst out of the room, slamming the door behind him with enough force to shake it and elicit several angry curses from the neighbouring rooms. Logan ignored them and took the stairs three at a time, skidding into the common room. The innkeeper gave him a lazy glance, as if large, unkempt men crashing into his taproom at sunup was a common occurrence.

'Where's Pie?' Logan said, slamming his hands on the bar. The tankards hanging above him clattered together like alarm bells. The man took a hurried step back, raising his eyebrows.

'W–what pie? We haven't served pie for three days now.'

'Not pie, Pie. Magpie.' Logan gritted his teeth, forcing himself to take deep breaths. He wouldn't achieve anything rambling like a madman. Except possibly a visit from the ever-friendly city guards. 'My *husband*, the bard. He played here last night. Where is he?'

The innkeeper's eyes widened.

'The bard? Are you talking about the fight last night?' He looked away, rubbing the back of his neck. 'Look, perhaps you better sit down for this. It was an argument over dice or something. Bunch of brutes they were, never seen them before. I don't think they took a liking to your bard's tone.'

A chill settled in Logan's gut.

'What are you saying?'

The innkeeper gestured to the chair again before giving Logan a resigned look when he refused to sit.

'Your bard got stabbed, pretty bad. I'm sorry.'

The room spun around him, words echoing in his head. *Stabbed.*

'I really am sorry,' the innkeeper retrieved his cloth from where it sat on a firkin of wine and went back to polishing. He lowered his gaze as Logan's world shattered in slow motion around him.

'Where is he?' Logan demanded. 'Where were the guards?' They'd been all over the city gates last night. Why didn't anyone try to stop the fight? More guards were seen every day, persistent in their hunt for spellcasters. No one was willing to risk a night in the cells because of a bar fight.

'Afraid I can't tell you more than that.' The innkeeper sighed, rubbing his neck. 'If you want to know, I guess your best bet is a necromancer. There's one living out west on the moors.'

'Where?' Logan asked.

The innkeeper gave him directions to the necromancer. Logan tried to focus, but panic squeezed at his heart. *Please, be okay Pie. I'm coming.* His vision faded in and out. Suddenly, the taproom was too hot, too small. The smell of last night's ale a stifling fog. Logan staggered through the inn's doors and into harsh daylight. Outside, the noise hit him like an axe blow. He managed two steps before doubling over and vomiting into the mud. People leapt out of his way, groaning and berating him as a drunkard. Logan didn't care.

With his stomach empty, his head felt clearer. The pounding headache faded to a dull throb at the back of his skull. It didn't make sense. He knew Pie gambled, knew he wasn't always good at it. The pale bands on his fingers from missing rings were a testament to that. As was the constant ache in Logan's leg, a gift from a disgruntled loser who'd accused Pie of cheating. But Pie hadn't even picked up a pair of dice since that day. Right? There was more to this. There had to be more to this.

How much had Pie been hiding from him?

He'd never paid much attention to Pie's tattoos, other than the marriage knot, and now he found himself regretting not knowing more about his husband. He knew Pie's patron deity was Mav, the god of open roads and weary steps, flipped coins and lucky finds. Unusual for a bard, though many travellers chose Mav, of course. But then so did less savoury types – pickpockets, gamblers, bandits.

Pie was a bard, not a bandit.

Your bard got stabbed, bad.

The thought made him retch again. Pie wasn't dead. Pie couldn't be dead. They had a life to live together. Logan pictured returning to their empty cottage and lying in their bed alone. The image squeezed at his heart, threatening to shatter it, until bile began to rise from his throat once more.

He spat a mouthful of sour saliva onto the street.

Necromancer.

He clung to the idea like the handle of his axe. A necromancer would know if a soul had moved on or not, right? And then he'd know for sure that Pie was alive. The rush of emotion made him giddy. And who knew, maybe it was a good way to find out where Pie was.

The dead were everywhere, after all.

The innkeeper's instructions had slipped from his mind, and it took a while to convince someone else to give him directions. When he mentioned the word *necromancer,* people cowered, swore or made religious signs at him. The few necromancers that were around these days seemed inclined to cause mischief on a much smaller scale, but stories of the empire lived around the campfire. And, of course, no one wanted to speak of magic of any kind with the guards looming. Eventually, with a few pointed comments about the axe on his back, a harried tinker gave him hushed directions to a place half a day's walk away.

I'll find you, Pie. I promise. If you're still in there, wait for me, Logan vowed as he strode from the city gates.

Half a day turned out to be most of a day at his pace. A horse would have made the journey smoother, but of the two of them, it was Pie who made the money. Logan mostly tended their animals and garden. Sometimes he managed to barter his skills around the village – a pile of wood chopped for a pail of milk. He only had a few sovereigns of change in his pocket.

When he got there, there was no doubt he'd reached the right place. The two-storey wooden house looked comically out of place in the empty moorland, as if it had been plucked from somewhere more civilised and plonked down here, out of the way. A yew hedge, neatly trimmed, separated the wilderness from an elegant flower garden, where two skeletons tended blood-red roses.

One of them wore a straw hat.

Logan did his best to ignore them as he mounted the uneven steps to the house. He pulled a rope by the door until a bell tolled a sombre tone somewhere inside. As he stood on the doorstep, he worried at a bit of loose skin on his thumb. By the time the door opened, he'd worked it off completely, and a tear of blood ran down his wrist. A skeleton stared back at him.

'Um,' he said, rubbing the blood away. 'I need to speak to the necromancer.'

They eyeballed each other, or at least, Logan eyeballed the skeleton, and the skeleton eye-socketed him in return. From inside the house, a voice dripping with refinement called.

'Who is it?'

A moment later, and with considerably less elocution and considerably more annoyance, it continued, 'By the Dark Mother. One moment.'

A gloved hand pushed the skeleton out of the way, and a woman in a long black silk dress stood before him, her greying hair piled high on her head in a style that reminded Logan more than a little of a gravestone.

'I'm terribly sorry,' she crooned. 'The skeletons make good servants but are absolutely appalling doormen. It's the lack of tongues, you see.' Her eyes widened, and she clapped her hands together with a giggle. 'Well, if it isn't Logan the Bear! Fancy seeing you again. I hope you haven't come to cause me trouble. I've got a special dispensation to practise my arts.

I have a charter.' She pronounced the word with at least three As and rolled both Rs.

Logan blinked. He stared at the woman, and a memory of a damp moor and a ravaged tomb surfaced. He resisted the urge to reach for his axe. He needed her skills, now, as unsettling as that felt. 'I remember you. I took you in for grave - robbing.'

She gave him a deep curtsy that somehow managed to also feel like an insult. 'Countess Ariadne DeWinter, at your service.' She looked up, a glint in her eyes. 'Unless you've come to try and arrest me again, of course.'

Logan shook his head. 'It's your art I need. I need to find out if someone's . . . passed on.' He choked out the last words, and his stomach lurched again. He pressed a fist to his lips.

'Poor boy. Come in, and let's see what the spirits can tell us, shall we?' The countess patted his wrist.

She bustled into the house, her silk skirts whispering as she moved. The skeleton doorman gave him a stiff bow and extended a hand. Logan entered, doing his best to keep as far away from it as possible.

Tiles of red, white and black covered the floor of the entrance hall, thrown down in a haphazard fashion. Every time Logan thought he caught a hint of a pattern, it changed. The walls were a more traditional dark wood panelling, with paintings hung at intervals: small birds, a pair of melons, and two eggs lying by a parsnip. Each one managed to be both entirely innocent and yet somehow deeply suggestive.

The countess led him to a wide room overlooking the roses, with plump, worn, dusky pink furniture and a roaring fire in the hearth. Vases of flowers dotted every surface, filling the room with a heady perfume that made his nose itch. She gestured to one of the seats and sat in the other, skirts and chair creaking merrily.

The hair rose on the back of Logan's neck. Something about the normality of the place set his teeth on edge; it was worse than if it had been decorated with skulls and tombstones. He perched on the edge of the seat, afraid he'd be swallowed up by the cushion if he sat back. A skeleton offered him what looked like a chamber pot. Someone had painted pink rosebuds around the edge.

'Wha—?' he asked, too out of his depth to fully articulate the word.

'We've found grief can be a messy business, especially coupled with some of the . . . visuals.' The countess waved a hand in a quick circle. 'And you're looking rather green already, dear. The skeletons don't like mopping the floor if they can help it.'

Logan didn't realise the undead had much choice in their labour. He shook his head.

'Someone slipped something into my drink last night. I'm fine now.'

The skeleton pushed the pot at him harder. Logan rolled his eyes at it.

'They call me the Bear,' he growled. 'I've killed many men and seen their insides splashed on the ground. I'm sure whatever you do will not turn my stomach.'

The countess gave the skeleton a dismissive wave and it stepped back. She smiled and patted her knee. 'Ossy? Ossy, where are you?' A skittering sound made Logan lift his head, his hand reaching for his axe. Something small and white shot into the room, leaping at the countess's skirts. She picked it up, a wide smile lighting up her face, and placed it on her lap. It appeared to be the skeleton of a small dog. She stroked her hand over its smooth skull, and its little tail wagged furiously. 'Ossymandias, you naughty boy, where have you been?'

'Can we get on with this, please?' Logan said. His headache had returned, along with an itch that ran from the back of his neck to his fingertips.

It took a special mind to be comfortable commanding the bones of the dead, and that sort of mind slipped easily to the sort of behaviour that adventurers were called on to stop. He could deal with that. He killed the undead and their masters. He didn't sit around in their comfy armchairs and pet their skeletal puppies. Every nerve screamed at him to get out, to get away from this place.

But he couldn't.

Not until he knew.

'Very well,' the countess said, her prim accent settling back down like the folds of her skirts. She gestured to the skeleton still hovering with the chamber pot. 'Go fetch my things. Now, what is the name of the person you wish to ask about?'

'Pie, er Magpie. He's a bard.' Logan's tongue felt too big for his mouth. A bead of sweat rolled down the side of his face, despite the fact his guts felt chilled. The countess smiled sweetly.

'I need his full name, Logan,' she said, as if talking down to a child. 'The dead are legion. If you're not precise then you could get misinformation.'

'It's . . . it's Al . . . Ala, no . . .' The chill in Logan's guts turned to ice. How could he not know his own husband's name? Sweat, dripped into his eye. He was going to fail Pie at the very first hurdle.

The countess's eyes widened. 'Al? You mean the bard with the red hair who was with you when you captured me? Oh, I liked him. Terribly dirty sense of humour.' She cleared her throat. 'Now, what was his name? Alistair? Alphonse?'

'Aloysius!' they both announced together.

'Aloysius Montague,' Logan said softly. Pie had been Pie to him for so long now.

The skeleton was back, holding an iron pot overflowing with items and smelling like an apothecary. The countess took the cauldron and handed the skeleton a piece of chalk. It knelt, knees knocking hollow against the wooden floorboards, and proceeded to draw an intricate circular design on the floor.

'I should really get that painted there,' the countess said, 'but I just haven't been able to find the right rug to cover it up when we don't need it. It doesn't fit with the aesthetic.'

She set the little dog on the chair and put the pot in the middle of the design, muttering under her breath. Then she shook out little cloth bags so a shower of dried herbs fluttered down. The air filled with a strange spicy scent that reminded Logan of the gods-square in the city. Next, she lit five black candles, placed them around the edge of the circle, and turned to Logan, knife in hand.

'Palm, please.'

Logan tensed, years of training, experience and muscle memory reacting to the presence of a blade pointed at him. The countess gave him another patronising smile.

'Do you want to complete the ritual or not? I just need a bit of blood. I'm not going to take your heart.' She held up a gloved hand and tittered behind it, as if she were at court and the most eligible man in the room had made a joke. 'I can use mine, but experience has shown the seeker's blood is far more effective.'

'Fine.' He reached out and she gripped his wrist with surprising strength. She drew the knife in a quick motion, opening a red line that crossed the other scar on his palm. The one that had been opened when he and Pie said their vows and mingled their blood at a wet and windy moorland shrine.

He closed his eyes, remembering Pie's face, his eyes shining, the smiles and tears matching the sunshine and showers of the day. A happiness so sharp and overwhelming it hurt far more than any cut. His insides knotted and he bit down on his lip. Suddenly, he didn't want to do this. He didn't want to know. Couldn't bear the certainty if the news were bad.

It would be better to search the world hopelessly for Pie than to know he was really gone.

'I call to those who listen and bind you with this blood,' the countess called out. She held Logan's palm above the circle so the blood dripped over the pattern. 'I seek the one named Aloysius Montague, known also as Magpie the Bard. If he be beyond the veil of mortal sight, then step forward and be known.'

Logan held his breath. Dark spots danced in front of his vision and his chest burned, but he couldn't let it go. If Pie spoke, he didn't want to breathe again.

'Nothing,' the countess announced, a smile creasing her face. 'Well, Logan dear, it seems like you're in luck. Your friend is still this side of the Dark Mother's gate. Isn't that good, Ossy?' She picked up the puppy and kissed it on its smooth white forehead.

Relief slammed into him, knocking the breath out in a noisy gasp. Pie was alive! He leaned forwards, trying to calm his heart, and caught the skeleton staring at him. Probably trying to decide if it needed to make a dash for the chamber pot.

Now what?

Pie was alive, but that was as much as he knew. He had no idea what Pie wanted in Tallywell, if he was meeting anyone, or where they might be heading. Had any of the innkeeper's story been true?

He'd been in too much of a panic this morning to think straight. Now, if anyone staying in the inn had seen Pie, chances are they were long gone too. He smacked a fist against his leg. The countess, seated once more in her chair, watched him, her hand moving rhythmically over the dog's skull.

'Can you find him?' He waved a hand in the direction of the chalk sketch. 'Can you ask them if they know where he is?'

The countess toyed with a loose lock of grey hair. 'Ask the dead? Well of course I can, but the dead do not tend to pay much attention to the matters of the living. Which is lucky, really, because the ones that do tend to try and push back through the veil. And I know you don't approve of such things.'

Logan shuddered. He certainly did not approve of things that should be dead bothering the living. No matter what the person had been like in life, death changed them and never for the better. But he'd do anything he could if there was even the slightest chance of finding Pie.

'It's worth a shot,' he muttered, and the countess nodded. She set the little dog down on the floor. With a dagger so fine and sharp it could have been an oversized needle, she pricked her thumb. Five drops of blood fell, extinguishing the candles one by one. The room darkened, as if someone had thrown a shroud over the window. Logan rubbed his arm as his breath came out in white clouds.

'I open the veil and call upon all who hear me. Enter my circle and speak freely if you have word of Aloysius Montague.'

Silence pressed against his ears, thick and heavy. His heart crept up his throat and it hurt to breathe. A faint smell, part dust, part smoke, filled his nose and something appeared in the circle.

It started as a weak light, four feet off the ground, until it expanded to the size of one of the skeleton's skulls. Sparks danced around it, moving up and down, forming bones. Then came the organs and the blood vessels, and then Logan understood the need for the chamber pot. It didn't disgust him as much as fascinate him, watching a person appear from their core to their skin – but then he'd seen the insides of more folk than most.

The figure stood in the circle, feet not quite touching the floor. Raising his gaze from the toes, he looked at a pair of angry eyes, drawn into a deep glare. And then he did feel sick.

'Oh shit,' Logan said to his ex-wife's ghost.

Interlude

Twenty Months Ago

Of course there'd be a bard. There was always a bloody bard. Logan cast his gaze over the assembled group and struggled not to let his irritation bleed through to his face. Five altogether – three nobles in bright silks and swirling cloaks on fine horses, a bodyguard who had far too few scars for Logan to have any faith in his accomplishments, and the bard, wearing a ridiculous wide-brimmed hat, perched on a tree stump, strumming a hand idly over his lute.

Logan cleared his throat.

The dark-haired nobleman on the lead horse turned to him, fixing him with a stare that left no doubts about his opinion of Logan. 'You're our guide?' He sniffed.

'Logan Theaker. They call me the Bear.' He held out a hand, but the man turned his mount away.

'I am in a hurry.'

Not enough of a hurry that you'd hire a horse for me, too. He didn't mind the walk, though, as long as his paymaster didn't spend the journey making pointed comments about speed. Logan liked horses, but they could be flighty, shying at anything and everything. And if they did encounter anything, he fought better when his arse wasn't numb from hours on the saddle.

'Let's get moving then. We'll have you in Southfalls by tomorrow,' Logan announced.

He set off at a brisk walk, leading the way down the wide road, his boots squelching through the churned mud. This kind of herding was his least favourite part of being an adventurer, but unfortunately the best paying. Logan gritted his teeth and put his head down, focused on walking. The three nobles didn't seem interested in conversing with a hireling like Logan, and as long as the other bodyguard wasn't chatty, and the bard . . .

The bard was coming towards him.

Logan pushed hard, trying to outpace him, but the bard had caught his eye and offered him a bright smile, revealing a set of impeccable white teeth.

'Good day, Mister Bear,' he said, sweeping off his hat in an elaborate bow.

Bards. Logan snorted. Couldn't even say hello in a sensible manner.

The man held out a hand. 'Pleasure to meet you. I'm Aloysius Montague.'

'That's a bloody stupid bard's name. The fuck am I calling you that.'

The bard blinked, staring wide-eyed. Logan tensed, waiting for him to storm off in a huff. He hadn't meant to be quite so blunt, but bards always set his teeth on edge.

'Well, I suppose . . . I suppose I go by Magpie sometimes. Would that suffice?' He offered the hand again.

'Guess it will do.' Logan shook the hand once. Magpie had long slender fingers, adorned by numerous rings, with a softness and cleanliness that confirmed affluence.

He'd hoped that the handshake would be enough to make the man move on, but he fell into step beside Logan, whistling in the sunshine. Logan glowered at the dirt. Of course there'd be a bloody bard.

Chapter Three

'Logan Theaker, I should have known I'd find you. Anywhere there's trouble, you're always at the centre of it.' The spirit waggled a finger, taking a step towards him. As her hand crossed the edge of the circle, it vanished as if it had been lopped off at the wrist. She snatched the hand back and glared at him.

'Hello, Ophelia,' Logan said softy. 'I'm sorry you're dead.'

It wasn't much of a greeting, but what else was there?

'You damn well should be. This is entirely your fault.' She shook her finger – more carefully this time – at him.

Logan blinked. 'How is this my fault?' Her words felt like sand, getting under his clothes, chafing his skin. Death hadn't changed that. 'You left me, remember?'

'You'd have to be there for me to leave.' She rolled her eyes. 'You'd rather spend your days hunting monsters through the mud than spend any time with me.'

He folded his arms. 'Hardly surprising. I got less of a tongue-lashing from the beasts.' He caught the countess watching them with undisguised amusement and growled under his breath. 'What are you staring at?'

The countess held up her hands.

'Apologies. There's a lack of gossip this far out of town. I didn't realise you had an ex-wife, Logan.'

'It was an *arranged* marriage.' He pushed his hand through his hair. 'It didn't work out.'

Ophelia flashed him a look of hurt and pain, laced with hate.

'It didn't work out because you have no heart. You only ever cared about killing monsters.'

'Enough. Make her talk.' He jabbed a finger at the ghost. 'Make her tell me where Pie is.'

'Only you would summon the dead to satisfy your stomach, Logan.' Ophelia tossed her head. Her black ringlets glowed with an ethereal light.

Logan ignored her and spoke directly to the countess. 'I don't care how you do it, but do feel free to make it as painful as possible.'

The countess clapped her hands together once, the sound muted by the black silk gloves she wore. She turned to Ophelia and gave her a warm smile.

'My name is Countess Ariadne DeWinter. You stand in my circle, summoned by my power. You must speak the truth and only the truth to me. What do you know of a man named Aloysius Montague?'

Ophelia fixed her attention on Logan. 'Before I tell you, I want you to promise me something.' She set her hands on her hips, her eyes boring into his skull. He pulled his gaze away, staring instead at a dark stain on the wooden floorboards. 'Come on, Logan. You dragged me from my eternal rest. The least you can do is one favour.'

'Fine.' He couldn't lift his head, couldn't meet her eyes and see that judgement. She made him feel unworthy, and he was. He'd let her down as a husband, all those years ago. But he couldn't fail Pie now.

'Good. Then you must agree that I come with you.'

Logan couldn't breathe. He gasped, struggling like a fish out of water. Ophelia folded her arms, no pity in her expression.

'What?' he managed, choking the word out.

'Ever the elegant wordsmith,' Ophelia said, with a smile that didn't reach her eyes. 'I'm sure we'll make a bard out of you yet.'

Bard was the wrong word to say to him. Logan propelled himself out of the chair, standing face to face with her. His eyes were level with her forehead, and he could see the ghostly impression of her brain and then the countess through her translucent form.

'Don't toy with me, *spirit*, or I'll send you back to the pit you crawled out of.'

'Oh, sit down, Logan. You don't scare me.' She folded her arms. 'Now, you agreed to my terms, so if you break your word, I can take what I know back to the other side. Or are you going to be an adult and let us help each other?'

He stared her down, breathing hard. His hand twitched, longing to pull the axe from his back and drive it through her. It wouldn't have accomplished anything, of course, but it was tempting to see what reaction it provoked.

'I rather like this one, too,' the countess said, breaking the staring match between Logan and Ophelia as they turned towards her. 'You are excellent at selecting your partners, Logan, even if you do struggle to hang on to them.'

He sank back into the chair, his guts twisted. Of course, the common factor was him. He was bad luck. Something touched his shoulder. Logan found the skeleton standing over him, patting his shoulder gently. He pushed the bony fingers away in disgust.

'I don't have any choice, do I? Fine, stay then, if you can. That's rather up to her.' He flicked his thumb towards the countess.

Ophelia tucked one foot behind the other, put her hands behind her back, and pivoted towards the countess, wide-eyed and with a pleading smile in full force.

'Please, Lady Ariadne, you'll want to hear this too.'

' I can bind you to myself keep you in this realm should you wish, but most ghosts don't enjoy it very much.'

If the words worried Ophelia, she didn't show it. She clenched her fists in triumph and gave them both a grin.

'Here's the deal. The word among the dead is that King Ervin is putting a team together to go after the Chalice of Vivax. That's where I heard the name Aloysius Montague mentioned. He's part of the king's team to retrieve it.'

The countess's hand shot up to her mouth.

'The Fleshpot? Someone's trying to find the Fleshpot?'

Logan choked. 'Are . . . are you sure that's the right word, Countess?'

'Just a nickname, Logan dear.' She raised an eyebrow, a teasing look in her eye. 'I shan't use it if you're a delicate soul. Anyway, the point is that thing is practically a myth. A story to tell young necromancers at bedtime.'

'Do you want to explain for those of us who aren't tainted by the dark arts?' Logan stomped a foot against the floorboards.

Ophelia shot him a dirty look. '*Tainted* my left foot. I'm only dead because—'

'Enough bickering,' the countess said in a firm tone that reminded Logan of his mother. 'The Fleshpot, er, the Chalice, is the ultimate necromancer accessory – it can create flesh bodies. Skeletons are all very well, but it takes power and concentration to keep the bones held together. And other things like ghosts, well, they have an annoying habit of keeping their own minds and their own agendas. But an army of fleshy bodies to control? A lady could do a great deal with that.' She stared out of the window, rubbing her hands together.

'Seems a very good reason to keep you far away from it,' Logan said. 'Keep anyone away from it. Why on earth would the king want something like that? And why would Pie be involved?' He narrowed his eyes at Ophelia. 'Why do you want to be involved?'

'Isn't it obvious?' the countess said. 'She wants to live again. With a body, I could cast her spirit into it, and she could live out the rest of her natural life.'

'Oh.' He sat back in the chair, the wind knocked out of his argument. 'I see.'

The countess clapped her hands together. 'Well, that settles it. We shall set out and recover the Fleshpot. Ophelia here will get her life back, Logan will rescue his husband, and I shall raise an army.'

'No army,' Logan said firmly.

She pouted. 'Not even a little one?'

He shook his head. 'Not even a little one. You start turning up with an army, and people are going to start getting antsy. That tends to lead to people putting their swords through your shiny new toys and setting big bonfires for you. Trust me.'

The countess gave him a theatrical sigh. 'Hmph. You're absolutely no fun, Logan. I'm sure Aloysius would let me have a very small army at least. But you raise a good point. People do tend to overreact a bit. I had to do some very fast talking when you brought me in, I'll tell you.' She tapped a finger against her chin. 'Of course, if I had an army . . .'

'There will be no armies.' Logan pinched the bridge of his nose. The countess opened her mouth and he held up a hand to stop her. 'I'll find something to reward you, if you help me find Pie. But I'm not letting you raise an army, because then no doubt I'll end up stopping that army. It just seems easier to skip that step, and then you can go back to your skeletons and I can go back to my home and my pig.' He hoped the animals were being looked after. They'd asked a neighbour to feed them, but that was only supposed to be for a day.

Her mouth opened and shut a few times.

'You keep pigs?' Ophelia asked, one eyebrow raised.

He scowled. 'Yes – well, one pig. His name is Bacon. And goats. See, I can look after things, not just kill them.'

'What are the goats called, Milk and Cheese?'

'Bastard and Other Bastard. Then Pie said I wasn't allowed to name any more animals.'

He thought she'd roll her eyes at him, or at least laugh like the countess. Instead, she gave him a thoughtful, almost wistful smile.

'It sounds like you have a nice home,' she said quietly.

'Yes, and I'd like to be back there as soon as possible.' He stood up, not meeting her eye. Something about her sudden change in demeanour made him uncomfortable. He could deal with her sniping at him. That was fair. Sympathy, if that's what this was, felt off.

'Come on, let's get on with it.'

'Logan, it's less than an hour until sunset,' the countess argued. 'Now's not the time to be setting off into the darkness unprepared. I mean, I'd be fine – skeletons don't need light to see by – but I'm not sure you want to be riding a living horse through the dark. Assuming, of course, you even have a horse?'

He did not, of course, have a horse.

'Stay here tonight,' she said. 'We'll have a meal like the civilised folk we are and set out nice and early in the morning. How about that?'

Logan paused. He could leave now, walk through the night, hope each step took him closer to Pie. But he had no idea where his husband was, so they could just as easily take him in entirely the wrong direction. He closed his eyes.

'Fine.'

Dinner was more meat than he'd eaten in a while, and Logan hated every minute of it. Instead of the low bench by the fire, the countess had a vast dining table with uncomfortable high-backed chairs. At home, he ate snuggled up close to Pie. Here, they sat at opposite ends of the table so Logan had to shout if he wanted to be heard.

Not that he did.

Skeletons carried food to the table, which made him twitch. He was more used to them coming at him with a sword than setting down a rare slab of meat. Part of him longed to smash the bones to dust, but, for the moment at least, he needed Ophelia, which meant he needed the countess. He hadn't seen Ophelia since the countess released her from the ritual circle, and he had the chilling suspicion she was watching him from somewhere.

The countess ate daintily, occasionally feeding titbits to the dog by her ankles. The morsels fell straight through the little dog's ribcage, and another skeleton with a brush and pan rushed in to clean them up. Logan had come to the conclusion that the countess's mind had slipped more than a little.

Which was probably for the best. Right now, she was an eccentric old woman, using her powers to provide the occasional talk with the dead for the grieving, or divination for the lost. She could have been doing much worse.

'I do hope the food is to your liking, Logan,' she called cheerfully. 'It's so nice to have company.'

Logan nodded and went back to finishing his food as fast as possible. When he was done, he pushed his plate away.

'We leave early tomorrow. I need to get to bed.'

She nodded. 'Of course. I'll have someone see you to your room.' She clicked her fingers and a skeleton appeared. 'The green room, I think.'

The skeleton gave Logan a bow and he followed it out of the room and up a creaking set of stairs.

'Are . . . are you a prisoner here?' Logan asked it when they were out of earshot. 'Do you want me to send you to your eternal rest?'

The skeleton stared at him, and Logan had the distinct impression that if it had had eyes, it would have rolled them. Instead, it pushed open a door and held it.

'I . . . see. Well, good night, I guess.'

The skeleton gave him a polite nod, handed him a candle, and left him alone.

Logan sank onto the bed. The green room had not been misnamed. Green velvet curtains hung over the window, and a green blanket covered the bed. Even the whitewashed walls had a green tint, though Logan wasn't sure if that was deliberate, merely reflection, or mildew. The room smelled old, like dust and forgotten secrets.

He curled up in the bed. Another night without Pie. The dusty, unused sheets made him sneeze, and they smelled wrong. Instinct and habit made him reach out for a warm body to draw close, and each time he encountered nothing but cold air, it sent shivers running right through him. Loneliness gnawing at his heart, Logan got out of bed, pulled his cloak around him, and slept on the floor.

He woke, stiff and empty, before sunrise the next morning. For a moment, his heart raced as he tried to work out where he was, and why he felt so miserable. Then yesterday came flooding back. He pulled himself to his feet, rubbing at the aches in his shoulders and back, as the eastern sky grew pink.

'Good morning.'

Logan startled a foot in the air at the voice behind him. He reached for the axe, which was propped up at the foot of the bed, bringing it swinging around on whoever had entered.

'Now, now. That's no way to say hello,' Ophelia said.

'Don't you bloody knock?' He forced his heart back out of his throat and strapped the axe to his back.

'Kind of hard when your hands go through everything.' She waved her incorporeal fingers at him.

'I could've been dressing,' Logan muttered, and she laughed.

'So? I've seen it before. It's not special. Did you forget we were married?'

'Not a bloody minute.'

'Do you think I did? Married to a half-bear with a temper and a bad smell wasn't exactly my dream either. And that's when you even bothered to show up.'

Logan clenched his hands into fists. 'Gods, give me strength. What was I supposed to do? There were all sorts of things lurking around on the land. What if they took a sheep, or worse, a child? Is that what you wanted, Ophelia? Some family to lose their children so you had more time to fumble in your husband's bed?'

She glared at him, her eyes dark and burning with hatred. 'I wouldn't want to fumble in your bed if you were the last person alive, Logan Theaker. You're a rude, selfish, arrogant brute who only cares about spilling blood and—'

A knock at the door cut her off. They both turned to find a skeleton standing in the doorway. It gave them a polite bow and gestured to the stairs.

'Guess it's time to go.' Logan strode past Ophelia, who was still glaring at him, as if she could set his clothes alight with her hatred. He didn't hang around to find out if that was something the dead could do.

Outside, the rest of the skeletons piled luggage into a wagon drawn by two immense skeletal horses. Given the number of boxes and chests, the countess must have packed half the house. Logan put a hand out to stop a skeleton holding a cracked leather case.

'Oh no. No. This is a rescue mission, not a court procession. You cannot possibly need any of this, Countess.'

She emerged from the other side of the wagon with a sheepish smile. 'I suppose I did go a little over the top. But it's been so long since I went on an adventure.'

'So long that you completely forgot all practicalities?' He turned to a skeleton carrying another wooden chest. 'Take that back. Take all of it back.'

'But those are my shoes,' she protested, hugging the case. 'Can't I take one little box? They won't take up much room in the wagon.'

'No shoes,' said Logan, who couldn't conceive owning more than one pair of most things. 'No wagon. I'm not sure you should even have one of those.' He waved a hand at the skeletal beasts.

'Why not? They don't tire, and you don't need to feed them,' she pointed out. 'If they get in the way, you can dismiss them down to a pile of bones. Very practical.'

'I . . . suppose. But people will make a fuss if you go marching into town with them. People are on edge enough with the magic ban.'

She waved a piece of paper at him. Logan didn't quite catch where it came from. 'Charter!' she said. 'They can't make a fuss. I have a legal right to use the bones of man and beast, as long as they're dead, and not used against the king's subjects.'

'Most people aren't going to give you the time of day, let alone stop to read that.' He sighed. 'Look, you make a good point about them not needing rest or food. And as long as we keep off the main roads, we'll probably be fine. Just be prepared to make them disappear if we need it. But no wagon, and no extra shoes. Just what you can fit in a saddlebag.'

'Has anyone told you that you're a frightful bore, Logan?' She scowled.

'Yes. My ex-wife. Frequently.'

By the time the wagon had been unloaded and removed, and the two skeletal beasts had been tacked up, the sun was well over the horizon. Every moment they stood there made Logan's skin crawl. Every moment they dawdled, Pie got further away. At some point, Ophelia had skulked out of the house and her shade lurked behind one of the bone steeds, throwing daggers at him with her gaze.

Two skeletons helped the countess, now wearing a simple black robe with a wide skirt, onto the broad back of one of the beasts. After a moment, Ophelia appeared behind her. Logan regarded the other creature, desperately trying to pretend it was a flesh-and-blood horse. Its head swung around, regarding him with empty eye sockets, its exposed teeth looking sharper and more dangerous than they had any right to on a creature that had eaten grass when alive. He flinched as the skull moved in closer, but instead of attacking, it rubbed itself against his arm. Logan reached out and scratched its forehead gingerly.

'Hello, girl.' He paused. 'Boy?' How could you tell on a skeleton anyway? He gripped the saddle and pulled himself up. He expected it to shift and slip, but when mounted, he discovered it sat securely. A glance down showed it had ridges that sat between the ribs, keeping it in place. He patted a hand against the horse's vertebrae. The creature shook itself, making its bones clatter.

'Ready?' the countess called. She held the reins between hands gloved in soft black leather, her back straight as an arrow. Logan saw his old foe in her now: not the simpering old lady with the ridiculous home and the little bone puppy, but a ruthless and determined woman who would not let things like life and death get in the way of what she wanted.

You better have a damn good reason for all this, Pie.

'Ready as I'll ever be,' he answered with a weak smile. 'So, where exactly is this thing?'

'First,' replied Ophelia. 'We need to find a unicorn.'

Chapter Four

'A unicorn?' Logan spluttered. 'Might as well try and capture a cloud. There aren't any unicorns left; they died out a hundred years ago. Everyone knows that.'

Pie had a song about it. Whenever he sang it, he got a faraway look in his eye, one of pain and sadness. Afterwards, he tended to be quiet and distant, and drank more than he should.

Logan hated that song.

He clenched his fist, tightening his grip on the reins and causing the horse to throw its bony head. 'If this is some ploy, or worse, a joke, I promise it will end very badly for both of you.'

'Don't be so bloody suspicious, Logan.' Ophelia rolled her eyes. 'The Chalice is hidden, right? No one's found it for hundreds of years. You'd need a powerful spell to do that. And the way to undo it, is with a unicorn. Because they're not extinct. They didn't die out. They're hidden. And you can find them, if you know where to look.'

'And I suppose you know where to look?' Logan asked, feeling very bloody suspicious still.

'Not exactly,' she admitted, drifting over to sit on the back of the countess's horse. 'But I know a way of finding them.'

Logan raised an eyebrow. 'Are you going to tell us, or keep us in suspense the whole way?'

'Patience. We need to find someone who can pierce the spell that keeps them hidden.'

'Countess?' he asked and both women looked at him as if he'd suggested she could fly.

'Spellcasters and necromancers work very differently, Logan dear,' the countess replied. 'We manipulate different energies. They are simply not interchangeable. Spellcasting energy comes from the caster's own lifeforce, whereas necromancy uses the latent energy produced when a living thing dies.'

'I didn't understand a word of that.' Logan rubbed his head. He turned to Ophelia. 'You're saying we need to find a spellcaster? I'm sure that'll be easy now the king's forbidden magic.'

She gave him a sweet smile. 'Just because they're not so public about it anymore, doesn't mean they've vanished.' She leaned over to the countess. 'Take the low road down towards the sea.'

The countess nodded and put her heels to her horse. Logan wasn't sure how the creature took the instruction with no flank to press, but nevertheless it started off at a brisk trot. He took a deep breath, collected the reins, and pushed his heels down. It had been years since he'd ridden, but the positions, motions, sensations all came rushing back.

His arse was going to be numb within two miles.

'Come on then . . .' He paused. It was no good. It had to have a name. 'Come on then, Bones.'

The creature turned its head towards him, as if judging him, but set off after the countess's mount. He urged it into a trot that jarred both their bones until they were alongside the other skeleton steed again.

'How do you know all this, Ophelia?' he asked. She turned her head away so all he could see was a mass of translucent black curls.

'The . . . the dead talk.'

'I see. What's it like being dead?' As a man who sought out danger on a regular basis, Logan had considered this question more than once. Everyone had an answer, of course. Priests of various deities squabbling over which god was correct and therefore which afterlife.

'I don't know.'

'You don't know?' Logan's jaw dropped. 'How do you not know? Have you had your head in a pot up there all this time?'

'Don't chide her, Logan dear.' The countess reached over to pat his arm. 'It's well known the dead cannot speak anything of the afterlife.'

'That makes no sense.' He shook his head. 'She knows all this other stuff.'

The countess shrugged her narrow shoulders. 'It's the way of things. Those who worship the Dark Mother believe she guards the secrets of her realm very carefully. Me, I believe it was a pact between all the gods. Think about it. If someone came back and said, "the afterlife is like this", then it would affect faith in the others. So, they conspired to make sure no one learns about it, not even the most powerful necromancer. It's rather elegant, really.'

Logan shook his head and urged Bones onward. His head and his back ached from the poor sleep, his arse was already protesting and the last thing he needed was a discussion on the nature of the afterlife. He'd never worried too much about it. Death would come for him, probably sooner rather than later. It wasn't something he could change or control. And any god capricious enough to be swayed by prayers or offerings wasn't going to stay swayed for long.

He led them away from the main road, down smaller paths that cut across the moors, criss-crossing the little and not so little streams that meandered over the landscape. Come winter, much of this would be impassable. They would have had no chance of getting a wagon over it. At least it wasn't raining, and as weird as riding a skeleton steed was, it was a damn sight more comfortable than walking.

They stopped for lunch at the edge of the moorland, where the gorse scrub gave way to denser forest. Logan wanted to keep riding, but the countess declared they were stopping, and Bones refused to listen to his commands anymore. Grumbling under his breath, he dismounted and gave the skeletal beast a glare. It ignored him and walked over to a tree for a scratch.

The countess dropped two teeth onto the ground and a moment later two skeletons stood there. She clapped her hands once, and they set about pulling a checked blanket from one of the saddlebags and spreading it on the ground.

'No reason why we can't be civilised, even out here in the wilderness.'

This isn't wilderness, he wanted to tell her. The wilderness had no roads, or paths. You had to fight your way through it with an axe or machete. And when you did find a space, it was usually filled with something with slavering jaws or poisonous skin, ready to pounce.

You didn't have fucking picnics in the wilderness.

'Sit down, Logan, you're making the place look untidy,' Ophelia said. She'd disappeared from the back of the horse and reappeared, cross-legged, next to the countess. The necromancer smiled and offered him a hunk of bread and some hard yellow cheese.

Logan sat, the muscles in his backside protesting loudly, and reluctantly took the offered food. He couldn't help Pie if he didn't keep his strength up. It wasn't like he could go anywhere at the moment, he thought, shooting Bones another glare.

'So,' the countess said, as Logan crammed half a chunk of bread into his mouth. 'When did you and Aloysius meet?'

Logan choked on his mouthful, spraying crumbs all over his beard. 'Why do you care?'

'Just passing the time,' she said politely, while nibbling on her own lunch.

Logan sighed, lowering his plate. A skeleton offered him a linen napkin and he waved it away.

'Fine. It was about two years ago. Pie was trying to earn his livery from a fancy house when I first met him. I'd been hired to escort the eldest son and Pie was part of the entourage. He annoyed me at first – he was so incessantly cheerful.'

'I can see why that would piss you off.' Ophelia scowled. 'We all know your views on smiling.'

Logan bit his tongue, keeping his attention focused on the countess.

'As I was saying, we didn't exactly hit it off at first. But the group was caught off guard by a monster and even though everyone else acted like a bunch of chickens, Pie kept his head. Impressed me.' The monstrous black cat, known as a parel, landed in front of them without warning. They were powerful, silent hunters; cunning, too. Their mouths filled with too many teeth and curled at the corner in a perpetual smirk. 'The next time I met him was before the battle of Boswothy, though neither of us made it to the actual fight. The idiot had drunk water downstream from a battlefield, made himself sick.'

'And you took care of him?' The countess clutched her hands to her heart. 'How sweet.'

Logan rubbed the back of his neck, heat rushing to his face. 'After that, we kept running into each other, every few months or so.'

'Fate had marked you out for each other,' the countess said with a smile.

Logan shook his head. 'Wasn't fate. We were just looking out for each other. Took a while to admit it.' He shoved the rest of the bread in his mouth, chewing hard. His stomach felt tied in knots. He didn't want to eat, didn't want to talk. They needed to get back on the road again.

'Something's coming,' Ophelia said, making everyone jump. Logan did a quick scout of their surroundings. No sign of travellers, no footsteps or hooves on the soft ground.

'Are you sure?'

'Yes, I'm sure,' she snapped, throwing him a glare. 'I can sense the living, and there's something living and very large coming towards us.' She pointed towards the river. 'Over there.'

Logan pulled his axe out of its holster. He glanced at Ophelia for any sign she was mocking him or setting a trap. Her eyes were wide, scanning the area along the riverbank. Her hand kept passing through her hair. On the blanket, the countess carried on with her lunch as if imminent danger were the most normal situation.

Logan took a tentative step towards the river, his axe hefted and ready. The water flowed swiftly, almost to the bank level, swollen from the recent rain. Thick green weeds swayed in the current like angry cat tails, and large brown fish darted in and out of them. Thoughts of Pie roasting trout tickled the back of Logan's mind, making his mouth water.

Suddenly, the river erupted in front of him as something surged over the bank. Logan leapt back. He squinted, drawing the axe in front of him, trying to make out the shape of the thing. Translucent and almost colourless, it looked like a blob of water crawling up the bank towards him.

'What is it?' Ophelia shrieked, backing away. She kept trying to clutch her hands together but they passed through each other.

'It can't hurt *you*,' Logan growled. 'It's a gover. A giant carnivorous toad. You should keep clear, Countess. They're not just slimy; they're poisonous as well.'

'I'm sure you can handle it, Logan dear.' She rose slowly and brushed down her skirt.

The gover slashed out with an immense black tongue, causing him to dance back a step. Flecks of thick spittle drenched the grass. The blades it touched shrivelled and turned brown. Logan gave a grunt of disgust. No one liked these things; he suspected even other govers didn't like them. Even the bards wouldn't sing about these creatures.

The gover flicked its tongue out again, its gaping mouth dark and cavernous. Logan leapt, coming down hard on the left side of the creature. He pivoted on one foot, swinging the axe and letting the momentum carry the blade. It entered the gover, parting it in two. The top slid off the bottom, spraying him in a thick, cold, jelly-like substance.

He stared down at what was left of its corpse, half expecting it to rise up and attack him again. The translucent jelly quivered as it slowly broke down to nothing. The grass under it, currently wilting, wouldn't be safe to eat before spring. He glanced down. Oh, shit. He was covered in the stuff, from head to toe.

'Well done, dear,' the countess called, giving him a delicate wave. Logan ignored her, pulled his boots off, and leapt into the river.

It wasn't deep, so he had to lie down to thrust his head under. The cold knocked the breath out of his lungs, and he swallowed a mouthful of icy water. He pushed his head out of the river, coughing and spluttering, before pulling off his shirt.

'Oh, my.' The countess gasped behind a gloved hand as Logan unbuckled his trousers.

He glowered at her, his face burning. 'Do you bloody mind? This isn't a show.'

'Turning away, dear, turning away' she said with a titter.

Logan pulled a rough length of weed from the river and used it scrub himself down. His skin reddened under the efforts, but there was no sign of the blisters or rash that came from the poison. His skin itched a little, but that would pass. Dripping and cold, he hauled himself from the river.

The countess still sat on the blanket, one hand held over her eyes, her fingers parted just slightly. Logan placed his hands over his crotch and scurried over to Bones to pull dry clothes from his saddlebag.

'You're both welcome,' he muttered, teeth chattering. He slipped into the treeline and used his cloak to mop up the water. Behind him, the countess whispered to Ophelia about his physique in less than hushed tones. Logan supressed a groan and squeezed the water out of his hair, shivering.

If Pie were here, he would have pitched a fire and handed him something dry. He would have laughed, without judgement, and found a time to tease Logan about it when they weren't cold and wet.

Aside from his physical touch, it was Pie's laugh that Logan missed the most.

They reached the port town of Cassten as night curled in around them. Despite Logan's best efforts, he hadn't managed to fully dry off, and riding in damp clothes had left him chilled and uncomfortable. He called a halt at the edge of the trees.

'We'll leave the, er, horses here,' he said to the countess. 'We go the rest of the way on foot. Ophelia? Can you be . . . less visible? I don't want us attracting any more attention than we have to.'

She scowled at him. 'This is discrimination against the dead – you know that. Right?'

'Call it what you like, but I'm not the only one with a problem. Do you want us driven out of town before we've had a chance to meet up with this spellcaster of yours?'

'Fine. I'll make myself scarce.' She faded away, her glare lingering after she'd vanished.

The countess dismounted and made a gesture with her hands. The two skeletal mounts disappeared, leaving a couple of horse teeth and the leather tack on the ground. Logan tucked the peculiar saddles and teeth under a bush and collected the saddlebags.

'Does it hurt . . . when you do that to them?' he asked the countess.

She threw him a wide grin and slipped her arm around his.

'Why, Logan, you sentimental thing. No, it doesn't hurt them. They just cease to be for a bit.'

Logan didn't feel terribly comforted.

'I hope there's a decent inn in this place,' the countess continued. 'I had to sleep in a barn once. I did not enjoy it.'

Logan, who considered barns in his top three places to sleep, didn't respond.

'Oh dear, what if they only have one room?' she said, raising a hand to her mouth. 'Whatever will we do?'

'I'd sleep in the barn,' Logan replied.

She punched his arm with surprising force. 'Well, that's no fun.'

'Did you forget that I'm married?' Logan growled.

'No, but he's not here, is he? I'm sure he won't mind.'

Logan rubbed his forehead. There was no malice or teasing in her voice. She seemed genuinely surprised that he wouldn't put her desires ahead of everything else.

'I rather suspect he would. I would, certainly.'

She stuck out her lip.

'I know, I know. I'm a terrible bore.'

The city gates stood closed as they approached. The countess marched up to the gatehouse and rapped on the shutter.

'Evening, my good man. We are weary travellers, and we wish to spend the night safe within the walls of your fine city.'

The shutter opened with a begrudging creak. 'Who's we?'

'I am Countess DeWinter, and this is my manservant.' She looked back over her shoulder at Logan, one eyebrow raised as if daring him to correct her. Logan decided not to rise to the bait. She shrugged and turned back to the gatekeeper.

'Fare's a sovereign each after dark,' the mysterious voice replied from the gloom.

'A sovereign's a bit steep,' the countess muttered. 'You wouldn't be trying to take advantage of a poor old lady now, would you?' She clasped her hands together and twisted on her foot.

'Do you want me to open the gates or not? Magic's banned, everything's harder to do, takes longer. Means prices go up.'

'I see.' She smoothed her hair and turned back towards Logan. 'Very well, pay the good man, Logan.'

Logan bit back a retort and pulled out two sovereigns. Pie earned them singing in the inn back home. King Ervin's face glared up at him from his palm. He slammed his hand shut again and dropped them into the gatehouse.

'Don't suppose you've had a bard come through here? Male, tall, auburn hair down to here?' he gestured against his shoulder. 'Plays the lute.'

'Very handsome,' the countess added with a wink.

'Can't say I have.' The man turned away, fiddling with something with a grunt, before the city gates swung open with a groan.

The countess patted Logan's arm. 'Don't lose heart, dear. We'll find your husband, don't you worry.'

Logan nodded half-heartedly and followed her into the town. He hoped so, he thought as the gates closed behind them with a dull thud. The town seemed quiet, subdued. Even the little village back home never went to sleep until the moon was high.

'Now, let's find us a nice inn, shall we? I fancy a bath.'

'We should find the spellcaster. I don't want to waste any more time than we have to.' He glanced around. 'Ophelia? You still here?'

She emerged out of a shadow.

'Where do we go?'

'Down to the docks. There's a resistance group pushing back against the king's ban on magic. They have a ship docked there.'

'How do you know all this?' he demanded.

She gave him a glare that radiated hatred. 'The dead talk, Logan. Weren't you listening before? Perhaps if you were to pull your head out of your own arse you'd keep up better.' She vanished, but her words prickled at him, like a grain of sand under a nail.

He still hadn't fully got his head around the idea that she was back in his life, let alone in this form. A mix of emotions ran through him every time he caught sight of her; it made his neck itch. He set off down the hill as fast as his legs would allow, the countess muttering about baths behind him.

The closer to the docks they walked, the busier the streets became. Music spilled out of a waterfront tavern, the gentle voice of a woman carrying across the still night air. Certainly not Pie. Dockworkers unloaded boxes of cargo under lamp-light, and a drunkard was yelling at a seagull. Nailed to a fence were a series of wanted posters.

'Spellcasters,' the countess offered, reading his mind.

On the far end of the fence, covering the last couple of posters, someone had scrawled a stick figure, a crown falling from his head, cowering from an incoming fireball.

'Logan.' Ophelia's hand materialised, passing through his wrist.

He shuddered at the icy flush against his skin.

'What?'

'Over there. I know that woman.' The hand pointed at a slight blonde woman in a blue dress. She paused at the statue of a dog sitting at the entrance to the harbour. It had large, pricked-up ears, and a paw raised in greeting. A plaque at the statue's base read 'Waylon'. The dog's bronze nose was a bright gold where people rubbed it for luck, and as he watched, the woman leaned down and gave it a kiss.

'She's your spellcaster?'

Ophelia shook her head. The woman turned away and headed towards an alley.

'Not the spellcaster I was expecting, but I'm pretty sure that's my cousin, Seraphina. She's the spitting image of my aunt.'

'You're not certain?' Logan asked as he started towards the alley.

'She was ten when I died, Logan,' Ophelia snapped, and he cringed.

He quickened his pace and rounded the corner of the alley just as she was unlocking a door.

'Hey, you!' he called, and she flinched, almost dropping her key.

'Back off. You're messing with the wrong person,' she yelled, shifting to a defensive stance.

Logan held out his hands. 'I don't want to hurt you. I just want to talk to you. Tell her, Ophelia.'

The woman paused at Ophelia's name, and several emotions flashed across her face. Ophelia stepped out from behind him.

'It's good to see you again, Phina. Last time I saw you, you were a little girl with daisies in your hair.'

The woman paled and the key shook in her hand. 'If this is some sort of sick joke . . .'

'It's no joke,' Ophelia said softly. 'It's really me. This is the Countess DeWinter and the skulking lump of muscle over there is Logan Theaker.'

The woman stared at Ophelia, her eyes wide. Her mouth moved silently as she took in the words. 'Wait, not Logan as in the Bear?'

Ophelia grinned. 'That's the one.'

'You called me the Bear too?' Logan asked. He'd been gifted his adventurer name after Ophelia had sent him away. That she'd come up with the same moniker raised a strange warmth in his guts.

'You act like a bear with a sore head, and you smell like one, too.' Ophelia folded her arms.

'Oh.' The warmth fizzled away.

'This reunion is all very sweet,' the countess said, coming up next to Ophelia. 'But we probably shouldn't be standing around on the streets after dark. Do you have somewhere we can talk, young lady? Maybe with a nice bath?'

Seraphina blinked at her, as if she were speaking another language, then nodded. 'I suppose you can come inside.'

She held open the door, which led into a small room with a fire burning in the hearth and a few cushions on the floor. A rickety flight of steps led up to another level. Seraphina locked the door behind her and gestured awkwardly to the cushions. She was young, maybe only twenty or so, Logan guessed, with blond hair bound in a braid and wide blue eyes that darted around the room like a butterfly unsure where to land.

'Are you a spellcaster?' Logan asked.

She tensed, sucking in a breath with a hiss.

The countess laughed. 'Now, now, Logan dear. It's not polite to ask a lady if she's involved in illegal activities the moment you meet her. At least buy her a drink first.' She jabbed him in his ribs with a bony elbow.

Logan's face warmed and he cleared his throat. 'I'm sorry. I didn't mean . . .'

'Perhaps you should tell her your story.' The countess selected the plumpest cushion, sat down and arranged her skirt. She looked up at Logan expectantly.

'My . . . my husband is missing.' He settled himself on the floor and, after a moment, Seraphina did the same. 'Ophelia believes he's been press-ganged into doing a mission for the king. We're going to find him and bring him back home.'

Seraphina's eyes widened and she bit her lip.

'I'm guessing you have little love for the king,' Logan said, 'with spellcasting being illegal.'

'And you could say we're not exactly friendly with him,' the countess added. 'Husband-stealing and all that.'

As if she hadn't been flirting with Logan from the moment he'd stepped into her home.

Logan shifted on the cushion, trying to make himself more comfortable. It was flat and too small, offering little protection from the cold floor. He explained to Seraphina everything that had happened since Pie disappeared from the inn.

'Ophelia says that you can help us,' he finished. 'I really hope you can.'

'The king's a monster,' Seraphina said softly. 'I saw him, and he was a monster.'

'What do you mean?' Logan asked.

She picked at her braid, twisting it between her fingers. 'I've just come from Mywin, the coast. It's predominantly a fishing town. Without magic, they're at the mercy of the elements. Over the last year, several vessels have been lost because they couldn't outrun storms.'

'The king even has watchers on the sea?' Logan couldn't quite believe it.

'No, but he's got big warnings hanging up, and promises of big rewards. It doesn't take much to convince someone to turn in his friends, especially if he's poor and hungry.'

Logan stroked his beard. 'I see.' He gestured for her to go on with her story.

'A few days ago, we got word that the king was passing by. A couple of spellcasters and I came up with a plan. We were going to show the king, show him magic could be useful. Set up a situation where we could save his life. He banned it because of an accident. We wanted to show him the other side.'

He'd never met the king, but from what Logan had heard, he was a man of unenviable bad luck. The fourth son of the previous queen, he'd been set for a life of comfort but little power. Then, one by one, those closest to him began dying. Illness, accidents, an unfortunate squabble over succession between a pair of twins. Logan had always considered such patterns suspicious, but Pie, who had met the king at least twice, said the deaths changed him so much he couldn't believe Ervin was involved. The final straw came when an argument between spellcasters flared into violence and a stray fireball spooked the horses pulling the king's coach, causing an accident that killed his fiancée. After that, he'd made magic illegal.

'You tried to trick the king?' Logan snorted. 'I can guess how that stunt went.' Seraphina was little more than a child and he'd come across this kind of impetuous and overly complicated planning before.

She glared at him with tears in her eyes. 'I'm the only one who survived.'

'I'm sorry,' Logan replied, head bowed, at a loss for more comforting words. Ophelia rolled her eyes, but what did she expect from him? Comforting someone was not his area of expertise. He was Logan the Bear, not Logan the Comforter. If only Pie was here.

He took a breath. 'So, what happened?'

Her face paled at the memory and she trembled like a frightened animal.

'The three of us were ambushed by the king's mercenaries and brought before him. He . . . he wasn't right. He stared like he was looking right through us, and I swear to every god he smelled wrong. Rotten. The king made everyone get out of the room. A–and then—' She choked down a sob. Ophelia moved to put a hand on her, then stopped. 'And then he killed my friend,' Seraphina continued. 'Cut his throat and let him bleed out on the floor. But that isn't the worst of it. We were in shock, and then he got back up again.'

'The king's a necromancer?' The countess poked a finger at the young woman. 'That can't be right. I would have felt something, I'm sure.'

'I know what I saw,' Seraphina said, her voice cold, daring them to doubt her. 'He killed my friend and brought him back, and I was too shocked to act. But when he killed the other spellcaster as well, I ran. I ran and I ran and I ran.' Tears flowed down her face. 'I don't know how I got away. Maybe I was lucky. Maybe he just doesn't care enough about one spellcaster. But I'm going to make him pay.' She curled her hand into a fist. 'I'm going to make him pay.'

'And I'm going to get my husband back, and then the king is going to regret messing with us.' Logan held out a hand. 'You should come with us.'

Seraphina shook her head. 'I can't. I have other plans.'

A cold flame ignited in Logan's guts. 'What do you mean, you have other plans? We have a common enemy; we can work together, we can stop him. What other plan is there?'

She shook her head again.

'What do you know of fighting?' Logan roared. 'Think you can be a hero, just because you're angry? Your silly plan got two men killed, and you still want to go off on your own?'

Ophelia strode across the room and kicked him, meaning her foot passed through his back. He gasped at the wave of cold.

'Stop yelling at her!'

'I'm not yelling,' he protested. 'I'm trying to make her see sense. I'm trying to get her to help us. Isn't that what you said we needed to do? To get a spellcaster?'

Ophelia kicked him again, and he rounded on her. 'Bloody stop that, Ophelia. You can't strike me. You're just giving my insides frostbite.'

'You're scaring her,' she replied.

'I'm not what she needs to be afraid of.' Pie's fate rested in their hands, and every new tale he heard about the king only filled Logan with more dread. Stubborn revolutionaries running off to save the day and getting themselves killed wouldn't change anything. Logan needed a spellcaster, and he needed to get to Pie.

'You're a monster,' Ophelia sneered. 'I bet your Pie isn't even in trouble. I reckon he just ran away and left you like I did.'

His guts twisted. Pie wouldn't leave him. Pie loved him. He got to his feet, reaching for his axe. 'You take that back. Now.'

'Or you'll do what, Logan?' She folded her arms.

The countess clapped her hands. 'Now, now, children. While you've been fighting, our host has . . . Well . . .' She gestured to Seraphina. The woman had curled up with her head on her knees, weeping.

Ophelia moved to her side, whispering softly to her.

'Logan dear? I know it does *wonderful* things to your muscles when you tense up like that,' the countess said. 'But perhaps you'd better sit down.'

Logan put the axe away and did as the countess asked, guilt sloshing with his anger and making him feel nauseous. He fought back the need to get up and pace. He itched to do something, anything to take his mind off the worries circling like carrion crows. How had Pie got himself caught up in this? What did he know? Why hadn't he come to Logan?

When he finally caught up with Pie, he was going to have a whole heap of wrinkles.

Seraphina lifted her head, her eyes red. 'There's a group of spellcasters in hiding. They have a ship and they're arriving at the port tomorrow. They've been building up support for rebellion, and when I tell them what the king is doing to his own people, they'll have to move against him.'

Logan pounded the ground with his fist. 'You're making the same mistake you made in Mywin. This won't work. You'll just spark a war. No one wins in a war.'

She stared at him, her gaze boring into him. 'I can see why Ophelia left you.'

Chapter Five

Logan smacked a fist into the wall. The pain, sharp and raw, was a comfort. He was fucking this up. The spellcaster was going to turn them out, and he'd lose his one chance to get on Pie's trail. Blood dripped from his knuckles.

'That was silly,' the countess quipped. 'If you want suggestions, I've got much better things you can do with those big hands.'

'Please. Not right now.' He felt hollow. Empty. Scared. Logan the Bear wasn't a man used to feeling scared.

She gave him a grin that was probably supposed to be reassuring. 'The spellcaster hasn't kicked us out yet, has she? I don't think you've blown it completely. Emotions are high right now. Let everyone sleep on it.'

He nodded and settled down against the wall, grateful for even a scrap of hope, despite its source. He closed his eyes and pushed away the pain in his leg.

'And if not, we'll make a villain of you yet, Logan,' the countess said.

He snapped his eyes open. She was pottering around the room, poking through the shelves, turning objects over in her hands before discarding them again.

'I'm not a villain,' he muttered, wrapping his arms around himself.

'No?' She turned, one exquisitely arched eyebrow raised. 'Isn't that what they call men who make young women cry?'

One of the words, he had to admit to himself. Villain was one of the politer ones at that.

'I didn't mean to upset her,' he muttered, feeling like a reprimanded child.

'I know, dear,' she replied. 'Doesn't matter what she thinks. The important thing is you didn't mean harm.'

Logan cocked his head. She was mocking him, but he'd decided that it didn't matter. Whether she was calling him out on his terrible manners or agreeing with him, he'd done a shitty thing and then tried to cover it over with a shitty attitude.

'Gods, I am a villain, aren't I?' A cold, hard lump spawned in his stomach, sending a freezing ache rushing through him. 'What if Ophelia's right? What if Pie just left? What if he doesn't want to be found?'

She picked up a little pot, gave it a sniff, then set it back down. 'You're asking my advice?' She rubbed her chin. 'Well, if it were me, I'd find that husband of mine, grab him by that firm yet supple arse, and then sling him over my shoulder. Bring him back where he belongs.'

'That's my husband you're talking about,' Logan said, unable to keep the growl from his voice.

She flashed him a hungry grin. 'Well, if he has left you, we'll see. You can't know anything until you catch up with him, so there's no point moping around pondering the worst. If you're going to imagine things, Logan, it's always much more fun to imagine the positive.'

Logan wrapped his arms around himself again and closed his eyes. The hard stone wall pressed against his back, poking at his spine. He'd never been good at imagining the positive. Quite the opposite. In fact, he'd credited his survival with always looking for the worst-case scenarios, being prepared to face them. Either he'd be right, prepared and smug, or pleasantly surprised.

Until Pie came along.

Pie with his soft smiles, and his dirty jokes. His fingers that sent tingles running down Logan's skin. Pie with his incessant declarations that Logan was attractive, funny, kind. Loveable.

Declarations that sounded like nonsense at first, but he'd heard so many times that he'd actually begun to believe them.

Bards. They got in your head. But that was the thing about believing something: once you started, you couldn't stop. Those beliefs took root, spreading through you, until they became a part of you. He had to believe Pie loved him. Had to believe in the life they'd promised each other. The person who couldn't believe those things didn't exist anymore.

Logan woke the next morning, shoulders, back and hips all aching in protest. There was a warmth over his chest, a familiar and comfortable one. Blinking sleep from his eyes, he reached out and touched the hand resting on him.

'Pie?'

The flesh was cool and papery to his touch, the arm thin and spindly.

'I could be, if you wanted me to be,' the countess said softly, running her hand up to caress his cheek. Her fingers dug into his beard.

Logan let out a startled cry, pushing her away. She remained kneeling on the ground, looking up at him, her thin lips twisted in a smirk. Logan groaned and pulled his shirt tightly around himself. Ophelia glided into the room to take in the scene, hands on her hips.

'This isn't what it looks like,' he said, looking down at his boots, hating himself for the way his face flushed.

'What? The old bat snuggled up while you were sleeping?' Ophelia replied. 'Because that's exactly what it looks like.'

'I just woke up with her wrapped around me,' Logan remarked, getting to his feet.

'Old bat?' The countess glared. 'You should have more respect. I can send you back across the veil with a snap of my fingers.'

'But you won't,' Ophelia said, 'because it amuses you too much when Logan and I fight.'

The countess's eyes widened, then she threw back her head and laughed. 'Ah, you have me there, dear. I do like my entertainment.' Her hand reached out to Logan again. 'Of all sorts.'

He smacked her hand away. 'Touch me again, Countess, and you'll lose an arm. You're not the only necromancer in the kingdom.'

'None quite as delightful as me, though.' She turned away, pulling some teeth out of a pocket and throwing them down on the ground. Within moments, skeletons were tending to her hair. It reminded Logan of the way a cat licks itself after it's been scolded, though few cats had skeletal henchmen.

They probably would if they could.

'Thank you for believing me,' Logan said to Ophelia, his face growing warm again.

She looked him up and down, her expression stern. At least she wasn't rolling her eyes at him. 'You have many, many flaws, Logan. But I don't think you'd betray a lover. Besides, that woman is a snake.'

'Snakes would resent that,' Logan said.

The door opened and he tensed as Seraphina entered. A cold hand squeezed at his guts as he remembered her in tears from the previous night. Her face was pale, her eyes puffy but not raw. She caught him looking at her and frowned, which only made the hand in his guts squeeze harder.

'I'm sorry,' he said, ducking his head. Everyone in the room was staring at him, setting off his combat reflexes. But reaching for his axe was most likely not going to ease the tension in the room. He pushed a hand through his hair, snagging it on three knots and a piece of twig. 'I was unfair last night. I shouldn't have said those things to you. After what you witnessed, I should have been kinder.'

She chewed her lower lip, considering his words, then spoke. 'I spoke with Phelie – Ophelia – last night. She explained how worried you are about your husband.'

It wasn't forgiveness, but at least it was understanding. Logan would take that.

'Can you help us?' he pleaded softly.

She dropped her gaze, fiddling with the end of her braid. Logan held his breath. Pie's fate rested on her answer. She raised her head and met his eyes.

'I can. I trust Ophelia, and she trusts you.'

Logan blinked, unsure how to take that revelation. He glanced at Ophelia and she gave him a small smile.

'But . . . I'm not coming with you.'

Beside her, Ophelia's eyes widened. 'But . . .'

Seraphina held up a hand. 'You have your plan, and I have mine.' She looked Logan in the eye. 'I'm still going to get on that ship. This is a spellcaster problem. It needs a spellcaster solution.'

Ophelia reached for her, before pulling away, her hands disappearing as she clutched them into her chest. 'You'll be careful, won't you?'

Seraphina smiled. 'Of course. I'm not a child anymore, Phelie. I know what I'm doing. Come and find me when you're done. We're sailing up the coast, past the capital, and collecting more spellcasters from the Bay of Sighs.'

'But you'll help us first? You'll help us find the unicorn?' Logan pleaded desperately.

He couldn't bring himself to meet her eye, or Ophelia's. The countess's words from yesterday still left him cold and unsettled. *We'll make a villain of you yet, Logan.* He was a monster killer, not a monster. His mother had raised him to be a hero, to protect those weaker than him. He knew now that hero was an unobtainable ideal, but the need to protect, to defend, was baked into his blood. He pulled his shoulders in, trying to make himself smaller, less threatening. If he was to find Pie, he needed her to believe he wasn't a monster, too.

Seraphina nodded. 'Yes.'

Logan let out a sigh and pulled on his memories of Pie's confidence. He raised his head and looked her in the eye. 'Thank you.'

The countess put a hand on his shoulder, one long finger tracing circles on his neck. 'Chin up, Logan dear. It's so much better for your posture.'

He shuddered and pushed her away.

'What do we do? How do we find a unicorn? How does that get us to Pie?'

'I'm afraid I can only really help with the first part.' Seraphina twisted her braid around her fingers. 'I can give you something that will get you through to where the unicorns are, but how to get one and what to do next, that's up to you.'

'Thank you.' It was a step in the right direction. One step here, then one step there, and soon he'd have Pie back in his arms.

'I have a house in Mywin, close to the cliffs. There's a blue rose growing around the door. Walk five paces into the house and turn west. Take another three paces and lift the floorboard. It's warded to look nailed down, but at that place it will lift. Under the floor, there's a box with a knife.' She took a key from a string around her neck and handed it to Logan. 'That knife will help you cut a way through to where the unicorns are. They're here, but not here, if that makes sense.'

'Not really.' Logan shook his head. This was bard territory, and he had no map.

'This knife will let you cut through the spell at a place where it's weakened. You'll be able to slip between the two points of reality.'

Logan raised an eyebrow. 'That sounds powerful. Where did you find this knife?' He didn't like this. He didn't like any of this. Magic. Unicorns. Portals. None of this was his area of expertise. He felt like he was scrabbling up a cliff-face, barely clinging on with his fingertips.

Logan wanted solid ground under his feet at all times.

'The unicorns live happily in that realm, but their human companions need supplies from our world. My grandfather was one of a network of trusted traders who'd supply the trainers. When my father died, we kept the knife safe and hidden. Unicorns in the wrong hands would be a disaster. They were driven almost to extinction a hundred years or so ago, so they'd be incredibly valuable now. Not to mention the issue of them being magical. I hope you understand what entrusting it to you means.'

'Thank you. This means a lot.' He slipped the key into his pocket.

'And where is this weak place?' the countess asked.

'Follow the cliffs north of Mywin, and you'll come to a tomb. It belongs to a renowned mage and the wards protecting him affect the surroundings. The magic they generate should allow you to cut through.'

The countess clapped her hands together. 'A tomb? Oh, goody.'

'Don't even think about it,' Logan growled.

'I really wouldn't,' Seraphina agreed. 'You don't know what sort of protections have been cast around those dusty places.'

The countess stamped a foot like a disappointed child. 'But if he was so powerful, there might be something useful there.'

'One, I doubt it, and two, we don't have the time.' Logan headed for the doorway, ushering them all out. The countess's gaze gave him an itch. 'I know, I know, I'm a terrible bore.'

The main road to Mywin led away across the open farmland, but Logan took them instead up a narrow coastal path. He walked beside Bones, guiding the creature over the rocky and poorly maintained path. Scrubby bushes, kept low by the constant wind from the sea, prickled at his legs and he had to stop the horse from trying to eat them every few steps.

Ophelia sat on the back of Bones, her arms folded, staring at the ground as if she wanted to punch it.

'What's eating you?' he asked, giving the reins a tug as Bones stopped to try and devour another shrub.

She turned her head back towards the retreating town. 'I'm worried about Seraphina.'

Shame flushed through him. 'Oh. That.'

'Yes, that.' Ophelia crossed her legs, her hips sinking into the horse's pelvis. She pointed a finger at him. 'Your head is jammed so far up your own arse you can't think about anyone but yourself.'

'I think about Pie,' he muttered.

She tossed her head. 'I cannot wait to meet the man who has managed to occupy a space in your tiny little world.' She disappeared from the back of Bones, and reappeared floating just above the road, her form mixing with the morning mist until she seemed less of a person and more of a smear of anxiety. Logan cleared his throat.

'She seems like a smart woman. I'm sure she'll be fine.'

'That's not what you said yesterday.'

He rubbed the back of his neck. 'No, and that was wrong. I was too worried about my own needs. Look, if she's related to you, then she's stubborn, strong, and not the sort to let anyone get in the way of what she wants. I think she'll do just fine.'

Ophelia gave him a stare, as if trying to work out if he was lying or teasing her, then slowly nodded. 'I hope so.'

'Thank you for talking to her. And, I . . . er . . . I am sorry, about my behaviour last night.' The words caught in his throat, tripped over his tongue, and spilled out into the air like scattered pebbles.

Her stare deepened, as if trying to see into his soul. 'Well. Good. So you should be. You're a monster, but at least you can acknowledge it.'

'I'm not a monster.' He sighed. The accusations of yesterday still nettled him, and he found her animosity did too. They'd been friends, once. Closer than friends, and he missed that. 'I guess I'm just bad at priorities.'

'You can say that again.'

'I try to do the right thing, Ophelia.' She'd told her cousin she trusted him. Maybe there was still hope for them both. 'I always have. But I get caught up on this one right thing, and I forget there are half a dozen other right things as well.'

'You're like a cart horse in blinkers,' Ophelia agreed, nodding vigorously, but there was a smile playing on her lips. 'Big, dumb, and only going one way.'

'Hey. I'm trying to bare my heart here.'

'And you smell,' she added. She stretched her legs out in mid-air and leaned back. 'But thank you.'

The town of Mywin nestled in a hollow between two craggy hills, laid out below them like a model. Logan wondered which house was Seraphina's. In the sheltered bay, fishing vessels waited at anchor, rocking gently with the swell. Ophelia had cheered up since their conversation, and now walked alongside the path, investigating the wildflowers. The countess appeared to be deep in a game of I Spy with one of the skeletons. It was pointing at things, while she shook her head and laughed at it.

The closer Logan grew to the town, the more the back of his neck prickled. Something wasn't right, though it wasn't until he reached the open gates that he could put his finger on it.

There was no smoke coming from any of the chimneys.

'Countess, is anyone alive out there?'

She shook her head. 'No, it's quiet. Oh. This isn't right.'

'No, it's not.' Logan hefted his axe, the weight of the hard steel a comfort in his hands. A town like this should have been loud and vibrant. The gates were open, but no one appeared to be in the gatehouse. 'Wait here.'

She hung back. 'Perhaps we should be cautious, Logan dear.'

'We don't have time to be cautious,' he snapped. 'We need that knife. You wait here; I'll be back shortly.'

'One day I'll make you trust me, Logan Theaker.'

'I severely doubt that.'

He took a step towards the gate, and she followed him like a shadow. Logan pinched the bridge of his nose, then gave her a pointed glare.

'All right, all right. I promise I won't raise anything unless absolutely necessary. But I'm not staying out here and missing all the fun.'

'That will have to do.'

The town gates had been carved with images of fish, and Logan felt every blank wooden eye staring at him as he passed through. He readied his weapon and glanced around. The main road wound down to the harbour in a gentle curve, lined with shops on each side. All closed up. A smithy sat to his left, the forge stone cold.

The countess sent her skeleton down the road, while she began peering through a shop window. Silence pushed in on Logan, wrapping around him like a shroud. Nothing seemed wrong: no fire, no damage to the largely wooden buildings, no sign of magic.

Nothing, apart from the complete lack of people.

Logan walked a short distance to check the guard post by the gate. As he slowly eased the door open, he expected to find a body. But like everything else, it was empty. The stillness made the hairs on the back of his neck stand on end. A ledger and quill lay open with notes from the day's passing traffic. Logan leaned over to take a better look. The previous day's entries ran the length of the page but this one stopped about halfway down. No blood, no sign of a struggle. It was as though the guard had simply wandered off for lunch and never returned.

A soft caw made Logan spin, axe raised. Muscles tensed and heart pounding, he realised it was a crow and cringed, half expecting a mocking retort from the countess.

'Countess?' he called when his dignity returned unscathed. Only the crow answered. Logan swore under his breath, glancing around for her, but she, too, had disappeared. 'This is not the way to get me to trust you.'

He left the guard's post and set off down the street, his footsteps too loud in his ears. Goosebumps rose over his arms, part chill, part fear. Still no sign of the countess, let alone anyone else. He pushed on towards the centre of town, where the shrines and boneyard lay.

'If I find you've raised so much as a rat, there's going to be trouble,' he muttered.

He found her storming back from the central square, her cloak billowing out behind her like bat wings.

'What's going on?' he demanded, standing in her path. 'If there's anything moving around that shouldn't be—'

She skidded to a halt in front of him. 'No, Logan, nothing's moving. Nothing's moving at all!' She waved a hand towards the square, her mouth set in a tight line, but her eyes wide. She wrapped her arms around herself, her lower lip trembling.

'What do you mean?'

'See for yourself. It's absolutely appalling, I tell you.'

Logan's stomach turned over. Something the *countess* found appalling?

He pushed past her to the open plaza. A large, low structure, built from odd-shaped logs and stones, sat in the middle of the cobbled square. Logan squinted; the twilight distorted everything into a murky silhouette. His body tensed, senses on edge, waiting for an attack. He felt as if he were back in combat. But this wasn't a battlefield. It was a town. A perfectly normal, undamaged town, with no evidence of fighting or death.

Except for the smell.

He approached slowly, realisation dawning. Those weren't logs, they were bodies wrapped in cloth.

Hundreds of them.

Chapter Six

The bodies were stacked five levels high, each level turned ninety degrees from the one below. Logan stumbled back from the grotesque structure, heart drumming wildly in his ears. This had to be the entire town. Hundreds of men, women and children. All dead. It wasn't just the overwhelming number of corpses that sent a chill through Logan, but the calm, methodical way they'd all been carefully stacked. Not with respect in mind, but practicality.

'Who could have done this?' His voice made him shudder, as if even the slightest whisper would bring whatever did this crashing down on him. As if the same thing would come and wrap him in a white sheet and place his body at the top of the stack.

'It's disgusting.' The countess folded her arms with a humph.

'I would have guessed something like this wouldn't bother you,' Logan muttered. 'Maybe there is hope for you yet.'

'Of course it bothers me,' she snapped. 'You can't treat the dead like that. All bundled up the same, like little parcels. Where are the rites? Who gave the Dark Mother her due?'

'That's what's bothering you? The lack of respect to your god? Not the, I don't know' – he waved a hand at the stack of corpses – 'huge number of dead right there?'

The countess took a step back. 'Well, I suppose that's terrible, too.' She fished in her bag and pulled out a lump of chalk. 'I'd better get on with things.'

'What are you doing?' His legs wobbled as if he'd run ten miles. 'I told you, no raising anything!'

She ignored him and began sketching out a crude circle on the cobbles.

'I'm serious. No—'

She held up a finger. 'Logan Theaker, do you want to know who did this?'

'Well, of course,' he muttered.

She continued. 'And do you want to know if they're still in the area?'

'I . . . er . . .' Logan's face burned like that of a scolded child.

'What was that, dear? I couldn't quite hear you.'

'You make a good point,' he mumbled.

'Of course I do. Now be quiet and let me work.'

Logan walked away, unable to bear the sight of the neatly wrapped packages of human corpses. This wasn't the work of monsters. Even the more intelligent ones couldn't do something like this. They killed to eat, to protect their territory. This was manmade. Had there been a war on, then he might think an enemy army had passed through here and taken no prisoners, but the last major conflict had ended before King Ervin's rule even started.

Logan had always been indifferent to the king's situation in the past. Falling in love with Pie had changed his mind on the matter. To lose so many loved ones over such a short period of time was bound to have a dramatic effect. Some said grief had driven the king a little mad, but Logan thought this was backwards. To lose the one he loved, and *not* change? That would have been madness.

Of course, that was before the king had dragged Pie into all this.

Pie had always spoken kindly of the king, described him as kind and thoughtful, the sort of man who had little interest in power for power's sake. Logan kicked himself for never asking questions about Pie's connection to the king. Perhaps if he knew more about how they'd met, he'd understand more about what Pie had got caught up in.

'Oh, look.' Ophelia's voice startled him. 'Logan's in the middle of death and destruction, once again. No surprises here.'

'This is serious, Ophelia – and it has nothing to do with me,' he snapped. 'People are dead. A whole town gone.'

She glared at him. "I can see that!"

'He's right, my dear. It isn't his fault,' the countess called. Logan and Ophelia turned to where she stood. 'Come over here and let's get some answers from the Dark Mother's newest children.'

Two skeletons from her home knelt on the ground beside her – at least, Logan hoped they were the same skeletons from her home. They arranged some candles around the intricate circular design etched into the sandy dirt. The countess lit the wicks and spread her arms.

'I open the veil and call to the new dead of Mywin. Step away from the Dark Mother's side and speak your truth to me.'

Logan paced beside the circle. What if none of the dead stepped through? What if too many stepped through at once? Could the little dirt circle hold them back? A spark flashed in the air and a shape formed, growing from a faint light to the shape of a figure.

It was a man, maybe ten years older than Logan. Even in his translucent form, the effect of years of wind and salt on his skin was visible. The countess moved to speak, but Logan cut her off, desperate for answers.

'Who killed you?' Logan asked the ghost.

The ghost opened his mouth and let out a blood-curdling scream that penetrated Logan's bones, echoing through his marrow. Before Logan could react, the countess clicked her fingers and the spirit vanished.

No one spoke. The air hummed with energy.

'Well, that was unhelpful,' Logan quipped with a nervous laugh.

The countess huffed out a frustrated breath. 'The dead often are, especially the newly deceased. Normally when people come to me, they're seeking someone who's been dead a while. Raising the newly dead is quite another matter. Let me try another.'

'No.' The scream still curdled his guts. And if the man was that recently dead, the perpetrators could still be around. 'There are other ways to find out who murdered these people.'

The countess snapped her fingers at a skeleton and pointed to the candles, which had toppled over. She pulled out her velvet pouch of sweet-smelling herbs, frowning at the contents.

'Well, I suppose you could grub around in the dirt for ideas – go ahead. But don't mock or spurn the greatest power we have access to. That would be extremely inefficient, if you ask me.' Both skeletons nodded in unison.

'Fine. Carry on.' Logan took another sweep of their surroundings. He found a doll discarded on the ground, a basket of eggs set on a wall, a handkerchief trampled in the dirt. Little signs of the people of the town, their lives cut off. Walking around the corpses, Logan tried to ignore the feeling that they were being watched. He'd seen enough of the countess's work to dispel any doubts he had about her powers. If she said there was no life here, she wasn't wrong. A cold breeze pulled at his clothes, adding to the multitude of shivers brought on by the situation.

A patch of pale blue caught his attention. The fabric, as well as being an unusual colour, seemed finer than most of the wrappings. It was bundled amongst the bodies. Curiously, Logan pulled at it. The fabric quickly unravelled.

It was a flag.

A blazing flame emblem was largely hidden, but he could make out the edges. Logan had seen this emblem before. It was held aloft proudly during battles, fluttering over armies, hung over guildhalls and in nearly every town and city. It was the flag of the king. Was that body a soldier? The body was dressed in simple clothes that smelled of sea salt and wore no armour. Had they simply run out of suitable shrouds. The stack was neat, almost methodical. It didn't suggest a slaughter in anger or hatred.

The realisation wasn't making him feel any better.

Could the king have done this? Was this the madness brought on by the death of his wife? What else would explain the systematic murder of his own citizens? If so, would he be back to raise the rest of the town, as he had Seraphina's spellcaster friends? And where did Pie fit in all this? Pie got queasy at the sight of blood, had no interest in battles or politics. What could Ervin possibly want with him? Logan's guts knotted with worry.

'Countess,' he called over his shoulder. 'We're leaving.'

'I'm not quite finished, Logan dear,' she answered back, muttering something to one of the skeletons.

'Stay out here if you want, but I'm pretty sure King Ervin's behind this and I don't want to be around when he begins awakening the dead. No offence, Ophelia,' he added quickly.

Her answering scowl told him offence had most certainly been taken. Logan shrugged and headed across town, striding away as quickly as possible. The road turned and he caught a glimpse of the sea, grey waves whipped into a white froth by the rising wind. It howled through the empty town and waves crashed in the distance like ghostly voices. Logan shivered again, despite his best efforts. The sea always struck him as bleak, even on a bright day. A vast expanse of water, empty of life.

Apart from fish, but he suspected they were cold, wet and miserable too.

He followed Seraphina's directions, heading up a steep cobbled street past thatched cottages towards the edge of the town. The countess followed behind, muttering to herself. Logan passed little gardens, full of vegetables that would never be harvested, herbs that would never be clipped. The home's hearths would remain unlit, the beds cold and empty.

The cottage with the blue roses was easy to find, standing at the end of the row. It reminded Logan of home and a sharp stabbing nostalgia hit him like a punch to the guts. Pie had always wanted roses around the door. It had been one of the jobs Logan had been tasked with, but every chance had come with a different reason to wait. He had wanted to create a trellis for them to climb on. He had thought he had all the time in the world.

'Stop smelling the flowers and come on,' Ophelia called, passing through the door.

'We can't all walk through solid wood, Ophelia!' he retorted. The door was locked, but a swift kick sorted the problem. Logan turned to the countess. 'Keep a lookout. The king was here recently, and we don't know how far he's gone. We can't risk them getting their hands on this knife.'

The countess nodded. 'You heard the man,' she said to the two skeletons. They took up position, one in front and the other behind the property. Inside, Logan carried out the instructions Seraphina had given him to locate the loose floorboard. As she'd said, it appeared to be nailed down, but when he dug in with his fingernails, it came away easily.

The box was made of dark, almost black wood, with nothing but a single brass keyhole to decorate it. Logan pulled out the key Seraphina had given him and turned it slowly. The air popped and crackled around him, as if a thunderstorm was building in the house.

The blade was made from a strange metal that reminded Logan of stone. It shimmered blue, green and purple in the light, the colours shifting and swirling. The handle was well-worn, and as he held it, a prickling sensation ran up through his fingers and down his spine. Magic. Power.

The countess approached and peered over his shoulder at the box.

'How interesting.' She reached a long finger towards the blade, and Logan tucked it into his belt, out of reach.

'We got what we came for. Let's get out of here.'

'Rude, dear,' the countess muttered.

They took a narrow sea path that led them far from town and along the cliffs. They walked in single file, silently, watching as a thick sea mist rolled in off the waves.

The countess took a deep breath, rolling her shoulders and breaking the long silence. 'Come on, Logan dear, cheer up. We got the knife.'

'I can't see my feet,' Logan replied, despondent. 'There's every chance I could walk right off the cliff and be smashed on the rocks before I even noticed.'

'That would be a terrible shame,' she said sweetly. 'But I'd make sure to put your bones to good use.'

He snorted a laugh that turned melancholy; cracking a joke like that was exactly what Pie would do. She sent one of her skeletal cronies up ahead to check the path. Despite his urgency, Logan would not be reckless on the narrow path. Grey tendrils of mist wound around his legs, a damp and dangerous caress. To his left and far below, the sea boomed against the cliff walls, howling like a mad beast longing to crunch his bones to sand.

Which at least would save him from an afterlife of servitude to the countess.

After hours of hiking and sore muscles, a hazy sun appeared through the remaining clouds, and the mist dissipated enough for them to see the path. Everyone had lapsed into a calm silence, apart from the countess, who was happily regaling them with a tale about being courted by a spellcaster and speculating what would be awaiting in the mage's tomb. Logan groaned under his breath. She was going to make this difficult, wasn't she?

The path rose so steeply that the passage of previous travellers had carved steps into the ground. Panting, his leg burning, Logan reached the top and came face to face with three immense blocks of stone, two standing and one placed on top of the others, like a door lintel. The base of the blocks was surrounded by little chips of black and white stones, and between them lay a brass plaque, set into the ground. The writing had long since worn away. Logan wondered just how old the tomb was.

'I'm guessing this is the place.' He wiped sweat from his brow. The pain in his leg throbbed, making his stomach churn.

'What a wonderful spot!' The countess spread her arms like a drunken bat.

Logan pulled Seraphina's knife from his belt. 'Right, let's get on with it then.'

'Are you sure we can't do a little grave-robbing while we're here?' she pleaded, clutching her hands together over her heart. 'We might find something useful.'

She walked over to the stones, running her hand across them. Swirling symbols were carved delicately into the stone, and Logan could make out the outline of what looked like strange, wild creatures. Nothing about the creeping, many-legged entities suggested that touching the tomb was a good idea.

'No grave-robbing. You can do that on your own time.'

'Well, you say that, but I seem to remember a certain someone taking offence to it last time and dragging me off to the authorities.'

'I won't bother with the authorities this time,' Logan said distractedly, staring at the knife in his hands, wishing he'd pushed Seraphina harder for information about what to do with it. How exactly did one cut a spell?

'Ooh, you're going to tie me up and leave me in your own personal dungeon?' She giggled. 'You're a wicked man, Logan.'

Logan slashed at the air. The blade moved through it with a whistle. His scalp prickled. In front of him hung a bright line, as if drawn by a pen. He swallowed.

'I guess that's how you cut a spell,' Logan murmured.

The countess came forward and raised a finger towards the bright line. Logan cringed, waiting for her to jump back in pain. She poked it again and giggled.

'Oh, it tickles.' The countess laughed.

'I don't see how this gets us through though,' Logan said.

'Have you considered cutting a door?' Ophelia said, condescension clinging like fog to every word.

'I . . . had not.'

Logan took a deep breath and readied the knife again. This time, he reached down to the ground and moved it in a straight line straight up to above his head. Then along, and down to the ground again. The bright line hung in the air like last time, but now, the space encased by it looked different.

And the same.

And yet different.

Logan closed his eyes, shaking his head twice, trying to clear his vision. The light directly in front of him had a pinkish tone, and on the other side was a world. Their world, only brighter, warmer. The sea path disappeared, replaced by rolling meadows of luscious green grass and vibrant wildflowers. He took a step to the side and peered around, checking that outside the doorway, the sea path and the stony cliffs continued uninterrupted. He checked several times, looking between lush meadow in one moment and craggy coast in another, until Ophelia slapped a hand through his arm.

'Let's get on with it,' she suggested, and he nodded sheepishly.

'Well, here goes nothing,' he said, and stepped through.

Interlude

Eighteen Months Ago

The warmth of the campfires drew Logan closer. It was easy in the dim light to tell the regimented camp of the army from the mess of mercenaries and adventurers. He sighed. What was he doing here? Squabbles between princes were no business of his. But agents from both warring princes had been putting considerable pressure on anyone who could wield a weapon, from financial incentives to direct threats. So here, soldiers and criminals lingered side by side.

He set up his tent and looked around for any familiar faces. A hand waved from across the campfire, beckoning him over.

'Bear! Didn't expect to see you here. Come join us.'

'Butcher.' Logan greeted the man with a nod. Duncan the Butcher was a burly bald man with a scar running down one cheek and a grin that revealed many lost teeth. Around this particular fire were six or seven other adventurers Logan vaguely recognised, and on the far side, a pale figure with auburn hair that was hard to miss. Unlike the worn and muddy leathers of the adventurers, he wore a clean linen shirt and a light cloak embroidered with autumn leaves. A hat with an enormous peacock feather sat on the bench next to him.

'What's a bard doing here?' Logan asked Duncan, taking the seat next to him.

'He's come to sing of our glory,' Duncan replied with a grin. 'He's got pre-battle nerves. Watch this.'

Duncan turned to the woman next to him, Meg the Ogre. She looked like she could lift a blacksmith in one hand and his anvil in the other.

'Remember the battle of God Hill?'

She gave a throaty laugh. The fire flared, highlighting the green face painted on her pauldron. 'When I put a knife right through that mercenary's eye? Took me weeks to pick clean the brains from my breastplate. Still doesn't smell right to this day.'

The bard clapped a hand over his mouth and hurried from their circle.

'You're an arsehole, Butcher.' Logan watched the bard stumbling through the dark. 'That was cruel.'

'Takes one to know one,' Duncan replied, though his voice held no malice. 'Beer for the Bear!'

'In a moment.' Logan left the warmth of the fire and soon found the bard leaning against a tree, wiping his mouth on a monogrammed handkerchief.

'Come to mock me as well?' the bard asked, before retching again.

'Came to offer you some water.' Logan held out his spare waterskin. After a moment, the bard took it.

'Thanks.' He took a mouthful and spat it over the gnarled tree roots. 'Hey, it's you. Our grumpy guide to Southfalls.'

'Aye, that's me. And you're Magpie, the bard who never shuts up.'

'Pretty sure you're describing all bards, there. Part of the job. I'm the *handsome* bard who never shuts up.' He took another drink, then groaned, wrapping an arm around his stomach, his pale face shining with sweat.

'You sure it's just battle nerves?' Logan asked, concerned. The bard looked green.

'I don't know.' He took another sip. 'Came on just after I got here. I can't stop shivering. Is that normal?'

Logan shook his head. 'Did you eat Duncan's cooking? I've seen it fell men before.'

'I haven't been able to stomach food, definitely not that slop he calls a meal. Haven't had anything apart from some water from the stream back there.'

Logan frowned. 'The one that runs parallel to the road? The one that runs from around the hill?'

'Why?'

'That stream flows past yesterday's battlefield.'

The bard paled to a ghostly white, doubling over and vomiting violently. Logan patted his back, trying not to mock the man. Bards. Who else wouldn't check where water had passed through before drinking?

'Am I going to die?' Magpie asked, his voice shaking.

'I doubt it,' Logan replied. 'Come and lie down until you feel better.'

Logan wrapped an arm around Magpie's waist and put the bard's arm around his shoulder, then led him back to his own tent. As they passed the fire, he grabbed a pot and took it with them. Magpie lay down on the bedroll, pulling Logan's blanket around himself until he was cocooned. The little tent barely had room for Logan's bed and pack, so he found himself squashed in a corner, the pack pushed out into the night. Risky, with this many strangers around, but he wasn't going to leave a sick man alone.

'How did you end up here in the first place?' Logan asked. 'You don't strike me as the sort of bard who enjoys this kind of work.'

'Gods, no. I'd never choose a job like this.' Magpie rested a hand over his eyes. 'I . . . I lost a game quite spectacularly and owed the Count of Veatherton a small fortune. He said he'd write it off if I composed some ballads for his troops' victories tomorrow. They better bloody win.'

Logan wasn't convinced the bard would be in any shape to witness anything tomorrow. 'Which prince is Veatherton backing?'

Magpie reached for the pot, retching painfully. He lay back with a groan. 'I don't even remember. Honestly, the best thing they could do would be to kill each other and leave the throne for Ervin. He's the best of the lot of them. What about you? You big on battles?' he asked.

For a moment, Logan pondered how a travelling bard knew the royal family well enough to make such a call.

'I was pushed into it when I really should have said no. Might still say no, to be honest with you. Killing monsters is one thing, but killing men, especially over the petty quarrels of high-born men, is another. Whoever sits on the throne makes no difference to me.'

There was no further response from the bard and when Logan looked, Magpie had fallen asleep.

Chapter Seven

Stepping through the portal was somewhat anticlimactic. He'd expected a reaction when he walked through. Sound, lights, a sudden three-part harmony. Something. But it was the same as every other step he'd taken in his life.

His leg still ached. And he had no idea if he was any closer to Pie.

He traced the lines on the knot tattoo under his shirt from memory, wondering if Pie ever did the same. Did he sit there, missing Logan's voice or touch? Logan hoped wherever he was, Pie was warm and dry and eating enough.

The countess and Ophelia followed him, as did the skeletons. Both women looked around them, eyes wide, darting their heads in quick motions to take everything in. The skeletons stared at him, as if they knew everything leading up to this moment, and anything that came after, was Logan's fault.

The bright line that marked their entranceway winked out of existence.

Logan's stomach dropped.

He made a slash with the knife, but no bright line. No change. No doorway.

'Guess we better find that damn unicorn,' he muttered.

He took another look at his surroundings. Everything around him looked similar, in the sense that the trees and the grass looked the same as the ones he saw every day. But the colours were warmer, more vibrant. And the sea had vanished. In its place were flower meadows, an odd, twisted oak tree, a gently flowing river winding its way across the landscape in the distance. He cast a glance at the sun, peeping through fluffier clouds. It even had a pinkish tinge.

Ophelia doubled over laughing.

'What? What's wrong with you?'

She pointed at him. 'Your hair is standing on end. You look an angry hedgehog.'

Logan passed a hand over his head, several pops of static tickling his fingers. His hair, normally an unruly mass of black and grey waves, now appeared to be doing its best to escape his head. He sighed and tried to push it back down.

'That's really not the most important thing right now,' he said, pushing away the skeleton who had come over with a comb. 'Which way?'

If this were the same world, only hidden, then the unicorns could be anywhere. They could end up walking for weeks before they realised they were going in the wrong direction. He'd end up wandering around blindly while Pie was alone in another world. Images flooded his mind, making his chest tight.

Pie lying in the dirt.

Hurt, bleeding.

Calling for him.

He squeezed his eyes shut, but the images remained. His heart pounded and his vision spun.

'Logan!'

He turned, the voice pulling him back to reality. Ophelia stood with her hands on her hips.

'Stop ignoring us, you dumb ox,' she said. He gave her a glare for appearance's sake, swallowing back bile.

'As I was saying,' the countess continued. 'Unicorns are animals, so we should look for where animals might live. My suggestion would be to head down to the river.'

'That makes sense.' He nodded slowly, forcing himself to breathe. His heart vibrated in his chest, and his whole body felt loose and wobbly, as if someone had boiled his bones. 'Yeah, that makes sense.'

The countess cocked her head, her elaborate gravestone hairstyle leaning precariously at an angle. 'Are you sure you're all right, Logan dear?'

'I'm fine,' he muttered.

Logan took a step in the direction she had indicated. He gritted his teeth, ready for the jolt of pain from his leg, but when it came, it was milder than he expected. He took another step. Not exactly comfortable, but no agonising pain either.

Huh.

He set off downhill at a brisk pace, not waiting to see if the others were following. He'd once convinced himself he was happy and content to be alone, not needing anyone else or wanting to have anyone rely on him. But Pie had torn that idea to shreds.

Gods-damned bards.

By the time they reached the river, he felt calmer. He'd pushed himself hard, but even after that, his leg barely complained. The river wound its way across the landscape in lazy serpentines. Instead of the dull, silt-laden water he was used to, here it sparkled clean and inviting.

'It's beautiful here.' Ophelia stood at the water's edge, a wistful expression on her face. Without her usual scowl, she looked much younger, more like the woman he'd been told he was marrying. He hadn't hated the idea back then.

Or her.

She had flowers and ribbons in her hair in the red and yellow of Founding Day the first time they'd really spoken. Her lips were the colour of rosehips, her green eyes bright and curious. He knew her, of course – everyone did. Her father was one of the town elders and she lived in the large wooden house set back from the rest of the town. She was beautiful, lithe and delicate, a year or so older than him.

'Dance with me,' she said, holding out a hand. It wasn't a question. Logan set down the tankard of cider, panic stealing his voice. But he took her hand and followed her out to the other dancers.

When she'd put his hand on the small of her back, he'd worried that his heart might explode. She smelled of jasmine, intoxicating. He'd never been good at dealing with people at the best of times, and now she occupied every sense.

'You were part of the group that caught that parel,' she said in his ears as the music started. 'My father was very impressed.'

'Was nothing,' he muttered, staring at his feet. His face flushed so hot he was sure it must be the same colour as her ribbons. They swirled around the dance floor in a dizzying pattern.

'Fighting off a giant cat that's been stealing lambs isn't nothing,' she retorted. She leaned in close, her breath tickling his neck. 'It's heroic.'

'I don't like it.' The countess rubbed her arms as if she were cold, despite the warm spring day. 'This place doesn't sit right with me.'

'Don't you think it's beautiful?' Ophelia said dreamily. She passed her hand through a patch of bright yellow buttercups. Logan understood what the countess meant. The place had a dreamy, ethereal quality. It was like a bard's song – lovely, but not real.

'Come on,' he said, pointing down the river. 'Let's find ourselves a magical horse.'

The sun rose higher, burning away the clouds, and the bright sunlight only added to the beauty of the place. Colours felt more vibrant and the water shimmered. Logan's leg felt better than ever. In the distance, he spotted a trail of smoke, possibly from a chimney.

Logan dared to hope.

He strode across the grass, taking full advantage of his fading injury. One more step, one more thing done, one move closer to Pie.

'Logan, wait! You're leaving us behind,' Ophelia called.

He turned back but didn't slow his pace, gritting his teeth. 'I don't want to wait. I want to get a damn unicorn and get my husband back. Hurry up.'

'I'm sorry, Logan dear,' the countess murmured. 'I'm afraid my old bones aren't moving as fast as they used to.'

She had her hand on one of the skeletons' knobbly shoulderblade, leaning heavily. The skeletons seemed different too. Stiffer, their movements jerkier. As he observed their odd behaviour, one of their teeth fell out. The countess caught it and put it in her pocket.

'What's wrong?' he asked, concern lacing his words.

'This place is draining, don't you think?' She pulled out a black lace handkerchief and began dabbing at her face.

'Quite the opposite,' Logan replied. 'I feel about ten years younger.'

'How nice for you,' she grumbled.

'Come on.' He held out his hand. 'We need to get to those unicorns and get out of here as soon as possible.'

'What are you proposing, Logan dear?' Her eyebrows were raised.

He suppressed a sigh. 'If you promise to keep your hands to yourself. I'll carry you.'

She let out a gleeful giggle. 'How delightful!'

'One inappropriate touch and I'm dropping you on your bony arse, you hear?'

'Completely understood, Logan dear.'

He took her gently into his arms, awkwardly at first as he tried to navigate the long black skirt to avoid any inappropriate touching on his behalf. She'd never let him live that down.

She laid her head against his shoulder, her breath tickling his chin. She felt like a ragdoll compared to the times he'd carried Pie. Delicate, floppy, light as a bag of feathers. They continued on toward the rising smoke.

As they grew closer, the small wooden hut came into view. Several horses grazed around it and Logan's hopes rose and then sank.

What if they were just horses?

'I think we've done it,' Ophelia said at his side.

Logan squinted. Were those horns? 'You're sure?'

'Benefit of being dead. My eyesight is much better than when I was alive.' She grinned, but it faded quickly. 'Of course, there are a few other drawbacks.'

'I'll see you get a body again,' he said. 'I'll make sure the countess here fulfils her promise.'

'You owe me that much,' Ophelia said. 'Maybe I'll take a big muscly one so I can beat you up.'

'That seems a little unfair,' he replied. In his arms, the countess laughed. He sucked in a breath, then let it out again in a sigh. 'You, er, you never told me how you died.'

She tensed up and then shook her head. 'Not now, Logan.'

Before he could say more, she hurried off, moving swiftly through the grass without bending a single blade.

'I have a feeling you might not like the answer to that,' the countess said. She tilted her head so she could stare up at him. 'Best to let it drop.'

'Never been particularly good at letting things drop,' he said. 'You might be a first, though.'

'Such a tease, Logan dear.' There was a hitch in her voice, despite her cheeky smile. Her face had a sheen of sweat that shone in the strange sunlight.

Beside them, the skeletons collapsed into a pile of bones.

'Oh dear,' the countess said, her voice weaker.

Logan stared at the bones. The skulls grinned back at him. The contrast of them beside the lush grass and sparkling river felt creepier than usual.

The countess shook her head. 'Let's go get our unicorn and get out of here before I need my hair doing again. Come on, noble steed, giddy up.'

They *were* unicorns.

Logan blinked several times but the long, elegant horns remained. There was a herd of them in a variety of colours from jet black to gleaming white, with several bay and even a piebald one. They were beautiful creatures, with long, arched necks, wavy manes and flowing tails. Their hooves were feathered like those of a draught horse, but instead of being large and stocky, these were graceful, willowy creatures built for speed. Several raised their heads as Logan approached, their ears pricked and alert.

No paddock contained them, but there was a wooden shelter nearby, as well as a small cottage where smoke rose steadily from the chimney. There were no people around that he could see, but he couldn't imagine these beautiful creatures were undefended. And even if they did manage to nab one from the herd, how were they to get back home if Seraphina's knife didn't work?

Suddenly the door to the wooden cottage opened. Logan's heart raced – the open meadow offered no cover. Still carrying the countess, he ducked behind the cottage, out of sight. He wanted time to work on an explanation that would convince them to hand over a unicorn, and he was never at his most convincing when surprised.

The figure headed away from them, towards a small stone well. It was a young man, maybe early twenties – a good couple of decades younger than Logan – dressed in a tight-fitting shirt and well-patched trousers. He appeared to be alone.

Logan relaxed slightly. If it came to a fight, he shouldn't be an issue.

Hopefully it wouldn't come to that.

The youth stripped off his shirt and hung it on a post. Logan glanced at his arm. Only a couple of tattoos, probably patron deities, nothing to suggest a life of adventure. No sign of marriage.

'Oh my,' the countess said, dragging out the last syllable. Beside him, Ophelia swallowed and nodded.

'What?' Logan asked, but neither woman answered him.

The youth picked up the bucket, leanted forwards, and tipped the contents over his head.

'He's going to do the head flick,' Ophelia whispered.

'He is, isn't he?' The countess leaned forward in Logan's arms, causing him to struggle to maintain his balance.

The youth straightened in one smooth motion, flicking his head back and sending a rush of water droplets through the air. They scattered like diamonds in the sunlight. Ophelia and the countess sighed.

Logan rubbed the bridge of his nose. 'What? What am I missing?'

Ophelia raised an eyebrow. 'You don't think he's attractive?'

He squinted. The youth had a chiselled torso, muscular arms, an open face with brown eyes surrounded by thick lashes, and glossy chestnut hair that reached to his shoulders. Attractive was a fair assessment, but . . .

'He's not Pie.'

Ophelia slapped the back of his head, or at least tried to. Her fingers slipped through his skull, sending a rush of cold air bouncing through his head. It faded, leaving behind a pounding headache. He rounded on her, almost dropping the countess in the process, and let out a growl.

'By all the gods, Ophelia, I swear . . .'

'Hello? Is someone there?'

'Now look what you've done!' Logan and Ophelia spat at each other.

The youth, still glistening from his shower, headed towards them. He appeared to be unarmed and his expression showed no concern at finding a group of strangers on his property. Logan eased the countess down and reached for his axe. She stood on her own two feet, swaying slightly.

'Leave the talking to me,' she urged.

'I will not,' he said quietly. 'I'm not having you propositioning us to get a unicorn.'

'Hello,' the stranger said again, rounding the corner and holding up a hand in greeting. He cocked his head at them. 'I've not seen you around here before.'

The countess put a finger on Logan's lips and took a step forward. 'Are you in charge here?'

The youth nodded.

'Of course you are,' she continued, taking another step. Logan's hands itched. 'Strapping lad like you. I bet your herd is the best around.'

'Oh, well, all unicorns are magnificent. But . . .' He gave her a conspiratorial grin. 'I suppose mine are particularly fine.'

'So I see.' She stood close enough to touch him now, and Logan was more than a little surprised she didn't. 'What's your name?'

'Gary,' he said with a nod. There was something equine about his motions, as if he'd spent more time in the company of unicorns than other people.

'Well, Gary, I am the Countess DeWinter and this is my handsome travelling companion, Logan Theaker. I come to you with a very important mission. It's a matter of life, death, and . . .' She reached out and ran a finger down one pectoral muscle. ' . . . Love.'

Logan suppressed a groan.

Gary's eyes widened as he took in the countess's words. 'That does sound serious. I suppose you'd better come in and sit down.' He grabbed a shirt from the rail and pulled it over his head. The countess took his arm and allowed him to guide her into the wooden cottage. For a moment, Logan wondered if he should intervene. Gary was clearly young and naïve, leading a complete stranger into his home with casual confidence. But they were already inside, so Logan hurried after them.

He stepped into the cabin, which was bright and airy and smelled faintly of fresh bread. There was a wooden table in the centre of the room, next to an open fire, and several neat cupboards were painted with delicate wild roses. The cabin had a dividing wall, but no door, and Logan spotted two beds on the other side.

'I can't believe that worked,' Ophelia whispered in his ear. He turned, but she was nowhere in sight. Probably for the best. The countess was one thing, but an actual ghost was another.

'He didn't even ask who we were,' Logan said. 'I don't think he's had a lot of human contact.'

'The countess is going to eat him alive, isn't she?'

'Quite probably.'

'Do you live with someone else, Gary?' Logan asked, as the youth helped the countess into a seat.

'My uncle,' Gary replied cheerfully. 'He's gone for supplies, probably won't be back until tomorrow.'

That made things easier.

Logan didn't want to hurt him. For a start, the youth seemed utterly unaware of the danger he was in. And he didn't think Pie would approve all that much of knocking him out and stealing a unicorn. But on the other hand, he couldn't see someone handing over one of these creatures, and he didn't exactly have the money to pay for one. According to Pie, the creatures had once lived wild on the island, but had been hunted to extinction a hundred years ago. Their horns had been prized both for their ability to open up portals, and their use as an amplifier for magic.

Gary set out a cup of water for everyone living, and then put a plate of warm pastries on the table, as if they were old friends, rather than an adventurer and a necromancer. Logan was almost sorry the skeleton was gone and Ophelia was hiding. At least then Gary might have had some inkling of what he was up against.

'So . . .' Gary picked up one of the pastries, breaking it in half, and putting it in his mouth. There was a long pause, where Logan reassessed the idea of just knocking him out and making a run for it. 'What brings you here?'

The countess straightened. She clutched the arm of her chair, her knuckles white, her face pale as bone, but she put on a smile.

'Well, you see, it's like this.' She gestured to Logan, her hand trembling. 'This man is Logan Theaker, a man who has dedicated his life to ridding the world of monsters who prey on the weak. A hero, no less.'

Behind Logan, Ophelia snorted. At the sound, Gary looked around, but shrugged and turned back to the countess.

'And then, just when he had retired and settled down to live a life with his beloved, his husband was kidnapped!'

Logan opened his mouth to say he wasn't entirely sure it was a kidnapping, but stopped. Whatever it was, Pie needed help. The countess's words were clearly having an influence on the young man, who sat wide-eyed, one hand lifted to his mouth in horror. He caught Logan looking at him, and gave him a look of pity.

'I'm so sorry.' Gary reached for another pastry. He licked a little of the flaky crust from his lip. Behind Logan, Ophelia sighed.

'So, we absolutely have to help him rescue his poor husband, and for that we need your help.'

'Of course.' Gary nodded vigorously, his words somewhat muffled by the mouthful of food.

Logan's breath caught in his throat. Could it be that easy?

'You'll give us a unicorn?' the countess asked, unable to keep the excitement out of her voice.

Gary blinked. 'A . . . a unicorn?'

Logan's stomach sank. Of course it was never going to be that easy.

The countess's smile didn't falter. 'Yes, a unicorn. Logan's husband, Aloysius—'

'Pie,' Logan said.

'—has been taken somewhere only the unicorns can reach. Will you help us save him, Gary? For the sake of true love?'

Gary looked away, his face drawn in a deep frown. 'I . . . I want to help, but I can't just hand over a unicorn. For a start, they won't obey anyone except their trainer, unless you use the enchanted tack, and that's just so cruel, to bind the will of a unicorn.'

Logan curled a fist. He'd let the countess try her way. Looked like it would have to be done barbarian-style after all. He needed to make sure the lad didn't see it coming, put him down quickly. He didn't much like fighting people, but he'd do what he had to.

For Pie.

'And they were my parents' herd, but my uncle manages everything now, so really you'll have to wait until he comes back,' Gary finished.

The countess reached for Gary's hand, drawing an elegantly manicured finger over his palm. 'I'm not sure Logan can be convinced to wait that long. He's an impatient soul at the best of times.'

Gary gave Logan a sideways glance. Logan shuffled in his chair, trying to make himself unassuming. If the youth could see any sign of aggression in him, it would make it that much harder to put him down.

A loud whinny from outside caused everyone at the table look up in unison. Gary leapt up and ran from the room. Logan cursed under his breath. Much harder to sneak up on the lad outside.

'Stay here,' he told the countess, and followed Gary outside.

Out in the paddock, four figures in black cloaks with well-fitted leather armour surrounded the piebald unicorn. One figure stood off to the side, while the three others tried to get a rope around the creature's neck. The unicorn tossed its head and pawed at the earth, twisting and jabbing at them with its horn.

'Get away from her!' Gary yelled. 'She'll run you through. You can't force a unicorn like that. They only answer to their trainers.' He was running toward the group, with Logan fast on his heels. Gary's bravery was only matched by his stupidity, Logan decided, racing out to meet armed fighters without a single weapon.

'Which, I suppose, you are?' asked a man with a slender goatee. He pulled a crossbow from under his fur-lined cloak. Logan gripped the handle of his axe tighter.

There was something so familiar about the man's face.

Logan planted his feet, assessing his foes. They were lightly armoured but moved with a confidence that demonstrated training. They were well equipped, too well equipped for the sort of bandits who haunted the roads. Mercenary company? How had they got here? Probably not the most important thing now. He tried to anticipate the fight. Crossbow would fire first. Then the archer would stay back, let the others rush Logan while he reloaded. So he'd be Logan's first target.

'Ah,' said Gary softly.

Logan pushed the youth aside and stepped forward. 'Get behind me, lad. You'll have to come through me if you want him.' He hefted the axe.

'Gladly,' the man said, raising the crossbow. The other three left the unicorn and turned towards Logan, drawing their own swords.

The archer's finger twitched against the trigger.

'Get back in the house, lad, and lock the door,' Logan whispered to Gary. He couldn't check if the youth had followed his instructions, couldn't take his eye off the crossbow. He tensed, waiting to dodge. If he mistimed it, he'd end up with a bolt through his neck.

A cry from across the field caught everyone's attention. A shiver ran down Logan's spine. That voice . . . surely it couldn't be?

Two figures waited on horseback some distance away. Logan couldn't make them out clearly over the glare of the sun on the river. The one in front wore a hood, low over his face, a scrawl of reddish facial hair over his jaw. The one behind was a woman, her hood down, revealing ginger hair pulled into a braid. She had one hand on the reins, the other over the hooded figure's mouth as he struggled in the saddle. Logan's heart raced in his chest.

Pie?

'Fix! Leave him be,' the woman called. She leaned forwards and whispered something to the man on the horse in front of her; he stopped struggling, slumped.

The crossbow wielder, Fix, muttered a curse and lowered his weapon. The other three men turned and ran. Fix threw one last glare at Logan before he hurried after them. Logan's heart hammered in his chest, his throat dry with panic. Could it really be Pie?

Logan broke into a run. Despite the healing effect the place had on his leg, it was clear within moments it was a futile attempt. He couldn't catch a horse, even one carrying two people.

He had to try. If it was Pie, he had to try.

The woman moved her hands and a bright doorway hung in the air. She urged her horse through, then the archer and the rest of the group followed. As Logan reached it, the doorway winked out of existence.

Chapter Eight

'Who were they?' Gary skidded to a halt beside Logan. He had a broom in his hands, brandished exactly like someone who'd never fought with a staff in their life.

'I don't know,' Logan said. His heart pounded and his mind whirled. 'But I think Pie was with them.'

Gary blinked. 'Your . . . your husband? But why would your husband be with a bunch of unicorn thieves?'

'That's the question, isn't it, lad?' Logan sighed, running a hand through his hair. *What are you up to, Pie?* Anger bubbled in a deep pit when Logan thought of him struggling against his captor. Had they hurt him? If they had, Logan would repay it tenfold.

Logan couldn't be sure it was Pie, but it looked like the hooded figure wasn't there willingly. Why would a mercenary group kidnap a bard? They didn't look the sort who wanted their exploits detailed in taverns across the land. Pie have something they wanted. 'Do you recognise them? Do you know where they went?'

Gary shook his head. 'They could be anywhere. This place is a pocket. You can step in and out of it anywhere you like, as long as you have the magic. Or a unicorn.' He frowned and scuffed at the grass with one foot. 'Thank you, for what you did back there. You were willing to put your life in front of that crossbow. I can see why the old woman called you a hero.'

'I'm no hero,' Logan said firmly. 'And don't you go believing a word that woman says.'

Gary cocked his head, brows drawn in confusion. Logan had forgotten that he was supposed to be playing the role of loyal guard for the countess, but Gary was already returning to the cottage. Logan followed him inside, where the countess waited at the table. Ophelia floated at her side but vanished as they entered. Logan hoped Gary had missed the spirit fading into the fireplace.

'I've decided. I'll lend you a unicorn. I'm coming with you.'

Relief flooded through Logan, followed by a cold wash of reality. 'I can't ask you to do that, lad. Besides, if they tried to steal a unicorn once, there's no reason to think they won't try again. You could be in danger. You should find somewhere safe.'

'I'll be safer with you.' Excitement danced in his eyes. 'Unless they've got a bridle studded with witch-stone – and good luck trying to get that on a unicorn – they're going to need a trainer. Which means if I'm here when they come back, they only have to overpower me to get what they want. If I'm with you, then you can protect me.'

'Wouldn't rely on that,' Logan said bitterly. He hadn't been able to protect Pie.

Gary appeared to not hear him. 'I'll go and pack my things right now and leave a note for my uncle.' He rushed to the bedroom at the back.

Logan couldn't decide if this was a victory or not. On the one hand, they had access to a unicorn, and someone who could work with it. On the other, he wasn't comfortable putting the lad in danger. The countess was still an evil necromancer, and who knows what else they might face on their journey. If they were to take Gary along, he was another person for Logan to watch over and protect. A sheltered romantic with no concept of the risk of strangers was hardly the best companion for a foolhardy mission.

But it was one step closer to Pie.

He let out a long breath. If Gary wanted to risk himself, it was his choice. Logan wasn't going to stop him.

'Logan dear, could you help me outside?'

Logan glanced at the countess, still sitting at the table. Her face had turned a sickly green. He offered her his arm. There was no sign of Ophelia – probably taking advantage of her invisibility to watch Gary as he packed. The countess leaned heavily on him, but he barely noticed the pressure of her grip. When they'd taken two steps outside, she bent over and vomited quietly into the dirt.

'You really need to tell me what's wrong.' Logan rubbed her back instinctively. Despite everything he disliked about her, a thread of worry nettled him.

She straightened up and dabbed at her mouth with a black lacy handkerchief. 'You're sweet to care.' Exhaustion turned her words dry and dusty. 'The magic in this place does not agree with me, shall we say? But it sounds like you've convinced young Gary, at least.'

'Not sure how I feel about that.' Logan rubbed the back of his neck. 'Do you need to leave?'

She gave him a sad smile. 'Yes, but I don't exactly have the means or the energy to do so currently. If our host hurries, I shall be fine.'

'And if he doesn't?'

'If he doesn't, I shall . . .' She made a wet sound in the back of her throat and pressed the handkerchief to her mouth. Her chest heaved as she took in several deep breaths. After a moment, she let out a sigh. 'I shall probably pass out, and you don't want that.'

Logan raised an eyebrow. 'Are you sure? Might be peaceful for me.'

'Yes, dear, I am.' She patted his arm. 'Because I am the only thing holding Ophelia's spirit here, and if I lose that connection, she'll float off, untethered, but trapped in this place. Unable to return to the realm of death, her spirit will simply decay here. And you did promise her.'

The implication settled slowly through Logan's mind, but when it hit the bottom, it hit hard. They were running out of time, and he couldn't let Ophelia down again.

'Shit!' He spun on his heel and hurried back inside.

'I'll be fine, dear!' the countess called behind him.

In the back room, Logan found Gary humming to himself as he stared at several apparently identical shirts laid out on the bed. They were all plain homespun cloth, unadorned by embroidery.

Logan sucked a breath through his teeth. 'We don't have time for this. Here.' He grabbed the closest one and thrust it at Gary. 'Put that on. Put that one in your bag. Then go get whatever it is you need to grab a unicorn. We're in a hurry.'

Gary blinked owlishly at him, then pulled the shirt over his head. 'You must be worried about your husband.'

'I am.' It wasn't a lie, but as much as he wanted to get to Pie, the situation with Ophelia was even more pressing.

Gary put a friendly hand on Logan's shoulder. He stood even taller than Pie, at least four inches taller than Logan. 'We'll find him, don't you worry.'

A sudden desire to shake the youth gripped Logan. *You don't know us*, he wanted to scream. *We're not exactly good people.* But he couldn't, not now. Not when so much depended on getting Gary's cooperation. Maybe later he could put the scares in, send him back here to his uncle and safety.

Logan took a deep breath. 'Thank you. Now, are you ready?'

'Just a few more things,' Gary said, oblivious to the tension turning Logan's nerves to lute strings. He picked up a tiny horseshoe, some smallclothes, and then headed to the other room, where he began carefully wrapping the remaining pastries in a cloth.

Logan pushed him out the way. 'Go ready the unicorn, I'll prepare the pastries.' Not a phrase he'd ever expected to say in his life.

If Gary took offence at Logan's gruff command, he didn't show it. As Gary headed outside, Ophelia whispered in Logan's ear. 'Why did you make him put a shirt on? I was enjoying the view.'

'You'll thank me when I explain later. Now hush before you scare the boy.' He didn't wait to listen to any pithy response. Pastries prepped, Logan walked out of the hut to find Gary. The countess stood where he'd left her outside the front door, her face pale and waxy. Sweat stuck grey tendrils of hair to her face. She gave Logan a brief smile, then turned away to be sick.

'What's wrong with the countess?' Ophelia asked.

'This place, it's making her sick.' Logan shrugged. 'That's what she said. That's why I'm trying to get pretty boy over there to hurry up.'

Gary had stepped out onto the grass where the unicorns grazed. They seemed unfazed by the earlier events. He held out his hand and three of them trotted over, ears pricked and tails held high. He touched each of their noses while Logan ground his teeth. Eventually Gary put his hand out to one that was jet black and slipped a halter over its head. He walked the creature over to Logan.

'This is—'

'No time.' Logan cut him off. 'Do whatever it is unicorns do. Open the doorway, get us back to the real world. Just south of Mywin.' The countess hobbled over to him and Logan scooped her effortlessly into his arms. 'Don't even think about being sick on me,' he said to her.

'Sully a handsome one like you? I'd never dream of it.' She wrapped her arms tightly around him. Despite her frivolous words, her whole body shuddered and he couldn't entirely push away a pang of worry he had for her. Gods, he was getting soft about a necromancer.

Gary placed his hand on the unicorn's shoulder and moved his palm in a circular motion. The unicorn stamped its hoof, then swung its head in a similar pattern. The air around its horn shimmered. Ahead, the void opened. The grass dull, the sky less vibrant.

'Come on, then.' Gary motioned. He clicked his tongue and the unicorn trotted forwards. Logan took a moment to appreciate the lack of pain in his leg, before following on.

His next step took him onto identical grass. Except it wasn't. Everything here felt flat, empty somehow. Lacking magic. Logan almost dumped the countess to the ground and threw himself back into that place of light and warmth, where everything sparkled.

To that place with no Pie.

He pulled his attention back to his current surroundings. The countess was curled in his arms, her face pushed against his neck.

'How are you feeling?'

'Much better,' she said, making no attempt to move. 'But let me stay here just a moment longer to get my strength back.'

'Ophelia?'

'Here, you ox,' her voice said in his ear. 'Why wouldn't I be?'

Logan let out a sigh of relief at hearing her again. He eased the countess down to the ground. She clung to his arm, whimpering in protest. 'Stop pretending,' he said with a growl, but with less intensity. She smoothed her skirts and gave him a grin.

'Can't blame a girl for trying.'

'Time to get on the road again.' He reached down and scratched at the scar on his leg. Already it was making its presence known.

From where they had emerged, it wasn't too far to walk back to the town gates where they'd left the rest of their belongings. Gary looked around him in wonder.

'Do you know where we go from here?' he asked Ophelia.

'North,' she said. 'The entrance is somewhere near the Kal mountains.'

'Ah, the early necromancers always had a flair for the dramatic,' the countess said. Logan raised an eyebrow. He wasn't sure the current ones had lost it.

Their peculiar saddles and a small pile of horse teeth still remained hidden under the bush where they'd left it, and Logan let himself relax a little at the sight.

Perhaps things were starting to go their way. He picked up the handful of teeth and handed them to the countess.

'Here you go. Let's get a move on.' He turned to the youth, but the words died in his throat. How did he explain what was going to happen? Perhaps it would be best to let him see, and show him he had nothing to fear from the countess's skeletons. Gary had trusted them so far.

She took them and clutched them to her chest. 'Ah, feels good to be back.'

She dropped the teeth to the ground and the two skeletal steeds sprung up. Bones regarded the situation with empty eyes, swinging his head from Logan to the unicorn and back again. Logan rubbed the skull, and the creature shook itself, a shuddering motion that started at the head and worked down the body to the tail. Logan hefted the saddle, ready to set it on the backbones.

'Necromancy!' Gary shrieked.

Logan sighed. No, things going their way was clearly too much to ask for. He let go of the saddle and held up his hands for peace. 'It's not like that. The countess is helping us. She's authorised—'

'I have a charter!' she said, waving it helpfully.

Gary backed away, his face pale. The unicorn pawed the ground with its hoof and lowered its head. The horn suddenly looked a whole lot sharper to Logan.

'Come on, lad, let's talk.' He took a slow step towards the youth, his hands held out. Gary took a step back. 'Let me explain,' Logan continued. 'There's no need to be afraid. We're not here to hurt you.'

Gary looked at Logan, then the countess, then back to Logan. He swallowed, before vaulting onto the back of the unicorn, poised to run.

'No!' Logan screamed. If Gary took the unicorn, they'd lose everything. He'd lose Pie.

Before Logan could react, Ophelia appeared behind the youth and threw herself at Gary. Logan expected the youth to plummet from the saddle, but she had disappeared *into* his body. For a moment, everything was still.

'Well,' said Gary, calmer now. 'This is weird.'

Logan stared at him. 'Ophelia?'

Gary's head nodded. His eyes shone with a greenish light. 'I panicked. I've never done this before; I wasn't sure it would work, but I just had to do something, or he was going to take the unicorn away.' He looked down cautiously. 'This thing is bigger than I thought.'

Logan wasn't entirely sure if she was talking about the unicorn or Gary himself. The unicorn had calmed now its master was no longer panicked. It had stopped the pawing and now lowered its head to crop at the grass.

'What do we do?' Logan asked. 'We can't exactly leave Ophelia in there.'

'I don't see why not,' the countess said. 'Strikes me as an ideal solution.'

'Is Gary *aware* in there?'

The countess shrugged. 'Probably.'

'Well then, aside from the fact that Ophelia knows nothing about unicorns, we are absolutely not leaving that poor lad as a prisoner in his own body. We need his help, but he's not our prisoner.'

'Suit yourself,' the countess said with a huff.

Gary, or Ophelia, dismounted awkwardly, almost falling. 'Sorry. It's been a while since I've had legs,' she explained to the unicorn apologetically, running a hand down its elegant neck. 'Logan's right, we can't keep him like this. I say we tie him up and convince him to help us. He was already halfway there.'

'I know I'm at my most pliable when tied to a tree,' Logan grumbled, but he didn't have a better solution. 'Better hide the skeletons for the moment – and Ophelia, make yourself scarce. Ophelia, are you listening?'

Gary's arm was flexed, the muscles of his bicep pushing back the shirt sleeve.

'Stop that,' Logan said.

Gary's face gave him a sheepish grin. 'Just curious how big these muscles were.'

'Well stop it. It's not your body to be curious about.'

The countess had rope in her saddlebag. Logan decided to accept that fact and not ask too many questions, though he could see from her expression that she was desperate for him to do so. Since returning to this realm, any sign of her illness had faded. She seemed stronger than ever.

He approached the tree. 'I'll tie him up, and you let me know if it feels secure but not painful,' he said to Ophelia. 'We don't want to hurt him. We just need him calm so we can explain.'

Gary's head nodded. Logan came around behind him, crossing the youth's hands over and binding them tightly. The youth stood, unmoving, as Logan bound him against the tree trunk. *I'm gonna have lots of material for your songs by the time we meet again Pie*, he thought.

'How's that?' he asked Ophelia.

Gary's hands wriggled in the bonds. The action made the muscles in his arms flex, and Logan caught himself staring. He shook his head, hard.

'All good,' Ophelia confirmed. 'Right, I'm going to step away now.'

She emerged from Gary's body and his body slumped, his chin resting against his chest. Logan crouched in front of him.

'Gary?' he called softly.

The youth groaned and lifted his head. His eyes slowly focused as he took in the scene. They'd lost their green colour. 'W–what happened?'

'We . . . er . . . had to subdue you,' Logan explained cautiously.

Gary took a step towards him, or at least tried to. His head whipped around to determine why he couldn't move, and his mouth fell open. A moment later, it snapped shut in a tight line. 'You're filthy necromancers! Help! Someone help me!'

'We are quite clean, I can assure you,' the countess harrumphed, dusting the sleeves of her dress for emphasis.

Gary struggled against his bonds. The rope creaked. Behind Logan, the unicorn snorted and stamped, as it watched its master struggle. Logan held up a hand to the animal in what he hoped was a placating gesture. The glistening horn lowered like a lance and he swallowed.

'Calm down, please. Ignore the countess, about this and in general. Please, lad, we need your help.'

'Rude, dear,' the countess muttered.

'Please, let me tell you my story. Give me a chance to explain,' Logan pleaded, his voice low, his manner as unthreatening as he could manage. Which was hard when he'd made a career out of being threatening and swinging an axe hard enough to decapitate a head in one blow. 'I wasn't lying about what I told you of my husband. Everything I do, I do it for him.'

Gary closed his eyes. His mouth moved as if he were arguing with himself. Logan waited, trying to hold back from drumming his fingers on his thigh. The unicorn had stopped its pawing, but the silence – broken only by punctured mutterings from the countess – raised the hairs on the back of his neck.

Gary opened his eyes.

'Fine, I'll listen,' he said. 'But untie me first. I promise I won't run – not *before* I've heard you out, anyway.'

Logan would take that. He studied Gary. Brown eyes, a darker shade than Pie's, stared back at him, open and honest. He decided Gary probably didn't have the capacity to lie, or else he was very, very good at it. He pulled out his knife and cut the knots, then sat down against the fallen tree. Gary rubbed at his wrists, looked over at the unicorn, then joined Logan where he was slumped against the tree.

'Pie is . . .' Logan sucked in a breath, pulling his arms around himself. A weight pressed down on his shoulders. 'Pie is the love of my life. I never thought I'd have another relationship of any kind before I met him, let alone a marriage. I always thought I belonged on my own, that I'd live and die by the axe.' The corner of his eye burned as if there was a cinder caught in it. He wiped it with the back of his hand. 'I don't know what he sees in me, but there must be something, because he pursued me relentlessly. Even turned up naked in my room one night.'

'Oh, now you have to tell me that story,' the countess called.

Another tear rolled down Logan's cheek, soaking into his beard. At the same time, he couldn't help smiling at the memory of Pie lying there naked, a rose between his teeth.

'And now he's missing, he's in trouble, and I can't work out exactly what's going on, but I know he needs me. And I have to pursue him like he did me, like he would if I was in trouble. I'm not going to force you to help us, lad. It wouldn't be fair. But I just want you to understand why I'd do anything to get him home safe, even if it means working with a necromancer and a ghost. Besides' – he gave the countess a smile – 'I don't think either of them are as bad as they'd have you believe.'

'I understand now.' Gary clapped a hand on Logan's shoulder. 'I'm sorry. I understand now, and of course Freddy and I will help.'

'Freddy?' Logan asked.

Gary gestured to the unicorn sheepishly. 'Fredrick Onyx-Heart the Third . . . Freddy.'

The beast swung its head at the sound of his name. He didn't strike Logan as a Freddy. Maybe a Stabby.

Logan cleared his throat. 'Right, I guess we go north, then. The city of Krensten is the last point of civilisation before the mountains. We can stop there and pick up supplies.'

'What are we going to do for money?' Ophelia asked.

Gary swung around at the sound of her voice. The colour drained from his face.

'G–gh—'

Logan sighed and gripped Gary's arm. 'Yes, as I said, she's a ghost. That's really not her worst quality. This is my ex-wife, Ophelia. She's acting as our guide.'

Ophelia rolled her eyes at him. 'And what exactly is my worst quality? At least I don't smell like a bear's last meal.'

'The point,' Logan continued, ignoring her, 'is that she's nothing to fear. She's going to help us rescue Pie, and she's very sorry about accidentally possessing you. It won't happen again. You have my word.'

Gary looked between Logan and Ophelia, before settling his gaze on the ground. 'If you say so, then I believe you, Logan Theaker.'

Logan nodded, a strange warmth spreading through him at the youth's words. People didn't trust him easily. He glanced around the assembled group and gave them a nod.

'Now, if we're all done screaming at each other, let's get on the road,' the countess announced jovially.

She summoned their bone steeds, and they all took a moment to pull themselves into the saddle. Gary sat on the unicorn, seemingly at ease riding bareback.

'You didn't answer my question,' Ophelia said as they set off at a trot. She sat sideways on Bone's back, her legs disappearing into its every time it took a step. It reminded Logan of the times they'd sat kicking their feet in the river in their youth.

'About your worst quality?'

She jabbed a finger into his ribs, making him wince.

'Ow, easy there, icy hands.'

She gave him a scowl, but her lip curled in a smile. 'About money, you ox.'

'Ah, that.' It felt good to talk like this, like equals, without the weight of their past pulling them apart. 'We're heading through some fairly wild country. If we're lucky, a few of the right creatures will attack us, regret their life choices, and I'll sell their *components* to buyers in the city.'

She raised an eyebrow. 'And if the wrong things attack us?'

'Then you'd better hope these horses are fast.'

Interlude

Seventeen Months Ago

Logan settled into a chair by the fire. The heat licked at him, raising a sweat on his brow, but he didn't care. After the last few days tramping through the cold and wet, he could put up with being too warm. The inn was heavy with noise, voices raised in good cheer, but he tuned them all out and focused on his plate of meat and the tankard in front of him. A man couldn't want for much more. His life was perfect.

'This seat taken?'

He looked up, recognising the voice but needing to see the face just the same. The bard looked thinner than he had previously, and his nose had been broken at some point. It had been set carefully – a pretty face was an important commodity to a bard – but Logan couldn't help noticing the slight misalignment.

'You're staring,' Magpie said, the corner of his mouth twitching.

Logan cleared his throat. 'Seat's free for a friend.'

'Thanks.' Magpie started to sit, but Logan grabbed his wrist.

'A friend would bring ale.'

A grin broke free. Magpie caught the eye of the serving woman and she set a couple of tankards on the table. He flicked her a coin and she snatched it out of the air. Logan pulled both vessels towards him.

'So, what brings you out here, *Pie*?'

Magpie made a grab for one of the tankards but stopped. 'You called me Pie.' His eyes were wide.

'That's your name, isn't it?' Logan took a drink.

'Well, no, but that's beside the point. You normally just call me *Bard*.' He imitated Logan's low inflection.

'Is that a problem?' Logan asked slowly.

'No. Do it again.'

Unthinkably, Logan laughed.

Chapter Nine

The river dwindled away from a wide, lazy serpent to a shallow torrent that tumbled down waterfalls and over large rocks with reckless abandon. The terrain sloped, gently at first, then steeper, with intermittent plateaus that never quite managed to feel flat. The skeletal steeds took everything in their stride, as did the unicorn. Logan knew nothing about the creatures – they'd been rare even before they disappeared from this world – so Gary would have to judge the creature's stamina.

The trees, dark and dense, pushed in, a constant whisper surrounding them. This was the sort of place where Logan felt most alive, before he had been civilised. Birds called all around them, a mixture of harsh croaks and sharp alarm calls. It was a good sign. Birds weren't usually afraid of men; they knew they could get out of the way, and it was mostly tiny, feathered bravado. It was the forest falling silent that Logan feared.

There was something comforting about being back in deep forest – adventurer territory. Slipping into that alertness, that readiness for danger, felt like slipping on a favourite pair of boots. The axe at his back was a constant companion, a comfortable weight of steel and edge. He was Logan the Bear, and killing monsters was what he did best.

Behind him, Gary chattered to the countess, asking questions about everything and everyone.

'Lad has no idea what he's getting into there, does he?' Logan said to Ophelia.

'You think we should do anything?' she asked. For days on the road they had slipped into a comfortable peace around each other.

Logan shrugged. 'What can we do? The woman isn't afraid of anything, and I suspect if we push her, she'll push back. In the most petty way possible.' He didn't want to treat Gary as a sacrifice to the countess's whims, but he most certainly did not want her to take away Bones. Already his leg throbbed, and he'd barely walked on it in this world again. Logan also had to admit that he'd miss her fireside tales. She could almost rival a bard.

Almost.

'I might have an idea.' Ophelia tapped a finger through her lip. She disappeared from the back of Bones and reappeared on the countess's horse. They had a quiet conversation, during which the countess's expression grew darker and darker. Eventually she threw up her hands, and Ophelia disappeared, leaving the trace of a grin.

'What on earth did you say to her?' Logan asked as she reappeared.

'I said the moment the countess said or did anything inappropriate, I'd hop back over the veil and have strong words with her god about cutting off her power. I have no idea if I can genuinely do that, but she doesn't have to know, right? Hopefully it's enough to get her to behave, around Gary at least. She'd eat him alive if she got the chance.'

Logan nodded. 'Good plan.'

'You actually sound impressed.' She tilted her head. 'Who are you and what have you done with the real Logan Theaker?'

He snorted. 'Don't let it go to your head.'

They rode on in, an easy silence lingering between them.

'Why do you hate me, Ophelia?' The question burst out of Logan like a bird from a bush, startling them both. Logan's face warmed. 'I mean, I know I'm a bit of a brute, and I probably do smell like a bear's last meal. But is that really enough to warrant hating me?'

She turned away sharply. Her hair didn't move with motion, the curls lying static as if she were merely a drawing.

'I told you. It's your fault I'm dead.' Her voice was flat, emotionless, but the temperature dropped as if winter had caught up with them.

Logan's hands tightened around the reins. 'What are you on about? You died long after you kicked me out. How can it be my fault? What happened after I left? Did someone hurt you?' He'd heard the news too late, coming back from an adventuring job. The knowledge had set off a strange sensation. Not grief or loss, but a peculiar feeling of knowing something that had always been there now wasn't.

As if a star had winked out of existence.

The house was cold and silent when he returned. The fire in the hall burned down to ashes. A bowl of soup, also cold, sat at one end of the long table. Logan took a sip, not bothering to sit down.

It tasted of loneliness.

It wasn't how he'd pictured married life. When she'd first come to him, he'd thought of companionship. Of coming home tired and muddy to a warm bath and a loving word. Not to a cold dish in a cold house, his wife long retired to her bed.

He traipsed down the passage towards the bedrooms, pausing at her door.

'Ophelia?'

'It's late. Go to bed, Logan.' The tears she'd shed lingered in the bitterness of her words.

'I . . . I thought . . .' he started, and she sighed.

'I very much doubt that. I'm sure you've got to get up early. Plenty outside the house for your attention. Perhaps I could get myself kidnapped, and then you might spend some time in my company.'

'You're not being fair.' The words dug under his skin, needling him worse than the cold and hunger. 'I'm doing this for you. To keep you safe. You and everyone else.'

'How many monsters did you kill today?' she asked, her tone flat and cold as a flagstone.

'None, but that just means I'm having an effect.'

'This isn't all on you, Logan. If there are any signs of monsters, there's a whole town of folk ready to go hunt them. This is your passion, not your job.'

'I . . . I don't know.' If he stopped, and something happened, how would he live with himself? If he stopped, would he know what to do with himself? 'You called me a hero once. Is that not how you see me?'

She shifted in the gloom of her room. 'Logan, I haven't seen you all day. I barely know what you look like anymore. When is it going to be enough? When will you spend your days in your house, not stomping around the woods?'

He didn't have an answer for her.

'That's what I thought.'

'Because you weren't there.' Her voice was a drop of icy water down his neck, dragging him back from the memories. 'I know you didn't love me. You made that abundantly clear. My father didn't care for you much either, but he did covet the land your mother had owned, so he was happy to set up the match. I don't know if I loved you, or if it was merely childish feelings. I did want to make things work, though.'

'So did I,' he snapped. 'Don't try and paint me as a monster. I kill those. I kill them to keep people safe. People like you. You wanted to be held. I wanted to make sure a parel didn't snatch you for its dinner.'

'Is it so wrong to want to be held?' Her voice didn't hitch, because she didn't breathe. 'Would you begrudge Pie that?'

'No, I wouldn't.' He shook his head. 'But it's different. I'm retired now. And Pie understands.'

She appeared, cross-legged, floating at Bone's neck. Her eyes bore into him. 'You don't think he worries about you? You don't think that when he bandages your wounds, he doesn't feel every cut himself?'

'I wouldn't let Pie anywhere near me with a bandage. Doesn't have the knack.' The one time he'd tried, Logan had ended up with a bundle of cloth wrapped continuously around his wrist while the blood soaked his trousers. But . . . he'd never stopped to consider how Pie felt, let alone Ophelia.

'It wasn't just that you ignored me, Logan. It wasn't just that you cared less for me than you did for going out killing monsters. It was because I cared, and I hurt, and after a while I couldn't take it anymore.' She wiped her face as if expecting tears that could no longer fall. 'You didn't seem too fussed sitting there while the priest marked out your tattoo.'

He glanced down at the mark, hidden by his clothes, but visible in his mind. A sun over an ear of wheat, symbol of Kaldyn, the fertility god whose worship prevailed in Ophelia's community, now crossed through neatly. His own mother had preferred to give her patronage to the Wild Woman, spirit of change and uncertainty.

Logan let the gods do their thing and they seemed content to let him do his.

'I don't know what you saw in me, Ophelia. I'd lived alone with my mother for twelve years, and then almost as long entirely on my own. I could barely hold a conversation. I knew nothing about managing a house. I knew about chopping wood and hunting and protecting people.'

She reached a hand towards him, her expression almost tender. 'I saw someone I thought cared. Might care for me.' Her hand dropped.

'I did care about you.' The need to make her believe that gnawed at him. 'I thought you were beautiful. Perfect. I wanted to protect you.'

'From what?' she snapped. 'There had been bad years for monsters, sure, but not since we were teenagers. Your mother helped take out most of the monster population and you did the rest.'

'It doesn't work like that,' he muttered. 'They move, change habitat, get driven into new areas.'

'After that,' Ophelia said, ignoring him, 'I was lonely, hurting. Vulnerable. Another man came to seek me, and I opened my heart to him. He seemed to be caring, to care about me. When the priest carved the mark a second time, I was happy. But over the years, he changed. He drank more, gambled more, lost more. He hit me once, calling me a bad luck charm.' She paused, closing her eyes. Logan didn't want her to continue, but couldn't bring himself to tell her to stop. 'I told him that was enough. That tomorrow I'd call the priest and send him away too. But he didn't give me the sad eyes like you did. He tried to hit me again, so I drew my dagger and told him to leave. I tried to be brave, to stand like you, to fight like you. Because you weren't there. I even got a good hit on him, but he shoved me and I fell. Hit my head on the table.'

'Ophelia . . .'

'And I lay there, my blood pooling around my head while he screamed at me, thinking, "He's a monster. He's a monster, and Logan kills monsters. Logan will save me." But you never came.'

Logan couldn't speak. His words had turned to stone and settled in his stomach. He wanted to hold her, to apologise with a touch. But he couldn't do that. Because she was dead. Because he killed monsters, but he couldn't protect his wife. He hadn't been there to protect her from the real monsters.

'You . . . You didn't deserve that,' he said finally. Stupid words. Empty words. Guilt raked at his insides. Gods, of course she hated him. He'd let her down worse than he'd ever believed. A knife twisted in his gut. What if he did the same to Pie? They both deserved better. People spoke about how Logan was a hero, but really he was little more than a mercenary. Real heroes protected people. Real heroes protected the ones they loved.

'Of course I fucking didn't!' She wiped her hands across her face. 'I didn't deserve any of it.'

He reached out to her, then snatched his fingers back. Nausea twisted his guts, bile burning at the back of his throat. Rage left him chilled. 'What happened to the man? Do . . . do you want me to kill him for you?'

She snorted. 'That's such a Logan response.'

It was, and he hated himself for only having that to offer her.

'Don't say anything. There aren't any words that can undo this. But I hope you understand now why I hate you.'

He did, and any previous judgement of her melted away, leaving only the weight of his guilt.

They rode on again in silence, punctuated only by the dull thud of hooves on the path.

'Oh, this is even worse!' Ophelia reappeared, sitting back on Bones' hips. 'I can't cry, you're a big mound of angst, the countess is sulking and Gary probably hasn't had a conversation with anything that didn't have four legs since he was a child.'

Logan said nothing.

'Tell me about Pie. Tell me about the man who actually got Logan Theaker to care,' she demanded.

He turned to stare at her, and she met his gaze with a baleful expression. 'Are you sure?'

'It's better than sitting here in this dark cloud. I thought when I told you . . . I don't know what I thought, but I don't want to sit here remembering dying over and over, so yes, tell me about Pie.'

Logan cleared his throat. 'Well, he's a little taller than me, auburn hair, hazel eyes. They change colour from more green to more brown. He's—'

'I meant what's he like as a person,' she chided, flicking a hand into his back.

'Pie is . . . Pie is funny. Kind.' Logan closed his eyes, remembering Pie's arms around him, breathing in the memory of the scent of him. 'When he sings, the whole world stands still. He gets under my skin, makes me believe in better things. Makes me believe in home and happiness. Makes me believe I deserve them, too.'

'Sounds like you love him very much.'

'I do. I . . .' He took a deep breath. 'I'm sorry I couldn't be that man for you. I'm sorry that you didn't get a chance to meet the person who could.'

She shrugged. 'I still have a chance, once I get my new body. I'll find them then, the person who makes me believe in love too.' She smiled at Logan, and the sight made his heart ache. Brave and headstrong, as she'd always been. She deserved her happiness.

'You will.' He had nothing to offer her but hope. The forest pressed in, trees leaning close as if to eavesdrop. Even the birds had gone silent.

Wait . . .

'Shit!' Logan spat. He'd been so caught up in Ophelia's story, so busy talking about Pie, that he didn't notice that activity around them had stilled. Something large was out there, and it had probably been able to creep right up on them.

'Gary, Countess, this way, quick,' Logan called over his shoulder. A clearing up ahead offered visibility and room to manoeuvre. He put his heels to Bones's ribs, and the skeletal steed leapt forwards. A quickening of hoofbeats told him the others were following.

Logan reined in at the centre of the clearing and dismounted. He handed the reins to the countess as she approached.

'You and Gary stay here. If I tell you to run, leave Bones and go. I'll catch up.'

'Bones?' A grin cracked her face. 'Oh, Logan, you big softie.'

He pinched the bridge of his nose. 'That's not important right now. What is important is there's something out there, maybe several somethings, and they're probably hungry for blood. Stay out of the way and leave this to me.'

'You seem to be mistaking me for a helpless old lady,' the countess said. 'I like roleplay as much as the next person, but let's not let it cloud our judgement. You don't make it to my age, Logan dear, without being able to defend yourself!'

The bushes rustled to his right. Logan turned slowly, one hand releasing the axe from his back. He watched the motion of the leaves, waiting for the change in pattern that would announce the arrival of their foe. He hefted the axe, his breathing slow and steady.

A flurry of squawking and whirring wings, and a bird flew out of the bush. Logan lowered the axe as the countess let out a nervous laugh. Freddy the unicorn snorted disparagingly.

Suddenly, a clap of thunder filled the clearing. The ground shook, and Logan threw out an arm for balance. They all looked at each other, wide-eyed. The countess most likely regretted her decision not to run. From the dense treeline, three huge creatures came rampaging through the clearing, snorting loudly.

Jonsfaks. Huge, carnivorous pigs.

Logan preferred goats. At least you could get milk from a goat. These things were toxic, their saliva and blood acidic to the touch, so neither the meat nor hide were any use. As far as he knew, no one had ever tried to milk one, but there was no way he'd put jonsfak cheese in his mouth even if they did.

'Get out of here,' he said quietly, swinging the axe in front of him. Three on one was going to be . . . An interesting fight.

'Logan dear, you're too attractive for me to let you get squashed,' the countess argued. A soft trickling sound came from behind him, like rain, and he sensed something else approaching. He resisted the urge to sigh. Her unarmed skeletons were going to be trampled to bonemeal.

The jonsfak to his right lowered its head, small, piggy eyes fixed on him. They had a thatch of blond hair that made them look deceptively comical. Misjudging them was a mistake – their bodies were solid muscle, and their teeth and jaws could grind bones to dust. Logan had heard enough tales of men who'd tried to shoo them on, then watched in horror as their own arms were eaten in front of them. He moved the axe, not wanting to take his eye off the other two.

A large skeletal cat slammed into the nearest pig's throat with a clatter. Logan almost dropped his axe as he watched it sink its teeth into the jonsfak's fat neck.

'A *parel*? You have a bloody parel skeleton?' he yelled. The countess said nothing, her concentration fixed on the fight, but he could sense her smug grin.

One pig pawed at the earth. It let out a series of waffling grunts and charged at him. Logan threw himself to the side, bringing the axe down on the side of its head. The creature snorted and snapped ugly brown teeth. The blow left a gash below its ear, but it didn't even seem to notice.

It came at him again, moving faster than something with that bulk should have been able to. It caught him on his injured leg, knocking him into the dirt. Logan held up his axe to shield himself as it swung its head, mouth open, teeth drenched in saliva.

'Logan!' Ophelia called.

'I can see it,' he muttered. Smelled it too. They stank like foetid ale for some reason. He pushed out with the axe, catching the pig on the lip. It squealed in pain and rage, striking him with its head. Hot, sticky blood sprayed over him, and, like a fool, he put his hand up to protect himself.

The jonsfak grabbed his arm, teeth digging into his flesh. Logan dropped his axe and grabbed the creature's upper jaw with his free hand, trying to push it back enough to get his hand out. Rancid breath ran over his arm with the blood.

The creature pulled harder, wrenching at his arm. Logan tried to brace himself, but pulling back only increased the pain in his shoulder as the creature tried to wrench his arm from its socket. He gritted his teeth and dug his nails into the thing's gums. Not like this. He wouldn't let it end like this.

A scream filled the clearing. Logan's heart raced. Either the parel skeleton had failed, or the third pig had attacked. He struggled harder until a sudden rush of air hit him, and the creature let go with an anguished cry. Logan lifted his head, unsure what could knock back a six-foot lump of stinking pig.

It turned out to be a unicorn.

Freddy's horn was buried deep in the jonsfak's side. The pig wailed and shook, trying to free itself, but it was clear from the wheezing and the blood spraying from its mouth that the horn had pierced its lungs. On Freddy's back, Gary looked dazed.

'G–good job,' Logan said, feeling somewhat dazed himself.

He snatched up his axe, surveying the situation. The parel skeleton had ripped the throat out of the first jonsfak, and now played with the corpse, blood dripping down its many, many sharp teeth. The second pig was on its knees, making revolting wet breathing sounds as it drowned in its own blood. That left the third.

Logan wasn't going to be the one left without a kill today.

He charged at the creature, which turned its malevolent piggy eyes on him and started to run to meet him. At the last moment, he dived out the way and swung the axe as the jonsfak lumbered past, severing its hamstring. It collapsed in a squealing heap, sliding along the ground with its momentum.

He leapt at it, bringing the axe down, and slashed the creature's jugular, which sprayed him in the face with blood.

Gods dammit.

'We did it!' Gary said, his voice only trembling slightly. 'Take that, swine!' He dismounted and began to clean the gore off the unicorn's horn. The action almost concealed the way his hand shook.

'I told you to stay out of it,' Logan said, wiping his sleeve across his face. Pain ran lightning bolts up and down his arm. 'What if you or the unicorn had been hurt?'

'I wanted to help.' Gary paused his wiping and turned to Logan, his stance stiff and defensive. 'I wanted to be a hero, too.'

'No such thing as heroes.' Logan softened his voice. He hadn't meant to raise it at the lad. He glanced at Ophelia. 'Only people trying to do the right thing and usually making a mess of it.'

Chapter Ten

They left the clearing quickly enough – the smell of three jonsfak was bad enough already, and the smell of them decaying wouldn't be any better. Up ahead, the river tumbled over a waterfall, creating a deeper pool. Logan stripped off, ignoring the comments from the countess, and stepped into the water. The temperature took his breath away at first, but the pressure of the water on his shoulders felt good. Not as good as Pie's hands, though.

Had adventuring always been so messy?

He looked down at his arm. The cold water had slowed the blood-flow, and the damage looked superficial, but the failure it represented chewed at his gut. A stupid mistake. And if Gary and the unicorn hadn't been there, he might not have been able to get his arm free at all.

Could he hope to save Pie if he couldn't even save himself?

Logan closed his eyes, sinking deeper into the water. It drummed over his head, berating him with every drop. *Logan kills monsters. Logan will save me.* Both of those claims were false, it seemed. He was injured, out of practice.

Old.

'Feeling sorry for yourself?'

He snapped his eyes open to see Ophelia standing in front of him. The river flowed through her stomach without so much as a ripple.

'Can't a man bathe in peace?'

She folded her arms. 'Stop sulking. So you only killed one out of three. Isn't it a good thing that everyone worked together and no one got badly hurt? Stop being a miserable arse and let's get on the road again.'

Logan let the waterfall batter his tired muscles for a moment longer, then pulled himself away. 'Why are you being so nice to me?' he questioned.

She cocked her head. 'I just called you a miserable arse.'

'Yeah, but you didn't mean it this time. Trust me, I can tell.'

She glared at him and vanished. Logan strode towards the bank. The countess stood waiting for him, holding out his cloak. He took it from her and used it to dry the worst of the water from his body. The weather wasn't too bad at the moment, but the further north they went, the colder it was going to get. Baths might be a luxury he would have to put aside.

They definitely needed to pick up more supplies. Gary thought Logan didn't notice him shivering in his thin shirt, which was barely enough right now, let alone for when the snow started to fall. And of course, the only thing they'd encountered were jonsfak, which were utterly useless.

'Let me see your arm, dear.' The countess held out a clean bandage. Logan wondered exactly what she had in her saddle-bags. At least it didn't appear to be an endless supply of shoes.

'I can do it.' He snatched the bandage from her hand. It wasn't the first time he'd patched himself up. He wrapped the cloth over the gashes, keeping it as neat and tight as he could manage. The countess pushed out her lower lip and he sighed, then offered her the two ends. He probably couldn't do it tight enough on his own. When she'd finished, she ran a hand up his arm and let it linger on the bicep. Logan pulled away with a grunt.

By the time the sun dropped low in the sky, the road had headed away from the river and deeper into the forest. Logan called a stop well before sunset, knowing that the dense trees would bring the darkness in that much faster. They found a sheltered spot under an overhang that would give them protection from the worst of the elements.

Logan set some snares in the bushes around the campsite, while one of the countess's skeletons built up a fire in the centre. The skeletons would stand watch, and Ophelia didn't sleep either, so he could look forward to resting the whole night. He settled down to warm his hands by the crackling flames. He'd slipped back into the routine of outdoor life easily. It had been a while, but it comforted him to know the knowledge hadn't faded away.

Gary hovered over his shoulder as he worked, asking questions about everything. Logan pushed down his irritation. The last thing he wanted to do was encourage the lad, but he had an earnest enthusiasm that felt cruel to punish.

The countess had summoned the littlelap dog and was now throwing it a stick, a look of blissful happiness crinkling her features. Logan decided he'd never get the measure of her. Right now, she could have been any other old woman, fussing over her pet – if you ignored the fact that this pet was undead. But when she wanted to be, she was sharp, determined and utterly ruthless. When Logan had caught up with her a couple of years ago, she was using the inhabitants of a wealthy tomb to rob their own graves.

She saw him watching her, and gave him a wave. 'Looks like we're sleeping together again tonight, Logan dear.'

Logan groaned. The unicorn lay down at the edge of the camp, something Logan had never seen horses do. The youth curled up against the creature's flank, and the unicorn nuzzled him gently.

'Cold?' Logan asked.

Gary shook his head. 'I'm fine. Freddy's warm.'

Logan took off his cloak and threw it over. 'We dragged you away from your home, lad. Don't suffer in silence. I'll be plenty warm enough by the fire.' *And no doubt I'll end up with the countess wrapped around me in the night.*

'It's true,' Ophelia called. 'Logan's got so much chest hair it acts like a second blanket.'

Logan half-heartedly threw a stone at her.

'Tell us about yourself,' he said to Gary.

Gary pulled the cloak around himself. He looked much smaller, sitting next to the dark mass of the unicorn, and younger still. 'My mother managed the unicorn herd, before she died five years ago. I don't know much about my father. I don't think I've ever met him. My mother said he was a hero, once, but that was the only thing she said.'

Logan nodded. The youth's obsession with heroes was more understandable now. Just as fool-headed and dangerous, but understandable.

'I've lived over there' – he waved a hand at the darkness – 'all my life. Since my mother died, it's just my uncle and the unicorns for company. Once a year we meet up with the other unicorn breeders who survived to trade stock, but that's it.'

'Sounds lonely.' Logan poked the fire, sending sparks spiralling into the sky.

'It is. I want to see the world,' Gary said with a nod. He dropped his gaze to his boots, as if guilty for wanting more than his lot. 'But it wasn't so bad. My uncle's a bard, so he's always got stories.'

A bard. Well, that also explained a lot. 'Look, bards, they have a way with words, and they make you believe things. Things that are fine for bedtime stories, but the real world isn't like that. It's messy, dirty, and everyone has their own agenda. Hopefully we'll get to where we need to go with minimal issue, and then you can just turn around and go home, but promise you'll be careful, and trust no one.'

Gary gave him a wide-eyed stare. 'Even you? But you're a hero.'

'I said there's no such thing as heroes,' Logan replied with a sigh. 'That's something bards invented to get them coin.

Everyone's got an agenda. Everyone wants something. No one's truly selfless in this world.'

Gary pulled the cloak around himself. 'Doesn't your husband think you're a hero?'

'Pie? Probably. But he's a bard, too. I'm just saying be careful. That's all.'

Gary lay his head on the unicorn's flank, pulling Logan's cloak around his shoulders. 'I will.'

Morning roused Logan with the scent of damp and decaying roses. Gently, he eased the countess off his chest and onto the ground, then sat up. The fire burned steadily, and the campsite seemed calm and still. Gary remained curled up next to the unicorn, which watched him with dark eyes. He wondered if it had awoken around the same time as him, or if they didn't sleep either.

The fire had kept the worst of the stiffness out of his leg, but he still limped across the clearing to check the traps. After yesterday's fiasco, he wasn't expecting much, but of the five traps, two had plump bush birds in, and the last one had a jewelled lizard. Both the skin and the meat of the latter were prized and would probably fetch enough to meet their supply needs, if he was careful.

Whistling to himself, he set about plucking the birds for breakfast.

'You're in a good mood,' Ophelia said, appearing in front of him.

Logan wasn't even mad she'd startled him. He held up the bird, feathers scattering on the breeze. 'Gonna enjoy this.'

She frowned, flinching away from the carcass. 'Looks delicious. Must be nice – eating.'

A stab of guilt twisted his gut. 'I'm sorry. But you'll get your body back soon. When this is all over, I'll get Pie to cook for you. He's much better at it than I am. He does this thing with a whole trout, baked over the fire, in a cream sauce . . .' He stopped to wipe his watering mouth.

She sat cross-legged on the ground. 'I'm not surprised you married a man who can cook well. You always did like food.'

'I liked that one you did with the pork and mustard,' he admitted, and her expression softened.

'You remember that, huh?' She reached up to play with her hair, her fingers passing through the dark curls. 'Logan, are you sure you should be doing this?'

He paused, feathers pinched in his fingers. 'Yes, of course. Got to pluck it or the stench of burning feathers will spoil the meat.'

'You don't know what happened to Pie,' she pressed. 'How much do you really know the man? You don't know what his motivations are or the people he's with. You don't know what might happen. You might not like what happens.'

Logan threw the feathers into the air. Several caught in the flames, sending up acrid smoke. 'Are you actually worried about me, Ophelia?'

She shook her head. 'No. No I'm not. I'm sorry I said anything.'

She vanished, leaving Logan alone to finish plucking. He understood her hating him. He could deal with that. He deserved that. But when her attitude to him changed like that, he didn't know what to say.

Logan went back to prepping breakfast. Pluck the feathers, clean out the guts, push a stick through it and set it over the fire. His style of cooking. Before long, the tantalising smell of roasting meat roused the others. Between his own appetite and Gary's, two birds barely satisfied the three living people. Fortunately, the countess was a delicate eater, even if she lacked delicacy in anything else.

Ophelia stayed away.

Logan didn't know if she was upset about her lack of body, or upset at him, or, more likely, a combination of the two.

Even when they broke camp and set off, she was nowhere to be seen.

The forest opened a bit more on this side of the hill, and the steep rocky paths meant they were unlikely to run into any more jonsfaks. Before long, the city of Krensten emerged below them. It sat, nestled into the base of the grey mountains and facing an equally grey sea.

It had been a while, but Logan had spent a good deal of time in the area when he was younger. The place was a confluence of passing travellers, a rock amongst hard places. People came through with stories, jobs, hopes. Others took one or more from them and only sometimes paid a fair price.

Before they reached the edge of the trees, Logan called a halt. 'I'll go into town, see what I can obtain. The rest of you should stay here.'

'I absolutely will not,' the countess argued, folding her arms. 'It's been too long since I was here. There's a beautiful shrine in the catacombs. I must at least go and pay my respects to the Dark Mother.'

'Fine.' He didn't think he'd be able to stop her if he tried, short of physically tying her up, and she'd probably enjoy that too much for his comfort anyway.

'I want to come too,' Gary said. 'I've never seen a city before. I want to see the gods-square, and walk through the market, and have a drink in an inn, and . . .'

'And walk in with a unicorn?' Logan said, halting Gary's stream of wants. 'You're not thinking this through, lad.'

Gary looked up at Freddy, his face colouring. 'I . . . I guess.'

'It's not like you can stick a hat on it and pretend it's just a horse,' Logan said, trying to keep his tone light. Gary had been out of contact with people in the real world for too long. Wasn't his fault he was overly curious and trusting. But those were the worst qualities to enter into a big city with.

'I'll stay and keep you company,' Ophelia said, surprising Logan with both her sudden appearance and her words. He'd expected her to want to stay near him, ensure he was keeping to his promise. He wouldn't argue with her, though.

'Just stay off the road and you'll be fine,' Logan said. 'We won't be long.'

The countess dismissed the two bone steeds and pocketed the teeth – 'Just in case,' she explained – and they set off down the road towards the city. The steep path made Logan's leg ache within minutes, and by the time they'd reached flat ground, he couldn't suppress his limp. He didn't like the idea of approaching with any sign of weakness.

Cities were a bad place for weaknesses.

Entrance to the city was slow going, with every person registered on the gate. Travellers and traders jostled to get through, and more than once he had to pull his feet away from a cart wheel or heavy hoof. At least the bustling nature was reassuring. They wouldn't be walking into another pile of corpses.

'Keep your eyes open for trouble,' Logan muttered to the countess.

'Trouble and I are very familiar with each other,' she replied with a grin.

Huge oak doors stood open, banded with iron that showed signs of wear and salt from the ocean. Every ten years they had to replace them, or they'd fall apart on their hinges. In the past, Krensten had been a spellcaster stronghold and the site of a vicious battle. The only signs of war now were the large craters in the ground that either repelled all plant life, contained a pool of lava, or faintly glowed.

The countess took his arm as they walked through the walls, smiling at one of the sullen guards who stood in the gatehouse. Logan decided not to protest – as long as she kept her hands only on his arm. The noise of people washed over him: footsteps, chatter, calls of goods for sale. The main market was up ahead, whereas the gods' district was over to the right. To his left, the charred and crumbling ruins of a tower loomed in a precarious manner – the remains of a spellcaster library or academy. The wall had been split open as if it were a cake and someone had removed a slice, revealing a wide circular room lined with shelves. Looters had long ago picked them clean, but a round table still sat in the centre, as if waiting for the books and readers to return.

'Go and do your god-bothering.' He motioned the way to the countess. 'I'll catch you up in a couple of hours. I'll meet you . . .' He looked around him for a suitable landmark. 'At the Unicorn's Head,' he said, pointing toward an inn down the street. That seemed like as good a place as any.

'Very well, my dear.' She patted his arm. 'Do try and stay out of trouble, won't you?'

He rolled his eyes at her and she gave him a grin before bustling off down the street, holding her skirts delicately above the mud. Hopefully she was just going to do what she said – pay her respects, as a good necromancer should – but he didn't believe that was terribly likely. He pitied whatever poor fool attracted her attention.

Better them than Logan.

The mountains squeezed Krensten like a girdle. The city had long run out of space to grow, and now it mostly clambered over itself, with buildings stacked precariously atop one another. Once away from the main gates and plazas, the streets narrowed, and houses perched higher and higher, pressed against the stone of the mountain face in a desperate attempt to hang on.

A few careful words in the right ears in the market square sent him up a set of steps to a narrow maze of tight streets. At the end of one, Logan found a small, dusty shop with a faded sign selling potions and amulets, and a very willing buyer for both the lizard skin and its flesh.

The man, a lizard-like fellow himself, counted the coins carefully on the stained wooden counter, his eyes darting around the room. When he handed them to Logan, the shopkeeper pressed them firmly into his hands.

'I'm always up for goods like this. Pay well, I do, better than the king's informants, I promise you.'

The words made him pause, remembering the stack of bodies in the square of Seraphina's town. While the spellcasters had been pushed underground or away like the unicorns, little shops like this, selling unction and ideas, had always been tolerated as they weren't actually magic themselves.

'I'm not going to sell you out. Been giving you trouble, have they?'

'Not yet. But the king's nervous. That's what they say,' he said, bobbing his head like a bird. 'I've heard it happen to others. We don't get many up this way, but it's enough to put a man on edge. I'm just plying a trade. Not causing no trouble to no one.'

Logan nodded, unsure what else to say. He took the coins and his leave, squeezing out the narrow, somewhat uneven doorway. Between the cloudy day and close tumble of buildings, mid-morning felt like twilight. He set off back to the main streets, keeping his senses alert. Whether it was the shopkeeper's story or just experience, something had his hackles raised.

Still, Logan made good progress acquiring supplies for the journey – warm clothing, more rope, tough trail food that would be a misery to eat but fill your belly. By the time he was done, he felt like a loaded pack horse.

He turned a corner and stepped out into a wider, brighter street, and allowed himself a moment to breathe. An old man pushed a cart of cabbages down the street with increasing difficulty, and his face reddened at the same rate as his swearing increased. Behind him, a man in a cloak lined with fox fur whistled a familiar tune as he crossed the road.

Logan had almost turned into the inn, but now he stopped. The cabbage man continued on and narrowly missed ploughing into the stranger. The old cabbage farmer skidded to a sudden stop, which caused the green orbs to wobble. He raised his fists at the man, unleashing a rattling torrent of abuse.

Logan barely registered the old farmer's words. His heart thudded against his ribs. The tune hat the man in the cloak been whistling wasn't just familiar.

It was one of Pie's creations.

Chapter Eleven

The man had vanished like smoke in a storm. Logan pushed through the people, ignoring angry shouts and one ill-considered kick to his shin. The snatch of song played over and over in his head, warping to match the beat of his heart.

He twisted, trying to see in all directions at once. Splashes of colour stood out, dragging his attention around like a poorly trained dog, straining at its leash. A flash of gold changing hands. Green vegetables. A red scarf on a woman's neck.

But not the ruddy colour of fox fur.

He pushed harder against the flow of people, swimming against the human current. That man had met Pie, and recently. He couldn't have known the song otherwise. It had only been composed a couple of weeks ago, as Pie sat on the wall of the pigpen while Logan pulled weeds from the vegetable patch.

There were two types of song, according to Pie. One was the folk songs, the traditional melodies, the ones that were owned by no one and belonged to everyone. The other type were the ones a bard composed themselves. No bard would take another's song. It was a terrible sign of having no skill of your own, of being nothing but a thief and a fraud. And given that bards were the gossip network of the country, it would be easy to spread that message far and wide.

He found himself heading down wide marble stairs and emerging into a vast plaza lined with small stone buildings. The plaza itself had scattered statues, some small and unassuming, others vast and gilded. The gods-square.

Something sharp pricked his back, just behind the kidney.

Logan froze.

'You've been following me, *friend*,' said a voice, drowning the last word in sarcasm. 'That's not very bright.'

'Neither is pulling out a knife in the sight of every god and all their worshippers,' Logan replied, keeping his voice level. The temptation to ignore the knife rose. To round on the man knowing he couldn't inflict a fatal wound from that position. Let him get that one hit in, and then Logan could beat any knowledge of Pie out of him.

'You've not been in Krensten for a while, then.' The voice oozed disdain. It was male, neither old nor young. Polished speech that only came from nobility or those that hung around them. 'No one cares. I could butcher you on the spot and people wouldn't bat a lash. Not worth it. I'd prefer not to, of course. Got a few things we want from you, and I'd prefer to take them while you're alive, which is why you're going to walk nice and quiet like, exactly as I tell you.'

'I don't think I am,' Logan replied softly. He took a deep breath, then dropped, bending his knees into a deep squat. His injured leg screamed but he ignored it, swinging his other foot around in an arc until it hit his attacker's knee. A soft *oof* told him he'd hit his mark hard.

Logan pushed himself back, rising to his full height as he retrieved his axe. The man in the fox-fur cloak knelt in front of him, a dagger in one hand and a scowl on his face.

'You were the one trying to steal the unicorn!' Logan owed him for that as well. Around them, people had taken note of the fight and stopped their daily business. As the stranger predicted, none seemed eager to get in the way. He took a step towards the man. 'And you were in Stowatt. Where's my Pie?'

The man grinned and pulled himself to his feet. He was small, wiry, with a scar running from his ear down his jaw. His eyes shone with a cold hunger.

'Your stomach's your own business. Last chance. Come along quiet like, and let's avoid this fuss. There's a good fellow.'

Logan's blood boiled. The man's sneer and casual expression mocked him, taunted him with knowledge of Pie.

'My husband is every bit my concern. And if you've hurt him in any way, I'll rip you to pieces with my bare hands.' His hands tightened around the axe.

Fox-Fur didn't move. 'I can see why they call you the Bear,' he said, examining his nails. 'Very well. Don't say I didn't warn you.'

The first arrow shattered on the flagstone in front of Logan's feet, sending pale stone chips flying into the air. The second grazed his shoulder before tangling in his cloak. Instinct took over and Logan rolled, ducking behind a statue of a lesser fertility god.

He scanned his surroundings, trying to pick out the archer. From the trajectory, they were at the top of the steps, which meant they had him trapped in the square. If the man in the fox-fur cloak decided to leave, there wouldn't be anything Logan could do that wouldn't involve him getting skewered.

He peered around the statue.

'What are we doing?' the countess asked.

Logan jumped at the sudden voice, his hands tightening on the axe. He spun around, the blade a hair's width from her chin.

She frowned at him. 'You could have told me you were planning a fight, Logan dear. It's been too long since I had a good scrap.'

'Where did you even . . .' He shook his head. Not important. 'There's a man out there. One of the ones who tried to steal a unicorn. He knows something about Pie.'

Her eyes widened. 'Well, isn't that fortuitous? Let's find out what he knows.'

Logan gripped her arm. 'There's more than one. At least one archer on the steps. Maybe more.'

'Say no more, dear. Let's go and even the odds, shall we?' She pointed behind her towards one of the shrines. This one was jet black, unlike most of the buildings, and the entrance way was lined with skulls. 'The Dark Mother provides.'

'You cannot be serious. Those are the catacombs!'

'Well, exactly. Did you think we were going to find a nice set of bones just lying around?' She raised an eyebrow. 'You're not scared, are you, Logan dear?'

'We can't just go around raising the dead in catacombs!'

Another arrow clipped the statue, turning the lesser fertility god into an even lesser fertility god.

'Would you rather stay here?' the countess asked. 'And besides, it's fine. I have a—'

'Charter, yes, I know,' Logan finished with a sigh. 'Lead on.'

They dashed across the flagstones towards the dark building. Another arrow slashed a burning line across Logan's calf. He stumbled down the steps into the gloom and the countess pulled the door closed behind them.

Logan blinked, letting his eyes adjust to the darkness. He stood at the foot of a steep flight of steps, looking down a corridor lined with bones. As his vision improved, he discovered that 'lined' was the wrong word. The passageway was *made* of bones.

'What's going on?' A priestess strode up between the skeletons. She was a little older than Logan, dressed in a simple black dress, her greying hair pinned with thin bits of bone. 'The Dark Mother is everywhere, and *Her* house is welcome to all. The doors must not be closed,' she said, waggling a finger in a matronly manner. A bracelet of tiny bird skulls rattled as she gestured.

'It's just temporary. No need to worry,' the countess said with a stiff bow. 'There are some unruly types out there trying to send us to the Mother's bosom before our time.'

The priestess folded her arms. 'Your time is at *Her* choosing.'

'Yes, but trust me, now isn't a good time,' the countess rebuked, bustling past the priestess. 'She wouldn't give us our gifts if she wanted us to just roll over. Come along, Logan dear.'

Giving the priestess a shrug, Logan followed the countess past the stacks of bone and into a larger chamber. Torches sat cradled in skeletal hands, fixed to the wall. At the far end, a large altar sat in a moon-shaped pool of water. Above it, a statue of a woman carved of black granite gazed down at him. Despite the gory surroundings, her eyes were soft, kind – fond, even. One hand reached out towards him as if welcoming him into an embrace.

Two more priestesses emerged from a side passage. Again, the countess gave them a stiff bow, the most deference she'd shown anyone. Before she could say anything to them, there was a heavy thud as the door was slammed open.

'Just borrowing some bones,' the countess reassured the holy women.

'Where are all the city guards?' Logan asked.

'Haven't you heard?' one of the priestesses said. 'The king's recruiting. He's offering better pay and less risk than being out here on the frontier.'

'I need blood,' the countess muttered, looking around the room.

Logan turned and pointed to the gash left by the arrow on the back of his leg.

'Very kind of you to offer.'

'I assumed you'd just take it anyway.'

She drew a finger over the wound, making him hiss in pain. Then she daubed symbols on her arms and face. The room rumbled, as if a heavy cart was passing overhead. The countess held up a hand, and bones assembled themselves into dozens of skeletons in front of her. The priestesses' eyes widened', one mumbled a prayer.

'Ready to cause some trouble, Logan dear?' the countess asked Logan with a wink.

'Just promise me one thing.'

She raised an eyebrow.

'If I die, here or anywhere else, you'll have me cremated.'

She barked a laugh, but it was cut short as three men pushed down the bone corridor towards them. None of them were Fox-Fur.

'Can you hold them off?' he asked the countess. 'I need to find the man who attacked me.'

'Logan dear, don't insult me.'

'Is there another way out of here?' he called to the priestesses, who nodded in triplicate. Logan set down his purchases. Hopefully they'd still be there when he could get back to them. 'I'll meet you back at the camp,' he told the countess, and then followed the priestesses, who headed down another passage.

The catacombs were made up of twisting passages of bones, branching off into all directions. If the countess felt overwhelmed, she'd easily lose them in the macabre maze. The thought calmed him a little as he ran. He wasn't worried about her, per se, but she had offered without question to watch his back, and he respected that, if not her methods.

A wall of skulls leered at him in the half-light, their eye sockets seeming to follow him as the torchlight flickered. He almost lost sight of his guides, and the thought of spending his last days wandering, screaming amongst the bones opened a chasm in his gut. Then a reflection of torchlight on a pelvis up ahead revealed them and he pushed himself to go faster.

The priestesses opened a door decorated in teeth and finger bones. The sudden shock of sunlight blinded Logan momentarily. He stood, blinking away tears, until the bright blur resolved itself into a street. He stood not far from the main gate, emerging from an unassuming building in a side street. Nothing about the door he closed behind him suggested it led to the catacombs.

He made his way around to the gods-square. The crowds had dissipated and there was no sign of where his attackers had gone. Fox-Fur hadn't been with the archers, so where had he run off to? A shout near the walls caught his attention.

A small group of men stood near the city gates. Logan's fist curled at his side as he noted the fox-fur cloak. *Now I've got you.* Fox-Fur was accompanied by a squat, burly man with huge cauliflower ears. And beyond him, another watched out towards the hills. His face was obscured by the shadow of the wall, but there was a green scarf around his neck.

It couldn't be . . .

Dark red hair streaked with white. A slight physique, obvious even under the layers of warm clothes. A lute slung over one shoulder. Before his body could react, Logan's heart raced towards his husband.

'Pie!'

All three turned towards him. The squat man scowled. Fox-Fur grinned. Pie paled. He held out his hands in front of him.

'No, Logan, you can't be here. You have to get away from here.' His voice shook with terror. 'They'll kill you. They'll kill you.'

Logan raised the axe. 'No, they bloody won't.' He hadn't come all this way, been through all of this, to be killed by a couple of ruffians. He hadn't pulled his ex-wife from beyond the veil, requisitioned a unicorn, endured the countess, to die here.

He hadn't found his husband only to lose him again.

The squat man moved quickly for someone of his build and stature. Before Logan had even registered it, he was in front of him, raising an equally squat hammer. Logan parried the blow and steel crashed against steel.

'Got no reach with that thing,' Logan said. He turned the axe, catching the hammer between the head and the shaft. He yanked hard, and the squat man lost his grip. The hammer clattered on the cobbles, and Logan kept going. Turning his back on the man wasn't the brightest move, but Pie wasn't going to leave his sight again.

'Logan! Look out!'

Pie's shout drove Logan's hackles up. He turned on Fox-Fur as the man fired a crossbow bolt. Logan flung himself to the side, and the bolt whistled past his cheek. He sat up and put a hand out to push himself back to his feet, but a boot stamped on his fingers. Logan cried out in pain as the squat man grabbed a handful of Logan's hair and pulled his head back, hard. Logan's skull collided with the cobbles and his vision faded to fuzzy grey.

'No!' Pie screamed.

The sound tore through Logan's heart, bitter and wretched. It wasn't right. He wanted to make Pie happy, would do anything for that smile that spread like the sun emerging from behind a cloud. He'd kill them for making Pie scream.

Still half blind, he lashed out. His hand closed on the squat man's leg and dragged it towards him. Logan bit hard into the thigh, tasting mud and hide. A cry of surprise and pain rewarded him.

'Animal,' the squat man snarled, moving back.

'So they say,' Logan replied.

He swung the axe in front of himself, making the man move back again, and jumped to his feet. Everything around him faded to a blur. His opponent was the only thing in focus. He came at Logan, a clumsy blow, easily deflected. Logan flexed his neck, causing his tendons to crack.

The squat man was a brawler, fast and strong, but too reliant on these traits. Logan had met plenty of that type in his life.

The axe cut a gash into the squat man's side, vibrating as it grazed a rib. He staggered back, clutching his wound, blood spilling over his fingers. He tried to take a step towards Logan, but his leg wobbled, and he sank to one knee.

Logan turned his attention back to Fox-Fur and Pie. The crossbow was aimed at Logan's chest, Fox-Fur's finger on the trigger. Logan froze, his body primed to evade. Fox-Fur's lips turned up in a sneer. Suddenly, Pie hit Fox-Fur on the back of the head with the lute. It shattered to splinters with a sad twang.

The crossbow bolt pinged off the cobbles harmlessly.

Fox-Fur turned and punched Pie directly in the mouth.

Logan charged.

With a growl that started at the base of his spine and emerged as a roar from his mouth, he stormed across the road and slammed his shoulder into the man. Fox-Fur hit the wall and slumped, the crossbow slipping from his hands. Logan raised his axe.

'No! Leave him! Come on.' Pie grabbed at his wrist. Logan stared at him but did not lower the weapon. Pie tugged at him again. 'Please, please, come on. We have to get out of here.'

'They hurt you.'

Fox-Fur lay on the ground, stunned. Logan put his foot on the crossbow, and it cracked in a satisfying manner. He reached out a hand to caress Pie's face, his palm coming away bloody from Pie's split lip. Pie gripped his hand and pulled, managing to drag Logan down the street, and soon out of the city walls and toward the forest. They didn't stop running, even as Logan's leg screamed at him to stop.

'Need to hide,' Pie said, his eyes darting around. His fingers shook around Logan's. Logan wanted nothing more than to wrap his arms around Pie, hold him tight, but a strange cry caught his attention. He turned towards the forest. *Ophelia. Gary.*

A man and a woman in black cloaks and well-fitted leather armour struggled with the unicorn. They managed to wrangle a rope around Freddy's neck, but the unicorn reared up and slashed out with his hooves, making them dance out of the way. A short distance away, a second woman with blackened teeth was pointing a wickedly sharp blade at Gary, who was bound and gagged.

Pie whimpered. He let go of Logan's hand, placed his palms either side of Logan's face and kissed him hard. Then he said the words that crushed Logan's heart.

'Go. Forget you saw me. Forget you ever met me. Please. If you love me, you'll get out of here right now.' He choked out a sob. 'Please, Logan. I can't watch anyone else get killed.'

Logan's head hurt. Pie's words hurt. He'd come all this way, and he'd found his husband! They were supposed to keep running, together, until they reached their cottage and their goats. His eyesight was still fuzzy from the blow. Logan had lost Pie once; he wasn't going to lose him again. Not ever.

He couldn't leave Gary out there to whoever they were, either. He tightened his grip on the axe, pushing down a wave of nausea.

Logan was just going to have to do this the old-fashioned way.

Behind him, a series of screams and crashes almost made him lose his grip on his weapon. Pie's eyes widened and Logan turned to see three men running from a dozen skeletons, all armed with bones which they wielded like clubs. The countess, mounted on her bone steed, stood behind them, laughing maniacally. Her face was daubed with blood and her hair had worked free of its normal style, falling in waves around her shoulders.

A dull, rhythmic thud pounded the insides of his skull. Logan dug his fingers into the axe shaft, trying to hold onto his consciousness.

'Oh good,' he said, his words slightly slurred. 'The undead cavalry's here.'

Many people had fled from the streets, but this being Krensten, others were eyeing the countess and drawing weapons. Two men brawling was one thing. An army of skeletons was quite another. Behind her, Fox-Fur pulled himself to his feet, leaning heavily against the wall.

'Adella!' he yelled at the woman holding Gary. 'Get the unicorn out of here. Let's leave them to the mob.'

Adella nodded and turned up the hill, away from the town and the forest. Gary was tied to the back of her steed, his screams muffled by the gag in his mouth. The other two struggled with the unicorn, pulling it with ropes while dodging as it thrust its horn at them. Up above her, the broken outline of a half-collapsed castle stood against the skyline.

Pie let out a sigh and slumped against Logan. 'They're gone, it's over.'

But Logan's heart was still rampaging in his chest. Where was Ophelia? Why wasn't she here?

'We need to go after them,' Logan replied firmly. He kissed Pie. 'Stay here. Stay safe. I'll be back. I promise.'

Pie gripped his hand so tight his nails dug into Logan's flesh. 'You can't. You can't go after them.'

'I have to. I can't leave that lad out there to deal with my mess.'

'Logan, you don't know these people like I do. We need to run,' Pie begged.

'Pie, *no*.' The words came out harsher than Logan intended and Pie flinched.

Pie closed his eyes, his lip trembling. He pressed his forehead against Logan's. 'No, you can't, can you? You'd break your own back to carry everyone else. But that's part of why I love you.'

A pressure lifted from Logan's chest at the words. He let Pie's touch linger a moment longer, then moved past him and set off towards the forest and the road up to the hills. Behind him, the countess let out a loud whistle. Skeletons clacked their teeth, and bone thudded against flesh.

Logan was halfway to the trees before he realised Pie was following.

'Go back,' he said through gritted teeth. His head throbbed, and his vision blurred at the edges until he blinked repeatedly. 'Go back, Pie.' He had to keep them all safe. But he couldn't do it while fighting that many on his own.

'I'm not leaving, Logan.'

Dammit. He spat a glob of blood on the ground. He couldn't waste any more time forcing Pie to turn back. Logan had to get Gary to safety. The armoured mercenaries were halfway to the castle by now, probably would have reached it already if it wasn't for the battling unicorn.

The woman turned in her saddle and let out a startled shout. A thudding filled Logan's ears. At first, he thought it was his heart, but the woman shouted again as something white barrelled towards him.

'Thought you could use some help,' the countess called from behind him.

Logan grinned as the bone steed rushed up the hill towards him. This would even the odds a bit. Bones reached him and skidded to a stop, prancing on the spot. Logan pulled himself into the saddle. Now they'd pay.

'New friends of yours, Logan?' Pie approached Bones cautiously. He glanced over his shoulder at the countess and her skeletal army. 'You'd better introduce me.'

Logan's stomach churned with emotions. Relief that Pie was alive, anger at his leaving, fear for Gary. But there wasn't time to feel. Only act. He clenched his jaw and held out a hand. Pie pulled himself up behind him and wrapped his arms around Logan's waist, pressing his head against Logan's back.

Logan put his heels to Bones's ribcage and the creature surged forwards, eating up the distance to the unicorn with long, powerful strides. Now he had them. Now they'd regret ever tangling with Logan the Bear's marriage.

He rode straight at the woman holding Gary. She knocked the youth aside and threw herself to the ground. As if sensing the change in situation, Freddy reared up, tossing his head and pawing the air, his hooves flashing majestically in the sunlight.

Pie drew in a sharp breath. 'Definitely going to write a song about that one.'

Logan dropped from Bones's back and strode towards the woman. 'You've made a big mistake, messing with me and mine. I'm going to see you regret every last moment of your short life for kidnapping my husband.'

She snorted, drawing her sword. 'Some *husband.* Al came of his own free will.' Her tone made Logan pause. He glanced over his shoulder. Pie ducked his gaze, his face pale.

'I don't believe you.' He struck a blow that she parried easily.

'Doesn't matter either way. Give up, Bear. I have no quarrel with you. You've done me a favour, delivering the unicorn and the trainer to me. Back down and no one else needs to get hurt.'

'I don't believe you're in a position to give orders,' Logan grunted, swinging another blow at her. His limbs ached, heavy as iron. The flashes of grey across his vision were getting more frequent. But it didn't matter. Pie was cutting the rope on Gary, the unicorn had freed itself, and the countess was riding up the hill towards them, the remains of her skeletons stumbling after her.

'It's over, we've won,' Logan announced.

A horn sounded ahead and Logan's blood ran cold.

'Did you think we were all there was? Stupid fool. King Ervin won't allow this mission to fail.' Slowly, Logan realised what she meant. They were being led into a trap.

'There's a troop of the king's men headed this way from the remains of the old Count of Krensten's estate. Thirty men, Bear. Thirty armed, trained men. You think you and your axe can stand against all of them?' She pointed, and Logan dragged his gaze to follow. Metal gleamed, swords and armour. He couldn't count the men, his vision blurred too much, but whether there were thirty or not, there were too many to fight against. He fought back the urge to vomit.

'Al, get over here,' she ordered. 'Get over here and I'll see your husband spared, as long as he drops his weapon.'

'Do it.' Pie's voice was barely a whisper. He brushed past Logan, head down, refusing to look at either him or the woman. 'Please.'

Logan froze. It couldn't end like this. Not now. Not when they'd found each other. Desperately, Logan cast a look around him for options. The countess had almost reached them, but most of the skeletons were far slower and many of them had been picked off by the townsfolk already. Gary stood by Freddy, his hand on the unicorn's flank. Freed thanks to Pie. That was an option. If the unicorn could open a portal back to the farm, they'd be safe there.

Gary caught Logan looking and nodded. Had the youth come to the same conclusion?

'You ought to be ashamed of yourselves!' Gary's voice trembled, but he squared his feet and stood firm. Beside him, the unicorn snorted. The woman raised an eyebrow, and Logan struggled with the urge to smack his face with his palm. Now all attention was on Gary, it would be harder to make the break with the unicorn.

'Is this how King Ervin instructs his people to act?' Gary continued. Logan couldn't tell if the quivering was fear or indignation now. 'Abducting good people going about their business? Splitting up husbands? Harassing old women?'

'Less of the old, Gary sweetheart,' the countess said as she joined them. She didn't stop, but carried on up the hill towards the king's soldiers.

Is she going to hand us in? Rip their flesh from their bones? Flirt with them? All options seemed equally likely.

'I've had enough of this.' The woman took a step forward. 'Seize the boy and the unicorn. If Logan or the old woman give you trouble, kill them.'

Logan raised his axe. Pie met his gaze, his expression pleading, but Logan couldn't bear to let him out of his sight again.

'No.'

Every single head turned at the sound of the countess's voice. She'd stopped her mount just before the group of soldiers, in sight of the crumbling remains of a large gate. She had a different air to the one she'd had in Krensten. No glee this time. Now, her eyes gleamed with tears, but her mouth was set. She raised her fist to the air, blood running down from a wound on her thumb.

The countess traced a bloody symbol on her forehead. The ground rumbled somewhere deep behind the soldiers.

'You do not belong in this place. You will not defile it further with your presence.' Her voice echoed off the stones and the trees. It didn't shake or hitch, and every word hit Logan in the base of his spine. 'The life is gone from here. So I'll give you the dead. All of the dead.'

The ground shook.

The soldiers turned and drew their weapons as the stench of decay washed over them. Logan took a step towards Pie as the woman looked around her, her smug expression melting away.

And then the dead came. They rushed through the gate, a wave of bones, some still half-wrapped in burial shrouds, caked with earth.

They broke over the troops like a wave, crawling, clinging. Smothering. Shouts became screams as they clawed and bit and chewed. The woman yelled at her companions, and they turned tail and ran down the hill. Logan started after her, but

Pie grabbed his wrist. So instead he turned his back on the carnage and held his husband close.

Silence.

Logan turned his head. The soldiers lay on the ground, blood seeping into the grass. The dead filed back through the gates. Meek. One, a small skeleton, paused by the countess's horse. She gave it a sad smile.

'Thank you, Charles,' she said. 'It was good to see you, too.'

Pounding filled Logan's head. The sun burned too bright, and he closed his eyes.

'Definitely not going to write a song about that,' Pie muttered. 'Logan?'

He tried to answer, but the ground shifted under his feet, and he stumbled and fell.

'Logan!'

He forced his eyes open. Pie's face blurred in front of him. Was it real? Was any of it real? He closed his eyes again and sank into unconsciousness.

Interlude

Fifteen Months Ago

Logan put his key in the door. It didn't turn. Had he been given the wrong key? He tensed, straining to hear anything in the room. Gods, he just wanted a meal and a warm bed without anyone trying to kill him. Was that too much to ask? It would have been nice to catch up with Pie, but the bard had disappeared after his set.

He put a hand on the door handle, took a deep breath, and shoved the door open.

Logan almost dropped his axe.

On the bed lay a figure. A very naked figure. A very, very naked figure with a rose between his teeth.

Reluctantly, Logan put a hand over his eyes. 'Pie, what are you doing?'

'Isn't it obvious?' Pie held out the rose. His hair was free from its normal tail, curled artistically around his shoulders. Candles around the room filled the air with a heady aroma, mixing with the scent of the open bottle of wine on the bedside table. 'I'm seducing you.'

Logan sighed.

'It's . . . it's not working. It normally works.' Pie frowned.

'Go on, you should get going.' Logan held open the door.

'Why?' Pie questioned, making no attempt to move. The candlelight traced the edges of his muscles in a golden light. 'I've seen the way you look at me. Saw the way you looked at me just now. Nothing wrong with a bit of fun, right?'

Heat crept up Logan's neck. He couldn't deny the stirrings in his body. But this was an invasion of his privacy.

Pie cocked his head. 'First time?' he asked sympathetically.

Logan growled. 'Of course not.'

'First time with a man, then?' Pie suggested, and Logan rolled his eyes. 'Ah. First time with a bard. Well, you're in for a treat!'

He held out a hand, and Logan glared at him. Pie sighed.

'Fine, fine. Not going to make you do anything you don't want to. But . . .'

Logan raised an eyebrow.

'But I don't suppose you'd see your way to letting me stay anyway? Just to sleep. Lost my room key in a game of dice, and I hate sleeping in the barn.'

Logan sighed, strode over to the bed, and dropped the blanket on the floor, doing his best not to look. 'You can sleep there if you want.' He turned his back, waiting for Pie to weigh up the options. When the bard shifted to the floor, Logan lay down on the bed, not bothering to undress. He held his breath, not wanting to risk opening his mouth and having the wrong thing fall out.

He wasn't quite sure what the wrong thing would be.

Logan wanted Pie to say something, to break the tension, crack a joke with his usual skill. But it seemed that as well as breaking into his room and throwing all his emotions out of whack, Pie was leaving him to have the last word.

'You know,' he said slowly, 'if you'd asked, I might have been up for this. I just don't like surprises.'

'Next time, ask to fuck in the common room, got it.'

Logan pinched the bridge of his nose. 'That was not what I said.'

'No, no, I understand. You're a simple man of simple tastes, and I respect that.'

Logan could hear the grin through his words. He sighed again and rolled over. 'Goodnight, Pie.'

Chapter Twelve

Logan raised his head, wincing at the pain that started behind his temples and raced down to the tips of his toes. *Where am I?* He tried to take stock of his surroundings. His vision was still fuzzy. Soft cloth underneath him, no wind or rain. Indoors then. Soft, regular breathing caught his attention. He tensed, not knowing if it was friend or foe, and the action set off a whipcrack of pain. A small cry escaped through his clenched teeth.

'Logan?'

The voice sent another jolt through him. Not pain, and not the opposite, because that would merely be absence of pain. This was another sensation, like the sun breaking through after a rainstorm or seeing home after a difficult journey.

'Pie.' Logan forced his heavy eyelids open. He'd dreamed of this moment so many times, dreams that felt so vivid he'd awoken each time in a panic and cold sweat, empty arms reaching out in vain. He blinked until a shape resolved itself into a figure sitting by the bed, not too tall, a little too thin. Auburn hair streaked with white at the temples, bound back with a leather thong. Hazel eyes more brown than green right now. Logan's stomach swooped like a swallow. 'It is you.'

He launched himself from the bed, wrapping his arms around Pie, pressing his lips against Pie's, the kiss hot and hungry. Pain swelled, blurring his vison, but it didn't matter. Pie's eyes widened for a moment, then closed, and he pressed himself against Logan.

'I thought I remembered you. But I didn't know if you were real,' Logan said softly. He couldn't bring himself to let go in case he was wrong and this was another Dream Pie who would melt away like the morning mist.

'I am real.' Pie pressed his forehead against Logan's, so they were eye to eye. Tears tracked down his cheek. 'I promise, I'm real.'

'What happened? Where am I?'

'You're safe. You've been asleep for a day now. The countess said . . . How did she put it . . . "He's not badly hurt, it's just that his body's had enough of his stubborn refusal to let it get enough rest and has taken control."'

Logan snorted. His head felt packed full of sawdust. He closed his eyes, trying to remember, snippets flashing across his mind.

Krensten.

A fight.

Pie telling him to leave.

Logan drank in the sight, the touch, the smell, the taste of his husband for a moment longer, and then he pushed him away. Pie stumbled back, his eyes wide in shock.

'How could you?' Logan yelled. Conflicting emotions and desires left him nauseous. A thousand thoughts whirled in his head, but Pie's voice telling him to leave was louder than any of them.

Pie gasped, then bit his lip, looking away. The pain in his expression would have crushed Logan's heart, but fear and anger had hardened it.

'I . . . I thought I was doing the right thing. I didn't mean to hurt you.'

'How?' Logan's hands curled around the bed sheets. 'How could leaving me drugged and alone, thinking you were dead, ever be the right thing? How could telling me to forget I'd ever met you be the right thing? Did the things we promised each other mean nothing to you?'

'Of course they did.' He held out his hand to Logan.

The door opened and Gary stood in the doorway with a cheerful smile and a tray of food. Beside him, Ophelia shook her head.

'We'll come back,' she said firmly, sweeping a hand through Gary's arm. The youth shivered. 'We'll come back later.'

'But . . .' Gary said, holding out the tray.

'Don't make me possess you. Come on, leave them be.'

The door closed again behind them. Pie gave Logan a quick smile. 'Everyone's been worried about you.'

Logan folded his arms. 'And I've been worried about you. Explain to me why you put me through all that. I was told you were dead! Explain how I can ever trust my feelings with you again.' His eyes burned. A dark hole in his chest sucked at him, and he pulled his arms around himself, afraid it would turn him inside out. *Leave me*, screamed Pie's voice in his head, cutting deeper than any knife wound.

'Please, please don't talk like that.' Pie wrapped his arms around himself, his lips trembling. When Logan said nothing, he took a deep breath and leaned back against the wall. 'I . . . I did something stupid, a while ago. After we'd met, but before anything happened between us. You know they don't call me Magpie for my voice, right? But I was never sure you knew why they called me that.'

Logan shook his head. 'Struck me as a stupid name for a bard.' Magpies were loud, coarse. Not something anyone wanted to listen to for hours on end.

'Because magpies like shiny things, Logan.'

Logan shrugged. 'Yeah, I've seen you preening like a peacock. Get to the point.'

'They steal things. That's what I do, too. I'm not just a bard, I'm a thief and a damn good one. Well, most of the time.'

'Oh.' Logan felt gut-punched. He thought he knew Pie, thought he knew him inside and out, but the truth was he'd barely scratched the surface. He clenched his teeth, tasting bile in the back of his mouth. 'You must have been laughing at how dumb I was to not notice.'

'It wasn't like that!' Pie's fist hit the wall with a dull thud. 'It wasn't like that at all. I thought about telling you, so many times, but I was scared about how you'd react, what you'd do. And I was right. You'd have marched right up to the palace and demanded Ervin release me from my debt. And he'd have killed you on the spot.' He lifted his gaze, as if hoping to see some forgiveness in Logan's expression, but clearly there was none, as he dropped it again quickly.

'So, what's this debt? What did you do?'

Pie closed his eyes. 'It's been like this since we were children. My brother, Matty, he was always pushing me to test my skills, steal things, first from around our home, then town, and then on to bigger and more dangerous prizes. It wasn't ever about the money. It was about the thrill. The prestige. His approval.' He took a shaky breath. 'Matty told me he'd been working for the king, getting his hands on old texts, books on necromancy, spellcaster history, that sort of thing. The king clearly didn't want people learning about his interests.' Pie shook his head. 'I should have known it was bad news, getting involved with someone else, and the bloody king no less, but Matty wouldn't hear otherwise, and I could never stand up to him. Next thing I know, we've got the plans in motion. But I . . . I messed up, tripped a magical alert, and we were both caught.

'Ervin paid our fine, had us brought back to the palace and locked up in the dungeon. And there . . .' Pie choked down a sob, pressing a fist to his lips. Logan's heart ached, but he couldn't bring himself to move.

'Ervin slit Matty's throat and let him bleed out in my arms. And then he told me he'd do the same to me, unless I agreed to do a favour for him, at a time of his choosing. If I didn't, he'd kill everyone else I loved.'

Logan lifted his head. 'That time in Runymarsh, when I found you drunk,' he said slowly. 'You told me your brother had died . . .'

' . . . But I didn't tell you it was my fault,' Pie finished. 'I was so miserable, and you wouldn't leave me alone, no matter what I did. And then time passed, and there was no summons and I wondered if maybe he'd just forgotten about me. I thought if I went far away, maybe he'd leave me alone.'

'That's why you insisted on setting up home on the far edge of civilisation, as far away from the palace as possible. It was nothing to do with good earth or quiet living. You used me.' A roaring sound filled Logan's ears. All those times Pie had made him believe in more. All those thoughts of home and hearth. It was a lie.

Everything was a gods-damned lie.

'No, I didn't!' Pie yelled, tears falling. 'I'd never do that. I should have pushed you away harder back then. I should have never fallen for you. But I did, and when the message came, the one that said I had to obey or they'd kill you too, what was I supposed to do? You'd have insisted on coming, and then I'd have your blood on my hands as well.' His voice broke, and he scrunched up his face. His voice dropped to a whisper. 'Gods, I paid the innkeeper to tell you I was dead. I thought that was the only way to stop you following. I love you, Logan. I only wanted to keep you safe.'

'What did you expect me to do? Go back home and live without you? Spend the rest of my life wondering what happened to the man I loved?' He wanted to shake Pie. The idea of working the garden with no singing to accompany him, of crawling into that big bed alone at night sickened him. The pounding in his head matched that of his heart. 'You could have told me. You could have trusted me. We could have dealt with this together. That's what marriage means.' He hung his head, staring at the twisted white cloth clenched in his hands. 'Please leave me alone, Pie. I need some time to think.'

'Logan, please, don't send me away.' He held out his hands, eyes wide and begging. The silence hung between them. Logan turned away.

'Fine.' Pie crossed the room in three strides and the door slammed behind him.

Logan buried his head under the pillow.

He'd almost fallen asleep, the weight of emotions crushing any strength he had, when Ophelia called his name. He pulled his head from the covers to see her disembodied head poking through the door.

'If you're going to yell at me, at least come into the room to do it. You look like a headless hag.'

'Bodyless hag,' she corrected, gliding into the room. 'You're being a bit hard on him, don't you think?'

He rolled away, staring at the wall. 'What business is it of yours?'

'Given that my only chance to be amongst the living again depends on you two recovering the Chalice, I'd say it's very much my business.' There was no creak, no movement from the bed, but he sensed from the drop in temperature that she sat beside him. 'Besides, he obviously cares about you. He hasn't left your side since we brought you here.'

'I know,' Logan said softly. 'I know he cares, and so do I. But I need time to deal with what he did.'

'And what was that, Logan?' she demanded. 'He panicked and tried to protect you from the mad king who murdered his brother. Are you really going to punish him for that?'

'I'm not punishing him,' Logan said with a growl. 'Stop eavesdropping and leave me alone, Ophelia. I'll deal with this in my own way.'

'You want my advice?'

Logan opened his mouth to say no, but she carried on anyway.

'You're feeling too much, and you don't know what to do about it. Well, there's a very easy way to deal with a lot of feelings at once.'

'What do you mean?' Logan asked, then stopped, a heat flushing through his face. 'Oh, no. No. You are my ex-wife. You cannot talk to me about that.'

She leaned in close. 'Fu—'

'No. I'm not listening. You can't make me.' He pressed his hands over his ears.

'Fumble,' she finished with a grin. 'You know I'm right.' Ophelia vanished through the wall as Logan threw a pillow at her.

He lay for a while under the covers, wallowing in the pain of a sore head and a bruised heart. He'd dreamed about finding Pie, about saving him. But Pie hadn't wanted saving. Had pushed him away. Logan sat up slowly, rubbing his thumb over the small knot tattoo on his bicep. Endless, interlinked. That's how it should be.

He sighed and pulled himself out of bed. The room swam as his feet touched the floor. He closed his eyes and took several deep breaths. When he felt safe enough to open them again, he took stock of his surroundings.

The room was small, with old furniture and a good quantity of dust over everything except the bed and the chair next to it. A slither of guilt wormed its way through his insides as he remembered the hurt in Pie's eyes.

Maybe Ophelia was right. Maybe he was simply feeling too much.

More memories were surfacing now – Fox-Fur, and the bandits trying to steal an angry unicorn. He tensed, aching muscles screaming in protest. What had happened after the skeletons attacked? Was the unicorn safe? He'd pulled Gary into this mess, and if anything had happened to his unicorn, it would all be Logan's fault.

He pulled on his clothes and grabbed his axe. Outside the room, he found a narrow corridor and another room opposite, and a steep flight of stairs to his left. Voices floated up from below. He took the stairs quickly and peered around the corner into the room.

The countess sat at the far end of the room, on what looked like a throne carved from black wood. It was cracked and charred down one side, but that didn't seem to bother her as she sat, stroking the skeleton dog. Gary and Ophelia were talking by a cooking pot set over the hearth. He breathed a sigh of relief.

'Logan? Is that you?' the countess called. 'What are you doing out of bed? And what on earth did you say to poor Al? If you've broken his heart, Logan dear, I'm not sure I can forgive you.'

He stepped into the room, feeling oddly sheepish. He cleared his throat. 'Pie and I have some things we need to work out, that's all,' he muttered. 'What happened out there? Who were those people? Where are we?'

The countess held up a hand. 'One.' She touched a finger. 'The Dark Mother's gifts saved us from visiting her realm too soon. Those people haven't given us any trouble since. Two.' She touched the next finger. 'Al can probably tell you more about them. And three.' She touched a third finger. 'You are in what remains of my ancestral home.'

'Oh.' He waited for her to elaborate further, but she said nothing.

'Logan, either come in and eat something,' Ophelia said, 'or go and talk to your poor husband. Either way, get out of the doorway. You're making the place look untidy.'

Logan set his axe down by the doorway and headed outside. He found himself near a crumbling and ivy-covered wall, where a pair of gates – more rust than iron – were hanging from their hinges. A dirt track ran from the gates through some woodland, and beyond that, he could see the ruins of a once-impressive castle. The setting sun cast long shadows over everything.

A movement caught his eye, and he spotted Pie sitting under a tree, his knees drawn up to his chest and his head resting on his knees.

'You'll make your back ache, curled up like that,' Logan called as he stepped closer to his husband.

Pie lifted his head with a jerk, a look of hope flaring in his eyes. 'I think I've already done it sleeping in that chair by your bed.' His face was a mess – dark circles under red eyes, a fading bruise on one side of his face. Lower lip still slightly swollen. If Fox-Fur was still alive, Logan would repay him ten times over for that punch.

Logan took a seat beside Pie. 'I've got a good cure for a bad back. You get a bard with magic fingers to massage it better.'

'I see.' Pie gave him a fragile smile. 'Know where I could get one of those?'

Logan shook his head. 'Sorry. Mine's very much taken.'

Pie leaned his head against Logan's shoulder. 'I'm sorry. I just couldn't bear the thought of what happened to Matty happening to you.' His voice hitched as he spoke. Logan wrapped his arm around Pie and pulled him close. 'I can't lose you, Logan. I can't. I love you so much.'

'I wish you'd talked to me. About all of it.'

'I know, I know. I got scared . . .'

Logan put a hand on Pie's cheek, lifting his head so they were eye to eye. 'You don't have to fear for me, Pie. I never want you to fear for me. Whatever happened in your past, whatever happens from now on. I will always love you.'

Pie's eyes closed, a tear running down his cheek. 'I love you, too. I . . . I didn't use you. I wanted our cottage too. A place that was just ours. I swear.'

'I guess I got scared too. Scared that one day you'll look at this big, hairy, uncivilised lump and wonder what you ever saw in me.'

'Never.' Pie gripped him tighter. 'I know what I see in you. One day I'll make you see it, too.'

Logan wasn't good with words – that's a bard thing. Instead, he was better suited to fighting and killing, and it looked like he wasn't very good at that anymore either. But he could do this. He could hold Pie while the sun went down and the stars came out, until the end of the world.

He'd thought Pie had fallen asleep and was contemplating whether to wake him or attempt to carry him back to the house, when Pie stretched and yawned.

'We should probably go back inside.'

Logan nodded and helped Pie to his feet. 'Probably. The others were worried about you. I don't want them coming out here with pitchforks looking for me.'

'They seem nice. Mostly. The countess is a bit of a character.'

'Has she been giving you grief too?'

Pie sighed and rubbed the back of his head. 'She's propositioned me three times in two days. Once right by your bed while you were still unconscious.'

'That bloody woman,' Logan mumbled. 'She's insufferable.'

'Don't be too harsh on her. She's just lonely. I guess those skeletons aren't into boning.'

Logan choked on his breath, his face burning. 'Pie!'

Pie gave him an innocent look. 'Something wrong with what I said?'

'All sorts. I could have gone a lifetime without those images in my head.'

Pie curled an arm around Logan's waist, pulling him in. 'How terrible of me. I guess you'd better punish me, then.' He leaned in closer, his breath warm along Logan's neck, sending heat racing through Logan's body. 'Bear.'

Logan grinned. 'Oh, that I can do.'

He put his hands under Pie's shirt, fingers tracing down his chest until they reached the stomach. Then he tickled. Pie's eyes widened and he fought desperately to push Logan's hands away, their laughter filling the air.

Pie fell back onto the soft, springy grass. Logan straddled over his husband. Pie gave up trying to force Logan's hands away and beat a fist on his chest instead.

'I yield! I yield, you brute.' He wiped away the tears of laughter with the other hand. Logan leaned in, kissing him hard. Pie always smelled like summer – warm days and comfort. Logan drank it all in as he wrenched the shirt over Pie's head.

Pie flinched, a groan escaping through clenched teeth.

Not a groan of pleasure.

'Pie?'

'It's nothing. Don't stop.'

But Logan had to stop. Had to look. Stamped on Pie's flesh was an ugly reddish wound, puckered around the edges – a flame.

The mark of the king.

'He branded you?' The words sounded distant, muffled.

'A warning of what he was capable of,' said Pie softly. 'As if I'd forget. It doesn't matter, Logan. Please, it doesn't matter.'

A new heat filled Logan. Not rich and warm like summer, but raging. A swollen river of anger.

Logan stood up, too fast, his head swimming. He stumbled away. His rage made him nauseous, blinding him. He reached for his axe and let out a roar of fury as he realised it was still inside.

'It's nothing,' Pie called again. 'It doesn't matter.'

'Of course it matters! He branded you, like an animal.' The words came out like thunder. Loud, abrasive.

'He's changed,' Pie said. 'He's violent. Cruel. I never knew him well, but I do know that he was never a cruel man until now. Quite the opposite. He hated ceremony, opulence. Even after Annabelle died, it was never like this. Something has caused this.'

'It doesn't matter what caused this. He's a damn cruel man now, Pie. He murdered the whole town of Mywin.' Logan turned back towards the house. 'I'm going to kill him. I'm going to kill him for what he did.'

'I know you are, love. And you're right: he needs to die. But not tonight. Logan, look at me.'

Pie stood on the grass, his pale skin glowing in the moonlight. He gave Logan a small smile, which did nothing to quell the rage burning through him. How could he be so calm?

'Look at me.' Pie pointed to a deep scar on the inside of his wrist. 'A parel did that to me.' He pointed at his crooked nose. 'Courtesy of Duncan the Butcher when I beat him at dice. To be fair, I was cheating.' He raised his hand to his forehead, pushing back the hair to reveal a small scar on the temple. 'I got this one slipping in the river, after Matty bet me I couldn't catch a fish with my bare hands. Turns out he was right. And this one . . .' He held up his right hand. 'This one I got cutting vegetables for dinner.'

'I don't understand.' Logan rubbed his temple. The river was slowing down now. Wide and deep, it sucked at his insides, but it didn't propel him along.

'You can't stop me getting hurt Logan.' Pie took a step towards him. 'Whether you're with me or not, it's going to happen.'

Logan said nothing. His husband inched closer and Logan wrapped his arms around him. His body felt heavy, and he was afraid if he let go, his legs might give way, pulled under by the river of emotions. Pie rested his head on his shoulder.

'That's better. Hold me, comfort me. Laugh at me if I deserve it.'

'I can do that,' Logan said.

'Good. Come on, let's go to bed. It's freezing out here.'

Logan sighed. 'Moment's passed, Pie.'

'I meant to just sleep!' he half-joked. 'I've missed sleeping beside you. It's rather difficult to sleep in silence when you get used to sleeping by a sawmill.'

'Cheek. I don't snore.' He pulled Pie into his arms as they set off for the house.

'Logan, there are people three villages away who will confirm you absolutely do.' He peered over Logan's shoulder. 'You know we've left my shirt back there?'

'You don't need it to sleep.'

'I suppose not. The countess is going to bring it up at breakfast, though.'

'Let her,' Logan grumbled.

'I love you.'

Logan held his husband as the river faded away to a trickle. 'I love you, too.'

Chapter Thirteen

The bed in the dusty room was narrow with barely enough room for them both. Logan was pressed up against the wall, Pie's arm wrapped tightly around him and his head on Logan's shoulder. Logan wasn't tired, so instead he lay there watching his husband sleep.

For the first time in days, he felt calm. Whatever happened now, they had each other. They could go home, back to the cottage and Bacon, and even the bloody goats. If anyone tried to follow them, Logan would see they regretted it.

Pie shifted in his sleep, muttering something. He'd always been a restless sleeper. Probably a bard thing. Logan found his hand under the covers.

'I don't care what you say, Pie. I'm going to do everything in my power to keep anyone from hurting you ever again.'

Logan eventually drifted off and awoke sometime later with the sunshine tickling his eyelids. He opened his eyes to Pie's face. Pie lay on his side, his hands under his cheek, looking up at him with a smile.

'Good morning,' he said, leaning forward to kiss Logan's cheek. 'I was worried you were going to sleep all day again.'

Logan groaned and stretched, every muscle in his body aching. Various joints clicked and popped.

'There's my grumpy husband,' Pie said cheerfully, making no attempt to move. Logan clambered over him.

'Aren't you coming to breakfast?'

'I would, but I'm not really dressed for breakfast,' he replied, lifting the sheet. 'Could you find my clothes? I should probably let these people get used to my face before I show off my arse.'

Logan pulled on his own clothes and reached for the door, just as someone knocked. Pie drew the sheet up to his chin.

'Good morning.' The countess stood beaming in the doorway. She handed Logan a neatly folded bundle of cloth and peered over his shoulder. 'Good morning, Al. I trust you two had a pleasant reunion.'

Logan snatched the clothes out of her hand. 'Yes, thank you.' He shut the door, and turned back to Pie, who still had his hand raised in a wave. 'Don't encourage her,' he muttered, throwing the clothes at his husband.

'She's harmless.' Pie pulled on a shirt as he sat on the edge of the bed. Logan's eyes flicked to the brand mark.

'She's bloody not.'

'Well, all right, yes, she's a powerful necromancer, but she's not doing anything other than flirting.'

'I don't like it.' Logan folded his arms over his chest. 'I'm not going to miss her one bit when we're back home.'

Pie's grin evaporated. 'Logan . . . we can't go home right now.'

'Don't see why not,' Logan replied with a snort. 'Went to find you. Got you. Nothing else to do now but return home.'

Pie sat back down on the edge of the bed, his hands tucked tightly in his lap. 'They . . . They know where we live. They'll find us. Kill you. Drag me back.' His body shivered as if he were feverish. 'The king is obsessed with the Chalice. He won't let me leave until he has it, Logan. That's what the brand means.'

Logan curled a hand into a fist. 'He won't get a chance to hurt you again. I'll put him down. I'll keep you safe, Pie.'

Pie shook his head, curling in on himself. 'You don't know these people like I do.' His hands shook in his lap, his knuckles white.

'We're never going to be apart again, you hear?' Logan put a hand on Pie's knee, leaning in close so their foreheads touched. 'Whatever happens, I've found you now and I'm not letting you go.'

'Sounds like you need a plan.'

They both turned towards the door, as Ophelia passed through it.

'Dammit, woman. Can't you—'

'No, Logan, I can't.' She waggled her fingers at him. 'Still incorporeal. Still incapable of knocking. Morning, Al. Hope this lug is treating you better today.'

Pie kissed the top of Logan's head. 'A perfect gentleman. He's just grumpy because he hasn't had breakfast yet.'

Ophelia rolled her eyes. 'Gods, yes, he's terrible before he's eaten.'

Logan looked between his husband and his ex-wife. This wasn't how he'd expected them to react to each other. The pair of them ganging up on him was hardly fair. He rubbed the bridge of his nose, suppressing a growl. 'I am not grumpy.'

Ophelia patted his arm, sending icy shivers across his skin. 'Of course you're not. Gary should be up with something to eat in a minute. In the meantime, I suggest we discuss what we're going to do next.'

Logan shrugged and sat on the bed next to Pie. He reached over and gripped Pie's hand, which trembled in his. Pie stared at a knot in the floorboards, his face pale. Ophelia leaned against the wall, her shoulders occasionally vanishing into the whitewash. Logan cleared his throat, waiting for her to start.

'Look, Al's right,' she said. 'You can't just march up to the king and knock him down to size on your own. And there's also the small matter of the fact you promised to help me get my body back. You can't do that if you throw your life away in a stupid way.'

Logan's cheeks warmed. He had been so intent on protecting Pie, on taking revenge, that he'd forgotten all about his promise to her.

'I propose we beat the king to the Chalice,' Ophelia continued. 'They've lost their best thief and I didn't see a unicorn with them. And then we use that to put an end to the king. We stop him from coming after you and Pie, once and for all.'

'With what army, Ophelia?' Logan couldn't hold back his snort. The rest of them weren't fighters.

'The one we raise from the Chalice, of course!' Ophelia said smugly. Pie lifted his head, and Logan saw hope in his eyes. He tightened his grip on Pie's hand, hating to be the one to dash that hope.

'You've got a point, but how are we going to raise this army? None of us know how to use this thing. The only one who stands a chance is the countess, and we are absolutely not giving that woman an army of undead bones to control. You know it will not end well.'

The room fell silent. When Gary knocked, no one seemed inclined to move. With a sigh, Logan stood and pulled open the door. Gary entered cheerfully and set a tray on the small table.

'Why does everyone look so down?' he asked.

'Because Logan's a big stupid-head,' Ophelia said, crossing her arms. Logan growled. Pie picked up a bowl and shoved it into Logan's hands.

'You're not a stupid-head,' he said, kissing Logan's cheek. 'Let's try and stay on topic. Look, are you sure about the countess? Has she ever done anything to threaten or hurt either of us?'

'She's a *necromancer*.' Logan folded his arms. 'And she's . . .'

'Forward?' Pie suggested with a raised eyebrow.

'Not the word I'd use,' Logan muttered.

'I agree with Logan,' Gary said. 'I don't think you can risk giving that much power to a necromancer. It's too dangerous.' Ophelia glared at him and he cringed over his breakfast bowl.

'Do we have another choice?' Pie ran a hand through his hair. Logan noticed for the first time how tired his husband looked. His hair was whiter and deeper lines creased his face. He'd definitely lost weight.

Logan pushed down his misgivings. 'She's never actually done anything against, us, I suppose.'

He would find a way to keep them safe, even if it meant he ended up facing an army of undead. He handed Pie a bowl of porridge spotted with dried fruit.

'Here, eat. I want to talk to her first,' Logan reasoned. 'We can't let the king get the Chalice.'

'She'll listen to you. She's as besotted with your big, muscly self as she is that little dog. Just flatter her a bit and she'll be eating out of the palm of your hand,' Pie suggested a little too eagerly.

Logan glowered. 'I do not like that image one bit.'

The mood in the room shifted as they settled into their breakfast and small talk. Logan didn't like any part of the plan. But having one felt like the right step. He couldn't fault Ophelia's logic, or Pie's concerns.

'You still want to do this?' he said to Gary. 'I'd understand your misgivings, believe me. We need a unicorn, but if you want to go home, I won't stop you.' They'd find another way.

The youth looked up, surprise making his eyes wide. 'Now that I've seen the world outside and know what's at stake, I can't go back. Freddy and I will stand with you, I promise.'

'That's a dangerous promise,' Logan cautioned. 'Do you have any experience with a weapon?'

Gary shook his head. *Of course not.*

'We'll pick something up, and I'll give you some basic lessons,' Logan said. 'But the best thing you can do is stay out of any trouble as well as you can.'

Gary nodded, his eyes beaming at the words 'weapon' and 'lessons'. Logan sighed, fairly certain that his most important message had gone in one ear and out the other. It didn't matter. Ultimately, he'd keep them safe, all of them.

Somehow.

When they'd finished, Gary stacked the bowls on the tray.

Pie stood. 'Come on. Let's go and see the countess and make sure she's fully on board with everything, including the plan to not run off with an undead army.'

The back of Logan's skull itched. 'She'd better be.'

'Just butter her up a bit first,' Pie suggested.

She wasn't in the room across the hall, or downstairs sitting in the throne. Eventually they found her outside, looking up at the ruined castle. When Logan touched her shoulder, she flinched, a shudder running down her body.

'Oh, good morning, Logan dear,' she said, dabbing her eyes with a black lacy handkerchief. 'Beautiful day, isn't it? The sun was getting in my eyes.'

Logan looked up at the sky. The early sunshine had faded away as heavy grey clouds moved in.

'Is it time to leave?' the countess asked, starting to turn. Behind her, Pie made a shooing gesture at him. Logan took a seat next to her and she let out a little gasp of delight. 'Why, Logan dear, so impetuous. What has gotten into you this morning? Or should that be who?' She gave him a sly grin.

Logan coughed, his cheeks flaming. 'Stop that. You, er, you . . . ahem. You said this was your family's land,' he deflected. He gazed at the scattered ruins, a burning sadness settling around him. 'What happened here?'

Her usual grin faltered. 'Oh, you know, the usual. Greed, fear, vengeance. I'll tell you about it sometime. I'm sure Al could make it into a lovely song.' There was a wistful note to her voice, and a darker tone under it.

'Are . . . Are you all right, Countess?' he asked. Beside him, Pie gave him an encouraging nod. 'Is there something you'd like to talk about?'

Her eyes widened in a mixture of surprise and delight, then she shook her head. 'For once, Logan dear, I don't fancy talking about myself. Let's talk about you, hmm? You want to beat the king's company to the Chalice, raise an army of the undead, and then pack that army away nicely when we're done. Is that about right, dear?'

Pie laughed. 'I'd say that about covers it.'

'You were eavesdropping,' Logan accused.

'I'm just a little old lady,' she replied, drawing her hands to her chest and looking at him from under her lashes. 'I'm merely looking out for myself.'

'See, this is exactly what I'm afraid of,' Logan said. This was a bad idea. They'd be trading one enemy for another.

'You don't trust me, do you, Logan?' She brushed a hand down his chest and he pushed it away. 'You think I'm a monster, like the necromancers of old.'

He thought of her in Krensten, on the back of her bone steed, an army of dead surrounding her. 'I wouldn't say monster, but . . .'

'I see.' She frowned, poking him in the centre of his forehead. 'For a man who trades in life and death as much as you, Logan Theaker, you don't seem to have a good grasp of either. I hope the lessons you learn are easier than the ones I faced.'

She picked up her skirts and turned towards the house. Logan pinched the bridge of his nose. She was going to make this as difficult as possible.

'What Logan is trying to say is that he respects your craft, Countess,' Pie said, stepping into her path. 'He thinks you're a formidable woman.' Pie glared at Logan pointedly.

Logan cleared his throat. 'Yes, that. Formidable.'

'Don't patronise me. You don't trust me!' She thrust a black velvet bag at him. When he just stared at it, she pushed it at him harder.

'What's this?'

'It's Ossymandias. You may not trust me, but I am entrusting you with my most treasured possession. I swear to assist you in your quest and not use my arts against you. Should I break my word, you hold what is dearest to me.'

Logan closed his hands around the bag as she stormed off. Five paces away, she stopped, turned, and shook a challenging finger at him. 'If you harm a single bone, I swear I'll put collars on the pair of you and keep you as my pets for the rest of eternity.' She stomped away.

'Anyone else feel like a terrible person, suddenly?' Pie asked.

Logan pushed the little bag at Pie. The countess's gaze still tickled the back of his mind, even though she'd disappeared into the building. An uncomfortable itch he couldn't rationally scratch. She'd chosen to do this. He hadn't forced her, had he?

He headed back to the house, Pie following behind. The countess had ordered the skeletons to tack up the bone steeds, and Gary was busy brushing down the unicorn.

'Isn't that the most beautiful thing you've ever seen?' Pie said quietly.

'You're talking about the unicorn, right?'

'What? Yes, of course I'm talking about the unicorn.' He put his arm around Logan's shoulder. 'You know I only have eyes for you. Matty always dreamed of seeing a unicorn as a child, but we thought they were all gone. I wrote the song "Long-Gone Unicorn" for him.' His expression clouded over for a moment, then he swallowed and turned to the countess. 'You have another one of those?' He pointed to the skeletal horses.

'No,' the countess replied. 'Only prepared the two. You can ride with Logan. They're strong enough to take two. I was going to invite you to ride with me, Al darling, but I think I'd rather be alone today.' Her tone was defiant, aggressive, even, but there was a slope to her shoulders, a sadness in her eyes that suggested a deeper hurt than she was trying to let on.

'The conversation went well, then?' Ophelia asked, appearing suddenly in front of Logan.

He couldn't stop himself from jumping. 'Dammit, you're doing it on purpose now.'

'Hey, I'm dead. Not a lot of joy in my life right now, so I'll take it where I can.'

Pie sniggered and Logan elbowed him in the ribs.

They mounted up, Logan at the front and the countess bringing up the rear. Ophelia vanished once more, but Logan trusted she'd turn up again, probably at the least opportune moment. It felt good to have Pie's arms around him as he put his heels to Bones. They might be on their way to steal a powerful necromantic item and take down a mad king, but at least they'd be together.

Interlude

Fourteen Months Ago

Logan drained the last of his drink and slammed down the tankard. Right. He was going to do it. Neither gods nor man could stop him now. Pie stood in the corner, showing the barmaid sleight of hand tricks. A gold coin flashed across his knuckles and then vanished from sight. Pie held out his empty hands and she gasped in delight. Logan had to move now, or he'd lose his chance.

The back of his neck itched as he stood, the confidence of several pints sliding off his shoulders. Logan fought to hold onto it. After his marriage had ended, there had been numerous one-night events – a bit of meaningless fun to warm the bed and nothing to leave them attached in the morning. As Logan had got older – and grumpier – and more set in his ways, they'd become few and far between. But why shouldn't he? At least he knew Pie was interested.

He wasn't quite sure what to say to make the barmaid go away, but fortunately Pie spotted him first and headed over. Logan's heart leapt into his throat.

'So,' Logan said as the bard approached. 'You still want to seduce me, right?' Immediately his ears burned, and he wanted the floor to swallow him up. That was smooth.

Pie grinned. 'You don't waste words, do you?' He put a hand on Logan's shoulder and the smile slipped a little. 'I do, definitely, but . . .'

Logan's heart sank. He'd left it too late after all. He tried to turn away, but Pie didn't release his grip.

'Hear me out. Last time you were pretty clear. What if this is the beer talking, and tomorrow you wake up and think differently?'

Logan shook his head. 'Ain't the beer.'

'I just want to be sure that you're sure.' Pie leaned in close, and Logan noticed for the first time that his eyes were both green and brown. 'I've been many people's bad ideas. I don't want to be anyone's regret.'

'What do you want me to do? Stand on one leg? Sing a song?' Frustration put a hard edge to Logan's voice. 'What will convince you that this isn't the beer talking, that I want this?' He lowered his voice. 'That I want you?'

'Tell me what's different this time.' The bard rested his hip against the table, and Logan tried not to focus on the way Pie's loosely laced shirt revealed his collarbone.

'Last time you surprised me. Didn't give me the opportunity to think. This time . . . This time . . .' He stumbled over the words, much harder to harness than feelings. 'I did good today. Saved those children. They went home to their families, happy. Why shouldn't I get some happy time too?'

Pie's eyes widened and so did his smile. He put a hand on Logan's cheek, drawing Logan's lips to his. He wore a citrusy scent that drove Logan's senses wild.

'Well, in that case, you've absolutely come to the right place.' Pie took his hand, pulling him towards the stairs. 'Happy endings are my speciality.'

Chapter Fourteen

The road took them around the countess's lands and into the mountains behind Krensten. The city, hard and grey below them, was the last they'd see of civilisation for a while. The wind whistled around Logan's ears. He pulled his cloak tighter, grateful for his purchased supplies. It was only going to get colder the higher they travelled and his leg ached in agreement.

The forest gave way to an open, rocky landscape. Short, grey-green shrubs and scrubby trees clung to the rocks out of what Logan suspected was largely stubbornness. No birds, only fat moths with whirring wings.

'So, Gary,' Pie called. 'I've got a question for you. Why did all the unicorns disappear?'

Gary frowned, his hands tightening on the reins. 'People weren't treating them right. They were racing them or killing them for medicine. Hunting the wild ones. Unicorns don't breed quickly, and their numbers were dropping fast. About a hundred years ago, a few spellcasters decided to make sure they survived. Moved small herds away to pocket spaces where they'd be safe. My great-grandmother was one of them.'

'Smart woman. It would be a crime to lose something so beautiful.'

Gary nodded. 'I just wish I was better at protecting Freddy and the others.'

'The best thing you can do in a fight, lad, is get out of the way,' Logan said. 'Let me handle the protecting.'

Gary bit his lip, his face contorted in a grimace.

Logan reached over to put a hand on his shoulder. 'Being a warrior isn't what the bards make it out to be.'

'Logan's right,' Pie said. 'You should become a bard instead.'

'Hey, now, that's not what I meant.'

'Teasing.' Pie leaned forwards and kissed his ear. 'Well, a little. With a face like that, he'd definitely be the centre of attention in a tavern. Maybe get his livery, spend his life in luxury until he's caught in a delicate situation with one of the family . . .'

Gary flushed a deep red.

'Let's not map out the lad's whole life for him.' Logan reached back and patted Pie's leg. 'Let him make his own mistakes.'

After the events in Krensten, Logan's nerves were taut, but nervousness had been his default state for much of his life. And as the day progressed with no further sign of being followed, he let his defences slip. The uphill path put them at an advantage against anyone approaching and nothing short of a mountain goat was likely to move around off the path.

There were legends of big creatures living here, but they were bard's tales. Such creatures were rare even before Krensten became an established stronghold – the mountains didn't hold much prey – and a large group of humans meant organised hunts.

When a break for lunch passed without incident, Logan even agreed to Pie's request to be allowed to sing.

Bones strode tirelessly up the path, clacking in rhythm to the song. A very different mood compared to the journey through the forest to Krensten. The rocks echoed with Pie's voice, and Logan leaned into the sound, enjoying the way it brightened his mood like the sun after the rain. Pie prodded him several times to join in, but Logan knew his strengths and weaknesses. Singing at home was one thing, but he wasn't ready to admit his complete lack of tune to an audience.

The day grew on, and the songs got bawdier. Whether the countess had forgiven Pie or not, she was apparently not going to miss the opportunity to join in with the Ballad of Elin and Hawk. It was a tavern favourite, with a chorus that consisted solely of the words 'balls, balls, balls, balls' sung with increasing vigour.

Logan called camp on a flattish plateau near a little waterfall that dropped several feet from the rock above, creating a soothing, pattering sound. The countess, still out of breath and giggling – she and Pie had sung the song three more times – dismissed the bone steeds, which set off an irrational flare of guilt in Logan's gut. It wasn't like the creatures needed to be rubbed down or anything.

He walked over to where Gary was letting the unicorn drink. 'How's he doing?'

'Fine.' Gary patted Freddy's shoulder. 'He might look delicate, but unicorns are strong.'

'I don't doubt it,' Logan said. Freddy swung his head around and regarded him with eyes like liquid night. Logan hoped he was never in a situation where he needed to battle a unicorn. 'How about you?'

'My butt is numb,' Gary admitted with an embarrassed grin.

'Arse. You mean your arse is numb,' Pie called from across the campsite. 'Butts are barrels.'

The countess laughed and Gary's ears reddened.

'Ignore my husband,' Logan said. 'Bards get drunk off their own talents. I expect your uncle is the same.'

'My uncle prefers to compose sonnets and epics,' Gary replied. 'There are definitely fewer . . . um . . . balls in them.'

Logan left Gary to tend to the unicorn and his embarrassment. Pie got a fire going, while Logan laid some snares at the edge of the camp; he wasn't particularly hopeful, but it didn't hurt.

'Ophelia?' he called to the empty air. The space at his back grew colder. 'Haven't seen you much today.'

'I was around.'

He turned, but she faded away. 'Feels like you're avoiding us.'

'Me, avoiding the big noisy living, with their loud, obnoxious songs? Never.' The air turned icy.

'Sarcasm isn't a good look on you.'

'I could say the same for your face.' She reappeared in front of him with a glare.

Logan sighed. He looked over to Pie, longing for some help, or at least moral support. But Pie was busy helping Gary feed the unicorn. 'You're still one of us, Ophelia. Being dead doesn't change that.'

She folded her arms. 'Really? That's why you were just going to take your Pie and run, leave me incorporeal forever?'

Shame itched down his spine. 'I . . . I let my emotions get the better of me. But I didn't leave, and I swear by any god you choose I'll get you a body.'

'First thing I'm going to do is punch you with it,' she said, but her voice was dull, flat. Logan longed to reach out and hold her, longed to know the right words to say to comfort her. But he just kept giving her more reasons to hate him.

'Ophelia?' he said to the empty air. There was no reply. Logan sighed and walked back to the others. 'I'm worried about Ophelia,' he said to the countess, expecting be mocked.

Unexpectedly, she agreed. 'I did warn her she wouldn't enjoy it here.' She reached up a hand to smooth her hair, then clicked her fingers at her skeleton servant. 'Ghosts still feel, Logan. But they have no body with which to dissipate those emotions. They cannot cry or stamp or break things. Those feelings can only build inside them until they overwhelm the personality, and all that's left is emotion, usually negative.'

A cold hand squeezed Logan's insides. 'That's going to happen to Ophelia?'

'Of course not.' Pie put his arm around him. 'We're going to get her a body, and she's going to have a long, fulfilling life. Right?'

Logan leaned into him. 'Right.' He could believe that. But it didn't help the stab of guilt as he stood there with his husband, while Ophelia floated somewhere in the growing gloom with only her rage.

'Come, sit,' Pie said. 'How's your leg?'

'It's been worse.' He eased himself onto the ground. It had, indeed, been plenty worse. He wasn't sure he'd have made it up this road without Bones. Pie dished out servings from the pot. 'Make sure you save enough for yourself,' Logan told him. 'You need to keep your strength up.'

'I have, don't worry so much.' Pie held out a full bowl for his inspection. 'See, plenty for everyone. Now, how are your socks? Any holes I need to darn?'

'What?' Logan growled, catching Gary and the countess staring at them.

'You two are adorable.' She clapped her hands together in delight.

Logan grumbled under his breath, his face warming at their scrutiny.

'You can't blame them.' Pie snuggled closer against Logan. 'We are sickeningly cute together.'

The firelight danced in his warm brown eyes and Logan was filled with a desire to knock the bowl out of his hands and kiss him. Push him to the ground and kiss him until the world faded away. Until the world was only Pie.

'Something wrong?' Pie asked.

'Nothing. Just love you.' Logan closed his eyes. 'Please don't leave me again.'

Pie sucked in a breath. He leaned his face against Logan's. 'I won't. I promise.'

Silence amplified the ache in Logan's heart. Emotions punched and kicked, physical things. He pressed into Pie, and thought of Ophelia, who couldn't even touch another.

'Perhaps we should have a tale?' the countess said suddenly. Logan let out a sigh of relief.

'That sounds good,' Pie said. 'Perhaps you could tell us about your home. There's definitely a tale there.'

She gave him a sad smile that didn't reach her eyes. 'Not tonight, Al darling. I'm not ready for that story yet.' She fiddled with a bracelet, twisting it back and forth, the knuckles on her hand white.

'No? Another time then. My turn.' Pie set down his bowl and got to his feet. He looked around the group. 'Some of you might know this one, I think it's a good tale.' He gave Logan a wink.

'Let me set the scene. It's springtime, about two years past. Our protagonist is a bard, of some renown, exceptionally handsome, and completely devoid of new material. He's sitting in a wayfarer inn at the edge of nowhere, listening to the chatter and desperate to pick up the threads of a new story to weave a song or two.

'The door to the inn slams open and a man enters, catching everyone's attention. He carries himself with a warrior's precision, his body rippled with well-used muscles. Hair dark as a thundercloud. Folk quickly move out of his way as he strides through, his trusty axe, Gut-Splitter, strapped to his back.'

'You're talking about Logan,' Gary said, eyes wide.

'Right you are, my young friend!'

'My axe doesn't have a name,' Logan muttered.

'Shush, love. Let me tell the story.' Pie cleared his throat and took a breath. 'So, anyway, our protagonist sees the mighty warrior and thinks, "This is a man who is full of stories. Here is the answer to all my problems." Doesn't hurt that he's a fine and attractive fellow, either.' He threw Logan another wink.

Logan, sensing all eyes on him, tried to shrink back against the rock. 'So, he buys the man a drink and uses his not inconsiderable charms to urge a tale or two out of him. The warrior says he has no time to sit and talk, for he has a pressing mission, but with a little more persuasion, agrees to let the bard come with him, to witness for himself.'

'That's not how it happened.' Logan pointed his spoon at Pie. 'I told you I was busy, ate my meal, and left. You followed me.'

'Ah, but if I'd said that, I wouldn't be presenting our protagonist as the handsome, charming character he is.'

Logan rolled his eyes, but gestured with his spoon for Pie to continue. The corner of his mouth tugged up.

'Our intrepid heroes set out across the moorland, away from the road and civilisation. Before long, there was nothing but silence. As if every living creature had hidden itself away in fear.' Pie dropped his voice to a dramatic whisper as he paced around the fire. 'Onwards they trudged, not daring to speak. The hairs rose on the back of the bard's neck, every sense heightened, alert for danger, his mind keenly recording the sensations for future listeners.'

'You complained your shoes were damp,' Logan said. 'Incessantly.'

Pie ignored him. He approached Gary. 'Despite the early hour, the sky was growing darker, the clouds the colour of iron. The air tingled, as if a storm approached. The warrior unsheathed his axe, and blue sparks danced along the edge of the blade.' He held out a finger to Logan to silence his interruption. 'With each step, their hearts beat faster, their mouths grew dry, sensing, anticipating, knowing that something was out there. Something unholy. Something . . .' He paused, making Gary lean forward, and then turned suddenly, and pointed at the countess. 'Like her!'

The countess gave Pie a round of applause. 'Ooh, now we're getting to the good bit.'

It grew dark and the fire cast shadows across Pie's face. The fire spat, sending a shower of sparks into the air. Gary jumped with a yelp. Pie grinned.

'Before them, in a hollow, were a pair of mighty standing stones, leaning against each other. A woman stood with her hands raised, her voice calling out commands to companions they could not see. Between the standing stones was a gaping wound in the earth, and the scent of something dark and deadly wafted out.'

'What was she like, this woman?' the countess asked gleefully.

Pie put a hand over his heart. 'Well, obviously, she was beautiful. Hair as black as a raven's wing and skin as white as a freshly uncovered skull.'

'Flatterer.' The countess blushed, tucking her hands up under her chin and batting her eyelashes.

'Bards,' muttered Logan. The countess had been as grey as she was today. He'd been hunting down a grave-robber in the area and finally caught her up at the ancient site. He hadn't expected a necromancer, just the usual out-for-a-quick-buck sort. When he'd seen her standing there, he'd known he was taking a big risk facing her alone rather than returning to the inn for back-up. But he couldn't let her slip away.

'The warrior put his hand on the bard's shoulder and proclaimed, "You should leave this place, for I would hate to see anything happen to such a handsome face." But our protagonist wasn't about to leave his new friend to face the wrath of the necromancer. The warrior called out and the necromancer whirled to face him. She called forth her unholy creations – no offence, countess.'

'None taken, Al darling.'

'They rushed towards the warrior, who fought them off bravely with powerful blows from his axe.' Pie swung his arms in wild imitation. 'The undead feel no pain, so they kept coming, again and again they swarmed. The brave bard had only moments to help, but what could he do? Largely ignored in the heat of battle – which is not an easy thing for a bard – he crept towards the necromancer. With her attention fully occupied by our hero, the bard caught her arm and held a knife to her throat.'

Logan nodded. That had happened, at least. Another moment where Pie had surprised him, in a good way. If Logan had gone alone, then things may well have ended up very differently. The fight seemed to fall away from her when Pie stepped in. She'd slumped a little and the tomb's occupants had clattered to the ground. And then . . . Logan groaned.

'Wait, Pie, do not carry on with this story!'

'You can't leave it there,' Gary said breathlessly, and the countess nodded.

'Absolutely. He's getting to the best bit.'

Pie threw him a grin. 'Sorry, Logan, can't disappoint the audience. First rule of being a bard. Give the people what they want.'

Logan huffed, wrapping his arms around himself, and pushed himself back against the rock.

'"I'll come quietly," the necromancer said. "For I am not ready to sit at the Dark Mother's feet and I tire of only the dead for company. But you must pay my price."' Pie leaned towards Gary. 'Can you guess what her price was?'

Gary swallowed and shook his head.

'A kiss!' Pie said with delight. 'Which the warrior readily agreed to.'

'Pie!' Logan protested.

'And so, the necromancer was taken away to face justice, and our brave heroes set out to find new adventure together.'

'Set out to wash the taste of old woman out of my mouth,' Logan muttered, but his words were drowned out by applause from Gary and the countess.

Pie gave them an exaggerated bow. As the applause died away, he returned to sit next to Logan, putting his arm around him.

'You enjoyed that, didn't you?' Logan said.

'I did,' Pie said, resting his head against Logan's shoulder. 'I think I needed it. It's been a while since I've been able to perform like that. You didn't mind too much, did you?'

'If it made you happy, then I don't mind.'

Pie gave a contented sigh and pressed in closer. 'You're too good to me.'

Logan watched the flames dance as the others settled down to sleep. The countess's two skeletons took up watch, one at either side of camp, their bones glowing in the moonlight. They no longer felt quite so strange and unnatural to Logan, enough so that he had stopped reaching for his axe every time they were near.

He stroked Pie's hair, drawing strength from the closeness of the man he loved. Whatever happened, he promised the stars above, he'd keep Pie safe or die trying.

Chapter Fifteen

Logan awoke before dawn, one side warmed by Pie, the other side chilled by the night. He gently eased his way out from under his husband and walked away from camp to piss. One of the skeletons gave him a friendly wave as he passed and Logan was surprised to find himself returning the gesture.

There was an unearthly stillness to the air, a sense of the world holding its breath. This whole plan, if you could even call it a plan, was stupid. And yet, what choice did they have? Maybe it wasn't too late to think about running away, taking Pie and starting a new life across the sea. Forget the king. Once they had the Chalice, Ophelia could have her body, and the countess could wreak havoc on the place to her twisted heart's content.

He'd miss the little cottage, but it was just a building. Home wasn't a physical thing. It was the place you felt safe falling asleep. The place you felt free to be yourself. Where you could belch and fart and laugh and cry, and nothing and no one in those walls judged you for any of it.

Home was wherever Pie was.

'Good morning, Logan.'

He jumped at the voice behind him, and then fumbled to make himself decent. 'Gary. Don't you know it's rude to sneak up on a man?'

Gary blushed, fiddling with the unicorn's rein.

Gods, the fucking unicorn has crept up on me, too.

'Sorry.' Gary's face brightened. 'Do you think we'll find it today? The Fleshpot?'

Logan groaned. 'Don't call it that. Don't you know what that means?'

Gary blinked at him. 'It's what the countess calls it.'

'Yes, but she's doing it deliberately.' He sighed. So sheltered. 'Look, a fleshpot is . . . well, it's a . . . it's not a good word. Pie will explain if you really want to know. Just call it the Chalice, please?'

Gary stared blankly at him for a moment, processing Logan's words. 'So, do you think we'll find the Chalice today?' he asked.

Logan rubbed a hand through his hair. 'I'm not sure. Maybe. Once we do, though, you take that beastie and you turn tail for home, you hear me? Go back through the gate and back to your uncle, where it's safe.'

Gary's face fell. He tightened his grip on the rein and Freddy snorted. 'You don't want me here.'

'No, I don't.' It was a harsh truth, but a truth nevertheless. Gary was too young, innocent and naïve. He wasn't built for this, and Logan wasn't going to let him become another victim. Better to have someone alive to hate you than dead because they believed you were something you weren't. 'We need the unicorn and we need you to control it. Once it's broken the spell on the necromancer's lair, we don't need either of you.'

Gary's features twisted between sadness and rage. 'You don't believe in me. No one believes in me.'

'You're not a god, lad. Belief doesn't mean anything to you. You're a sack of blood and guts on a fine horse, and there are a thousand things that would like to rip you apart like paper.'

'I'm not afraid of monsters.' Gary puffed out his chest. The unicorn pawed at the ground.

'You should be.'

Logan kills monsters. But you never came.

The words were bitter in his heart. He wouldn't let that fate fall on anyone else, but the more people he had under his watch, the harder it would be. No, this was better.

Gary opened his mouth to say something, before snapping it shut and striding away, yanking hard on Freddy's rein. The unicorn snorted and shook his head.

'You're being a bit hard on him,' Pie said, approaching Logan. He had his shirt in one hand, hair and shoulders still wet from the waterfall. Logan took in the sight hungrily.

'I don't want to see him get into trouble,' he muttered.

'Yeah, but he's young,' Pie replied. 'The young don't take warnings well. I broke five separate bones the year I was eighteen. People kept telling me to be careful. Let me tell you, it did not help.'

He reached out to Logan, who pulled away. He was emotionally frustrated. He didn't want to be physically frustrated too, especially not once they were on horseback.

'You're not helping.' He bent to check the snares he'd set up. Nothing. Typical.

'I'm just trying to lighten the mood.' The hurt in Pie's voice needled him.

'Why?' He straightened, his leg sending a shock of pain up to his knee and down again to his ankle. Well, that was an excellent addition to his morning. 'This isn't a story, Pie. There's no guarantee of a happy ending. There's only me.'

He stalked back to the fire, trying to suppress the limp as much as possible, and began shoving things back in the saddlebags. They didn't get it. None of them did. Too drunk on bard fantasies. Things didn't just work out. People like Logan made them work out. And then things went wrong for other folk somewhere down the line.

'There's not only you,' Pie said. 'There's me, and the highly skilled necromancer, and the resourceful ghost, and I heard Gary and Freddy are a pretty damn impressive team too.' He reached for Logan, who shrugged away and kicked dirt over the fire. 'Fine, be like that. Give me the bad-tempered bear routine. But you know I'm right.'

'Do I? It seems to me I don't know a damn thing about you, Pie.'

As soon as the words were out of his mouth, he knew he'd gone too far. They'd had this discussion, and he'd forgiven Pie.

Hadn't he?

Pie flinched as if Logan had struck him. Then he turned away, hiding his expression, and called out to the countess.

'Got room on your horse today?'

Why couldn't they see the situation like Logan did? He kicked more dirt at the fire pit, already smothered, sending dust clouds into the air.

Yesterday's singing and laughter felt like a lifetime away. Today, even the weather was surly, grey skies and crabby winds. The countess and Pie rode at the head of the line, while Logan took up the rear. The sound of their chatting reached him, but the wind refused to carry any of their words.

Probably discussing the fact that Logan was a terrible bore.

The road wound higher, the air grew colder, the landscape scrubbier. The land was a dirty pale yellow, the colour of spoiled milk. Several times they had to dismount and lead their mounts over piles of scree that had slipped down the mountainside. The skeletal horses might have been tireless, but they still had to be manoeuvred over slippery rocks, and breaking a bone would only cause them further delay.

He wondered what sort of person would willingly choose to live here, but quickly came to the conclusion that it was most likely the same sort of person who would create a powerful necromantic item from the dawn of time. Pie and the countess would know more about it, not that Logan wanted to speak to either of them.

Ophelia appeared from time to time. She floated in front of the countess, and she and Pie gestured as they discussed directions. She perched on the back of Freddy, and another time she materialised in front of Bones, studying him with an inscrutable expression.

'Where do you go?' Logan asked her.

'Wouldn't you like to know,' she replied, and vanished.

The countess called a halt at a windswept plateau. She took Logan to the edge and pointed down. 'Al says our destination is down there. Another couple of days, I think, and then we'll reach it.'

Logan squinted. It looked like more mountains to him, but that was what the unicorn was for – to undo whatever spell made the lair blend in with the surroundings.

'Good.' The sooner it was done, the sooner they could all go back to their lives. He looked over at Pie, who stood near the bone steeds, shoulders slumped, kicking at a rock. Seeing his husband so morose was like a punch to the guts, but Logan couldn't bring himself to call out. In the back of his mind, Pie screamed at him to leave again.

The countess clapped her hands. 'Gary sweetheart, I have a present for you.'

The youth looked up from tending the unicorn. 'Present?'

The countess unwrapped a cloth parcel from the back of her horse and handed it to Gary. A sword.

'I took it off one of those men who attacked us,' the countess said. 'I thought you might like to use it.'

Gary's eyes widened and a delighted grin spread across his face.

'I didn't agree to this,' Logan argued.

'You don't have to.' She summoned up a skeleton and gripped Gary's arm. 'Come along now. Let's go and test it out. You,' she pointed at Logan, 'stay here.'

She bustled down the road a bit, until all three were out of sight. No sign of Ophelia, which just left—

'Pie.'

He lifted his head forlornly. 'Save it, Logan. I know I fucked up. I don't need to hear it again and again.'

'You broke my trust,' Logan said, his voice louder than he'd expected.

'You don't have any trust!' Pie straightened up, folded his arms. 'You think you can carry the weight of the world on your shoulders and no one else can ever measure up to you.'

'That's not true.' Of course it wasn't. Pie was wonderfully talented at many things. Not killing, though. Not stopping others being killed. 'But I've lived this life. I know what's involved. You're just . . .'

'Just a bard?' Pie kicked the rock toward Logan. It bounced off his shin, but Logan barely felt it.

He clenched his fists. 'I love you and I don't want you to get hurt. Why is this such a bad thing?' His voice echoed off the mountains. 'Why are you punishing me for it?'

'Yeah? Well, I love you too.' Pie's face was red, and his voice shook. Logan wasn't sure he'd ever seen Pie angry before. Not like this. 'That's why I left. I didn't want to watch you bled out in front of me, watch the light leave your eyes while you stared at me.'

'That wouldn't happen to me,' Logan said, softer now. He'd keep them safe. Had to keep them safe. The idea of anything happening to Pie twisted his gut.

'Yes, it would!' Pie kicked another rock. It clattered down the mountainside, chiding them as it went. He pointed at Logan's leg. 'You're not invulnerable. You bleed as much as the next man. I close my eyes and I see it every day. I thought it would get easier when I found you again, but you're so damn Logan about things, I swear it's worse.'

'I'm not trying to make it worse.' Logan's heart thudded in his chest, and his hand opened and clenched at his side. Blood roared in his ears. 'I don't want to lose you.'

Pie's eyes widened. 'That's it, isn't it? You think I'm going to leave you. Even after all this, you won't believe me, won't trust that I won't run off with the next thing that catches my eye. That's how little you think—'

'You did leave me!' Logan roared. Pie took a step back. 'You did leave me. Everyone leaves me. My mother died, Ophelia sent me away, and you. Left. Me.' His whole body shook.

Pie ducked his head, shame flashing across his features. Then he looked up again, defiant. 'No. You're not the only one with fears.' He took a breath, his lip trembling. 'Yes, I left, because if I didn't, you'd be dead. Lying there with your throat cut and your eyes open, bleeding over my arms. I won't allow it. Don't you understand? If anything were to happen to you, it would kill me.'

Logan opened his mouth to speak, but nothing came out. He couldn't imagine living without Pie. He'd do anything, give anything – including his life – for Pie. He wanted them to grow old together, but if it came to it, a world where Pie lived and he didn't would always be better than the alternative. Right?

They stood facing each other, breathing heavily. Pie's jaw was clenched, his hands in fists at his sides. It made every muscle in his arms press against the fabric of his shirt. A pressure built in Logan, hot and heavy, pushing at his skin from the outside. He took a step towards Pie, not sure what he was going to do, and Pie took one towards him.

'So what do we do now?' Pie asked.

Logan shook his head. 'I don't know.' He felt like a pot in the fire, ready to explode.

'I don't know, either.' Pie pushed a hand through his hair. 'Gods, I wish I had a drink.'

He walked past Logan, down towards the sounds of steel on bone where Gary and the skeleton were sparring. Logan let him go. He hated himself for it, but he couldn't face more yelling. Part of him wanted nothing more than for the earth to open and swallow him up. It seemed easier than feeling.

This was why he'd kept to himself after Ophelia turned him out. He wasn't built for this sort of thing. And sooner or later he'd end up on the outside again. He clutched his bicep, fingers digging into his tattoo.

A shout of triumph, followed by applause and laughter. The temptation to mount up and ride away welled up, almost uncontrollable.

'I can't do that to Ophelia,' he muttered.

'Do what?' she asked, appearing beside him. Logan's heart felt too heavy to be startled. 'Oh, just go and say you're sorry.' She slapped a hand through the back of his head.

Logan scuffed a shoe across the ground. 'Ain't going to say I'm sorry for wanting him to be safe. He should apologise for not listening to me.'

She threw up her hands. 'The pair of you deserve each other. You're both hopeless. You've just spent the last five minutes yelling "No, I love you more," at the top of your lungs, and now you're not even going to speak? You were never that emotional with me.' She faded away. 'I can't be dealing with the living, I swear.'

More cheering made his insides clench. He grabbed the reins and pulled himself into Bones's saddle. 'Play time's over!' he called. 'We need to keep moving.'

He ignored the sighs and the sounds of dismay and put his heels to Bones. The steed set off at a brisk pace. A glance over his shoulder told him the others were following, but he didn't dare risk anything more in case he caught Pie's eye.

A soft throat-clearing caused Logan to turn in his saddle, a mixture of fear and hope rushing through him.

'Pie? Oh, it's you, lad.' He moved Bones over so Freddy could walk alongside.

'I . . . um . . . I thought since no one was talking to you, maybe you could use some company,' Gary said, his ears quickly changing from pink to crimson.

'That's kind of you, but I'm fine.'

'The countess said you'd say that,' Gary said. 'She said I shouldn't believe you.'

'I bet she did,' Logan growled. 'Go on, say your piece, or her piece.'

Gary stared at a spot between Freddy's ears. 'What's it like being in love? It seems . . . fraught.'

Logan barked a laugh. 'You're not wrong.' He risked a glance over his shoulder. 'How is Pie?'

'He seems upset. The countess is talking to him.'

'Probably trying to convince him to divorce me and run away with her.' He meant the words as a joke, but his stomach clenched.

'I don't think so,' Gary replied. 'I don't think either of them would do that.'

The path narrowed, so Logan pushed on ahead. Focus on the road. Keep riding. *Just say sorry*, Ophelia whispered in one ear. *Leave me!* Pie screamed in the other.

The path narrowed again, now little more than a crumbling ledge clinging defiantly to the mountain. Far below, the river raced around giant boulders, a frothing ribbon of blue dotted with grey. Logan slipped down from the saddle and lifted the reins over Bones's head. The creature gave his arm a friendly rub.

'Careful. You trying to send me over the edge to my death?'

It shook its head, which was silly, because it wasn't even a living horse capable of conscious communication. Logan put one hand under its chin and clicked his tongue, walking out onto the ledge.

'Watch your feet,' he called over his shoulder.

He focused his gaze straight ahead. Looking down never did anything more than set your imagination whirling. Better to focus on the goal. Focus on the positive, as the countess would say. He was grateful the skeleton horse seemed to have none of the fears of a flesh-and-blood one. They could be flighty creatures, prone to panic. He patted the immense shoulder blade, wondering what the creature would have looked like when it was alive.

Overhead, a hawk called, a piercing, haunting cry that matched the desolate mountain path. It circled above them, as if optimistically hoping to snatch one of them away. Logan strained, hoping to hear something of the conversation between Pie and the countess. Did Pie ache like he did? Did he still burn with anger? Was he terrified everything was going to come tumbling down like a landslide?

Logan took a step and his foot caught on a smooth, rounded stone. His ankle twisted, his bad leg giving way, pulling his weight down over it. He stumbled, falling, the river suddenly filling his vision. *I can't die*, he thought as he flailed desperately. *I can't die and leave it like this.*

'Logan!'

Something caught his shoulder, digging in hard. He twisted to find Bones's teeth gripping him. The creature pulled, dragging him back. He threw his arms around the skeletal neck, and closed his eyes, waiting for the shaking to pass.

'I'm fine,' he called, when he felt more certain his voice would hold. 'I'm fine.'

He took a step and a bolt of fire shot up his other leg, almost spilling him over the edge again. Dammit. He gritted his teeth, letting the skeleton horse help him over to solid ground.

One by one, the others made it safely over the ledge. Pie rushed over.

'What's wrong? You're limping. Is it your leg? Have you broken something?'

Logan gritted his teeth and tested his weight again. It hurt like hell, but it wasn't broken. 'It's just a sprain. I'll walk it off.'

'You'll do no such thing,' the countess announced. 'Sit.'

His body obeyed her, even as he protested. They found a flattish rock and wrapped some clothing around it, placing it under his injured ankle. 'Take his boot off, Al darling. Gary sweetheart, fetch a waterskin.'

'Stop fussing.' Logan winced as Pie pulled off his boot. His ankle was swelling. 'Shit.'

'Does it hurt?' Pie wrapped his fingers around Logan's. Any trace of anger driven out by concern.

'Not much.'

'So that's a "yes it hurts quite a lot" on the Logan Pain Scale.'

Logan raised an eyebrow.

Pie sat down next to him. 'I've got used to how you speak. "No" means it hurts a bit, but you'll ignore it. "Not much" means it hurts a lot and you need to be encouraged to rest. At least it's not at "I'm fine" levels.'

'Oh.'

Pie's fingers tightened around his hand. 'You're quite predictable, love.'

'Here.' The countess handed him a couple of flat, waxy leaves, oval in shape and dark green in colour. 'Chew on those.'

He took them, turning them over in his hand. 'You trying to poison me?'

She sniffed. 'Logan, if I wanted you dead, I could have killed you a thousand times over. These are just to ease the pain, help you relax.'

'I don't need anything like that.' He tried to hand them back and she slapped the back of his hand. 'Ow.'

'See? More pain. I don't think listening to you wallowing in agony is any way, sensible or manly. Besides, until you've squeezed out five children, you have no idea what pain truly is. So, chew and rest, then we can get this fellowship back on the roads.'

She stalked off, calling for Gary.

'I think we might have found the one person who can out-stubborn you.'

Logan stuffed the leaves into his mouth and almost spat them straight back out. A bitterness filled his mouth, numbing his lips and shrivelling his tongue.

'Gah. Pretty sure she *is* trying to poison me.'

'You'd better do as you're told, or she'll have one of the skeletons hold you down and feed you herself,' Pie replied. Logan shuddered.

Whatever it was, it seemed to be helping. The throbbing in his ankle faded away, and when someone wrapped a cool cloth around the swelling, he could barely feel it at all. He settled back, the ground beneath him soft and cushioning. Around him, people moved about, but they seemed far away. Something deep down insisted this wasn't right, but he felt warm and cosy, like someone had wrapped him in a fluffy cloud.

Pie peered at him. 'What, exactly, did you give him, Countess?'

'I told you. Something to ease the pain and help him relax.'

'He does look very relaxed,' Gary agreed.

'I think he's less relaxed when he's asleep,' Pie said.

'I'm fine,' Logan said. His words came out slurred. Mumbled. Fluffy. Everything was fluffy. 'Not "ow" fine. *Fine* fine.'

'Maybe try and get some sleep,' Pie suggested, a frown creasing his features.

Logan reached out and brushed a lock of Pie's hair with his finger. 'Heh. Fluffy.' A memory tugged at the back of his mind. 'I'm mad at you.'

Pie's frown deepened. 'I know. But that can wait.'

'No. No wait.' He couldn't leave it like this. Logan pushed his knuckles into his temples. 'I don't think you'll leave me. I think you'll leave *me*.' He drew the last word out.

'I really think this should wait until you're more . . . coherent.' Pie gave his hand a squeeze and tried to stand up. Logan held on tight.

'It's me. Everyone leaves me.' He took a breath, trying to shape the words in his mind first. They raced like unicorns. Little white fluffy unicorns. 'I make people leave.'

'You want to do this? Fine.' Pie put a hand on Logan's face, forcing him to look into his eyes. 'There is only one thing in the world that would make me leave you, and that's if it would save your life. And I'd do it again in a heartbeat. Because that's the only thing that matters to me. I'm sorry I hurt you. I'm sorry the world has given you this idea that you're unworthy of loving. I'm trying really hard to undo it, but you're a stubborn man, Logan Theaker.'

The sky was spinning, doing loops around the ground in ever decreasing circles. He forced himself to focus on Pie, on the ring of green in his eyes. 'I don't . . .'

'Let me put this in terms even you'll understand.' Pie kissed him, lips lingering on Logan's. A taste that made him hungry for more. 'I love you, and when it comes to keeping you alive, I can be just as stubborn as you. So shut up and accept it.'

Logan woke with the dawn. His head felt packed with sawdust, and his mouth slightly numb, but a calmness pervaded him, a sense of peace he hadn't experienced since leaving the cottage. He craned his neck to find Pie asleep with his head on Logan's chest.

He shifted his position, trying to check his leg without waking Pie. The swelling had gone down, and when he flexed it, there was no pain.

Pie stirred with a groan.

'Sorry,' Logan said. 'I didn't mean to wake you.'

'I'll never get used to this waking-up-at-sunrise business.' Pie sat up, wiping drool off his mouth with the back of his hand. 'It's not natural.'

Logan stood and tested his ankle. Even the scar on his leg didn't hurt as much today. 'Feels good as new.' He stretched. 'Feels like I've slept for a week, too.'

'Not quite that long, but whatever that plant was, it knocked you out since yesterday afternoon.' He glanced down at the floor. 'How much do you remember?'

Shut up and accept it.

'A bit,' Logan admitted.

'Are . . . are you still mad at me? Honestly?'

Logan searched the jumble of feelings, pulling through them for the hard knot that had burned in his gut yesterday. 'No. I don't think so. Mad's the wrong word. It's more . . .' He rummaged some more. The feelings were shapes, colours, textures. They didn't come with words attached.

'Scared? Frustrated? So in love you spend your time alternating between floating in the air and terrified that these feelings are too massive to ever get a handle on and they'll consume you utterly?' Pie suggested.

Logan rubbed the back of his head. 'Yeah. Yeah, that's closer.' He held out a hand, and when Pie took it, Logan pulled him close. 'I'm sorry about yesterday. I'm sorry about the things I said.'

'But you meant them, didn't you?'

'Not to hurt you. But I do love you, and I don't want to see you hurt.' He put his hand against Pie's face, running his thumb down the jawline. Pie reached up and pulled the hand down with his own, bringing it close to his chest.

'I wish you could see things like I do. I wish you could see I'm not as weak or fragile as you think I am. And I wish you could see how amazing you are, how worthy you are. I'm just scared that anything big enough to make you change your mind is going to end up hurting us both.'

Interlude

Twelve Months Ago

Logan lifted his head to see Pie running a finger down his tattoos.

'What are you doing?'

'Reading your life,' Pie replied with a smile. 'I like learning other people's stories. You were married?'

Logan flinched. 'I don't talk about that.'

'Oh, come on.' Pie's smile didn't faulter. 'Everyone's got a past. There's no shame in it.'

'I. Don't. Talk. About it.' Logan gritted his teeth, each word a growl. This time, Pie did pull away, wariness crossing his features. Of course. He'd push Pie away like he had Ophelia, because that's the sort of man he was.

But it hurt this time. Much more than it had with Ophelia.

Pie leaned in, brushed a lazy kiss against Logan's cheek. 'Are you heading off today?' Another kiss, less lazy this time. 'Or can I persuade you to stay?' He wrapped a leg around Logan's. 'I can be very persuasive, you know.'

'Got a job,' Logan replied, a little sharper than he'd meant to. He sat up and pushed Pie's leg off his own.

'So have I.' Pie yawned and stretched, the action somehow ending with his arms around Logan. His teeth nipped delicately at Logan's throat, the gentle pinch sending shivers down Logan's spine. 'My brother's got something big and exciting planned.' Another kiss. Another nip. 'He can wait, though.' He breathed out, a cool rush over the heat of the kisses. If he stayed another moment, Logan would never leave.

'I can't.' Logan slapped his hand away, stood up. Pie pulled the blanket back around him with a sigh.

'Fine, fine. I'll catch up with you at the Hind in Runymarsh, then?'

Logan pulled on his clothes. He didn't dare look around. 'I don't know if that's such a good idea.'

A hand gripped his heart, squeezing it to pulp. It was better this way. They'd got too close, and Logan had let down his walls too much. He knew how this ended. With resentment. With hands on hips. With shouting and accusations. He'd already started to push at Pie. Better to finish the job now.

'What do you mean?' Pie asked slowly. Logan risked a look over his shoulder. The bard sat up in bed, the blankets pooled around his waist, watching Logan with an expression somewhere between wary and hurt. His loose hair caressed the muscles of his shoulders.

Logan looked away again. 'This has been fun, but it isn't a good idea. I don't know how to let people in.'

'You let me in last night,' Pie replied. 'Twice.'

'I'm serious,' he snapped. 'I'm not a good man. I know how to fight, how to kill. I'm not the sort of man people get close to.'

'Don't I get to decide?' Pie asked. 'Isn't it my choice as much as yours?'

'You'll change your mind. I've seen it.' He pushed his things into his pack and put on his boots.

'Logan, you don't get to decide for people.' Pie stumbled out of bed, the blanket still wrapped around his waist, trailing around his feet. Logan couldn't say anything; his throat had closed up. He pulled the pack on his shoulder and opened the door.

'Logan!' Pie stumbled towards him, tripping over the blanket.

'See you around, Pie,' Logan said softly, and closed the door behind him.

Chapter Sixteen

Three more days passed, travelling between the skirts of two dominating mountains. The path rose at a gentle slope, easy travelling, which put Logan on edge. He reluctantly took over Gary's training, sparring in the mornings, and for longer when they broke for camp at the end of the day. The youth had sharp reflexes and was quick on his feet, but he lacked the instinct to attack, to see an opportunity to wound first.

Logan was not surprised, but it did strengthen his conviction that he was the main line of defense for the group. Possibly with the countess. If she got up after being struck down, he wouldn't raise an eyebrow, but then again, he wouldn't if she decided she was bored of the whole affair and took off in the opposite direction.

Still . . . She'd stayed this long, been a great help, even. Perhaps he was being unfair.

'We're close,' Pie said suddenly.

Logan reined in, letting Bones sniff at the scrubby vegetation. Being a skeleton didn't seem to quell the most primal instincts of the creature. 'You're sure?' The landscape looked identical to the ground they had covered yesterday: loose rocks the colour of old bone, low vegetation more grey than green, a path that descended in a winding spiral but never seemed to get any closer to the valley below.

'I remember the discussions, the maps. Bards have good memories.' Pie tapped his temple with a finger. He dismounted and approached a tree, leafless and dead, but still anchored to the rock. He ran his hand down the bark and paused a couple of feet from the bottom.

'See. There's a mark here.' He paused, running his fingers over it again. 'Two more miles.'

'You never said why the king wanted this thing,' Logan said as Pie mounted up again.

'I never asked. I just wanted to get the job over with in the hope that he'd let me go home again.'

Something in his voice told Logan Pie didn't think that would ever happen.

'What about the people you were with? Who are they?'

'The Black Company. The king's personal mercenaries.'

Logan shuddered. He'd never met a member of the Black Company but he'd heard of them. They did the king's dirty work, or so people said. Lately they'd been known to bring in spellcasters. They were ruthless and utterly loyal to King Ervin.

'Countess, how come you got set free?' Logan called. 'Given the king's desire to control every magic user, how come you got a fancy house and a bit of paper to wave in people's faces?'

'Charter,' she said. 'Because I'm nobility? Because he thought he could have use of my powers? Because death magic is not the same? He said I might be useful to him, but who knows. Probably just charmed by my beauty and grace.'

'Yeah, sure,' Logan muttered. 'Definitely that one.'

'What do you mean, death magic is different?' Pie asked. 'Magic is magic, is it not?'

'No, Al darling, it absolutely is not.'

Gary nodded in support. 'They're different things. Real magic draws on life. It draws from the caster. Necromancy is wrong.' He cringed under the countess's stare. 'I mean . . . it is, but . . . well . . .'

The countess gave him a benevolent smile. 'Yes, yes, I know how it gets told. Is a sword wrong, Gary sweetheart?' Her voice oozed sweetness, but there was a sour note underneath. 'Of course not. Day and night, light and shadow, life and death. These are all opposites, yet part of the same thing. You can't have one without the other. Neither is good or bad.'

'To be fair, Countess,' Pie said, 'no sword ever pulled a body out of its grave and made it a servant.'

'And?' She fixed him with a sharp gaze. 'Is that somehow worse than taking a man's life? Leaving him to bleed out on the ground?'

'You, er, make a strong point.'

'My point' – she held out a hand in front of her, as if examining her nails through her gloves – 'is the wielder is the issue, not the tool. Look for your evil there.'

'And which are you?' Logan asked.

She grinned. 'Me? I think we've stablished I'm a very naughty person.' She clicked her tongue. 'Come along everyone, there's a tomb to be robbed!'

Around half an hour later, the path moved around a sheer face in the cliff, where a section of the mountain sloughed off.

'Here,' Pie said. 'It's here.'

Logan cocked his head. 'Don't look like much.'

'That's why we need the unicorn,' Ophelia said.

Logan flinched at her sudden arrival, making Bones snort. 'Sorry.' He patted the vertebrae.

Ophelia moved in front of the unicorn. 'Come on. Your time to shine.'

Gary slid down from Freddy's back. He glanced over his shoulder at Logan, who shrugged.

'Just do what you need to do,' Logan said, 'and then you can go home.'

'You can do it, Gary.' Pie clapped a hand on the youth's shoulder.

Gary nodded, his hand on the unicorn's flank. Freddy stamped, his ears laid back. Logan couldn't see anything off about this place, but clearly the unicorn sensed something. Gary spoke softly, and after a moment or two, the unicorn settled. Freddy moved his head in a circle, and the air in front of him shimmered.

'Well. That's more like it,' Pie murmured.

A circle appeared on the stone, glittering like sunlight on water. It expanded, rainbows rippling around the edge, until it was large enough to encompass the entire cliff. The rock face, the unicorn's magic revealed, was not a solid cliff. An immense gate had been carved into the stone, large enough to have three carts pass abreast and still leave room. Around the gateway, a series of bas-reliefs depicted skeletons and robed figures. Across the top, a huge skull leered down at them.

'The lost city of Sarem, last seat of the Ancient Necromancer empire,' the countess said softly.

'What?' Gary asked.

'You young'uns never learn your history. The Necromancer Empire, Gary sweetheart,' the countess said, her voice dripping with derision, 'ruled this island and many other countries until their collapse, around five hundred years ago.'

'If it was that long ago, how am I supposed to know anything about it?' Gary muttered.

The countess sighed and put her heels to her horse, walking through the great gate. Logan stared up at the skull, trying unsuccessfully to supress his shudders.

On the other side of the gate, they found themselves in a wide plaza. To the left and right, buildings had been carved into the rock face, row upon row, with narrow steps cut into the stone to reach the higher ones.

In the centre of the square, an immense statue of a robed figure towered over them. It had a skull for a face, and two green gems set in the eye sockets, each as large as Logan's head.

'Think how much those must be worth,' Pie said with a whistle.

'Think about how much they'd weigh carrying them back to Krensten,' Logan replied.

'Spoilsport. They'd look lovely over the hearth.'

'History is important, Gary sweetheart,' the countess continued. 'You'll find it repeats itself if you don't learn from it.'

'What happened to them?' Pie asked. He slipped down from Bones and walked across the plaza towards the countess.

'The empire ran on gold, mined here and then spread across the territories. You can't manage an empire with skeletons alone: they don't have the brains for it, figuratively and literally. When the gold dried up, so did the empire. They pulled back to the island, and here they died. Something seems to have happened to them, quite suddenly. Perhaps they all turned on each other.'

'Does your god tell you all this?' Pie asked.

The countess raised an eyebrow. 'No, darling. I read. I had a beautiful library before it was burned to the ground.' She sighed wistfully.

'This is all fascinating, I'm sure,' Logan said. The gaze of the statue sent shivers down his spine. 'But where's the Chalice?'

'Ugh. No appreciation for the magnitude of a place, your husband,' the countess muttered to Pie. She pointed beyond the statue. 'I'm going to take a wild guess and suggest over there.'

Logan bristled at her tone, but followed her finger to a low, pyramid-shaped structure on the far side of the plaza. It had two large wooden doors, warped by rain enough to allow a person to pass through, traces of gilt still visible on the surface. More skulls decorated the lintel – real ones.

Logan handed Bones's reins to Gary and joined Pie and the countess at the doorway.

'Wonderful,' the countess said, taking a step towards the entrance. 'Such a sense of theatre. I'm sure you approve, Al darling.'

'Not really my style,' Pie replied. 'For a start, you'd struggle to get that into the average inn.' His tone was light, but he shivered against Logan.

'Gary, stay here with Ophelia. Hopefully this won't take long,' Logan said. 'I don't suppose I can convince you to stay outside?' he asked Pie.

'Not a chance. Besides, if this was something you could just walk in and pick up, the king wouldn't have sent me in the first place.'

Logan suppressed a sigh. Of course, Pie was right, but the idea of letting anyone he cared about walk through that building sent chills though him.

Pie put a hand on his shoulder. 'Let's get this over with.'

The countess passed through the entrance, humming to herself. The light from her lantern flickered behind her.

'I'll never understand that woman,' Logan muttered.

He paused at the threshold, peering into the inky darkness. The countess had vanished, as if she'd been eaten, a distinct possibility in Logan's mind. Pie's fingers closed around his own. He looked up and Pie gave him a small smile.

'Come on, before she gets to work on making her own army.'

Hand in hand, they entered the pyramid.

The passageway immediately turned right, and the light of the outside vanished. The darkness pressed in, dizzying. Logan kept one hand tightly gripped around Pie, the other pressed against the wall. His fingers brushed against more bas-relief, and he couldn't decide if he was grateful or not that he couldn't see it. He took small, stumbling steps, as if the darkness itself clutched at his feet. When he looked back over his shoulder, the light seemed ten times further away than it should have been.

Just when Logan was convinced his next step would send him spinning into a bottomless pit, the passage turned again, and a faint light licked the edges of his vision. It was a greenish colour, soft and faint to begin with, but as he blinked, it grew stronger and he could see more clearly.

The passage widened out into a vast chamber, almost circular, as if someone had pulled the core out of the mountain, the way you would an apple. A series of wood boards formed a crude staircase, descended into the depths, spiralling around the wall. Pie approached the edge and peered down, making Logan's stomach twist.

'Damn, that's deep,' Pie said, then sniggered.

'I was afraid you'd say that,' Logan replied.

'Come along!' the countess called, somewhere ahead and below.

'She's in a good mood,' Logan said. 'That's got to be a bad sign.'

Logan put a foot on the first step gingerly, expecting it to go tumbling into the gloom. But it held firm, and he stepped onto the next one. And the next.

The walls of the cavern were covered in carvings of skeletons, and every now and then, a real one set in the stone, like a macabre tapestry. Some were human, but most were animals – birds, fish, even a parel at one point. The skeletons gave off the greenish light, their bones glowing.

'This place is incredible,' Pie breathed. He reached for the wall, his fingers hovering over a bone.

'I wouldn't,' Logan said. 'No knowing how this place is trapped.'

'Fair point.' Pie snatched his hand back. 'It is amazing though. And we could be the first people in here for hundreds of years. Think about the stories these walls could tell.'

'You're starting to sound like the countess,' Logan muttered. Pie laughed, a sound that felt very much at odds with the place.

The steps spiralled down and down, until Logan felt dizzy from the turns and sick from the pain in his leg. He clenched his jaw and pushed on after Pie, not wanting to let him get too far ahead, and definitely not wanting to find himself left behind in the strange place.

At last, the spiral reached another passageway into the dark. The pit continued on downwards, too dark to see how far it went, but the steps stopped here. Water dripped down the walls, and there was a smell of mildew in the air. The countess stood waiting, tapping her foot. Logan stepped onto the stone, leaning against the wall to take the weight off his leg.

'Maybe *you* should have stayed behind.' Pie put his arm around Logan's shoulder.

'Not a chance,' Logan replied through gritted teeth.

The countess lifted the lantern. The warm orange smothered the green light and threw the rough walls into sharp relief. Drops of water glittered like crystals. She took a step forward, but Pie grabbed her wrists.

'Hang on. It's not safe.'

She raised an eyebrow. The shadows on her face made her older and more skeletal. 'What gives you that impression?'

'Well, them for a start.' Pie pointed across the chamber to a lump Logan had taken for fallen rock. As the countess moved the lantern, metal gleamed. Not a rock. A corpse. 'I guess we're not the first ones here, after all.' Pie took a cautious step. 'I need you to be quiet. Both of you.' He glanced back over his shoulder and gave Logan a smile. 'Trust me.'

Logan nodded slowly. The hairs on the back of his neck prickled. He wasn't used to standing at the back. Bears didn't wait. Bears attacked.

Pie licked a finger and held it out in front of him, moving it in a slow arc. Then he closed his eyes. Logan watched, his heart heavy in his ears, so loud he suspected Pie could hear it too. He hoped it wouldn't put him off.

After what felt like an eternity, Pie let out a sigh. Logan unclenched his jaw.

'Definitely traps. There's air moving across the chamber; I can hear it whistling. I suspect, looking at that poor sod, there are one or more pressure traps on the floor.'

The countess bobbed her head. 'That's very impressive, Al darling.'

'It's just listening. Bard skills and thief skills overlap more than you might think.' But he flashed her a proud grin.

'What do we do?' Logan asked.

'You two go back a bit and let me handle this.'

Logan shook his head. 'No. Not letting you put yourself at risk alone. That's not how this works.'

Pie's eyes narrowed. 'I can do this, Logan. This is what I do. What I'm good at. I don't need you protecting me.'

Logan took a shuffling step next to him. 'Not letting you do this alone. Tell me what to do, and we do it together.'

'Fine.' Pie sighed. 'But do exactly what I say.'

The countess let out a happy squeal and clasped her hands together under her chin. 'Ah, it's so romantic. Two lovers, robbing a tomb together. It warms my old heart, I tell you.'

Logan rolled his eyes.

'Get down,' Pie said, dragging Logan back to the task at hand. They both dropped to their knees. 'Now, we crawl forwards, very slowly. And if anything goes click, drop as flat as you can.'

Logan eyed the corpse. 'Will that be enough?'

'All the air currents are higher up, around chest height, so I hope so, but there's really only one way to be sure.'

'Couldn't we just send the countess?' Logan said.

'I heard that, dear!'

Pie's hand closed around his, then let go. 'Come on.'

They crawled forwards, the gravel littering the cave floor digging into Logan's knees. He dragged himself onwards, on hands and elbows, every nerve stretched taut. The process was agonisingly slow, but he suspected rushing things would only lead to a more excruciating fate.

At his side, Pie crawled with a determined expression, his face as focused as when he played his lute.

When the first click came, Logan was ready for it. He flung himself flat as the sound echoed across the chamber. The air above him whistled as several darts or bolts flew over his head, then clattered into the wall.

'One down,' Pie murmured.

'Keep going, boys!' the countess called. 'You're doing marvellously.'

Logan could picture her waving that black lace handkerchief like a favour.

He reached out, pushing on the hard ground. Cold and damp numbed his fingers, and the incessant stones that littered the floor all managed to have sharp edges. His sleeve stuck to him with blood. Inch by inch, they progressed across the chamber.

'Get down!' Pie pushed at his shoulder, knocking Logan flat against the floor. The air filled with the piercing whistles again. 'Didn't you hear that?'

Logan shook his head. Projectiles hummed over them. 'I didn't. Thank you.'

'Not just a pretty face.' Pie grinned, then the smile faded. 'I didn't hurt you, did I?'

He shook his head again. 'Not with a little shove like that.' Pie's smile returned, and they pushed on, but Logan's stomach knotted. Pie was five years younger, his hearing sharper, reflexes faster. Logan could never have crossed the floor without his help. The knowledge bruised his pride.

He glanced at Pie, his jaw set as he crawled, a smudge of dirt on his cheek, and hated himself for that jealousy.

Four more traps went off before they reached the edge of the chamber. Pie helped Logan to his feet.

'That was more than a little terrifying,' he admitted.

Logan reached out and brushed the dirt from Pie's face. 'You did great.'

'I know. That's why I'm here.'

'Do you miss it?' Logan asked, dreading the answer.

'Do I miss scraping the skin off my flesh crawling through caves?' Pie stroked his chin. 'I mean, I'd forgotten the thrill of knowing one misstep could cost me my life. But if you're asking me whether I prefer this to our cottage, then I'll always choose the one with you in it.'

Logan hated himself harder for his jealousy. He wrapped his arms around Pie and held him tight. 'I love you.'

'Love you – oof. Ow, Logan, I'd like to keep my ribs intact, please.'

Logan eased his grip and Pie leaned into him.

'You did well,' Pie said. 'We'll make a thief out of you yet.'

'Please don't.'

A narrow passage bent around to the right, and they quickly came to two huge, wooden doors, studded with iron.

'Should we knock?' the countess asked with a grin. She'd followed their trail to safety.

'I hope no one's in,' Logan replied.

Pie slipped his arm away from Logan. 'Leave it to me.'

'You can open that?' Logan asked.

Pie shrugged. 'It's just a door. A bloody big door, but a door nevertheless. Never met one I couldn't open.'

Logan leaned against the wall, his whole body tense as Pie approached the doors. Pie had to reach up to the lock. Logan's heart pounded in his ears, his mouth dry. Dark situations flashed across his mind. Pie fiddled with the lock, muttering curses that became less and less under his breath as time went on.

'Something's not right,' he said, slamming a fist against the wood. It reverberated with a deep hum.

'What's wrong?' Logan called.

'Something's stopping the lock from turning. I should have this.' Pie smacked the door again, making Logan wince, and the same hum filled the passageway. Pie paused, closed his eyes, and hit it once more. 'Interesting.'

He moved around the door, tapping and slapping at the wood in different places. Eventually he hit the same spot, just below and to the left of the lock, several times, and nodded. 'Logan, come here. When I say, I need you to hit this exact spot.'

Logan walked over and put his hand on the door where Pie pointed. 'Here?'

'Right there. Ready?' He leaned over the lock again, adjusting the picks. 'Now.'

Logan struck the door with his fist. It vibrated with a low sound, more of a growl than a hum. Pie twisted the picks and a click filled the air, reverberating through Logan's bones.

'There. Told you there wasn't a door I couldn't get through.' Pie crossed his arms and gave a satisfied nod.

The countess raised her head. 'Al darling, are you sure that was a good idea?'

The door swung open on its own with a grating, grinding groan.

Pie turned and stared at what stood on the other side. He paled. 'Oh, shit.'

The skeletons might have been waiting for hundreds, maybe thousands of years. But that didn't slow them down. They flooded over Pie, knocking him to the ground, swarming over him.

'Pie!' Logan drew his axe and charged into the mass. Bones cracked and shattered as he drove the axe into them, through them. Skeletons crumpled, but as one dropped, three more moved in to fill its place. They had no weapons, only teeth, but that was enough to make him bleed.

A skeleton grabbed his wrist with a bony hand. Two more had his legs, and some gripped his clothes, pulling him backwards. They were trying to drag him to the hole. He planted his feet, pushing down with all his strength.

His injured leg wobbled.

Logan fell to his knees, and the skeletons dragged harder.

The ground disappeared under his foot. Logan dug his nails into the ground. His own voice echoed in his head, but he didn't even remember opening his mouth.

'Obey me!' The countess's voice echoed off the chamber walls. 'By the power of the Dark Mother, I command you to set aside your former instructions and listen only to me.'

The skeletons dropped Logan.

He scrabbled in the dirt, desperately seeking purchase as his feet kicked over empty air. The void below sucked at him.

Pie grabbed his hand.

Logan let out his breath in a sigh as Pie helped him to his feet. The pair of them were covered in dirt, scratches all over every exposed inch of flesh.

'Probably should have checked for the army of angry skeletons,' Pie said with a shaky grin.

Logan said nothing, but let the hammering of his heart fade to a more normal rhythm as he held Pie's hand. Until now, he'd never considered he might use the phrase 'We were lucky to have a necromancer with us,' but if it hadn't been for the countess, he and Pie would have been swept into the pit. He thought about the Black Company. Did they have a necromancer? Ervin was, of course; but surely the king wouldn't accompany them here. And that raised a new question: What did he want with the Chalice, if he could raise people as easily as Seraphina said?

Logan tightened his grip on Pie's hand.

The countess ordered the intact skeletons to form up around them, and they moved through the giant doors. The room beyond was almost as bright as the world outside, though the light still had the same greenish quality. Thousands and thousands of bones covered the walls, the floor, even the ceiling. Skulls grinned at them from all around.

In the centre of the room stood a black iron casket. It drew Logan's gaze, holding it there as if something gripped the sides of his head. Pie took a step towards it.

'Why don't you let me have a look first, Al darling?' the countess suggested. 'Just in case.'

Pie gave her a bow. 'Please, be my guest.'

The countess approached it slowly, almost reverently. She ran her fingers over the strange markings covering the surface.

'Can you read it?' Pie asked.

She shook her head. 'Alas, this is old. Very old. I wish I had the time to study it. Or a way of taking a copy. I'll have to try and commit what I can to memory.'

'Is it safe?' Pie shifted from one foot to the other. 'Can I open it?'

'I don't sense any undead, or feel any magic.' She brushed a finger over the surface. 'In fact, it almost feels like . . .' She shook her head. 'No, that's silly. Go ahead, Al darling. Let's take a look at this Fleshpot!'

Logan reluctantly let go as Pie moved towards the casket. He knelt, holding the immense padlock. It was bigger than his hand.

Logan scanned the perimeter, walking slowly around the chamber and assessing the bones fixed into the stone of the walls and floor. They were mostly human, but he saw dogs, horses, even monsters amongst the remains. How many thousands of skeletons were here? Why were they all here? What had happened to kill all these creatures at once?

For a moment, Logan assumed the bones were scattered at random, but the more he stared, the more patterns seemed to jump out. Logan stepped back, and an image emerged. Hooded figures (he guessed they were necromancers) and hordes of skeletons stood facing something huge and dark that was crawling out of a hole in the ground.

'I've got it,' Pie called.

Logan hurried to his side, axe drawn ready, as Pie lifted the padlock away and stood up.

'Perhaps we should let the countess open it?'

'That sounds like a very sensible idea.' Logan nodded.

The countess sniffed. 'Stand back, boys. This is definitely a job for a woman.'

She tried to lift the lid off the casket, grunting with the effort. Logan was about to come and assist when she summoned over a trio of skeletons. Between the four of them, they managed to slide the lid across. It hit the ground with a thud that echoed through the darkest parts of the cave.

'The Chalice of Vivax.' The countess's voice was soft and barely audible. She lifted a half-wrapped bundle of black cloth from the casket, cradling it to her chest like a newborn.

She frowned. 'This . . . isn't right.'

The cavern shook.

'I believe that's our cue to get out of here,' she called over the din. Still clutching the object in one hand and hitching her skirt with the other, she ran for the main chamber and scampered up the steps.

'Go!' Logan cried to Pie. He shoved his husband towards the exit. The room shook again as bones dropped from the ceiling and cracked to pieces on the floor.

Logan put a hand over his head to try and protect himself from the worst of it. He sprinted after Pie, ignoring the pain in his leg as best he could. The passage above looked impossibly high, the little wooden steps spiralling upwards hopelessly fragile. Logan gritted his teeth and started up the wooden steps.

The cavern shook again.

Logan stumbled, falling to his knees. The impact sent a sickening pain shooting through his joints. He clutched at the wooden steps, his heart loud in his ears. As the shuddering faded, he began to climb on his hands and knees.

The steps whirled around and around. Grimly determined not to make this place his tomb, Logan climbed up and up. Stones fell from above, dropping down like arrows into the depths, and the air tasted of grit. He paused to wipe sweat and dirt from his eyes, already reaching for the next board.

It cracked under his hand.

Logan fell forwards, his chin smacking into the boards. His teeth crashed together and he bit his tongue. He let out a startled cry of pain, and above, Pie turned back, calling his name.

'Keep going!' Logan yelled. 'I'm fine. Don't you dare stop.'

Defying Logan's instructions, Pie remained where he was. Logan groaned, and forced himself up, reaching out for the next step.

The board beneath his foot gave way, falling into the dark depths.

Logan slipped back, clutching desperately at the step, his feet dangling over the empty chasm. The nothingness pulled him down, sucking at him like a mouth.

'Logan!' Pie cried. 'Hang on. I'm coming back for you. Just hold on.'

'No, stay back!' he shouted. He tried to pull himself up, but with nothing to brace against, his arms and shoulders screamed in protest. His feet scrabbled against the wall, trying to find purchase. 'Get back to the surface.'

Above him, the countess yelled, but Logan couldn't make out her words over the rumbling and grinding stones. He hoped she was convincing Pie to keep going, to make it out to the daylight with her. He suspected she wouldn't be successful. There was no way he'd leave Pie in this position.

Above, more boards broke free from the wall, tumbling down into the darkness. So deep he couldn't hear them hit the ground.

A cracking echoed above his head. More dirt rained down on him. Logan could do nothing but close his eyes and hang on.

Something grabbed the back of his shirt.

'Pie?' he said, but when he opened his eyes, Pie was still standing in the same place, staring at Logan with a peculiar mixture of hope and horror on his face. Logan twisted his neck to try and peer around.

The parel skeleton had come away from the wall and had Logan's shirt tightly clamped in its jaws. Clinging to the rock like a spider, it dragged him up and up. Logan let out a cry of unadulterated terror and squeezed his eyes shut.

The parel dumped him unceremoniously at Pie's feet, back in the stone passage. Logan kissed the ground, his body shaking too much to move any more than that. Pie knelt down and offered him a hand.

'You all right?'

Logan put a hand on his back. 'Got some pretty big holes in my clothes, but I'll take that over plummeting to my death.'

'You're welcome, Logan dear,' the countess called.

'Come on,' Pie said, slinging an arm around Logan's shoulder.

The sun had never looked so golden or bright as when Logan stepped out of the pyramid. He blinked tears out of his eyes. As they cleared the threshold, plumes of dust followed behind them, and Ophelia approached cautiously. He raised a hand in greeting but froze as she stepped past him and disappeared into Pie. When Pie's eyes opened again, they were a pure green.

'What are you doing, Ophelia?' Logan asked. His hand twitched, his stomach turning somersaults. 'What's the meaning of this?'

At his side, the countess murmured a faint, 'Oh dear'.

The Black Company had them surrounded.

Ophelia had betrayed them.

Chapter Seventeen

'Let him go,' Logan warned the bullish man clutching a bound Gary. The youth was gagged and a purple bruise was already framing his right eye. Logan's hand itched to grab his axe, but the wrong move could kill them all.

Pie's body took a step behind the countess, a knife at her throat. 'It's better this way, Logan,' Ophelia said. 'Just do as you're told, and everything will be fine.'

Logan felt like he was seeing double. Pie's body. Ophelia's soul. The two would not fully merge in his mind, leaving things fractured and disjointed. He coughed, his mouth dry.

'Ophelia. This isn't right. Let him go, and we'll deal with this. Between us.' The company members moved closer. He was running out of time.

'None of this is right!' Pie glared at him, his expression so cold and unlike Pie, it made Logan feel sick. 'None of this is right, but this is for the best. Now get down on your knees before someone gets hurt.'

'You can't hurt me, dear,' the countess said, her voice soft and calm. 'If you do, you'll be lost back to the veil and the Dark Mother's embrace.'

'You're right.'

Pie's hand dropped away from her neck, and Logan breathed a sigh of relief. In his peripheral vision, one of the company stalked towards him. Logan tensed, ready to strike out.

Pie pushed the blade against his own neck, the knife glinting against his auburn hair.

'No!' The world slipped beneath Logan's feet as he took a stumbling step forward. 'No, gods, don't hurt him. I'll do as you say.' Logan dropped to his knees, smacking the dirt with a fist. He couldn't take his eyes off Pie, the metal blade at his jugular.

Someone grabbed Logan's wrists, tying his hands behind his back. Every instinct urged him to fight back, but he gritted his teeth and let them bind him, the rope biting into his flesh.

'Drop the skeletons, too,' Ophelia ordered as the countess knelt beside Logan. With distaste scrawled across her face, the countess waved her hand and the two skeletons toppled to nothing, leaving only teeth behind. Pie slipped them in to his pocket.

Logan recognised Fox-Fur at the front of the group, a triumphant sneer on his face.

Not impossible odds, but highly unlikely at the very least. And he couldn't risk moving an inch until Ophelia released Pie's body.

Rage mixed with fear, fire and ice racing through his veins. They'd come so far, so close to their goal. Why now? Why had she helped for so long, only to turn on them?

The mercenaries tied Pie's hands, then bound them to the saddles of the bone steeds.

The mercenaries turned on Gary. The youth struggled defiantly in his bonds. The unicorn stomped and pawed, stabbing its horn at one of the men, who leapt back in alarm.

'Angry buggers, ain't they?'

Freddy tossed his head, pulling hard. One of the men holding the rope lost his footing, and the unicorn charged forwards towards Gary.

'Stop it!' someone cried.

Gary hurriedly pulled himself to his feet as Freddy skidded to a stop next to him. He threw himself awkwardly over the unicorn's back and, with no hesitation, a shimmering portal appeared in the air. Just as they passed through, Fox-Fur leapt in after them and disappeared. *Good lad*, Logan thought as

Ophelia glared at him. He hoped that between Gary and the herd of unicorns, Fox-Fur would find himself with several new orifices.

'Let us go, Ophelia. Please. We can still help you.'

'No, you can't, Logan. You treat every problem like a nail and you're a gods-damn hammer. Stop fighting before some-one gets hurt. Again.' She looked across at the bundle of cloth hiding the Chalice, now held by a woman dressed in green. 'I don't want just any body. The king has promised me mine, my old one, my old life. You come along quietly, we hand it over, and everyone gets to go home. That's what we all want, right? You can't win this, Logan. You can't win against a man who will murder a town to get what he wants.'

'He's not going to stop,' he yelled at her, but she ignored him, turning Pie's body away from Logan.

'Let's get this over with,' she murmured.

The mercenaries, instead of turning back and heading towards Krensten the way they'd come, continued down the path past the cave, a steep slope that wound sharply down to the river.

'So,' the woman in green said. She was broad-shouldered and muscular, her ginger hair bound in a braid. 'Logan the Bear. We finally meet properly.'

He fixed her with a cold stare. 'I'm not interested in conver-sation with someone who has me bound to a saddle.'

She grinned. 'I understand. I'd feel the same in your posi-tion. Still, this is the end. Once we deliver the Chalice to King Ervin, that's it.' Her voice was a little too high, the words a little too fast.

'You don't believe that. You can't believe that. If that thing can do half of what it's alleged to be capable of, you're put-ting a weapon in the hands of the king that even the ancient necromancers were afraid of. All it's going to do is kick off a war with the spellcasters. How can you believe it'll be over?'

She tightened her grip on her horse's reins, staring down the road ahead of her.

'Why are you working for the king?' Logan pressed. Find a weakness. Stick the knife in. Twist. 'He's clearly mad with power. I passed through a town where he'd butchered all the inhabitants. Were you involved in that as well?'

She stopped, pulling her horse across the path. A snarl distorted her features. 'How dare you? You know nothing of the man, but you'll do your best to cut his character to shreds, simply because he has power over you. No, none of us has been out slaughtering innocent townsfolk, and neither has the king.'

'Someone did,' Logan replied. 'And one of the bodies was wrapped in his flag.'

'That means nothing.' She snorted, then kicked her horse and carried on down the road at a swift trot.

At the end of the road, a barge waited. Logan was pulled unceremoniously from the bone steed and dumped on the vessel. The countess had been bound and gagged, and clearly no one wanted to risk ungagging her to allow her to dismiss the bone steeds, so they were loaded on as well.

'Let him go, Ophelia,' Logan said softly. 'Please.'

Pie stiffened as Ophelia emerged from his back. She vanished without a word. Pie blinked as if waking, let out a strangled cry.

'No. No, no, no.' Pie tried to stand, but his hands were bound behind his back, and he only succeeded in falling against Logan. 'Adella, let them go. You have to let them go.'

The woman in green shook her head. 'Sorry, Al. You should have come with us like you were supposed to.'

Pie choked back a sob, his body shuddering against Logan's.

Adella's expression softened. 'You got the Chalice, right? It's what Ervin wants. Hopefully he'll settle down once he has it.'

Yeah, a powerful necromantic item is exactly what will calm someone down, Logan thought.

The barge, for something so flat and bulky, moved quickly down the deep, fast-flowing river. Boulders as tall as men dotted the shores, gifts from the snowmelt in spring, when the river would be a raging torrent, rather than smooth and glassy as now. Logan watched his captors, trying to learn what he could about them. Adella steered the boat. At the rear, a man named Ivan and another woman named Liana pulled out handlines and sat fishing over the rail. The last member, a man called Kain, regarded the bone steeds with open curiosity.

Logan might have enjoyed the trip, if he weren't being held captive. It was a lot swifter and more comfortable compared to being jolted along on horseback or worse, walking. And the river had a plentiful supply of bass and pike.

Pie slumped against his shoulder. He hadn't moved from that position in hours, hadn't said a word. The silence terrified Logan. All he could do was lean back and hope that his touch helped.

The barge pulled into Krensten and moored at the river dock. Already a crowd had bloomed, drawn in by the sight of two horse skeletons. Some looked fascinated, others prayed loudly to their god of choice. If the countess had not been gagged, she'd have had a few words for them.

Logan suspected those words would have included *charter.*

Patiently he waited for an opportunity to grab Pie and run, but the sheer numbers made that impossible, especially bound. Ophelia appeared on the docks.

'You can let them go now,' she said to Adella. 'I did what you asked. I made sure Logan got to the Chalice.'

A white fury built in Logan's chest. 'That's why you were so helpful? You were manipulating us the whole way.'

'King Ervin wasn't going to take any chances. He's been watching Al, ever since the failed theft. Both of you in your happy little cottage. When he learned of the Chalice, it made sense that Al would be the one to fetch it. And you, Logan, would be the back-up plan,' Adella said. 'He knew kidnapping Al would spur you to act, to do whatever it cost to bring him back. Then it was a simple matter to direct you to the necromancer, and have her raise Ophelia, who would send you after the Chalice.'

'You knew about this, countess?' He glared at her, and she shook her head in horror. Then her eyes widened, and she dropped her head, her face paling further, past bone to porcelain. Adella gave her a cold smile.

'That's right. We sent her a message the day before saying she had to cooperate with you as a condition of her charter. I doubt she gave it a second thought. Her mind was probably consumed by the idea of the Chalice. The plan was to take the unicorn from you at Krensten, but when that didn't go to plan, Ophelia suggested letting you go the whole way and having you collect the Chalice for us.'

A tear rolled down the countess's face.

Rage burned brighter and choked Logan's lungs, boiling his blood. He wanted to shout, punch and bring his axe down through Adella's skull.

'Let them go.' Ophelia twisted her hands through each other. Her feet bobbed in and out of the dock. 'Please.'

'Sorry, not my call.' Adella didn't meet her eyes.

'Who's the monster now, Ophelia?' Logan said. She pierced him with a look that skewered his soul and vanished. He struggled against his bonds. His sheer anger was almost enough to burst them open.

The crowds parted as a group of soldiers approached the dockside. And finally, Logan came face to face with the king.

He was younger than Logan had expected. A youth, roughly the same age as Gary. Logan's second thought was that the king looked haunted.

He was thin, features pinched. Dark circles beneath his eyes as if he hadn't slept in days. His expression was cold, not anger, or even contempt. Just cold.

'Untie that one,' he said, pointing to Pie. Kain shrugged and cut the ropes around Pie's wrists. The king cocked his finger. 'Come here.'

Logan went to grab his husband, forgetting for a moment his hands were tied. He stumbled, and Adella put a hand on his shoulder to steady him.

'Best look away,' she whispered.

'Fuck you,' Logan said. He took a step towards Pie. And another. Adella kicked the back of his knee, knocking him to the ground. His shoulder hit stone, sending a jolt of pain through him. His teeth clacked together so hard he was sure everyone in the area heard it. She knelt on his back, holding him down.

'I tried to warn you,' she said.

Pie approached the king, each step slow and shaking. 'Please. Don't kill Logan. I'll do whatever you want. But please, please let him go.'

Ervin smiled, his expression sickly sweet. 'That wasn't our agreement, was it, little bard? You were supposed to fetch me the Chalice.'

'And I did!' Pie's voice cracked. 'I did. It's over.'

The king snapped his fingers and the Chalice was brought over. A calm smile spread across his face as he took it and peeked inside the fabric. 'So you did. Now my sadness can end. Perhaps I should reward you instead? There's someone here I think you know.'

The dock fell silent as shuffling, stumbling footsteps grew closer. Pie, already pale, turned white. He swayed on his feet and Logan feared he'd pass out. A single word escaped his lips.

'Matty,' Pie whispered.

Logan tried to get up, but Adella and Ivan had him pinned. All he could do was watch as a figure shuffled into view. He was a little stockier than Pie, had the same auburn hair, cut short, and his face matched his brother's, aside from a couple of missing scars. His eyes stared blankly ahead, unseeing.

Pie's legs gave way and he crumpled to the ground. 'How?'

Matty said nothing. His lips were slack and a fleck of drool dripped from his left side. His skin was the colour of spoiled milk.

'Isn't this touching?' The king smiled. 'Show your brother how much you've missed him, Matteo.'

Matty, or the thing that had once been Matty, swung its fist, hitting Pie in the face. Pie grunted, putting his hands up to shield his face, but didn't try to fight back or even move out of the way. Matty continued to rain blows on his brother.

'How can you stand for this?' Logan demanded from the onlookers. 'How can you follow someone who'd do something so sick?'

'You're not in a positin to talk' Adella said, nodding at the countess, but she sucked in a sharp breath as Matty kicked his brother in the ribs. Pie curled up, hands over his head, and every grunt or gasp of pain was a knife to Logan's heart.

'The countess would never make a man fight his dead brother. This is evil.'

'Get him on his feet,' the king ordered.

Matty grabbed Pie's arm, yanking him upright. The king stepped forwards and gripped Pie's chin, forcing him to look into his eyes.

'I told you that if you disobeyed me, I'd kill everyone you loved.' The king's voice had a sing-song quality, as if he were talking to a child. 'Betray me once, and you'll only do it again. I think I'll let your husband watch me kill you, and then I'll kill him.'

Pie's mouth moved, but no sound came out.

'Let me go,' Logan said again, struggling against his captor's weight. He bucked and twisted, trying to gain leverage against Adella. 'You know this ain't right.'

She froze, her body tense above him. 'I heard the rumours of necromancy. I didn't want to believe it, but . . .' Her voice trailed off with a choked sound.

To Logan's surprise, she stood, and pulled a knife from her pocket. He cringed, but instead of feeling a piercing in his gut, the ropes that bound his hands went limp.

Logan pulled himself to his feet as the king handed Matty a gilded knife. 'No!' he bellowed, charging towards them.

Hooves clattered across the docks. Bones cantered into view and crashed into the guards blocking Logan's path, knocking them sideways as Logan ploughed through the chaos.

Before the thing that had been Matty could plunge the knife downwards, Logan brought his axe down into the flesh of Matty's shoulder. The creature dropped the knife with an inhuman hiss.

'Don't kill him!' Pie cried, and Logan wasn't entirely sure which one of them he was speaking to.

'Protect the Chalice!' Ervin called. 'Don't let them take it. Protect the Chalice above all else.'

Logan pulled Pie into his arms. The king and his guards pulled back. Logan was well and truly outnumbered. He desperately glanced around for an escape.

'I'm sorry, Pie.' He kissed his husband's hair, before something caught his eye. A simmering crater, the remnants of old magic. He fingered Seraphina's knife in his belt. Could it be enough? Only one way to be sure.

Gripping Pie's hand tightly, Logan cried before pelting towards it. 'Countess!' He hoped both she and Bones would understand.

Logan and Pie crossed the dock as lumbering steps pursued them. Pie gripped Logan's shirt with a trembling hand. At the crater's edge, Logan pulled out Seraphina's knife, slashing three quick motions and praying to any god willing to listen to grant him this one thing.

The bright lines appeared, flickering and faint. Beyond them, the crater and the docks vanished, revealing the luscious grass and winding river of the unicorn farm. Logan murmured a thanks and stepped through.

Hoofbeats announced the countess astride the other skeleton steed, Bones at her side. Logan let out a sigh of relief, which he quickly regretted as the Black Company poured towards the portal. He waved the knife, hoping he could somehow get it to close, but it remained stubbornly in place.

He pushed Pie at Bones. 'Get on, get away. I'll try and hold them off.'

'Don't be silly, Logan dear, you can't fight that many,' the countess argued.

'No, he can't.' Logan turned to see Fox-Fur approaching. Of course–he'd followed Gary through the portal. Now he was stalking towards Logan, knife at the ready. 'And I'm looking forward to paying him back for the lump he gave me in Krensten.'

Logan gritted his teeth and raised his axe as four members of the Black Company advanced through the doorway, before it winked out of existence.

Suddenly, hoofbeats thundered across the field towards them. Logan's heart lifted as Gary and the unicorn came galloping over the hill. Fox-Fur swung at Logan, but he parried the move, narrowly avoiding a blow.

'Fix, let him be!' Adella cried, blocking the Black Company from approaching any further. 'It's over now. The king has what he needs, let's go!'

Fox-Fur shot her a glare. He thrust low, under Logan's guard. Logan threw himself out of the way and the sword narrowly missed taking a lump out of his hip.

They couldn't stay here. They needed help. *Think. Think, dammit.*

'The Bay of Sighs!' Logan yelled as Gary reached them. 'Get us to the Bay of Sighs. The water!'

'In . . . the water?' Gary blinked owlishly at him.

'Do it.'

Freddy tossed his head and the portal appeared, water drenching the grass as waves broke against the edge. Logan watched as Pie, the countess and Gary leapt through.

Fox-Fur blocked Logan's way. His hands tightened around his axe. If he wanted to die first, Logan would happily oblige. He raised the axe, but before he could swing, Fox-Fur staggered back as Adella hit him in the jaw. She followed it with a knee to his solar plexus.

'Don't just stand there,' she hissed at Logan.

Logan threw himself at the portal as the cold sea water snatched his breath away. His head slipped beneath the surface, and he came up coughing and spluttering. Another splash, and Adella landed nearby. The portal winked out of existence.

He trod water, looking around him. Pie, Gary, the countess, two bone steeds and a unicorn. Everyone. And a tall ship, floating not too far away.

Logan punched the air. 'We did it!' He swam over to the countess, who had her arm around Pie. Neither of them seemed to share his elation. The countess's mouth was set in a stern line, and Pie shivered against her. 'What's wrong?'

'Sorry,' Pie murmured, his voice barely audible. 'Seem to have got a little stabbed.'

He reached for Logan, his arm slipping off the countess. Logan made a grab for his husband, but Pie's eyes rolled up and he sank beneath the surface.

Chapter Eighteen

'Pie!' Logan cried, diving under the water.

It was as dark and cold as the cave in the mountains. He swam deeper, following a trail of red. Something white floated in the gloom and he grabbed it, fingers closing around Pie's hand.

The surface seemed miles away, Pie's weight pulling them further into the darkness. Logan set his jaw, tightened his grip and swam. The air burned in his lungs.

He broke the surface with a gasp and pulled Pie close. The bard's skin was pale as bone, his eyes closed. His hair floated in the water like blood.

'Pie. Come on, don't leave me like this. You can't leave me like this.'

The only sound was the waves, and the splashing from the unicorn and the two bone horses. No one spoke. Logan's heart felt heavy enough to pull him under the water again.

Pie coughed. At first it was a delicate sound, so small Logan almost missed it. Then Pie coughed again and again, spewing water. He lay his head against Logan.

'Fuck, that hurts.'

'You're safe.' Easy words, but they were treading water in the middle of the bay.

'They've spotted us,' the countess reassured. 'They're sending a boat.'

Logan looked up as a small boat headed from the ship towards them. No one appeared to be rowing, but it moved impossibly fast across the water. Gary and the countess shouted and waved.

'See, a boat,' Logan said to Pie. 'We're being rescued.'

'Good.' Pie closed his eyes. 'Wake me when it gets here.'

'No. No sleeping.' Logan patted Pie's face, harder than he meant to in his panic. 'I need you to stay with me.'

'I'm so tired, Logan.' His voice was almost washed away by the waves.

'Stay with me. Talk to me. No, sing. You're a bard, sing me a song. The one about the mermaid. I like that one.' Logan glanced over at the boat. It would be there within moments, but moments would mean nothing if Pie lost consciousness again.

Pie took a breath and began singing

Logan nodded. 'Good. Keep going.'

'Logan.'

He turned as the boat pulled alongside them. He recognised one of the occupants.

'Seraphina.' The relief of seeing a familiar face sent a jolt through him that almost knocked him underwater. 'I was hoping it was you.'

'Get on.' Her face was set in grim determination. She raised her hands, and the water lifted both him and Pie up and over the gunwale of the small boat. One of the other spellcasters helped the others.

'What about her?' Seraphina pointed to Adella.

'Bring her,' Logan said grimly. 'She's got answers.'

Seraphina turned the boat around, heading towards a larger vessel out in the bay.

'I . . . I didn't know, Logan,' the countess murmured, shivering from the sea water. 'I didn't realise . . .'

He shook his head and put a hand on her shoulder. 'We were used. All of us.'

She rested her head against him. 'What can I do to help?'

Logan bit his lip. In the little boat, there wasn't much. He pulled his shirt over his head, wrung it out once and handed it to her.

'Here.' He pointed to the knife wound in Pie's side. 'Put pressure here. Hard. We need to try and slow the bleeding.'

She said nothing, just took the cloth and did as he asked. If the countess couldn't bring herself to make a jibe, then the situation was dire. Pie winced, and the song died away.

'Come on, Al darling,' the countess said. 'Keep going. You can't leave your husband alone. You know he'll be utterly unbearable.' She gave Logan a wink, and he returned a grateful smile.

Pie's eyes flickered and he moaned. 'So cold.'

Logan's chest tightened. 'That's just because you're soaking wet,' he said, hoping he sounded more confident than he felt. 'Come on, keep singing.'

Pie coughed and winced but started the song again. His voice was a shadow of its usual self, weak and trembling like a guttering candle.

The ship loomed black against the night sky. Lanterns on deck looked like floating fireballs. The spellcasters raised their hands and the water gripped the boat, pushing it up to the deck. A second blob of water lifted the unicorn. Freddy tossed his head, kicking out until his hooves touched the deck.

Sailors hurried to secure the boat and help them. Logan laid Pie gently down.

'Healers!' one of the sailors called. He turned to Logan. 'How bad is he hurt?'

'I've had worse,' Pie replied, his words slurred.

'Keep singing,' Logan ordered. A greying man knelt beside Pie, examining his wounds

Logan hated to sit back and watch. He needed to keep busy, keep doing something to push the screaming voice of terror from his mind. The man met his gaze, held it with cool sea-green eyes for a moment.

'It's deep, but I don't think it's fatal.' He turned to another sailor.. 'I need bandages, needle and thread, something to bite down on. And alcohol. Bring something strong.'

Sailors rushed to fulfil his request. On the more stable ship, Logan took the opportunity to examine Pie's injuries more carefully. The gash in his side was long, extending from hip to halfway up the ribcage. Despite the blood, it didn't seem as deep as he'd initially feared. He leaned in close and sniffed, but couldn't detect anything more than blood and seawater. Good. That was good.

'H–how b–bad is it?' Pie asked through chattering teeth.

'I didn't tell you to stop singing,' Logan replied. 'You've got an audience now. That's what you bards like, right?'

Pie gave him a tired smile. His whole body shivered, and Logan wasn't sure if it was from cold, fear or pain. Either way, it wasn't a good sign.

A sailor hurried over with the bundle of items. The healer set them all down on the deck within easy reach and passed Logan the bottle. The countess helped Pie to sit up.

'You're not going to enjoy this very much, take a big swig,' Logan urged Pie.

'You always say the sweetest things,' Pie replied. Logan handed the bottle back, and the healer used the rest of the bottle to clean the area around the gash. Pie hissed in pain.

'Sorry,' Logan said. 'That was the easy bit. Here.' He placed the wooden spoon between Pie's teeth. 'Bite down on this. It will make it easier. Just remember I love you.'

'I don't think you're helping the mood, Logan dear,' the countess said. She took Pie's hand and patted it. 'Don't worry, Al darling. You're in good hands.'

The healer went to work, stitching the wounds. Logan focused on Pie, speaking softly, holding his husband's hand tightly. Everything faded away as the healer worked. The countess's soft voice, Pie's grunts and groans of pain, the waves hitting the ship, all blurred with the beating of his own heart.

And then the healer was tying off the last bandage and the job was done.

He reached down and eased the spoon handle from Pie's mouth. The wood had deep teeth marks now.

'Is it over?' Pie asked.

'It is.'

Logan gathered his husband into his arms. He felt lighter than ever, as if part of him had drained away. The deck below was stained with blood. Pie shivered harder, his skin hot and his face slick with sweat.

'Is there somewhere I can let him rest?'

'Follow me.' One of the sailors led them deeper into the ship to a cabin with a chair and two narrow fixed beds, then left them alone.

Logan removed the wet clothes, laid Pie on the bed, and fussed with the blankets until his husband was tightly tucked in.

'Are you comfortable? Warm enough? I can go and find more blankets if you want?'

Pie's fingers tightened around Logan's. 'Don't leave me.'

'I'm not going anywhere.' He leaned over, checking Pie for any of the signs that his injuries were more severe – blue lips, shallow breathing, erratic heartbeat.

'Can I stop singing now?' Pie asked sleepily.

'For a little while.' Logan kissed his forehead. 'Get some rest.'

There was a knock at the door, and the countess entered, carrying a bowl of water and a cloth. She set them down on the table by the bed.

'I'll take first watch if you like. Get some sleep or eat.'

'You don't have to do that.' His limbs felt leaden, and the idea of crawling into bed had never felt so appealing.

'Psh, don't have to turn down the opportunity to get my hands all over your husband while he's all weak and vulnerable, you mean.' She settled herself down in the chair and began dabbing the sweat from Pie's forehead. His eyes were closed, his features slack.

'Wake him in an hour, make sure he drinks a little water. Then wake me. An hour, you hear?'

She waved a hand at him dismissively. 'Sleep as long as you want. I need less at my age. And he's looking better already. He'll probably be up and demanding breakfast by morning.'

'I don't know about that.' Logan slipped off the bed again, uncertain. If he fell asleep and something changed in Pie's condition, he'd never forgive himself. 'I don't think there was any internal damage. If a weapon's nicked the bowel, there's no coming back from that. It's a slow, horrible death. Better to put a man out of his misery there and then.' He'd done it too, a couple of times over the years. He paused, his fingers hovering over Pie's face. Could he do it now, if needed? Logan snatched his hand back. It shook at his side, knocking painfully into his thigh. His face flushed hot, and he retched, bile burning the back of his mouth.

'Logan?' the countess asked. 'What's wrong?'

He closed his eyes, tears prickling the edges of his vision.

She put a hand on his shoulder, gently and without any of her usual teasing. 'What's got you so worked up?'

'I was thinking . . .' Logan dug his fingers into his palm. His stomach felt like a rock, but at least its contents stayed down. 'I was thinking of those men I've had to kill, because their wounds were too bad. And I looked at Pie and I knew I couldn't do that for him. It might be a kindness, but I couldn't—' He put his hand to his mouth, his gut constricting. 'I couldn't.'

'Oh, Logan, you big silly.' She gave him a sad laugh. 'Al will be fine. You don't need to worry about any of that. I told you before, it's much better to imagine the good things. Think about when he's feeling stronger, and well enough for you to rip his clothes off and—'

'Countess!' Logan cried.

She grinned back at him, not even flinching. 'There, that's better, isn't it? Much more the Logan we all know and love.'

Logan looked nervously at Pie, but he did not stir.

'Besides, death is just another journey,' she said. 'It's not the end. When the time comes, somewhere down the line, you two will find each other again on the other side of the veil.'

'You can't know that.' He wrapped his arms around himself. 'How can you believe that?'

'Because I have to. I have a family, waiting for me. I have to believe that too.' She stared past him at the cabin wall, as if watching the sea beyond. Waves slapped against the hull, again and again. Thud, splat. Thud, splat. Like a heartbeat. Five children, their husbands and wives, eight grandchildren. Charles, the youngest, was only seven.

'Death is simply life in reverse,' she continued. 'When a baby is born, it's quiet, still, and then it's not. It's loud and wriggly. When someone dies, they go quiet and still again. Death is the only certainty in life. One day, the Dark Mother's embrace will open for me, and I'll cross that stillness to my family again. But until then, I intend to be as loud and wriggly as I can be.' She patted his shoulder. 'You should do the same.'

He nodded slowly, unable to find anything to say.

'Go to sleep, Logan.'

He turned towards the bed, and then stopped. Pie's clothes lay in a pile on the floor, oozing seawater. He rummaged through the pockets and pulled out a little pouch. 'Here.'

Her eyes widened and she snatched it from him, shaking out the little teeth onto her palm. 'Ossymandias!'

'I don't think we need any leverage anymore.' He rubbed the back of his head.

She grinned. 'I told you I'd make you trust me, Logan Theaker.'

Later, Logan awoke in the dim cabin with the countess asleep in the chair beside him. He got up and lifted her gently into the bed. She curled up like a cat in the warm dent his body had left.

'I told her to go to bed,' Pie said.

'You should be asleep, too,' Logan said, settling down in the chair. He laid a hand on Pie's forehead. Still too warm, but he was conscious and coherent.

'Can't sleep. Hurts too much.'

Logan's heart ached. 'I'm sorry, Pie.'

'Don't be. You were amazing.' He reached for Logan's hand.

'I didn't do anything. I couldn't stop them hurting you.' He closed his eyes, fighting back the memories.

'I tried to tell you that you couldn't. But that's not the important thing. You saved my life,' Pie said softly. 'You were so calm, so strong. You kept me going.'

He shook his head. 'I just did what needed to be done. You'd have done the same for me.'

'I'd have panicked.' Pie gripped his hand. 'I'd have run around, screaming, probably thrown up. I'd be a mess. Not like you. Giving orders and taking charge. If it wasn't for all the blood trying to escape my body, I'd have probably been very aroused.'

Logan snorted. 'I think you're still a bit loopy from blood loss.'

'Possibly.' Pie tried to sit up, and Logan pushed him back down. 'But I'm not wrong, either. Not about you. Whenever I'm at my lowest, you're always there. Always. You beat yourself up about only being good for fighting and killing, as if you're a barbarian and nothing more. But that's not true. You're Logan the Protector. Logan the Healer. Logan the Leader.'

'Huh.'

'Believe me.' Pie squeezed his hand. 'I know you better than you do. I love you so much.'

'I love you, too.' Logan leaned down and kissed Pie's lips. 'But you need to go to sleep.'

Obediently, Pie closed his eyes. Logan sat back. Logan the Protector. Logan the Healer. Logan the Leader. It had a nice ring to it.

Interlude

Eleven Months Ago

The rain came down in heavy sheets, leaving Logan half blind and half drowned. The heavy cloak kept the worst of it from his head and shoulders, but his boots had given up long ago, and his toes swam in their own personal puddle. If he didn't get out of the rain soon, he risked his flesh rotting.

Up ahead, lantern light in the distance warmed his heart and gave him hope, until he saw the sign. The White Hart, the inn he'd agreed to meet Pie at, before their stupid fight. Logan almost turned away, then sighed. He needed to get out of the rain and Pie probably wouldn't even be there.

And if he was . . .

Well, Logan was good at ignoring people.

It was for the best.

As he approached, the door flew open and three people struggled on the threshold. The one in the centre clung to a bottle, as the man on the right tried to wrench it off him. He was clearly very drunk, swaying and stumbling. The rain had stuck his brown hair to his face.

No, not brown. Auburn.

'Pie?' Logan called, hurrying through the mud towards the group. His previous resolve melted away with the rain and a new chill spread through him. 'What's going on here?'

The man on the right managed to free the bottle from Pie's grip and another man pushed him away. Pie fell to his knees, head bowed in the rain.

Logan pulled Pie's arm around his shoulder, struggling to get him to his feet. Pie slumped against him, as if all the bones in his body had turned to mush in the rain. His breath stank of hard liquor. Logan dragged him towards the door and one of the men held up a hand.

'Oh no. You can come in, stranger, but he's . . .' He turned his head and spat. 'He's barred from the Hart.'

'Can you bar him after the rain's stopped? What's the problem, anyway?' Everyone liked Pie. He could walk into a room and charm anyone's life story out of them, make them feel like he'd been their friend for years.

'He's a thief,' the other man said, mimicking the spitting action. He held up the bottle. 'Stole this from right under our noses.'

Logan suppressed a snort. Couldn't have been watching the bar very well then. Bards didn't do subtle. Wasn't in their nature.

'You can't turn him out on a night like this. He'll die. Let me take care of him. We'll stay in the barn, and I'll pay for any damages.' He handed over his purse and the landlord jingled it with a frown. Logan held his breath.

'Fine. But if there's any more trouble, you're both out on your arses, rain or no rain.'

Logan slung an arm around Pie's waist, pulling him towards the barn at the back of the inn. The rain soaked his shirt until it was transparent, and he shivered violently, his eyes closed.

Not good.

There was no way he'd be able to get Pie to the hayloft, so he found an empty stall and laid him down in the straw. At least it was dry in here, and warmer than outside. He opened his pack and found a couple of blankets near the bottom that had escaped the worst of the rain.

'Pie, talk to me,' he said, as he pulled the sodden shirt off Pie and hung it over the top of the stall door.

The bard opened one eye. 'Piss off, Logan,' he slurred.

'Not going to do that,' Logan replied with a shrug. He used one of the blankets to dry the bard. Pie still shivered, though not as violently now, and his skin was pale and cold. 'On account of it still pouring out there, and also on account of the fact someone I care about is clearly having a bad time. I'm going to take your boots and trousers off now.'

Pie hit him. Or at least tried to. The swing was too wide and missed Logan by a good inch. 'You don't care. Go away,' he yelled, his voice raw. 'Go away like you did before.'

'You'll catch your death if you stay in wet clothes.' Logan kept his own tone level.

'Would that be such a bad thing?'

The misery in Pie's voice caught Logan by surprise. 'Yes, it would be a terrible thing. How could you say that?' He pulled off the last of Pie's wet clothes and laid the second blanket over the bard. 'Pie, what happened?'

Pie pulled the blanket around him, curling up, half buried in the straw. He rolled over, turning his back on Logan. If Logan hadn't been leaning in, he might have missed Pie's words.

'My brother's dead.'

The grief hit Logan in the stomach. He rested a hand on the bard's shoulder. 'I'm so sorry.' Pie had barely mentioned a brother before, never really spoken about family at all. Thinking about it, Logan had never asked Pie much about his background. Before he could ask anything further, Pie was fast asleep.

Logan watched Pie's chest rise and fall, each breath trapping him, binding him. He couldn't leave. Not just because he was worried about Pie's health. He couldn't walk away from him a second time.

When Logan had left Ophelia's home, he'd felt anger, shame, frustration at himself for failing her. Now, those same emotions returned, only this time stronger. After Logan had left Pie, his thoughts constantly drifted back to the bard. Wondering what he was doing, who he was with. Remembering that smile that chased the clouds away from his soul.

It wouldn't end well.

It was a mistake.

He wasn't strong enough to not to make it. He was in love with this man.

'Why won't you leave me alone?' Pie asked. He lay there, still curled on his side in the straw. Logan hadn't realised he was awake again. He put down the shirt he'd been mending, the uneven stitches scrawled over the fabric. 'I've sworn at you, spat at you, even hit you. Why are you still here?'

'It's all right. You don't hit very hard.' The joke provoked no reaction, which was worse than being screamed at. He'd seen men lose hope before, and once they did, pulling them away from the black edge of death became much harder.

In the next stall, a horse snorted. Sunlight trickled through a knothole in the barn wall. Was this the second or the third day? He'd lost count.

'You should hate me,' Pie said quietly.

'For grieving? Seems a strange thing to hate a man over.'

'Because I'm worthless.'

Logan reached a hand towards Pie's shoulder, then stopped. Much as he wanted to offer comfort, he didn't want to risk the wrong reaction. He felt as though he were crossing over a ravine on a beam, and if he slipped, it would be Pie that fell.

'You're not worthless. And I'm here because I care about you.' The words tumbled out before he could fully reflect on them. Next to him, Pie tensed. Logan took a deep breath. 'More than I've cared about anyone, in a very long time. I was wrong, the last time we met. I thought the meetings between us were just about . . . Well, you know.' Logan blushed. 'I thought

I was fine with that. But they were more than that. They were a reminder that there's more out there than monsters and killing. I'll always cherish that. Cherish . . . you.' This time he did reach down to put a hand on Pie's shoulder. 'I know you're hurting, and I wish I could take that pain away. But I can't, so all I can do is make sure you're not alone.'

Silence filled the barn. It pushed at Logan, eating at his nerves. Even the horses were still and quiet, as if they too waited for Pie's response.

'Please don't go,' Pie said, his voice a whisper. 'I cherish you too.'

Chapter Nineteen

Logan woke to the sound of footsteps on the deck above. Snatches of song echoed through the ship. He yawned and stretched, his back a mess of knots from spending most of the night in a chair. Pie had slept fitfully through the night, waking frequently from pain or fever dreams. He didn't mention his brother, though, and Logan didn't want to bring up the matter until Pie did.

Now, he seemed to be sleeping more peacefully. Logan rested a hand on Pie's forehead. Not as warm. That was good. Hopefully he'd sleep for a couple of hours more.

Logan glanced at the countess, who was equally fast asleep, one hand resting on the skeleton dog snoozing beside her.

'Strange woman,' he muttered to himself, shaking his head. He still didn't know what to make of her. She was the same person he'd met back in the house on the moor, the same person he'd taken in for grave-robbing. And yet, he felt he understood her a little better now. He straightened the blanket over her thin, bird-like shoulders.

'Never thought I'd end up friends with a necromancer.'

He slipped out of the cabin, almost knocking over a sailor.

'Where's Seraphina?'

'Galley,' the sailor replied. When Logan continued to stare blankly, she sighed. 'Follow me.'

She took him to a larger room, with rows of tables bolted to the floor. Sailors sat around, eating, drinking, throwing dice. He spotted Gary in the corner, listening to a tale about a storm in rapt attention. Seraphina didn't react until Logan sat down opposite her. She seemed lost in thought, or perhaps she was trying to divine the future from her bowl of oats. Her face was pinched and dark circles hung under her eyes. He suspected she hadn't slept much more than him.

'Oh, Logan,' she said as he dropped onto the bench opposite. 'Good morning. How's your husband?'

'Sleeping. He'll recover fully with time and rest.'

She nodded. 'That's good to hear.' She grabbed the arm of a passing sailor. 'Could you bring over another bowl, please?'

Someone shoved a bowl of cinnamon oatmeal under Logan's nose and his stomach growled like a starving beast. He dug the spoon in and devoured half of it.

'I wanted to thank you,' he said, after swallowing the mouthful. 'I wasn't sure if you'd leave us in the sea. I wasn't exactly the nicest person last time we met.' He shovelled more food into his mouth to cover his discomfort.

'We might not have spotted you, if it wasn't for Ophelia. She told me you were in the water and needed help.'

Logan dropped his spoon. A spatter of oatmeal decorated the table. His heart beat heavily in his ears, a dull boom that drowned out the buzzing of the rest of the room.

'She told you? She's here?'

'I think so. I've seen her around a couple of times since yesterday, so I think she's still here. Why? What's happened?'

'She betrayed us. Handed us over to the king's mercenaries.' The thought sent angry shivers, hot and cold, racing through his blood. 'Watch out for her. If she did this, who knows what else she could do.'

'Ophelia wouldn't hurt me,' Seraphina replied firmly. 'And she helped rescue you.'

'Everything you said about the king was right,' he said, as much to change the subject as to apologise. He couldn't deal with the thought of Ophelia right now. Not when everything she'd done to them was still so raw.

Her eyes widened. 'You saw him?'

'In Krensten.' He closed his eyes, the memories rushing through his mind, dragging him again through the thorns of the experience. 'He was with Pie's brother, only Matty died months ago. Murdered by the king.'

Her lips moved, chewing over his words, then she stood. 'Let's continue this discussion elsewhere.'

Logan shovelled the last of the oatmeal into his mouth and followed her. She took him up a level to the captain's quarters. After a moment, a warm voice called out for them to enter.

Inside, a uniformed woman sat behind a large oak desk. Scrolls of maps and sea charts were littered around her. She was older than Logan, judging from the grey in her short, tight curls, but her dark skin was flawless, and there was a timeless beauty to her face. She stood up as they entered, and Seraphina gave a quick bow.

'Captain, this is Logan Theaker.' Seraphina introduced. 'Logan, this is Captain Williams, of the *Avenging Arrow*.'

Captain Williams gave Logan a warm smile, but a chill remained in her eyes. 'The Bear. I've heard many tales of you. Come, please sit. Erin, could you bring drinks?' She turned to another woman Logan hadn't spotted in the back corner of the room. He thought about protesting the idea of drinking this early, then remembered the night he'd had, and decided he'd probably earned it.

When the young woman returned, it was with a tray carrying a small, metal pot and four handle-less cups. She poured a steaming liquid into each. Disappointment tickled inside Logan's chest as he was handed the steaming cup of tea. Then he decided that if a lack of booze with breakfast was the biggest disappointment he was facing, that was probably a good thing.

'We must stop the king.' The words spilled out of Logan in a wave. Next to him, Seraphina gave a little gasp, and the captain raised one eyebrow.

'You have a peculiar way of saying thank you for the rescue,' Captain Williams replied.

Logan wrapped his hand around the little ceramic cup, heat warming his palms and his cheeks. 'Don't get me wrong. I'm grateful. If you hadn't come to our aid, I'd have lost my husband. But I've been chasing folk tales and mysteries for days. Always following or hunting for something. I'm tired of that. It's time to put my foot down.'

The captain nodded. 'I understand. You're not the only one who wants to see Ervin fall. The *Avenging Arrow* this is one of the few places where magic is practised openly. The spellcasters have been hunted down; now we can only take to the seas for solace.' She waved her hand at the diminutive, dark-haired woman who had retreated to the corner of the room with a book. 'Not me, but my wife Erin is a spellcaster, and Seraphina of course. Many of the crew here have had to flee from their homes. After King Ervin's announcement, the Black Company have been causing havoc in villages, stirring up anti-magic sentiment and killing innocent spellcasters. We barely escaped with our own lives. For months, we've been gathering support, passing messages between rebel groups.'

'The spellcasters never wanted trouble,' Seraphina said, twisting a lock of hair in her fingers. Her quiet voice wavered. 'We've lost so many, Logan – friends and family members. All gone. Our forces were dwindled, with many spellcasters choosing to just leave the country and head for a new life on the continent. First it was the glass artisans, the wealthy and influential. But now it's anyone who can. There's a flour shortage in the larger cities because the mills have to wait for the wind, the fishing boats have no protection from storms, there's no one to light the mines so they have to risk lanterns. The king won't see reason, even as the country falls and his people starve.'

'Our only hope now is that Ervin's position is untenable,' Captain Williams continued. 'Sooner or later, the people will start to push back, especially because of the food shortages. But we can't wait for the country to start ripping itself apart. '

Logan took a sip of his tea. The hot liquid had a floral scent and a slight bitterness. The warmth moved through his insides like a comforting hug. Pie would like this, he decided. 'We've got another reason to hurry, the king has the Chalice. He'll raise a necromantic army if he's not stopped. He's already slaughtered a whole town.'

Logan explained the situation as best he could. Mostly clumsily, having to repeatedly backtrack and explain when the captain pressed him further. If Pie had told the story, they would be on the edge of their seats, desperate for every word.

'So now Ervin needs no support from the people.' Captain Williams slumped in her high-backed chair, her lip curled in disgust. 'It really is over . . .'

'There's something more.' Logan stroked a finger against his cheek, unsure how to explain. His beard felt rough and untidy under his touch. 'The king said it would end his sadness. I think he wants to bring back the ones he's lost.'

Both Pie and Adella had said the king had changed, but surely nothing less than the loss of the woman he loved could change a man that much. And if he thought he had a way to get her back . . .

Captain Williams raised her eyebrow again and Seraphina turned towards him. Even Erin came closer.

'The king said he could get Ophelia's body back – her actual body. I'm not sure how, but I think he seeks to do the same for his fiancée, maybe other members of his family. His grief has consumed him, completely.' Logan couldn't blame the man for wanting to hang on to his loved ones. If he'd only asked, Logan might have even considered fetching the Chalice for him. But any sympathy Logan had for the king was crushed to dust under the weight of what the king had done to Pie. For that, king or not, Logan would see him dead. For the people in Mywin he had slaughtered. For the pain he had caused countless others through his turmoil.

Seraphina twisted the lock of hair faster and faster between her fingers, and Logan wondered for a moment if she was trying to create sparks. 'But . . . I can't believe that's all there is to it. Not after he butchered every living soul in the town. My town.' The last two words were swallowed in a sob. Logan put his hand on her shoulder, wishing he could do more to comfort her.

'The countess mentioned something, right before we were interrupted by the Black Company,' Logan said, his mind trying to process through the chaos of his memories. 'She said the Chalice wasn't . . . right. I never got a chance to ask her what she meant.'

'We could always ask the captive?'

'Who?' Logan wondered before the realisation come to him. *Adella!* 'Where is she?'

'We threw her in the brig,' Williams replied. 'I haven't had a chance to deal with her yet.'

'When you speak to her, I'd like to be there,' he said, and she nodded.

'I don't see why not. Speak to the necromancer, find out what she knows about the Chalice, and then we'll confront the captive. Might as well squeeze any useful information out of her before she's put to death.'

Logan froze. 'Put to death?'

'The Black Company are not welcome on this ship, Bear,' Captain Williams replied with a dark hatred behind her eyes. 'She's a mercenary for the king, sent to butcher spellcasters. Her hands are covered in blood. Is that not fair?'

Logan nodded, but the idea weighed uncomfortably in his gut, as if he'd swallowed a hot rock. Adella had helped him escape. He stood up. 'Let me bring Pie some breakfast and I'll speak with the countess.'

'I'll send Seraphina to fetch you when I'm ready to speak to the prisoner,' Williams said.

Logan turned to leave, then stopped. 'Do you think I could get a pot of that?' He pointed to the kettle on the desk.

They made a quick stop at the galley for more tea before Logan made his way back to their assigned cabin. Slowly, he carried a tray loaded with bowls of honeyed oatmeal and plates of blood sausage and lightly cooked salt pork.

As he approached the cabin, he heard Pie and another woman speaking, but as he got closer, he realised the female voice wasn't the countess. A shiver rushed down his spine. He kicked open the door to the cabin and strode in.

Ophelia turned, staring at him like a caged rabbit.

'*You*,' he hissed, almost dropping the tray. 'How dare you show your face here, Ophelia.'

She hung her head. 'I wanted to make sure Al was all right.'

The dishes rattled as Logan's hands shook with rage. 'Does he look all right to you?' he yelled. 'Look at him! Is that your definition of all right?'

'Logan,' Pie said softly, but Logan barely heard him.

'This is your fault. You betrayed us, and you almost cost Pie his life, and then you have the audacity to come here to see if he's *all right*? You deserve to be dead after what you did!' Oatmeal spilled from a bowl.

'Logan!' Pie called again.

Ophelia vanished from the room without a word.

Chapter Twenty

'Don't say a word. Not right now, Pie. Not this time,' Logan warned his husband.

'Is that breakfast?' Pie asked gently instead, snapping Logan back to reality. Logan nodded and set the tray on Pie's lap. 'Do you really expect me to eat all that? Just because you have the appetite of a large parel doesn't mean everyone else does.'

'I brought some for the countess, too.' Logan looked over at the empty bed. 'Where is she?'

'She said something about visiting the little skeletons' room. I haven't seen her for a while.'

'Probably out having fun harassing the sailors. If she's not careful, the captain's going to clap her in irons and throw her in the brig.' Logan filled Pie in on his meeting with Captain Williams while Pie picked at his food. 'Come on, Pie, eat up. You need to get your strength back.'

'I'm trying.' Pie set down his spoon. 'But between the pain and the motion of the ship, I don't have much of an appetite.'

Logan placed the tray on the side table and poured Pie a cup of tea. 'At least drink this. I didn't know you got sea-sick.'

'I try and avoid ever getting on a boat; that way no one has to find out.' He took a sip and let out a sigh. 'I'm not as bad as some, though. Matty had it worse, and I swear just looking at the sea could make Lucius, my older brother, puke.'

Logan hadn't even known there was a second brother. He'd learned more about Pie's family in this conversation than in their entire relationship.

'Don't be mad at Ophelia,' Pie said quietly. He stared at his toes.

'Why bloody not?' Logan smacked a fist against his palm. 'It's her fault you're like this, Pie.'

Pie shook his head. 'No, it's not. It's the king's fault. He did this. It's Matty's fault for concocting that stupid plan. And it's mine for being dumb enough to follow him. Ophelia just wants her life back. She didn't know any of this would happen.'

'You're too soft.' Logan folded his arms.

'*I'm* soft? Really?' Pie reached over and poked his shoulder. 'This coming from the man who has to name every animal he meets. Including a skeletal horse?'

'Bones still thinks he's a real horse,' Logan muttered.

Pie laughed, then winced. 'I rest my case.' The smile faded and he reached for Logan's hand. 'I know you're mad at her, and I don't blame you, but I'm asking you please, let it go. For me.'

Logan stared into Pie's eyes. They were greener today, wide and pleading. Anger sloshed in his veins, bitter and cold. How could he possibly forgive Ophelia for betraying them, for hurting Pie, for pushing them further away from home? At the same time, the idea of disappointing Pie, of looking into those eyes and defying his wish . . .

'Dammit, you know I can't say no to you when you look at me like that.'

'Bard powers,' Pie said smugly.

'Pie powers,' Logan corrected, kissing Pie's forehead. 'The rest of your kind have no sway over me.'

A knock at the door announced Seraphina.

'Captain's ready,' she said.

'I have to go,' Logan said. 'I'll be back soon.'

'I'll be fine.' Pie waved him away. 'Don't worry about me.'

'Yeah, that's never going to happen.'

Pie grinned and kissed his husband's hand, before settling deeper into the blankets. Logan followed Seraphina. She led him down a level, deeper into the ship. The scent of caulk and sea salt tickled his nose, and the darkness pressed in. Seraphina held out a hand, and a small ball of light winked into existence. It lit the walls of the narrow passage with a soft peach glow.

'Neat trick,' Logan commented. Anything to break the silence between them. Ophelia's betrayal hung in the air, unspoken but heavy as a storm.

She shrugged. 'Has it's uses.'

'The stuff with the boat was even more impressive. Is the ship powered by spellcasters?'

She shuddered. 'No, wind and sails like a normal ship. We can take over in an emergency, but we'd rather not if we can help it. Fortunately, Captain Williams is very good at her job.'

'You'd rather not do it by magic?' He cocked his head. You'd never hear a bard say, 'I'd rather not sing.'

'Would you rather run everywhere if you could just walk?' She paused, the light bobbing with the motion of the ship. 'Magic needs a life force, usually the spellcaster's. It's draining. Something small like this is no worse than carrying an extra weight, but a big spell can render the caster unconscious – or even dead before too long.'

Logan thought of the spellcasters who'd raced the boat across the waves. 'Thank you, for rescuing us.'

She shrugged again, then opened a door. Captain Williams and another sailor stood between two barred doors. The captan looked up as they entered and gave them both a curt nod.

'Let's get this over with,' she ordered.

The sailor unlocked the door. 'Come out slowly,' he said. 'Any funny stuff and you'll regret it.'

There was a soft shuffling, even a sigh, as Adella stood at the threshold. She carried her head high, her posture ramrod straight, but when her eyes met Logan's, they lingered there for a moment longer than anywhere else.

'I'd rather you drowned,' Captain Williams said. Her words dropped the temperature in the room from cool to frosty. 'But I'm led to believe you might have information about the king. It would be pretty easy to hang you from the yardarm, so if you'd like to keep your neck attached to your spine, I suggest you cooperate to the fullest of your ability.'

Something in Adella's posture changed. A slight loosening of the shoulders, a miniscule drop of the head. Logan suspected most people probably wouldn't have caught it, but he'd seen it in enough things he'd hunted to recognise it. An acceptance of loss. She knew she wasn't getting out of here alive. It didn't make her less dangerous, though. A cornered animal rarely backed down. And if they weren't fighting for their lives, they were fighting to hurt you as much as possible before they succumbed.

'Adella, you said the king had changed,' he asked gently, which surprised him. 'What did you mean?'

Captain Williams cut him a glare but didn't interrupt or try to change the subject.

'Have you ever loved so much it hurts?' Adella asked. Both Logan and Williams nodded, and Seraphina closed her eyes, looking away. Adella shook her head. 'I don't mean in a romantic sense; not a shared love, but a singular adoration of everything they stand for. I mean, have you ever loved someone's very essence: their soul, not their heart?'

She looked around the room, and met confusion from Logan and Seraphina, irritation from Williams. Adella took a breath.

'King Ervin is a good man. I know you're not going to believe me, but it's the truth. You can cut out my tongue, but it's the truth.'

'That's not going to happen, Adella,' Logan assured her.

Williams raised an eyebrow that said it very much wasn't his place to make that call.

'He's a good man, but . . .' Adella hung her head. 'He's changed in the last year or so. Become obsessed. Cruel, even.'

'Cruel?' Williams snapped. 'He turned against his own people. He sent the likes of you to hunt us down, imprison and even kill us.'

'That's not how it started. The king is grieving. Whatever anyone did, whatever anyone said, nothing could pull him from the darkness that had consumed him.' Adella folded her arms. 'It wasn't just Annabelle who died when that fireball spooked their carriage horse. Ervin was gone too, just a shell of himself. All because of a stupid accident. An accident that left people dead. It wasn't the first time careless magic use had caused trauma. Our mission was initially to just bring people in, stop the use of reckless magic. I didn't have a problem with that.' Adella glared at the captain.

'But it didn't stop there, did it?' Seraphina said softly. 'It wasn't just the careless or the reckless. Ervin banned all magic.'

Adella grimaced. 'You're right. At the time, I didn't think about how things would escalate. As I said, I love Ervin and I trusted his judgement.'

'Why?' Logan asked. 'Aren't all kings the same in the end? Only interested in power, wealth, glory?'

'Maybe the ones that expect it. The ones that are born to it. Ervin never expected to take the throne. He never cared about ruling, didn't have his siblings' arrogance. Two of them nearly ripped the country apart in their stupid civil war after his father died. Ervin wanted to improve things.'

'But not anymore,' Logan pointed out.

She turned her gaze to him, scrutinising him. 'Not anymore. It's a harsh thing to love someone and not trust them.'

Logan felt that in his heart. The argument he'd had with Pie on the mountain came rushing back. If Pie had just trusted him, opened up rather than running away, how different would things be now?

'Don't suppose I could get some food?' Adella asked, changing the subject. 'Or even some water? It's been a long night.'

'Let's see if you're worth it.' Williams gave her a sneer. 'No sense feeding you only to string you up. Give us some details. Something we can work with.'

Adella held up her hands. 'Look, I understand your feelings. I don't have anything against you. All I want to do is help Ervin, and that's going to mean going against his judgement for a while.'

'What caused the change?' Logan asked. All the animosity between the spellcasters and the mercenary was pushing them off track. Adella wasn't the issue here, and neither was magic. King Ervin was.

'Almost a year ago, we were on a ship when a storm hit, hard and fast. Ervin isn't the sort to hide below deck like a coward. We were on deck, trying to help get the sails down before the wind ripped them off. A wave washed him clean overboard.' Her voice quivered at the last word, and she closed her eyes for a moment. 'We thought he was dead. The waves pulled him under, and we didn't see him for hours. The captain did his best to stay in the area, but we couldn't risk anyone else in the water. I wanted to try anyway, but Fix said Ervin would never tolerate anyone throwing their life away for him.'

The reverence in her voice didn't match with Logan's concept of the man who had murdered a town. Who had almost had Pie killed. By his own dead brother.

'Go on,' he encouraged.

She wiped away a tear from her eye. 'The storm died down, and then we saw him floating. At first, we assumed he was dead, but when we brought him on deck, he was still breathing. Sailors said the cold water must have helped him survive, and you don't question a miracle, other than which god to assign it to. But he wasn't the same.'

'Injury can change a man.' Logan nodded. He'd known a man who'd started life as miller, a small and unassuming fellow, until he'd been kicked in the head by a horse. After that, he'd been possessed by such rage, he had to leave his home and life behind, lest he ended up hurting anyone he cared for.

'I think it was more than that,' Adella replied. Her posture stooped further, shoulders visibly slumped. 'For a start, it wasn't immediate. For a while, he was mostly himself; he'd just forget where he was, or he'd stop talking and just stare into space. Then he started getting cruel. Ervin loved dogs, but a few months after the accident, he started yelling at them, kicking at them. Until they'd no longer tolerate being in the same room as him.

'He started looking into spellcaster magic and books. Before, it had just been about stopping the misuse of powers, keeping the dangers away from ordinary folks so no one else had to die because of a misplaced spell. But he got interested in the magic itself, looking for something, I think. He got obsessed with the history of the necromancer empire, and the legends of the Chalice. He ordered the countess's release, told her he'd call on her skills sometime. I'd find things in his chambers. Dead things. Dissected.' She swallowed hard. 'And then some of the servants started going missing. Could have been nothing, though. Could have been . . .'

'And you did nothing, of course,' Williams said pointedly.

'Like what? Accuse the king of necromancy, of murdering his own people?' Adella barked out a laugh. 'Besides, the Black Company were ordered on pain of death to find the Chalice. It sounds silly, but I was relieved, honestly. He started hiring thieves to find him ancient texts. Murderers to work as his personal guards. People who were cruel, like him. Who wouldn't question his darker orders. I couldn't stand to be in court any longer, to watch him change further. I hoped that when he got what he wanted, maybe he'd go back to being the man he once was. I didn't know what else to do.'

'Did you kill all the people in Mywin?' Seraphina asked. 'Was it you?'

Adella shook her head, hard. 'No, of course not. We were on the road to Krensten at that point. If I'd known, if I'd been there . . .' She raised her head and met Seraphina's eye. 'I'd have tried to stop him. Even Ervin, even my king. I'd have tried to stop him.'

Seraphina took a step back under the intensity of her gaze.

Williams clapped her hands together. 'Right, that's enough of this. Put her back in the cell. Bring her some bread and water. Your neck is safe for the moment.' She gave Adella an icy smile.

Without another word, they were ushered back towards the captain's quarters. 'If there's necromancy involved, I want the countess's opinion,' said the captain. 'Then, when I have it, I'll have no more reason to keep her on my ship. Her magic is tainted.'

'She takes some getting used to,' Logan said, worried for the countess. The captain's words were taking a dark turn. 'But once you know her, she's a decent enough person in her own way. Don't send her away. She doesn't deserve that. She's been helping us. Please.'

Logan put a hand on the captain's shoulder, but she twisted out of his reach. 'Touch me again, Bear, and they'll be calling you Logan No-Fingers. She was released on order of the king; who's to say she's not still on his side? Necromancy is a dark art, dangerous. Between that one defending a murderous king and you speaking for a necromancer, the world feels like it's gone mad.'

Logan couldn't quite disagree with that.

'Find the necromancer,' Williams yelled to a passing sailor. 'Bring her to me, and don't take any trouble from her. Use handcuffs if you have to.'

'There's no need for that, is there?' Logan protested, a panic bubbling up in his guts. 'She won't be any trouble.'

'She'd better not be, Bear,' Williams replied, stalking off.

The countess was brought roughly into the captain's quarters, the skeleton puppy clasped tightly in her hands. She gave Logan an enthusiastic wave, before turning nonchalantly to Williams. 'Good morning, Captain. You have a beautiful ship, and a lovely crew, I must say. Very firm hand, if you know what I mean.'

Williams regarded her disdainfully, her brows drawn in suspicion. After a moment, she huffed out a breath. 'I don't normally allow necromancers on my vessel,' Williams said, staring down at the countess, who met her gaze without flinching. 'Your abilities disgust me.'

'And your crew's magic makes me sick,' the countess retorted in a sweet voice. Logan swore she almost batted her eyelashes. 'That's not a judgement, just a fact. We're two sides of the same coin, but those sides never meet.'

'I'll have no raising the dead on my ship.' Williams said, smacking the desk with a thud.

The countess dismissed Ossy, carefully putting the teeth away under the captain's suspicious glare. 'My hair will be a terrible mess, but your ship, your rules.'

Logan wondered if the countess was aware Williams wanted her off the ship as soon as possible. Or worse.

The two women glared at each other until Logan cleared his throat. 'What did you mean, Countess, when you said the Chalice wasn't right?'

The countess's eyes widened and she smacked a fist into her palm. 'That's right! It's not right. Not right at all.'

The whole room turned towards her, and Logan cleared his throat again, encouraging her to continue.

'We were expecting a necromantic item,' she said. 'But the Fleshpot wasn't. It was alive.'

Chapter Twenty-One

'Alive?' Logan and Williams said at the same time.

'How can it be alive?' Logan questioned. 'It was locked in a box for hundreds of years. It's a cup.'

'And yet, it is.' The countess lounged back comfortably, looking at them, daring them to contradict her. Logan bit back a smirk at her irrepressible nature.

'What does she mean?' Williams glared at Logan.

'It was definitely a necromancer who locked the Chalice up down there,' the countess continued. 'Which rather suggests they didn't want anyone getting hold of it. Well, until we broke in. I think the Chalice might be something more than we expected. Maybe even more powerful.'

'And now you've just handed it over to the king,' Seraphina murmured. Her hands writhed in her lap like eels.

'"Handed it over" is a bit of a stretch.' The countess waggled a finger. 'Brutally taken from us, I think. Oh, if you see your ex-wife, Logan, tell her I want a word. Possessing poor Al like that.'

'Is she still . . . attached to you?' he asked.

'Yes. I could discard her like old clothes, but I have the feeling you'd like to get some answers from her too.' The countess frowned sadly. 'I fear her grip on herself is fading. Her emotions are overcoming her, destroying everything that makes her Ophelia. But I'll only do as Logan requests.'

'What are you saying?' Captain Williams demanded, her patience wearing.

'I'm saying I'll dismiss her and send her back to the dead. But only on your word, Logan. I won't do it unless *you* ask me.'

Do it, he almost said. She'd be gone, one less problem to worry about. Ophelia died a long time ago. She didn't belong here with the living.

But he couldn't bring himself to speak the words.

It wasn't just Pie's pleading. He'd made a promise to Ophelia, one he'd almost broken, then re-sworn. He hated what she'd done, but at the same time, she'd been betrayed by the king as much as any of them. If she was still on the ship and not walking around in her body, then either Ervin had lied to her, or she'd made the decision to stay here, with them.

'How much time do we have left?' he asked.

The countess shrugged. 'I'm guessing days. A week if she's strong enough.'

'And after that?'

'I can still dismiss her, but it gets much harder, and there's no telling what she might do in the meantime.'

Logan swallowed. 'I understand. Don't do anything just yet.'

'Is there a problem?' Williams asked. 'If there's a problem on my ship, then I want to know about it.'

'No problem.' Logan shook his head. 'I won't let there be a problem.'

'I'll explain,' Seraphina said to the captain, and Logan gave her a grateful nod.

Logan wasn't even sure where they were right now, other than on the ocean. His mind whirled with thoughts about Ophelia, worries about Pie, the revelations about the Chalice. The thought that it would enable the king to raise an undead army had been bad enough, but it seemed the king could raise people without it, so what could the Chalice possibly do that was worse? Why did Ervin crave its power so much? And what did the countess mean when she said that it was alive? He'd been picturing a gold cup up to now. What did it really look like?

'Are you part of my crew now, Bear?' Williams asked. 'Seems to me you and yours have caused nothing but trouble.

My job is to protect these people, and yet you bring a dangerous necromancer on board, and now there's a vengeful spirit? I ought to tie weights to her feet and throw her into the ocean.'

Before Logan could react, the captain's wife stepped in, whispering in the captain's ear. She stroked her wife's hand as she spoke softly, her expression soft and loving. Captain Williams sighed.

'Erin reminds me that we need all the help we can get, so the necromancer can stay for the moment. But I reiterate my previous question: are you part of my crew now?'

Heat flooded Logan's face, but his guts felt icy. She might be right, but it wasn't like they'd set out to cause issues for the spellcasters. All he wanted was to bring Pie home safe. All he wanted was for them to go home, together. 'I'm not sure; are we?'

'I think what Logan's trying to say is we're at your disposal, Captain,' the countess replied politely, reaching over and patting Logan's arm. That seemed to placate Williams a bit, as she settled back in her chair.

'I might know? something about the Chalice,' Erin said suddenly. She had a soft voice, like the rustle of paper. 'The legends say that the necromancer empire ran out of gold and collapsed in on itself, but there were always whispers . . .' She perched on the edge of Williams' desk, tapping her chin. 'I remember reading an account that mentioned the empire collapsed because something attacked their home country and killed most of them. Then there was a legend of a creature sealed away by a spellcaster and a bard. Morigen and Hale, I think their names were. Something living, sealed away? Could that be the Chalice, or something connected to it? I can't remember much, but if I could get to the library, then maybe I could find out.'

'The library in the capital?' The countess folded her hands under her chin and looked up at Erin. She nodded encouragingly in return before the countess laughed. 'The library in the capital right next to the king's palace? That library?'

Erin nodded again, glancing uncertainly at Williams. The captain sighed.

'I get your point, necromancer, but unless you know any more than you've said, I don't see we have a lot of choice.'

'Just making sure everyone knows what's involved,' the countess said cheerfully. 'Sounds terribly exciting to me.'

'Morigen, at least, is real, no matter the truth behind the rest of the legends,' Seraphina said. 'His tomb is the one outside Mywin, the one I directed you to use to get into the unicorn realm. Maybe there's something there?'

The countess punched Logan's arm. 'I told you we should have gone grave-robbing!'

Logan glowered at her, but guilt nibbled at his insides. He couldn't have known at the time, but if he had given in, could they have done anything to prevent the Chalice being taken?

'Which one?' Williams asked. 'Library or tomb?'

'Why not both?' the countess suggested. 'Hedge our bets.'

'I'll give the word to change course,' Williams announced. 'We can reach the capital in a couple of days, then sail on to Mywin. I assume you'll be going to the library?' she said to Erin.

Logan recognised the note of pain in her voice. Knowing she'd be sending her wife off into danger.

'You know I have to,' Erin replied quietly.

'I know.' Williams let her gaze linger on her wife a moment longer, then snapped it back to Logan. 'Bear. You'll go with her. Keep her safe. That's your price of passage.'

He nodded. 'Fair. I swear to you, I'll keep her safe.'

'I'm team tomb-robbing,' the countess announced, to Logan's utter lack of surprise. 'I suspect I'm the one with the most experience, after all.'

Williams raised an eyebrow. 'That doesn't exactly fill me with confidence about your intentions.'

'You can trust her,' Logan replied. 'She's trying to keep her image up, but she'll do the right thing, I promise.'

'Not helping with that image, Logan dear,' the countess sniffed. 'But I'm very good in a fight, which Logan can confirm. I've saved his arse more than once.'

Logan sighed, but nodded.

'Very well.' Captain Williams settled back in her chair. 'Your husband's a thief, right? Might be useful too, perhaps in the tomb.'

Logan glared at her. 'My husband almost lost his life yesterday. I'm not risking him losing it again.'

Williams laughed, though there was no humour in it. 'Lower your fists, Bear. I won't force him to do anything.'

Logan looked down at his hands. He hadn't meant to clench them.

'Go,' the captain ordered.

Logan stood, his chair scraping on the floor as he did. All eyes turned to him and he saw his own hurt and fear reflected in their eyes. He cleared his throat.

'I know it seems bad right now,' he started, and Williams gave another empty laugh. Logan's resolve grew. 'But we'll defeat Ervin. I swear it. And we'll do it together. Spellcasters and necromancers. Sailors and fighters. It will be a story for the ages.'

'Led by Logan the Legend,' the countess said with a smile.

'Well, I don't know about—' Logan started, but she shouted the name again and Erin and Seraphina joined in. The captain caught his eye and gave him a nod.

'People need something to believe in,' she said. 'Be that for them.'

Logan headed back towards the cabin. Williams's words bothered him. She wouldn't have any power to order Pie, but that didn't mean that if she suggested it, he wouldn't jump at the idea. Logan's heart weighed heavy in his chest. Perhaps Pie would recognise the idea was stupid; perhaps he was in enough pain that the lure of breaking and entering would have no hold. But Logan had noted his excitement in the necromancer's cave, his desire to break into the chest. Perhaps the best Logan could do was hope Pie didn't find out about it.

As he approached the cabin, he heard Pie's voice. Logan's first thought was that Ophelia had returned, but he quickly realised he couldn't hear anyone else. He quickened his step.

'Ow . . . ow . . . fucking—'

Logan slammed open the door. Pie flinched, then groaned. Something slipped from his fingers.

'What's wrong?' Logan's gaze darted around the room, looking for whatever had hurt Pie. 'Was it her again?'

'Dammit, Logan, open the door like a normal person.' Pie pressed a hand against his side, his teeth gritted in pain.

'Sorry, sorry.' Guilt nibbled at his insides. 'I heard you call out. I was worried.'

'I'm fine,' Pie muttered. His hand curled around the blanket. 'No, I'm not. I'm not fine. I'm tired and I hurt and my face itches and my hair's a mess.' He rubbed at the stubble on his jaw, tears prickling his eyes. 'I don't know how you stand it.'

Logan brushed a finger over his own beard. 'It's not so bad after a couple of days. I like it. You look good.'

'I look like a mess. I can't even comb my hair.'

Logan spotted the object Pie had dropped. 'That's what you were trying to do?'

'Every time I raised my hand it was like getting stabbed all over again.'

Logan picked up the comb. 'Well don't do it then. You'll open your stitches if you carry on like that.'

'But it's all knotty and horrid,' Pie said. Logan supressed a laugh. Bards. Always so dramatic.

He sat on the edge of the bed, and gently eased the comb through Pie's hair. Pie wasn't wrong; it was a mess.

'How's that?'

'Start at the ends.' Pie winced.

'Sorry.' Logan had never let his own hair get longer than an inch. Too much risk of someone or something grabbing it in a fight. 'How's that?'

'Better.' Pie let out a sigh. 'Yeah, that's better.'

Logan continued to comb, the slow rhythmic motion relaxing. For a moment, there was only the sound of waves against the hull.

'You're not so bad at this,' Pie said.

'Any time. You only have to ask.'

'You're not exactly good at asking for help yourself,' Pie said pointedly.

The corner of Logan's mouth twitched. 'No, I'm not. Maybe that's something we both need to get better at. Being honest with each other. Neither of us are as strong as we like to think we are.'

Pie said nothing. He closed his eyes. Logan carried on combing, but made a decision.

'Speaking of being honest, it's probably only fair you hear this from me.' He told Pie about the discussion with Adella, and then what was decided in the captain's office about the library and the tomb.

'And you don't want me to go.' Pie pulled his arms around himself.

'I don't. In the spirit of honesty.'

'But you don't get to choose, right?' Pie's hand tightened, twisting the blanket. 'It's my choice, right, Logan?'

No, it's not, Logan wanted to yell. *Because you'll choose the wrong thing. Because then you'll be out of my sight again and I can't bear the idea of that.* But it wasn't his choice. It wasn't a marriage if he was controlling Pie, forcing him to act for Logan's needs and desires. Treating him like that would be worse than the way he'd treated Ophelia.

He brushed his hand down Pie's arm, his fingers lingering over their marriage tattoo. 'It's your choice.'

'Part of me thinks you're right.' Pie clenched his fist. Logan let out a sigh of relief, but Pie shook his head. 'But I have to. I have to make amends for what I've done. To you, to my family. If I can help at all, then I have to do it.'

His body shook. Logan put down the comb and wrapped his arm around Pie, pulling him close.

'You don't owe anyone anything. You need to concentrate on your health.'

'My family . . .' Pie sucked in a noisy breath. Tears dropped onto the blankets, leaving little marks. 'My family disowned me after Matty's death. The news hit my mother hard, Logan. She didn't speak a word after I told her. I don't know if she ever spoke again. Lucius said it was all my fault. That he didn't want to see me again.'

Logan said nothing. He held his husband tight as Pie trembled against him.

'I lost Matty, my family, almost lost my own life. And I'm so damn scared I'm going to lose you too. I can't just sit around in bed.'

'You're not going to lose me,' Logan said.

Pie pulled away. 'But what if I do?'

'You won't.' Logan wiped a tear away with his thumb. 'And I won't lose you. If you want to go, if you think you'll be fit enough, then go. I saw you when we went for the Chalice. I know you're skilled. And the countess will be with you. Look.' He closed his hand around Pie's. 'Maybe we're not as strong as we think we are, but I do know we're far stronger together than we ever were apart.'

Pie gave him a tired smile. 'Gonna make a bard out of you yet, Logan Theaker.'

'Yeah? How long do you think that will take?'

Pie rested his head against Logan's shoulder. 'Probably the rest of my life.'

Pie fell asleep and Logan took the opportunity to nap himself. His dreams were plagued with unpleasant visions – Pie being stabbed; Ophelia melting away to a puddle of nothing; the countess leading an army of skeletons to wreak havoc over the land. And in the background of each one, watching him, something lurked. Something dark and hungry.

Logan jolted away dripping with sweat, the blankets tangled around one ankle. The room was dark and quiet. On the other bed, Pie snored gently. Logan did his best to wash up and pulled on the clothes the sailors had lent him. His own clothes were still in the pile in the corner where he'd left them, damp and smelling of the ocean.

Logan reached for his axe, but of course, that was gone too. Lost beneath the waves in the Bay of Sighs. The thought hadn't even crossed his mind at the time. He'd have to see if the captain had a weapon to lend him.

He somehow suspected she would.

Now he'd noticed it was gone, he felt strangely naked. It wasn't like he'd had much to do with the axe at home – it had decorated the wall most of the time – but wearing it on his back constantly while looking for Pie meant it had quickly gone back to being part of him again.

Logan moved over to check on Pie. His cheeks were still streaked with tears and he mumbled something in his sleep. *Not the only one with bad dreams.* Which wasn't exactly surprising. He found Pie's hand under the blanket and gave it a squeeze. Pie's lips curled up in a smile.

'Thank you for sharing your life with me,' Logan said. He understood now why Pie had kept so much of his past hidden. And while Logan hated to see the pain those memories had caused his husband, at the same time, there was a selfish glow of pleasure in Pie finally opening up to him.

A flash of movement caught his attention. Ophelia stood at the back of the room, watching them. When Logan lifted his head, she vanished.

'Ophelia,' he whispered. 'Can we talk?' He held his breath, waiting to see how she'd respond. His heart thudded in his ears.

She appeared at the doorway, then walked through it. Logan sighed and let go of Pie's hand. 'I'll be back,' he whispered.

Outside, the corridor appeared empty until he saw her disappear at the stairs to the deck. If she wanted to play hide and seek, Logan would do his part.

On deck, he lost her again. He walked slowly across the boards, dodging the sailors going about their business. Being out in the open lifted his spirts: he hadn't noticed how much being in the dark and cramped cabin had been weighing on him until he stood out here and felt free. The day was fresh and bright, and the ship rose and fell on the undulating waves. Seabirds followed the topsail, keening mournfully.

He caught sight of her at the front of the ship. She was watching the waves break against the hull.

'Ophelia. Please, don't go.'

She turned on him, and Logan took a step back. Her eyes, once a delicate green, were almost black, her expression hard and cold.

'I . . . I just want to talk.' He held out a hand to her. A pointless gesture, but he couldn't help it. 'I think you do too.'

She glared at him but didn't attempt to move.

He took a breath. 'Pie's getting better. He said to say thank you for checking up on him.'

She frowned. Her shoulders swayed from side to side as she considered him, a motion that put in Logan's mind the image of a snake about to strike. Despite every instinct in his body fighting him to run or attack, he took a step towards her. She hissed at him, a feral sound. Logan paused. Had she already gone too far?

'Ophelia. Talk to me.'

She shrugged, drawing in on herself. 'What do you want me to say, Logan? I betrayed everyone. I nearly got Al killed. I should have stayed dead.'

Goosebumps rushed up Logan's arms. She'd been cold to touch previously, but now that cold emanated from her, as if she sucked the very sunlight from the air.

'You shouldn't have died in the first place.'

She opened her mouth and let out a wailing cry that echoed in his skull. Sailors stopped and turned to stare at them.

'Stop trying to be nice! I know you don't mean it.'

The back of Logan's neck prickled as those around them watched. He didn't know if the spellcasters could do anything to Ophelia, but he didn't want to risk anyone trying, especially if it could loosen her tether on her sense of self. He took another step towards her, suppressing a shiver.

'I'm not being nice. I'm being honest.' He tried a different track. 'I did love you, Ophelia, and I like you as a friend, if you'll have me. You didn't deserve what happened to you. You didn't deserve to die. I'm sorry for what I said.'

'I don't like you.' She stuck out her tongue at him. Logan wasn't sure, but it felt as if the air warmed a little. 'But I like Al, and I'm sorry too. I didn't mean for any of that to happen. I'm so scared, Logan.'

'Why Ophelia? Why would you betray us?' He tried to keep his voice level, keep any accusation out of it. It didn't work.

'I thought you'd fuck it up!' she cried, the air turning icy once more. Logan couldn't help but shudder. Her words buried themselves in his flesh. Was it getting darker? She moved towards him, drifting over the deck. Logan stood his ground. 'I thought about telling you everything, but it seemed better to do what the king wanted. I thought it would be safer for everyone. He's stronger than you can imagine. We can't stop him. You'd only try to get in the way, to be Logan the hero, taking on the king all by yourself. You'd sacrifice yourself, and watch the people around you suffer in their grief. You only ever leave, Logan.'

Logan gritted his teeth. The cold made them chatter. He pulled his arms around himself, shivering. 'I know.' She'd tried so hard when they were married, he knew that now. She'd tried to be there for him, tried to be a partner for him, and he'd been so caught up in trying to keep her safe that he'd hurt her worse than any monster. 'I know, Ophelia.'

She raised a hand to strike him, then paused. Her eyes narrowed. 'You know *what*?'

'That I would have fucked it up. The Logan you knew would have absolutely rushed in and made everything worse. You're right.'

She lowered her hand, watching him suspiciously, like an animal trying to determine whether to attack or flee.

'But I'm not the same person you knew. I'm not sure I'm even the same person you met in the countess's house.' He forced himself to stand up straight, push down the shivers. 'I'm not going to promise to save you, Ophelia.'

She hissed at him again, lips pulled back in a sneer.

'*We're* going to save you. Me, and Pie, and the countess. Gary. Seraphina. None of us will abandon you again.'

Her eyes widened. She opened her mouth, but no sound came out. Logan waited, hardly daring to breathe. Spray from the sea drifted against him. Ophelia closed her eyes, murmured something, and vanished.

Thank you.

Interlude

Ten Months Ago

Logan watched the door to the inn, his drink untouched at his elbow. Pie had said he'd be here, that once he'd attended to his family, he'd come back to Logan. But the doubts nagged in the back of Logan's mind. He couldn't blame the man if he didn't show.

Logan wasn't a good man.

Logan was a fighter, a killer.

Logan wanted to change. For Pie.

The door opened and Logan's head snapped up, hope and fear wrestling in his heart. For a moment, the sinking sun caught him full in the face, blinding him. He couldn't make out the features of the person who had entered, only their silhouette, and the shape of a wide-brimmed hat.

Then he blinked and Pie stood in front of him.

'You came,' Logan said softly.

The bard gave him a smile soft as spring. 'I told you I would.'

'I . . . I wasn't sure . . .'

'Sure enough to buy me a drink,' Pie pointed out, picking up the second tankard on the table. He took a hefty swig, then held out a hand. 'Walk with me? It's a lovely evening.'

The sunset streaked the sky with vivid ribbons of orange and gold, reflected in the river, swollen with snowmelt. Little white flowers with bell-like petals lined the bank, swaying in the gentle breeze.

'It is a lovely evening,' Logan commented, not knowing what else to say. He was far too aware of his heart. It pounded in his chest, echoing in his ears.

Pie tightened his grip on Logan's hand. 'Always trust a bard on such matters.' He glanced away, staring at the river. 'I wanted to come out here, to talk first. If we'd stayed in the common room, I'd have dragged you upstairs before we got halfway through the first pint. I think it's important to talk first.'

Talk. Talk was bad. *Logan, I have something to say to you. I have summoned the priest. I am dissolving this marriage. You cannot be what I need, and it is unfair on both of us to maintain this charade.*

'I . . . I understand.' The crushing pressure on his heart made his chest ache.

Pie put a finger on his lips. 'No, Logan. You don't understand anything.' His lips quirked in a smile, softening his gaze, but there was an intensity to it that Logan had never seen before. 'Look, I get it, what you said, about being bad at letting people in. I'm not good at opening up either. Until now, it's been about sex, about fun. A night here, maybe a few weeks somewhere else. A string of places I really can't show my face in again. But it's different with you. I keep coming back to you. And you do the same.'

Logan said nothing.

Pie laced his fingers together, pressed them against his lips. 'I've had a lot of time for thinking, recently, after what happened with Matty . . . About who I am, about what I want. About what's important to me . . . And I came to the conclusion that it's you, Logan Theaker.'

Logan's heart raced like a rabbit released from a trap. Even though they were outside, there didn't seem to be enough air. He pushed past Pie and put a hand on the rough bark of a willow tree, his mind whirling.

'Not exactly how I was hoping that confession would go.' Pie's tone was light, but his voice had a hitch in it. 'Kinda hoped for more kissing, at least.'

Logan said nothing. He didn't trust himself.

'If you want me to go, just say,' Pie said sadly. 'If I've said too much. If I've scared you.'

'I . . . I don't want you to go.' Logan spoke to the tree, not trusting himself to turn around. 'I don't want that at all.'

A crack of twig broke before Pie's breath tickled his ear. 'So, what do *you* want, Logan?'

This time he did turn. Pie took a step back and held out a hand. Logan took it, gripping it tightly. He wanted . . . He wanted Pie. Every inch of his body. Every note in his soul. He wanted to go to sleep each night with his arms wrapped around his man and wake up with him every morning to check if Pie's eyes were more green or brown today. He wanted to protect him from anything the world might throw at him.

'I want . . .' He ducked his gaze, face heating under Pie's scrutiny. 'I want to make you happy. I'm just not sure I can.'

Pie's face lit up with the force of the summer sun. 'You're doing a good job of it so far. Believe me.'

Logan tightened his grip. 'I want to.'

Pie leaned in and whispered in his ear. 'Let's go back inside and I'll show you how else you can make me happy.'

Chapter Twenty-Two

In the distance, barely visible against the night, a small light glowed.

'Land!' Logan called. A beacon on the headland to warn ships of the coast and a sign his journey on the ship was almost at an end.

'Thank fuck, a break,' Pie muttered next to him. 'I've had entirely too much of ships right now.'

The wind had picked up in the late afternoon. Better to reach their destination, but it meant the ship moved in a series of lurches. The downward motion felt like falling, and Logan didn't have the rolling gait the sailors adopted to compensate. It was an exhilarating sensation, a bit like riding a giant, galloping horse.

Pie, on the other hand, did not find the experience exhilarating.

The ship dropped again, and Pie closed his eyes with a groan, leaning out over the rail. Logan rubbed a hand over his husband's back. He'd been reluctant to let Pie out of bed, but when the wind picked up, Pie had declared that he was not staying shut up in a box to puke, and if Logan got in his way, he'd throw up on him too.

As the ship moved closer, a second light appeared in Logan's peripheral vision. This one was lower and larger. The capital city. Williams had told them she'd bring the ship in just around the coast, and they could make their way to the library from there, then meet the ship again at Mywin.

'All ready for your next adventure, Logan?' the countess called from behind them. Logan rolled his eyes as she crept up on them. She stood next to him at the rail, closed her eyes and took a deep breath. 'What a beautiful night.'

'No, it's not.' Pie sighed queasily. 'There's fuck all beautiful about anything right now.'

'I see you've reached the "feeling well enough to be absolutely miserable" stage of recovery, Al darling.' She chuckled and reached past Logan to pat Pie's shoulder. 'Look at the horizon. It'll help.'

'Once we're off the ship, he'll be composing ten verse ballads about the glories of sailing,' Logan said with a smile, clapping Pie on the back.

'No I—' He paused to retch. 'I bloody won't.'

'Can you keep an eye on him for me?' Logan asked the countess. 'There's something I need to sort out before we leave.'

'Of course.' She put her arm around Pie. 'One more day, and then we'll be tomb-robbing. Try to focus on how much fun we'll have.'

Logan staggered across the deck and headed into the ship. Before he could reach his planned destination, someone called his name. He turned to see Gary coming up from the galley.

'We want in too,' the youth said. 'Me and Freddy. We want to come to the library.'

'Not sure a library is the best place for a unicorn,' Logan commented. He had enough to worry about with Seraphina and Erin, not to mention being away from Pie again. But . . . 'Still, you're getting better with a sword. Perhaps having another strong hand would be useful.'

Gary's face lit up. 'I am, aren't I? I've been practising with some of the sailors. And Freddy can get us instantly to Mywin, save travelling there on foot.'

That sealed the deal for Logan. He held out his hand and Gary shook it firmly. He left the youth and carried on to the captain's cabin.

'Come in,' Williams's voice called as he knocked on her door. She looked up from her desk as he entered. 'What can I do for you, Bear?'

Stop calling me that, he almost answered, but held his tongue. Logan the Bear had been his identity for so long. He couldn't shed it like an old cloak.

'I need a weapon,' he explained. 'I've managed to lose mine.'

'Careless,' she chided, but a smile danced on her lips. 'I thought you might be after something, and I think I have just the thing. Wait here.'

She entered a side door that probably led to her personal cabin and walked out a moment or two later with an axe. It was a single head, and a longer shaft than his previous one. But the blade had a wicked edge to it and the steel was clean and unblemished. She handed it to him.

'I took this off the man who tried to kill my wife. Seems fitting that someone should protect her with it.'

He took it from her carefully, feeling the weight and balance of it. It would be different to using his old axe, which was a heavy, thunderous thing. A barbarian's thing. If he was going to change himself, then a new weapon was an excellent start.

'I'd be honoured to protect your wife,' he said. 'Thank you.'

'Use it well then, Logan the Legend.'

The ship dropped anchor in a small bay off the coast from the sprawling city. On deck, Freddy opened up a portal. Logan looked at the gathered group.

'Let's get some answers,' he said.

'The ship will head to Mywin,' Captain Williams confirmed. 'We'll meet everyone there. Everyone, you hear, Logan?' She wrapped a hand tightly around her wife's.

Logan held Pie's hand just as tight. 'Everyone.'

Williams kissed her wife one more time, and both groups stepped through the portal into the twilight of the unicorn ranch. The two spellcasters looked on in awe. Logan pulled Pie into his arms.

'Be safe,' he said, his voice rough and unsteady.

'I'll be fine.' Pie wrapped his arm around Logan. 'Especially now I'm off the ship. You're the one heading off into danger. I'd come with you, but we both know that isn't a good idea.' He glanced down at his side, as if he could see the bandages through the shirt.

Logan stroked a thumb across Pie's cheek, then over his lips. 'I promise I'll be careful. And you take care too. Don't let the countess push you into staying in that tomb a minute more than necessary.' He leaned in and kissed Pie, savouring the moment. 'I love you.'

Pie closed his eyes, pressed his forehead against Logan's. 'I love you too.'

Logan let go and turned to Gary. 'Time to go, lad.'

'Logan!' Pie called. 'That's a powerful weapon you've got there. You'd better come back and show it to me properly, you hear?'

Behind him, the countess let out a laugh and Logan's ears warmed.

Bards and necromancers. A friendship to be feared.

Gary moved a hand on Freddy's shoulder, and another portal opened, showing the cliffs above Mywin. The countess hurried towards it, then stopped and tapped a finger against the side of her mouth.

'While you're here, Gary sweetheart, you should probably check up on your uncle. You might not get a chance for a while.'

The youth's eyes widened, and he looked to Logan for approval. Logan found he couldn't say no to that earnest expression. He couldn't exactly complain about someone worrying about their loved one.

'Go on then, lad. But don't take too long.'

'Oh, the night's young yet, Logan. Plenty of time. Why don't you show the ladies around, Gary sweetheart?'

'What are you planning?' Logan whispered.

She gave him a wink. 'Just thinking we don't know what's coming, or how much time we'll have for relaxing. Might as well enjoy the moment while we can. I'll be waiting on the other side, Al darling, as this place doesn't agree with me. I'm sure you can fill the time while Gary checks up on his uncle.'

Logan snorted. She was the least subtle person he'd ever met. Still, she had a point. He offered a hand to Pie. 'Come take a walk with me.'

They walked down the path into a wooded valley.

'You know everyone there knows what you mean by "take a walk", right?' Pie gave him a wink. 'Well, with the possible exception of Gary.'

'I'm sure the countess will explain at length if he asks.' Logan shrugged. 'Who knows what tomorrow will bring? I'm long past caring if someone feels affronted by me spending some alone time with my husband.'

'Good for you.' Pie's hand tightened around Logan's. 'I'm going to get some good stories out of this.'

Logan laughed. 'We'll be living off this one for the rest of our lives. You'll pack out the pub. Old Man Weaver will have to expand his common room to fit in everyone coming to hear you. We'll be—'

Pie stepped in front of him, pressed his lips against Logan's. 'I'm scared too,' he said as they parted.

Logan nodded. He took off his cloak and spread it on the ground under a sprawling tree. Pie sat down next to him.

'I'm sorry,' Pie said. His voice cracked. 'I'm so sorry I got us caught up in this. I—'

Logan put a finger on his husband's lips. 'No more sorrys.'

Pie kissed him, softly, tenderly, begging forgiveness with actions rather than words now. Logan put a hand on the side of his face, looking into eyes of green and brown. Looking into home.

'You want this?' he asked softly.

'More than anything,' Pie replied.

Logan lifted Pie's shirt over his head. Logan kissed him, then moved his lips down Pie's chest. Pie stiffened against him. Logan's eyes traced the journey his lips had taken, enjoying the lines of Pie's muscles, the swirling collection of tattoos that started on his shoulder and moved down his arm, mapping events in his life. The V-shaped lines that drew his attention from the hips to further down.

In the tree, a bird scolded them, harsh cries echoing through the leaves. Logan ignored it. It didn't matter. Nothing else mattered right now. One hand dug into Pie's hair, pushing their lips together again. The other undid the buckle on his trousers with practised ease. It didn't matter.

When they returned, Gary and the spellcasters were waiting for them. Gary's face blushed and he couldn't quite meet Logan's eye. Pie stepped forwards and gave the unicorn a bow.

'One quick trip to Morigen's tomb please, Freddy.'

The portal shimmered into existence. Across the hazy border between realms, the countess played fetch with Ossymandias. She raised a hand in greeting. Pie pulled Logan's hand to his lips.

'You better come back to me in one piece, Logan the Legend.'

Logan scowled. 'How have you heard about that?'

'Gonna make sure the entire country hears about it,' Pie replied with a grin. He let go of Logan's hand and stepped through before Logan could protest further, and the portal winked out of existence.

'How was your uncle?' Logan asked Gary to distract himself from seeing his husband disappear.

'He seemed fine, but . . .' Gary swallowed. 'Something's wrong. I know it is. He's nervous.'

'Do you want to stay here?'

He shook his head. 'No, I want to come with you.'

'Good.' Logan put a hand on his shoulder. 'Let's go and investigate this library, then. Can't imagine many places are safer than a library.'

Chapter Twenty-Three

Without checking to see if anyone else had followed, Logan stepped through the portal. It took him to the top of a coastal path that looked down on the sprawling capital city, Iveirrel. The library stood on the edge by the walls, tall amongst the clustered buildings, made of white stone that glowed faintly in the moonlight. It stood in the centre of a well-tended garden across the city from the palace. Around him, the woods were quiet. Nothing but his footsteps on the path, no sign of any living being. Yet the creeping sensation of someone watching him raised the hairs on the back of his neck.

One by one, the others emerged on the path at his side. Seraphina and Erin eyed each other nervously. Logan wondered how much experience either of them had in dangerous situations. He'd always preferred to travel and fight alone, not having to rely on anyone else to pull their weight or hold their own.

'Don't worry,' Gary said cheerfully. 'Logan and I have been in lots of danger. We'll protect you.'

Logan suppressed a groan.

'I'm perfectly capable of protecting myself, thank you very much.' Seraphina snapped her fingers and a spark zipped in front of Gary's nose. His eyes widened and Freddy snorted.

'I wasn't saying you couldn't,' Gary said, staring at his boots. 'I was just trying to be reassuring.'

She sniffed and set off. As she walked, she waved a hand down in front of her, and her blue dress changed to a dark green to blend in better with the woods.

Logan patted a hand on Gary's shoulder, then set off after her.

'There's an old wellhouse not far from here,' Erin said suddenly. 'We should be able to get in that way. It dried up years ago, so it hasn't been used.'

Logan nodded. 'That sounds promising. Lead the way.'

The path to the wellhouse was overgrown by the surrounding thick foliage, which was busy crawling up the walls. It didn't take long for nature to force its way back to the spaces humans had once claimed.

Logan held up a hand and motioned for the others to stay back. He crept forwards, alert for any sound. The night pressed in, his heartbeat loud in his ears. Every shifting shadow caught his attention, every shiver of every leaf.

He made a circuit of the building and returned to the others. 'I don't see anyone around.'

The door to the wellhouse was locked, but the wooden frame was so rotten it only took a few kicks to break down. Every blow seemed to echo and amplify off each tree until Logan was sure they must hear it in the capital. He pulled away the broken planks and ushered the spellcasters inside.

'Stay out here, lad,' Logan whispered to Gary. The youth's face crumpled into a pout and Logan gave his shoulder a squeeze. 'I don't think unicorns belong in libraries. Besides, if anyone does show up, you're our warning. You could be instrumental in saving our lives.'

That seemed to do the trick. Gary nodded and stepped back, scanning for any threat. Logan prayed for a quiet night for both their sakes.

Seraphina held up her hand, a little glowing ball of light once again dancing above her palm. They stood at the top of a set of steps leading down into a small rectangular room that smelled of damp and mud. The walls of the wellhouse were decorated in soft blue and dove brown tiles that swirled around each other. In the centre of the room sat the stone well, hidden by a wooden cover. And beyond that, another door.

The passage to the library ran straight as an arrow. By each wall was a channel, and Logan suspected the spellcasters had simply done some magic to bring the water from the well to wherever they needed it, rather than carrying it like mundane folks. It felt endless, just more of the same blue and brown tiles as they walked and walked.

Eventually it ended in a nondescript wooden door. Given the wealth of information that waited on the other side, it felt plain and shabby to Logan. He eased Seraphina out of the way and put his ear to the door.

Silence.

Of course, the door could have been too thick, or whatever was on the other side was aware and waiting for them. Maybe whatever it was moved with the stealth of a unicorn or . . .

'Are we going to go in or stand here admiring the woodwork?' Seraphina asked. 'It's a very nice door, I'm sure, but we are on a bit of a schedule here.'

'Just checking,' Logan growled. 'Better to be safe than sorry.'

He stepped out into the library and his breath caught in his throat. He was in a vast, roughly circular room. It rose up high, to a domed glass ceiling. The moon above drenched everything in silvery light. Immense shelves divided the room into four quadrants, but they didn't quite connect in the centre. Instead, there was a gap large enough for two people to walk through side by side, so you could see a little way into each quadrant. And each of the four shelves ended with a spiral staircase of iron steps to allow readers up to the next levels.

Books and scrolls lined the walls from floor to ceiling. They covered the curved exterior walls, and the four dividing ones up to the staircases. At regular distances, narrow walkways ran around at a higher level.

Seraphina choked back a sob. 'It's so beautiful.'

It was kind of beautiful, Logan agreed, with the stark moonlight catching the curves and flourishes of the ironwork. But there was something *other* about the place too. It was not a place for the likes of him, and he had a feeling it knew that.

'Where to?' he asked Erin. She checked a directory on the counter at the entrance.

'History, so that quadrant, second floor.' She pointed towards one of the staircases. 'Follow me.'

Logan let her lead, bringing up the rear. He hated the spiral staircase – tight and constricting, it gave him no room to do anything but go up or down – but he hated the hanging walkways more.

He'd never considered himself afraid of heights, but then he'd never been on anything suspended before. A cliff or tree might be high, but they were solid. They didn't wobble under your feet, threatening to spill you down onto the cold marble below. He clung to the rail, trying to ignore the fact that if the walkway did collapse, holding the rail would do absolutely nothing to save him.

What kind of mad man had built this place?

Logan huffed a sigh and focused on a single point on the bookshelf, not on the thirty-foot drop beneath him. His jaw ached.

'I've found something,' Erin called.

Logan relaxed and the walkway wobbled. He tightened his grip again in a hurry, breathing heavily. Erin hurried over, making the planks bounce with each step. Logan concentrated on not being sick.

'What did you find?' he asked, a cold bead of sweat running down the back of his neck.

'You all right?' the spellcaster asked, raising an eyebrow.

'Not important.' Logan shook his head. 'Will it help us, and can we examine it on the ground?'

The woman gave him a grin. 'Of course.'

One claustrophobic trip down the spiral staircase again, and Logan was back on the solid marble floor. He resisted the urge to kiss it. Erin laid the book on the floor and Seraphina brought over the light, softening the harsh shadows of the moonlight.

'It's an account of the founding of the capital,' Erin said. 'I remembered some of the legends about this place. When the necromancers ruled the island, the capital used to be further down the coast. A star fell and smashed into the ground there, creating the valley we see today. It turned the sky dark and scorched the earth, destroying all that was here. Nothing has ever grown there since. The whole valley is dead.'

'How does this help us?' Logan asked.

'This book goes into more detail about the events of the star. According to this, something came out of it, something that killed and ate everything in its path.' She opened the book and flicked through a few pages, long fingers manipulating the paper with practised ease. '*And Adphega entered the earth and became part of the earth and from the earth spawned things that took human shape that were but empty shells.*'

'That sounds like the Chalice,' Seraphina said. 'And it would explain why the countess said it was alive. It was part of this creature, Adphega. And if the Chalice is alive . . .'

'Then the creature is likely alive as well,' Erin replied.

'Does it say how to kill it?' Logan asked. If it was alive, then it could be killed. He clung to that thought.

Erin ran her finger down the pages. 'It ran amok, killing and destroying. Every life it took made it stronger. Eventually, there was a battle. Hale, the bard, distracted the creature and the tail was cut off with a knife made by Morigen. Spellcasters drove the creature into the ocean and bound it down there. And the last necromancers sealed the tail deep in the mountains.'

'So, when King Ervin fell overboard, could he have made a connection with this *thing*, still living under the waves?' Seraphina said. 'Perhaps their shared hatred of spellcasters was what brought them together.' She shuddered. 'And we've delivered the Chalice right into its hands!'

'Who's to say it even has hands?' Logan said. Seraphina turned on him and he shrugged. 'I guess that's not important right now. Let's have a quick look around, see if there's anything more on this thing, then head back to the ship.'

Seraphina gave him one last glare, then spun on her heel and strode towards the staircase. The others picked themselves up and followed after her. Logan glanced at the hanging platforms and shuddered. Hopefully he'd never have to see those again in his life.

He glanced towards the passage to the wellhouse, anxious not just to be away from the library but to get back to Pie.

A humming sound caught his attention. It swelled, becoming a rapid drumbeat. No, not a drum, hooves. The unicorn burst through the doorway and skidded to a stop on the marble floor.

'Someone's coming!' Gary called, slipping down from Freddy's back. He drew the sword the countess had given him, but Logan shook his head. Could Ophelia have betrayed them again? No, he had to have more faith in her.

'No time to fight. Open a portal and get us out of here, now.' He turned his attention to the spellcasters on the gantry. 'Get down here! We're leaving!'

Something clattered across the floor from the door behind him and smashed with a musical tinkle. A thick blue smoke rose up in front of Gary. He coughed and staggered, his knees buckling. He hooked an arm around Freddy's neck, fingers tangling in his mane. The unicorn trotted backwards, and Gary slumped at Logan's feet.

Logan pulled Gary close to him. The unicorn pranced, making Logan nervous that it would step on its trainer accidentally. The two spellcasters hurried over to him.

'The Black Company,' Erin said, her voice shaking. She wrapped her arms around herself, her face pale in the gloom.

Logan didn't care who they were. He raised the axe, ready to charge. If he had to do it alone, so be it. The bluish smoke dissipated, spreading out from the vial. His head ached, a sharp throb that started in one temple, and quickly spread to the other, then to the back of his head. The room swayed like a ship in a storm.

'Cover your mouths,' he said to the spellcasters, holding his shirt up to his nose. He couldn't fight like this, and the plumes of smoke were thickening by the second.

'Come out quietly and you won't get hurt!' A familiar voice called across the library, echoing around them. Logan peeked behind a shelf. Fox-Fur stood in the doorway, a crossbow raised, but he was alone. 'You have no way out of here. The other entrance is covered. Play nice, Bear. This is for the best.'

'How the fuck did you find us?' Logan demanded.

'Spotted your group checking up on the ranch,' Fox-Fur replied smugly. 'I'd been there to have a little chat with the owner. Don't worry, I sent men after your pretty husband and the necromancer as well.'

Logan's blood chilled. He needed to get out of here, get to Pie. No time to muck around or play nice. But without Gary, they couldn't just get out of here. He eased Gary's unconscious form onto Freddy's back and turned to Erin and Seraphina. 'Can't get a portal open with Gary unconscious. Get out. I'll keep them distracted.'

The unicorn regarded him with dark eyes. Logan had no idea if it understood anything he'd said, but at the end of the day it was an animal, and a slap on the arse would make it run.

Fox-Fur twisted as the unicorn flew past him. He lashed out at Seraphina, but she flashed up a ball of light and threw it at his face. The man cried out, covering his eyes, and Logan cheered in his heart.

Logan crept around the shelves, keeping close to the books. Fox-Fur shouted for him again and kicked out at a stack of books close to him, his insults getting coarser. Logan gritted his teeth and pressed on. He took another step, his legs as heavy as iron. The edges of his vision faded to cloudy white, his head throbbing in beat with his heart.

Couldn't pass out here. Couldn't abandon Pie.

'I owe you for punching my husband,' Logan said, stepping out from the cover of the shelf.

Fox-Fur grinned and set down the crossbow. He held his arms out wide. 'Come and get me, *Bear*.'

Logan raised his axe with a snarl and charged. The room swayed around him, but his hatred kept him focused. Fox-Fur ducked under a clumsy swing and came up inside his guard. His fist collided with Logan's jaw, setting off an explosion of colours behind Logan's eyes.

He stumbled back but caught his balance and tightened his grip on the axe. He couldn't see how he was going to get out of this, but if he could get the others out, then they could get to Mywin, help Pie and the countess. It might be enough.

Not for Pie.

The thought thundered through his mind like a unicorn. He'd been preparing himself mentally to be the sacrifice, to be satisfied if he saved others. But that wasn't fair on Pie. Dammit, it wasn't fair on him. Why shouldn't he get the happy ending for once?

With a growl, he threw himself at Fox-Fur, grabbed the front of his shirt, and rammed their foreheads together. Logan's head was already ringing, so it made little difference. Fox-Fur howled in pain.

He staggered back into the shelves, sending a pile of scrolls scattering. Logan pointed the blade of his axe against the man's exposed neck.

'Do it,' Fox-Fur hissed. 'You won't win. You can't defeat Ervin.'

Logan charged past towards the doorway and ran for his life.

'Bear, you coward!' Fox-Fur yelled.

But Logan didn't care. The ship was waiting for them. Pie was waiting for him.

So close to the outside. He couldn't stop now. Couldn't fail now. He took another step, rubbing a hand over his eyes. Three figures outside stood by several horses. Three. He could take three more down. Had to take three more. For Pie. The world span faster now. He stumbled, catching himself on the cool tiled wall.

Those weren't horses.

Logan's knees buckled and he fell to the forest floor, in front of the troop of unicorns.

Interlude

Seven Months Ago

Logan opened his eyes to a strange face.

'Ah,' it said. 'You're awake.'

The face didn't seem particularly threatening, with thin white hair and an abundance of wrinkles, but Logan ached from head to foot, so something had to have hurt him. He tried to assess his situation. White walls, white sheets. Lots of white. The scent of camomile and willow-bark. The man placed a rough hand on his forehead.

'Your fever's going down, but I imagine you still feel like shit.'

'Fair assessment.' Logan struggled to sit up and waited for the room to stop spinning. 'Where am I?'

'Healing house of Panae the Benevolent. I'm Healer Frakes. You took a nasty blow to your leg, but I think I've saved it. Gonna hurt like a bitch for the rest of your life, though,' he added cheerfully.

That sounded about right. Through the fog of fever, Logan pulled at his memories. Walking through the city with Pie. Someone jumping them. Getting in the way of the hand axe.

'What about the man I was with?' he asked.

The healer snorted. 'Oh, there's no helping that one.'

Logan's gut constricted. He'd saved Pie, hadn't he? 'Wh–where is he?' He made an attempt to get off the bed and the healer pushed him back down.

'Hmm? Oh, I sent him out to get some supplies because he was pissing me off being underfoot. He's not hurt, if that's what you mean. If he was, he might shut up for five minutes.' He snorted again. 'Bards.'

'Bards,' agreed Logan, but his heart soared. He lay back, let the healer check the bandages on his leg.

The door opened and he lifted his head. Pie entered, saw Logan staring, and dropped the basket he had been carrying. The healer swore loudly. Pie rushed to the bed and gripped Logan's hands.

'Logan! You're awake. I've been so worried. How's your leg? Does it hurt? Did the grumpy healer say if you'd keep it?'

Logan laughed. 'Pie, breathe. The grumpy healer said my leg will be fine.'

'No, I didn't.' Frakes peered at the discarded basket and shook his head. 'Said it would hurt like a bitch.'

Logan wasn't sure the man had quite the right temperament for healing, but he'd done a good enough job to save Logan from losing a leg, so there was that.

'I didn't want to leave you,' Pie continued, 'but he said you needed a few things, like eggs . . . oh.' He shot a guilty glance at the basket.

'Oh indeed,' the healer muttered. 'There goes breakfast.' He left the room, still grumbling to himself.

'Anyway, when I was walking around out there, I got to thinking.' Pie tightened his grip on Logan's hand and took a deep breath. 'Well, you're going to need some time to rest and recover, whatever happens with your leg, and maybe you should ease off the adventuring for a bit. Perhaps we can find a nice little cottage; I can play in the village inn, you know, just for as long as you want, and what I wanted to say is, um, maybe . . .' His grip on Logan's hand threatened to break fingers. 'Marry me, Logan Theaker.'

Logan's breath caught in his throat. He let the words play in his head over and over again. He didn't want to risk them being the product of pain or fever.

Pie looked away. 'I'm sorry. I shouldn't have. I just thought, after everything, that maybe . . .'

Logan pulled a hand free. 'Pie. Breathe.' A smile broke across Logan's face, and he feared he'd never stop smiling. He rested his palm against Pie's cheek. 'Yes.'

'Yes?' Pie asked, a tremor in his voice.

'Yes, I'll marry you.'

Pie punched the air with a delighted cry. Logan grabbed his wrist and pulled him in for a kiss. His head ached, still fuzzy with fever, but a warm, comfortable feeling rushed through him.

'It should have been more romantic,' Pie said. 'Flowers or starry skies. But I could have lost you back there and I didn't want to waste another moment.'

'I don't need flowers or stars. Just you. Tell me more about this cottage,' Logan said, patting the bed next to him.

Pie sat, snuggling close to him. 'It will be on the edge of a village, just you and me. We'll grow roses around the door and keep chickens.'

Logan wrapped an arm around him. 'Can we have a pig?'

'As many pigs as you like. Goats too. I can make cheese.'

'Not sure about goats,' Logan muttered. He'd never trusted anything with weird eyes. 'What about inside?'

'A hearth and a table. I'll cook for you every night. No more burned bread. And in the corner, one big bed.'

Logan closed his eyes, picturing it. 'Sounds perfect.'

Chapter Twenty-Four

Logan opened his eyes to a dark sky. Ophelia's face swam into view and he started with a yelp.

She scowled. 'You're such a pig, Logan.'

He sat up and clutched his aching head. 'What happened?'

'Saved your arse, didn't I?' Smug glee warmed her words. 'Got Seraphina to dump a bucket of water on Gary, got back to the ranch and collected a bunch of unicorns to rescue you. Turns out people find them pretty threatening.'

'Pie.' Logan got to his feet, looking around the lush meadow of the unicorn realm. Erin grabbed his arm as he stumbled. 'Got to get to Pie.'

'We need Gary for that,' Seraphina said. 'He went to speak to his uncle. Wanted to know why the Black Company were here. I told him it wasn't wise, but he wouldn't listen to me.' Her tone suggested she took that personally.

'The lad's tougher than he looks,' Logan said.

'He's so . . .' Seraphina twisted her braid. '. . . *Gary* about these things. He's always thinking the best of people.' She stamped her foot down. 'It's stupid.'

'Sometimes you just have to let men be stupid and stubborn,' Ophelia replied. 'It's in their blood. They don't know any better.'

Logan rolled his eyes at her, and she grinned. Despite his fears, it felt good to interact with her like this again.

They rushed down towards the cottage and Logan was once again thankful for the way the place seemed to wipe away his pain and injuries. His head felt clearer with every step.

'I don't know why the countess hates this place so.'

'The countess is a necromancer,' Erin said. 'Her power comes from drawing on death energies – the power released when something dies or decays. Spellcasting is based on life. It draws energy from living things, usually the spellcaster themselves, but particularly powerful ones can draw from other living creatures. This place is built from life magic. It cuts her off from the source of her powers and weakens her.'

'Gary?' Logan called as he knocked on the door. 'Time to go, lad.'

'He isn't going anywhere,' an unfamiliar voice replied.

Logan sighed. 'Not speaking to you. Gary. We need to go. Pie and the countess could be in trouble. We need you, lad.'

There was no answer, so Logan kicked the door open. Almost immediately, an apple hit him in the face. Logan staggered – fruit was surprisingly hard – and wiped juice from his eye. Gary stood on the far side of the table, and slightly in front of him, a tall man with a dour face. The uncle, Logan guessed. Gary clearly didn't get his looks from that side of the family.

Another apple flew off the table by itself and narrowly missed hitting Logan, smashing to pulp on the doorframe. *Of course, another spellcaster.*

'Come on, Gary. Let's go.' Logan noted the knife in the man's hand. He hoped he wouldn't raise it against a family member, but he couldn't take the risk.

'Gary's a good lad. I raised him from a small boy. He won't disobey me. Will you, boy?'

'That true?' Logan asked. He met Gary's eyes, and Gary looked away. 'Seems to me, if someone raised you it should be because they care, not so they can stop you from living your life. Family shouldn't be about control.'

Gary glanced between Logan and his uncle.

'Your place is here. You think I can manage all this by myself?' his uncle demanded, looking furiously at Gary, who was shrinking by the moment.

'That's his choice to make,' Logan replied. He kept his voice soft and reasonable, his eyes on Gary.

'He'll spoil the plan!' his uncle shouted.

'What plan?' Gary asked. 'What are you up to? Why were the Black Company here? They hunt spellcasters. Why are they here, in the sanctuary?'

'Get out of my house!' The uncle raised his hands, moving them in a complex, circular motion. The air pushed against Logan with the force of a gale. The cupboard doors rattled and slammed. Logan gripped the doorframe, fighting to keep himself from being blown away.

'What are you doing? Uncle, stop! You'll hurt him. He's my friend.' Gary cried.

'I'm doing what needs to be done.' His uncle's arms moved faster, and Logan dug his fingers into the doorframe. Dust in the air made his eyes water.

'Stop it!' Gary pulled at his uncle's arm and the wave of air buffeting Logan slowed a little. He pushed forwards, reaching for the solid wooden table in the centre of the room.

'Enough!' Seraphina shouted. A blinding white light flashed, making everyone cry out and clutch their eyes. By the time Logan had cleared the dancing colours from his vision, she'd crossed the room and grabbed Gary by the arm. 'We need to go, now. Go get on your shiny, pointy horse and get us a portal. If you want to keep your pretty face here, that's your business. But we're leaving.'

'It's a unicorn,' Gary retorted. 'Wait, you think my face is pretty?'

Logan could almost hear the eye-roll from Seraphina. He approached the man, who was still clutching his face and groaning. 'What plan?'

'None of your business.' The man groaned.

'Yes Uncle, what plan?' Gary pulled away from Seraphina and stood over the man. He clenched his fists. Logan had never seen the youth so angry before. Threaten the boy's unicorns, and there was hell to pay.

Logan hefted the axe in his hands.

The man cowered and his shoulders slumped in defeat. 'The king wanted the unicorns. All of them. It was meant to be my ticket out of here and back to the real world. Enough money to pay off my debts, get my creditors off my back, and still live in comfort for the rest of my days. I was doing it for us,' he said to Gary.

The youth was growing angrier by the moment. 'What does he want with them?' Gary asked, anger making his voice soft.

'How should I know? He can eat them for all I care.'

Gary rounded on his uncle, but the man slapped his hand away.

'I'm supposed to bring them to him this morning.'

Logan paused. 'Where?'

The man shrugged. 'Teclif beach. On the cliffs overlooking the wastelands. The Black Company were supposed to take them, but they've all run off for some reason. So I need Gary. If I don't get them there, the king will kill me.'

Logan nodded. Now they knew where to find and stop Ervin. 'When?'

'At dawn.'

'Then we need to hurry,' Logan muttered.

'I want you gone,' Gary said to his uncle. 'I'm going to go and help be a hero, and when I come back, I want every trace of you gone from here.'

He turned away and hurried towards Seraphina. Logan gave the man a last glance to make sure he wasn't going to try anything, but he was broken and sobbing on the floor.

Logan caught up with Seraphina and Gary as they reached Freddy.

'Get us out of here,' Logan ordered. 'Send Erin back to the ship. Erin, go tell your wife to bring the ship to Teclif. The rest of us will go to Mywin. We've only got hours before the king tries to raise Adphega.'

The unicorn moved its head, and Logan stumbled through onto the cliffs by the tomb. His stomach twisted, dreading what he'd find.

Down below, the sea smacked against the cliffs like a hungry caged animal. Away from the unicorn farm, weariness gripped at his limbs. His leg throbbed in a way that almost felt judgemental. Nothing moved, but blood splattered the grass, dark in the moonlight.

'Pie! Where are you?'

'Logan!'

At the sound of the voice, Logan told his injury to go fuck itself, and started to run. He caught sight of Pie barrelling up the path towards him. He stopped, digging in his heels, and held his arms out. Pie leapt and threw himself at Logan, grunting in pain as Logan wrapped his arms around him.

'Ow, ow, stupid injuries.'

'Idiot.' Logan pulled his husband close. Pie rested his head against Logan's shoulder. Logan breathed him in, warm and welcome, the scent of long summer days and winter nights huddled under furs. He tightened his grip. 'What happened? Where's the countess?'

'I'm fine, Logan dear, thank you.'

Her voice sent waves of relief through him.

'The good thing about a tomb is there's a nice lot of useful bones in there,' she said with a grin. 'Spellcaster Morigen and his family were most obliging in dispatching the king's men. And Ossy bit a man's finger off, didn't you, you good boy!'

The skeleton puppy danced around her feet in delight.

'I'm glad you're both safe,' Logan said.

'What happened? How did they find us?' Pie asked.

'Hush.' He kissed Pie hard, running a hand through his hair. Pie closed his eyes, one hand caressing Logan's cheek. 'Let me have a moment. It's about all we've got.'

'Things didn't go well?' the countess asked. 'What did you find out?'

Logan gestured to the ground and they sat down. Gary, Ophelia, and Seraphina joined them. Pie gave them both a cheerful wave.

Logan described what they'd learned in the library, the encounter with Fox-Fur, and the subsequent escape to the unicorn farm. At each detail, Pie tightened his grip, until Logan had to gently extract his arm and rub away the pins and needles.

'What was my uncle thinking?' Gary asked. He ran a hand down Freddy's shoulder and the unicorn snorted.

'He's a bad man.' Seraphina crossed her arms.

'He's not!' Gary turned on her. The unicorn snorted again, louder this time. 'After my father died, he took me in, cared for me. You take that back.'

She rolled her eyes.

Logan held up a hand. 'This isn't the time. Gary, I don't think your uncle is a bad man. I think he's a tired man, who saw an opportunity for a change of life and seized it. He's not our enemy. King Ervin is.'

'Not even him, I think.' The countess stroked at her chin. 'This thing, that was sealed beneath the ocean. That's what we're fighting against. I fear what is left of Ervin might not be possible to save.'

'How do we beat Adphega?' Logan looked around the group. 'Last time it took a powerful group of spellcasters and necromancers to just lock it away.'

'Well, we've got a group of spellcasters, and a necromancer,' Pie pointed out. 'And you and me, and a ghost, and a ship with an angry name. That's a good start, right?'

'And a herd of unicorns,' Seraphina pointed out.

'I don't think we need to involve the unicorns again,' Gary protested.

'But they're creatures that tap into magic itself.' Seraphina threw open her arms to emphasise her point. 'Creatures that can control the boundaries between dimensions.'

'When did those two notice each other?' Pie whispered in Logan's ear.

'Pretty sure they hate each other,' he replied with a shrug.

'Nah, I bet you anything they'll be kissing in a day or two.'

Logan thought about that. 'Two weeks cleaning out the goats says you're wrong.'

Pie held out a hand. 'You're on.'

'You haven't told them the best bit, Al darling,' the countess said. 'Tell them what we found.'

'Oh, right.' Pie gave Logan's hand a squeeze and stood up. 'So, after being freed from retching my guts up on the stupid ship—'

Seraphina narrowed her eyes.

' —We reached the wonderful dry land and town of Mywin. The lovely Countess Ariadne and I made for the tomb of Morigen. With the stars as our witnesses, we stole into the tomb.'

'Could you get to the point?' Seraphina remarked impatiently.

The countess glared. 'You have absolutely no sense of theatre, do you?'

'No. What I do have is a mad king, armed with a powerful necromantic item, who seems intent on raising something horrific in a few hours.'

'She does have a point,' Logan admitted.

'I suppose.' Pie's shoulders slumped. He handed Logan something wrapped in a dirty rag. 'We found this in the tomb. Ariadne believes it's the weapon Morigen used to cut the Chalice from the creature.'

Logan unwrapped the rags and held up a knife with a curved edge. The blade glittered, and he felt the same pricking sensation on his scalp as he had when he touched Seraphina's knife. But there was something else, a coldness that reminded him more of Ophelia.

'Be careful. It's very sharp.' The countess held up a bandaged finger. 'Ask me how I know.'

'So, what do we do?' Gary asked.

'We have to stop Ervin,' Logan replied. 'Stop him using the Chalice to bring the . . . Adphega back.'

'What if we don't? If we don't have the power to kill this thing, what then?' Seraphina asked. 'Look, I don't like the idea any more than you, but the question needs answering.'

'We could try and evacuate Rekmin?' Ophelia suggested. 'Once people are aware of the threat, we can build up numbers, but if it comes on them unawares, thousands could die.'

'That's a good point,' the countess replied. 'But are we any more likely to be able to do that? Who's to say they'd even believe us if we could get through to anyone?'

The mining town of Rekmin, sat between Teclif beach and the edge of the wastelands, wasn't large by any stretch of the imagination, but there would still be hundreds of lives, men, women and children, all at risk of being snuffed out. If only there was some way to get the word out about a threat – even if the threat they warned about was a different, more believable one.

'We need a performance,' he said, looking at Pie.

Every head turned to him.

'You've got an idea, haven't you?' Pie said, his eyes shining with pride.

'Countess, how many skeletons can you control?' Logan asked.

'If I've got the bones, then as many as you need.' There was no boasting in her voice this time.

Logan nodded. 'I can't believe I'm saying this, but we'll need as many of the dead as you can raise. Send them through the streets of Rekmin. Get them to drive the citizens away, make them fear the city as much as possible and they'll run. That's as much as we can do right now.'

'The Night of the Walking Dead.' Pie waved a hand in front of him as if announcing his next song. 'Has quite a nice ring to it.'

'This isn't a story,' Logan said.

Pie gave him a grin. 'That's where you're wrong. Everything's a story, love.'

'What about the rest of us?' Seraphina asked. At her side, Gary nodded. 'Even if we get the city cleared, we've got to stop that thing. Right?'

'Right,' Logan agreed. They were going home. They were going back to the cottage. Back to Bacon and the bloody goats. He wasn't going to let anything, no matter how big and ugly it was, stop that from happening. 'Don't suppose there was anything in that book that gives us any more information on how to stop this thing? Or why the king would want a herd of unicorns?'

'I think it feeds off their magic,' Seraphina said. 'I think that's why the area where it landed ended up so dead. And it would explain why the king wanted the unicorns. A meal of a dozen magical beasts would be just what it needs after being dormant so long.'

Gary's face turned a sickly green. He stood and hurried over to Freddy, winding his fingers through the unicorn's mane.

Pie got to his feet and put his hand on the youth's shoulder. 'We're not going to let that happen, are we, Logan?'

'Damn straight.' Logan smacked a hand into his palm. 'That unicorn's saved my life several times now. No way am I going to let anyone turn it into a snack.'

Gary bit his lip. 'Thank you.'

Pie squeezed his shoulder. 'That's it. Don't worry. We'll find a way to stop this, you'll see.'

Logan was less sure, but Pie's optimism was infectious. That's what a bard was. A wave of hope you couldn't avoid. A wave that went crashing through your mind, washing away doubt, spreading glory behind it. You couldn't help but feel good, no matter the reality.

A bit like the unicorn farm.

Unless you were the countess.

'I think you've given me an idea,' Logan said.

Chapter Twenty-Five

Pie and Gary looked hopeful, Seraphina surprised, and Ophelia dubious. Logan cleared his throat, suddenly uncertain under their gaze.

'Come on, you great lug,' Ophelia said. 'Don't keep us all in suspense. You aren't the bard, remember?'

Logan cleared his throat again. 'Fine. I was thinking about how the countess gets sick at the unicorn farm. You said it's because the magic doesn't agree with you, right?'

'That's correct, Logan dear,' she said. 'You've been paying attention.'

'Well . . .' He rubbed the back of his head. 'If this thing eats magic, then it's the opposite of the countess, right? If we let it loose on the farm, it would feast and get stronger.'

'I hope you're not suggesting we give it a good meal and hope it gets sleepy,' Seraphina said. 'I don't think that's likely.'

Logan shook his head. 'If there was a place like the unicorn farm, but for necromancy, and we sent it there, wouldn't that weaken it, if not kill it?'

'Send it to a realm of death magic . . . By the Dark Mother, Logan dear, that actually makes sense.'

He glared at her. 'I'm not stupid, you know.'

She patted his arm. 'I know, I know. Brains and brawn. You got quite the catch, Al darling.'

Pie puffed out his chest. 'Don't I know it.'

'Is it possible?' Seraphina asked. She turned to Gary. 'Could you open a portal like that?'

He rested his face against Freddy's neck. 'I . . . I don't know.'

'I believe in you.' Logan said. 'But be quick. We need a solution by the time we've dealt with Rekmin. We've got maybe a couple of hours before Ervin arrives at dawn.'

Gary's eyes widened and a grin broke out on his face. He nodded. 'I will.'

Logan picked up a piece of driftwood and sketched out a rough map of the landscape. 'Teclif beach is where the king will summon the thing. The spellcasters will head up on to the cliffs, overlooking the battle but not in it. Their job is to help me drive that thing towards the portal, or help protect me from anyone who might interfere.'

Pie nodded, though the motion was stiff, awkward.

'Once Ervin works out what we're doing, he'll try and stop you – he'll kill you,' the countess cautioned, fear lacing her words.

'Most likely.' Logan replied. 'Whatever has control of Ervin isn't going to let him go so easily. We need to be prepared for a battle for all our lives.'

Seraphina paled. Her hand closed around Gary's.

Logan cleared his throat. This wasn't the time. Dawn inched closer.

'Gary, Seraphina,' Logan continued. 'Once that thing appears, you'll bring the unicorns onto the beach, here, and create the biggest portal you can.' He tapped his stick at the narrowest point. 'Keep the portal to the death magic realm open as best you can. We'll do the rest.' He looked around the group. 'We won't let this creature win. Adphega dies today.'

'Once you've evacuated the city, you'll need to stop Ervin on the beach. If you can't . . .' Seraphina twisted a lock of hair around her finger nervously.

'I've got a feeling I'm not going to like this, am I?' Pie muttered.

'Assuming we can even get a portal up in the first place, it's not going to walk in willingly,' Ophelia pointed out. 'You'll need to tempt it in.'

'I was right,' Pie said. 'I don't like this at all.'

Logan wrapped his arms around Pie. 'That'll be my job then.'

'Why?' Pie shoved his face against Logan. 'Why does it have to be you?'

'You said it yourself. Logan the Legend. That's me now. And I can't ask anyone to do a job I wouldn't do myself.'

'You're an idiot,' Pie said bitterly.

Logan lifted Pie's face gently, forced him to meet his eyes. 'Don't be miserable now. You've got the most important job of all. You're the bard. You're the hope.'

'Dammit, Logan.' Pie pulled away, a tear streaking down his face. 'This isn't fair.'

'It's not supposed to be.'

'Why can't you be the bard?'

Logan laughed. 'Swap places? Have you heard me sing?'

Pie lightly thumped a fist against Logan's chest. 'You've thought of everything, haven't you? Fine. But you're not getting away from me again. Morigen had Hale to distract the creature. If it rises, I can do the same.'

Logan wanted to protest, wanted to demand Pie stayed as far away from the portal as possible. But they'd come this far together. If everything ended in a few hours, they'd end it together. 'I know you can.'

'When this is all over, I'm going to write the ballad of Logan the Legend,' Pie said, punctuating each word with a tap on Logan's chest. 'They're going to be singing it right across the country. Every time you walk into the room, it'll start up.' He shook a finger in Logan's face. 'You're going to fucking hate it.'

Interlude

Six Months Ago

'Don't look,' Logan said.

'I can't look,' Pie replied. 'Your very large hands are completely smothering my face. How much further? Are we even in the same village?'

'It was a bit further out than I thought. I think the privacy will be nice. Watch your step here.' He guided Pie over a bump in the path.

'Mmm, just you and me, and no one to interrupt us. Sounds wonderful.'

'Right.' Logan stopped and Pie bumped up against his hands. 'It's . . . well, it's got a bit of work that needs doing.' His heart beat rapidly in his chest. Suddenly, this didn't sound like such a good idea. What if Pie mocked the price Logan had paid? What if he hated it?

'Do I get to see it, then?' Pie elbowed him in the ribs. 'Or am I condemned to spend the rest of my life blindfolded? Actually, I don't think I'd particularly mind that idea.'

Logan took a deep breath and lowered his hands. Pie blinked and rubbed his eyes. He went rigid.

Logan's heart sank. Of course, he hated it. It was a low, run-down building with a hole in the roof where last winter's snow had broken a beam. The window frames were warped from damp, and the whitewash peeled on the walls.

Pie gripped Logan's face between his palms, smothering it in kisses. 'It's perfect. I love it.' Before Logan could react, Pie bolted for the cottage. 'Look, we'll have a vegetable garden here, an apple tree over there! And a pig pen there! Oh, oh, and if we clear down that bit of bramble, we could put up a shed for goats or even a cow! What shall we do first?'

'Probably fix the hole in the roof,' Logan finally muttered, a smile breaking across his face at his husband's pure joy.

Logan followed after him, caught in a dream. His feet glided across the ground, bobbing along in the wake of Pie's happy enthusiasm. He didn't want to even blink, in case it was all a dream.

Pie paused at the cottage door, his hand on Logan's wrist. 'What about furniture? A bed?'

Logan shrugged. 'I'm not sure. I don't think there is one.'

'Not to worry.' Pie took off his cloak. 'We'll improvise.'

Chapter Twenty-Six

The portal opened in the city graveyard. Logan, the countess and Ophelia stepped out. On the other side, Gary, Seraphina and Pie remained. They'd head to the cliffs and signal the *Avenging Arrow* when she came into view. Logan raised a hand to Pie, who was still visible through the shimmering gateway. Pie gave him a shaky smile in return. He couldn't bring himself to say anything else. They'd said their goodbyes, their I love yous, and anything else would have to wait.

The portal winked out of existence.

'Let's get down to business,' the countess said. While others had been saying their goodbyes, making their peace, she'd been working on her appearance. Her hair had returned to its familiar gravestone style, and bits of animal bone decorated it. Her lips had been smeared with a vivid rouge, and her eyelids darkened. She bit her thumb and pushed back her sleeves, daubing symbols across her arms and face.

'Now,' she said, turning to Logan with a wicked smile. 'Let's scare some folks!'

She held up her hands. The ground beneath Logan's feet vibrated, softly at first, then more violently. It shook so hard Logan had to throw out his arms to steady himself.

'Come forth, skulls and bones!' the countess called into the night.

A stone marker rocked, then fell, shattering loudly. Startled yelps came from several nearby houses.

'Rise up and remember your shape!'

The ground next to her cracked open and more yells sounded across the night. Suddenly, a skeletal hand emerged.

Then another, and another. All Logan could see was bone, rising, heaving itself from its resting place. Slender finger bones, curved ribcages, gleaming skulls grinning and shaking the dirt from their bones.

Despite his best efforts, Logan's heart pounded in his chest, his throat dry. This was different to the one or two skeletons who normally accompanied the countess. It was easier to dismiss the threat when they wore a straw hat or worked a comb through their mistress's hair. Now, he felt them watching him through their empty sockets. Did they begrudge his life? Did they covet it?

'Go!' the countess cried, her voice piercing his thoughts. 'Go. Knock on every door, drag everyone from their beds. Send them from the city and out into the night!'

The skeletons turned in unison, sending the hairs racing up the back of Logan's neck. They marched from the graveyard, dragging their shrouds with them. Tall, small, some with flesh still clinging, others missing bones or even whole limbs. Logan's stomach turned when he spotted the small shapes crawling through the grass behind the masses.

'That's the first lot,' the countess announced. 'Let's head down to the gods-square and the catacombs.'

The countess dropped some teeth on the ground, and the two bone steeds sprung up. 'For old time's sake?'

Logan nodded. He gave Bones a friendly scratch and pulled himself onto the horse's back. With no saddle, he sat directly on the vertebrae, his legs banging against the ribs. Incredibly uncomfortable, but appropriate for the moment.

'Onwards!' The countess raised a fist in the air and put her heels to her horse, Ophelia perched behind her. The beast leapt into a canter and Bones followed with no instruction from Logan. The sound of hooves echoed as they raced down the streets. They were wider than the streets of home or Krensten, overlooked by dark red houses, constructed of clay bricks. Logan couldn't stop himself associating that ruddy brown with blood.

The skeletons had been noticed now. Cries, shouts and screams punctured the night. The sounds penetrated Logan's heart and soul. He wished there'd been a more humane way to convince people, but being dragged from their beds by a skeleton was better than being consumed by Adphega.

A shutter opened from one of the buildings ahead and a man in a nightshirt peered out. Ophelia rose from her position behind the countess and stood in front of the man. He rubbed his eyes and the colour drained from his face as she remained, suspended in the air.

'The night belongs to the dead!' Ophelia threw back her head and laughed. The sound chilled Logan to his bones. Ophelia reached for the man in the window, her fingers growing longer, sharper. Her mouth opened, twisted and dark, the teeth elongating to become a row of knives. 'Leave the city or become one of us.'

The man in the window slammed the shutter shut so hard one of the hinges buckled.

'She enjoyed that,' Logan muttered to himself. 'A little too much.'

The bone steeds clattered into the gods-square. Much smaller than the one in Krensten, the shrines here were made of the same deep red stone as the houses. Torchlight glistened off iron symbols. The countess dismounted in front of the stones that marked the catacombs, engraved with bones, and the Dark Mother's house of worship. Only those with wealth were buried in cemeteries. For everyone else, the Mother's attendants would store the bodies of the dead down here without price or question.

The countess dropped to her knees.

'Lend me your strength and your cold children, Mother,' she said to the night. 'All things are yours, in time, and I beg for a little more of that time for the people of this city.'

A breath of air, cold but soft, whispered past Logan, caressing his cheek.

The countess stood, a smile on her face. She clapped her hands over her head, and the sound was like a thunderbolt.

Bones the horse stumbled as the ground trembled, then shook. Skeletons spewed from the mouth of the temple, a rush of bones clicking and rattling into the night.

'Hey,' a voice called. The word died in the speaker's mouth as two guards ran into the square. They took in the sight, eyes wide with horror. Logan reached for his axe, but before he could warn them off, Ophelia rushed the smaller one and disappeared into his body.

'Dan?' the other guard said slowly. He took a step back.

The smaller guard turned on his colleague. In the blink of an eye, he'd drawn his sword and held it at the other's neck.

'Leave,' he hissed. 'The city belongs to the dead now.'

The other guard swallowed. 'Dan? It's me. What's wrong with you?'

Ophelia's face protruded from the guard's own head. 'You're not welcome here.' She dropped the sword as the man let out a strangled scream. Then she grabbed the top of his breastplate and slammed the smaller guard's head against his. The larger guard staggered backwards, blood streaming from his nose.

Ophelia, still half in and half out of the guard named Dan, roared with laughter. The other guard staggered back a couple of paces, then turned and ran from the square.

'Run!' Ophelia called. 'Run as fast as you can! But you'll never outpace death, little man. I'm coming for you!' She chased after him.

'Oh dear,' the countess said. 'You better get after her, Logan dear.'

'What's happening?' he asked.

'She's losing her grip.' The countess shook her head. 'I should have seen this coming, but I thought she was doing so well. The emotions of tonight are too much for her. She's feeding off it. If you don't talk her down, there will be no Ophelia left. Just a spirit of vengeance and punishment.'

'Shit.'

He dug his heels into Bones. The horse leapt forwards, almost throwing him. Logan wrapped his arms around the snaking vertebrae and hung on for dear life.

He caught up with Ophelia as she chased the guard down an alley. She'd shed the body of the other guard, leaving him quivering on the ground in a foetal position. Logan dismounted and knelt down at the man's side.

'You need to leave the city,' he said.

The man stared at him, his mouth working in a soundless scream.

'Go. And get as many other people out as you can.'

The man fled screaming down the street. Logan sighed. He'd tried; there wasn't much more he could do. He pushed down the alley towards Ophelia.

She towered over the other guard now. Her form seemed stretched – she was thinner, more translucent – but she'd grown to a height of around seven feet. Her hand reached for him, slashing through his leg. The man let out a cry and his leg crumpled beneath him. He fell to the ground, pulling his arms around the spot she'd injured.

'Ophelia!' Logan called.

Whether she didn't hear him or didn't care, he wasn't sure, but she didn't react. She reached down and grabbed the guard's wrist, hauling him to his feet. Where her fingers touched him, the flesh turned pink, then black. Logan's heart raced. She could touch now?

'Ophelia, let him go!'

This time, she did react. With a hiss, she threw the guard aside like a child discarding a toy. The man hit the wall and slumped to the ground, his eyes rolled back in their sockets, blood staining the cobbles beneath him. Ophelia rushed up the alley towards Logan. She moved like a serpent, headfirst, her body twisting behind her.

'We're just supposed to be scaring them,' he said softly, trying to keep the tremor out of his voice. 'Not hurting them.'

She leered at him, her face no longer human. Her eyes were narrow, glowing a sickly yellow. Her mouth was wide and filled with dagger-like teeth. She flicked out a hand, reaching for him. Logan threw himself out of the way as an icy breeze raced across his skin.

'Can touch now,' she hissed at him. 'Touch, grab, take, hurt.' The last word came out as a hungry sound.

'You're so close, Ophelia.' He tried to hold her gaze, to ignore the monstrous appearance and remember the woman underneath it. 'You're so close. Please don't give up now.'

'Give up?' She laughed, a grating sound that turned his insides to ice. 'This isn't giving up. This is power, Logan. Why should I be denied that? Why shouldn't I hunt them, hurt them, after what happened to me?'

Her voice rose, louder and higher, until he was forced to put his hands over his ears.

'Because that isn't what you want.' He pulled himself to his feet, forced himself to face her.

Her eyes narrowed to slits. 'You dare to tell me what I want?'

Logan shook his head. 'No. It's what you told me you wanted. You told me you wanted to be able to eat again, to pet a unicorn, to find the person who made you feel like you were home. You told me you wanted to live, Ophelia.'

She paused, her eyes fixed on him. 'You lie.'

'No, I don't. That's why you came all this way. That's why you stayed with us. Because you want to live. Because you deserve to live. It was taken from you, and you should take it back. But you can't do it like this. If you carry on like this, you'll lose everything you ever were, and then everything you – Ophelia – are will destroyed.'

She turned her head away. Another breath of frozen air wended through Logan's hair. 'You'd like that, wouldn't you?'

'Gods, no.' He shook his head. 'Ophelia, I want to show you my home. I want to have Pie cook you dinner. I want us to stay up late telling tales of the time we brought you back from the dead. I'd like to one day visit your own home, meet your partner, maybe even your children if you choose to have them. I'd like to be able to give you a proper hug.'

He held his breath, waiting for her response. Was she too far gone? Was this thing, twisted features and frostbite hands, all that was left of her? Or was there something in there to save?

She pulled away, her face contorted in to a scowl. 'I don't want to hug you. You smell like a bear. But . . .' She shrank down until she was her normal size. Her eyes still had a faint glow, but they'd lost the cruel hard look. 'I do want to hug a unicorn.'

The corner of Logan's mouth tugged up. 'They are beautiful, aren't they?'

She looked up at the sky. 'What I want is to feel the sun again. I'm so tired of being cold, Logan.'

He felt the longing in his heart. Logan held out a hand to her. 'Then let's make sure that happens. Don't lose yourself here.'

She stared at him, as if waiting for a trick, and then slowly held out her own hand until their fingertips brushed through each other. Cold, but not enough to trigger frostbite.

'Go wait with Pie,' he told her. 'We can handle clearing the city. You think about the first thing you want to do when you get a body.'

'It's still to punch you, Logan,' she said, but she smiled as she vanished.

Chapter Twenty-Seven

Logan and the band of skeletons pushed through the city. Banging on doors. Chasing anyone they found in the streets. Driving them away from the beach as best they could. Pockets of resistance sprang up, usually around the city guards, but the sheer numbers of dead were enough to overwhelm any brave soul. Plus there was something about facing down a skeleton that shredded most people's courage.

Logan hoped they weren't giving some future villain any strategy ideas.

Dawn stained the horizon and Logan turned to head to the beach. The skeletons carried on the way they'd been going. He assumed they'd do that as long as the countess told them to. He didn't want to risk missing the action.

A gate near the docks led directly out onto the sand. The guard tower was abandoned, the occupants either engaged with the skeletons or long since fled for the hills. Logan approached the gate and peered through the spyhole.

The breath caught in his throat.

Out on the sands, hundreds of figures gathered. Another boat pulled up on the beach, from a galleon out in the bay. It was much too big to be the *Avenging Arrow*. The figures on the beach were armed, but they didn't look to Logan's eyes like soldiers. They lacked the pose and discipline for military. Mercenaries, then? The shopkeep in Krensten had said the king was looking to recruit. But even then, something didn't sit right with the idea.

They'd been in a fight already, he noted. Blood stained the clothes of pretty much everyone he could see, and quite substantial amounts too. No one seemed injured, though. No bandages, no limping. They mostly came across as disinterested, features slack and unfocused.

Like Matty.

Gods . . . Logan put a hand to his mouth, his mind spinning. They weren't soldiers or mercenaries. They were the dead, the bodies he'd seen piled high in the town square at Mywin. It was the dead townsfolk.

He'd seen plenty of necromancy recently, but this felt different to what the countess did. The skeletons were creepy and unnatural, but it wasn't the same as looking at the face of someone you might have known, a friend or family member, and having to put them down because their body was now empty of their soul.

At the water's edge, he spotted the king, flanked by the Black Company.

Hooves on the road announced the countess's arrival.

'How does it look out there?' she asked.

'Not good,' he admitted. The king had an army of dead bodies, and his mercenaries. Logan had a necromancer. A unicorn trainer. A few spellcasters. A ghost. And Pie.

That would have to do.

'Logan?'

He turned in surprise to see Adella walking towards him.

'What are you doing here?'

'Told Captain Williams I wasn't sitting in a cell as the world ended. She could kill me or set me free. She told me to seek you out, and that my fate would be your choice.'

'I could make you an offer,' Logan said. 'As you said, the world is probably going to end.'

Adella raised an eyebrow and folded her arms. 'So, what's the deal?'

'You help me, we defeat this thing, and then the Black Company is disbanded and you're free to do whatever else you want to do with your life.'

She scowled. 'No deal.'

'Your choice, but Captain Williams will almost certainly hang you if we somehow make it out of this alive. Things won't go back to the way they were. If I can put in a good word for you, it might help your survival chances.'

Her eyes narrowed. 'Fine,' Adella said suddenly. 'I'll do it. I can't speak for the rest of the company. I can't stop them if they want to carry on. But – if I don't end up eaten – I'll retire.'

Logan nodded. He had no reason to trust her. But at the same time, he didn't think he could doubt her, either. She stood, hands clenched at her sides, her expression defiant. If she made the wrong move, Logan wouldn't hesitate to put her down, but there were enough actual enemies out there without throwing her on the pile.

'What's going on out there?' she asked. 'Where's Ervin?'

'He raised the dead townsfolk from Mywin. We'll have to get through them, and your old friends.'

The countess pushed him out of the way to get a better look, then glanced over her shoulder at Adella. 'Where do your loyalties lie? If we step out there, will you go straight back to your friends?'

Adella met her gaze calmly. 'I won't fight them. But I won't help them either. I'm doing this for Ervin, and the thing he needs most is to be free from this thing's control.'

The countess went back to glowering through the spyhole with a look of utter distaste on her face.

'Not used to facing another necromancer?' Logan asked.

The countess's expression darkened further. 'We thought Ervin was a necromancer but we were wrong. That's magic. He's controlling those bodies with life magic.'

'I didn't think life magic worked on living things like that?' Adella asked. 'That's why you can't use magic to heal wounds.'

'It doesn't.' The countess smacked a fist into her palm. 'That's why Ervin had to kill them first. Life magic is limited by the wielder's own strength. If whatever's out there is controlling that many bodies, it's incredibly powerful.'

Logan mounted up again. 'Get ready. We'll try and put a stop to this before he can do what he needs to do. Push through. Get to the king.'

'Don't kill him,' Adella begged.

'I hope it won't come to that,' Logan said, but he wasn't sure they had any other options.

'I wonder,' the countess said thoughtfully. She stared at the gate, as if trying to see through it. 'Never mind. It doesn't matter now.'

The skeletons pooled around them, called forward by the countess. They filled the streets. Logan hoped it would be enough. He raised his eyes to the cliffs on the far side where the spellcasters would be waiting and Pie would be watching.

I love you.

'Open the gate,' he ordered.

Bones pawed at the ground as Adella moved to open the city gate. The creature could feel the tension in the air. If it had still had ears, they would have been laid back against its head. He patted its neck gently. One last fight.

The gate swung open, and Logan and the countess put their heels to their horses. They surged forwards, hooves kicking up a spray of sand. The dead rushed behind them, clicking and clattering as if they spoke some old language.

Perhaps they did.

The Mywin townsfolk didn't react, but Ervin and the living guards did. Then the king raised his hand and the dead surged forward like pieces on a chessboard. Ervin pointed and they turned and began shambling towards the incoming skeletal hoard. Then he turned back to the sea.

'Logan, go after the king!' the countess called. 'We've got this, haven't we, darlings?'

Logan turned Bones, driving around the lumbering pack of animated flesh, and headed up the beach towards the king. He had no fight with the dead of Mywin, and slashing at those who might have been Seraphina's family and friends felt wrong. A few rogue corpses stumbled after him, but they had no chance of catching the bone steed.

Ervin stopped a few feet into the sea, the waves lapping around his ankles, drenching the bottom of his robe. He held the Chalice out in front of him. As Logan approached, mud-coloured ooze dripped from the Chalice. It rolled across the sand, a few feet from the waves and uncoiled itself. The oozing mass stood up and took the form of a human, but only in as much as a bad drawing in the mud might appear human. It had two legs, two arms, a head, skin the colour of terracotta. But that was where the similarities ended. There was no hair, no genitals, no ears. No face at all, just a blank oval that nevertheless stared into Logan's soul. Logan rode on harder.

As he got closer, the guards moved into formation around the king, swords held aloft. Logan drew his axe, urging Bones on. More of the oozing things emerged from the Chalice. They all stood up and started to walk into the sea until the water covered their heads.

'I hope they don't hurt you,' Logan muttered as the horse closed the distance. He swung his axe.

One of the guards threw himself out of Logan's path and another struck Bones with his sword, catching it in the steed's scapula so it was ripped out of his hands. Logan urged Bones to a stop on the far side of the group and dismounted.

He put a hand on Bones's shoulder. 'Off you go.' He tried to push the creature away, but Bones snorted and pawed at the ground.

Logan grinned. 'I guess it's you and me, then.'

He kept his eyes on the king as the guards continued to attack. Logan was heavily outnumbered, and the Black

Company had broken away from the dead and were heading towards them too. If he could just get close enough to the king, get the Chalice out of his hands . . .

He caught a motion out of the corner of his eye, but it was too late; the sword scraped across his ribs, opening a chasm of burning pain across his chest. Logan drove the axe back, driving the handle into his attacker's solar plexus. The man stumbled back with a grunt, but another took his place.

Logan stepped back, parrying hard against two guards. His lungs heaved, sweat running down his face from the exertion. The clash of steel against steel rang heavy in his ears. The sand shifted under his feet and he lost his balance, slipping down to one knee. Behind him, the countess cackled and bone smacked against flesh. Another blow bounced off his shoulder, narrowly missing his neck. Through vision blurred by perspiration, he watched the figures closing in.

A flash of light made Logan duck and close his eyes. When he opened them again, the guard in front of him had dropped, a smouldering crater in his chest. Several more flaming missiles whistled over his head, striking down more of the king's guards.

Logan rubbed his eyes and looked over his shoulder.

The spellcasters had made their way onto the beach. They stood in a line near the cliff, and the sight set off an explosion of delight in his chest. *Fuck yeah, we have this now!* One spellcaster was levitating a rock, while another launched a flurry of fireballs and a third sent the fiery boulder flying across the sand.

Logan pulled himself to his feet. His body ached all over, from exertion as much as injury, but with friends and allies at his back, he had a second wind.

Logan ran across the beach toward the shore, throwing himself hard at Ervin. They tumbled across the sand, rolling over and over. A wave hit Logan's back, and he gasped as the cold water ran down his neck.

'You're too late!' Ervin grinned maniacally. It was the same grin as the skeletons. All teeth and no humour. He seemed to stare through Logan, as if barely seeing him. 'I'll be free soon. There's nothing you can do to stop me, *Bear*!'

'We'll see about that, won't we?' Logan drove his elbow into the king's face and Ervin crumbled. Logan wrestled the Chalice out of his hands.

It was shaped nothing like a cup, more like a horn. Three segments, small as a fist at one end, large as his head at the other. It was coloured a greyish green, like decaying flesh. Veins pulsed along its surface, oozing purple fluid onto the sands.

Logan pulled out Morigen's knife and drove the blade through the Chalice. It parted with a fleshy squelch that churned his stomach. The larger end convulsed, as if trying to vomit up another of the hideous fleshy things, then lay still. He glared at it, daring it to move.

'I killed it,' Logan said breathlessly to the air. 'That wasn't so hard.'

Logan turned to the king, but he was staring out across the waves. It took a moment for Logan to realise what he was looking at.

The sea was boiling.

Chapter Twenty-Eight

The sea bubbled and churned, slate-grey water turning white in a vast circle. And it was heading to shore.

Logan staggered back a step, then another. Every instinct in his body screamed at him to run, run and never look back. But he couldn't take his eyes off that patch as it drifted closer. His mind whirled, desperately ploughing through years of experience to find something useful to face whatever it was.

He had nothing.

On the sand next to him, the king had gone limp. His eyes stared blankly at the sea.

'What have you done?' Adella exclaimed, rushing to Ervin. She pulled him into her arms, dragging him away from the waves.

'We need to pull back. It's coming,' Logan muttered. He'd focused on the wrong target. He'd been so intent on the Chalice, he hadn't realised its true purpose. Those things it had spawned had crawled into the sea and it was them who had released Adphega. 'Something's coming.'

She shot him a glare, but Logan let it pass. If she wanted to waste her energy getting mad at him, that was her business. He glanced around the beach. The spellcasters had seen the change in the sea, judging from the pointing that was going on. Further down, the skeletons were still battling the people of Mywin, and it was hard to see who was winning. Bodies and bones covered the sand.

'Countess!' he yelled. 'Get ready!'

She raised a hand in acknowledgement.

At the far end of the beach, the air shimmered and a herd of unicorns stepped out. The sight sent a ripple of hope though Logan. A small one, admittedly, but it was there in his heart.

It rose out of the sea.

At first, it was just a black mass, curved and glistening from the water. Waves struck its side, sending plumes of obscuring mist into the wind. Logan's stomach dropped. It was massive. Big as a house, at least. Instincts took control and he backed away, stumbling over the sand.

More of the creature was visible now, and it reminded him of a dung beetle, though one horrifyingly immense. The black mass appeared to be a carapace, and the thought of an insect that could scuttle over buildings sent ice racing through his veins. The water surged and a huge black head emerged. Six glittering eyes, round and faceted like jewels. Vast mandibles clacked absently.

It didn't see him. Or didn't care about him.

At the sight of the unicorns, it let out an earthly screech. Its legs, curved and pointed like daggers, sank into the sand. Logan threw himself out of the way as one almost pierced his leg. He screamed as it raked down his flesh.

He rolled to his feet and whistled for Bones, who cantered over to him. Logan pulled himself onto the horse's back.

'Hey!' Logan yelled as he set off after the creature. 'Hey! It's me you want!'

Bones ran alongside the thing. It moved ponderously on the sand, but its size meant that didn't matter. It still ate up the ground as it headed towards the unicorns. Logan forced himself to stand, wobbling precariously, on Bones's back. He leapt, reaching for the black carapace. For a moment, he was falling, the sand rushing up to meet him, then his fingers hooked around hard chitin and he hung from the beast's shell.

Muscles straining, shoulders burning, he pulled himself onto the thing's back. Up here, it wasn't black, but myriad swirling colours, twisting in and out of each other in a mesmerising pattern. Stars of white and blue appeared, swelled, blossomed into patches of red and gold, then dwindled back down to darkness.

A fireball struck and the beast rocked, breaking him from his reverie. Logan threw out his arms to keep his balance. The beast stopped, swinging wildly from side to side. It started for the unicorns again, then stopped and turned towards the spellcasters on the far side of the beach. Logan glanced towards Gary.

A huge circle hung in front of the unicorns, a swirling vortex of purples and blacks.

The portal was open.

'Oh no, you don't,' Logan said. 'You're going this way now.'

He brought his axe down hard on the carapace. The blade barely scratched the thing, bouncing back and almost catching him in the leg.

Well, fuck.

He raced across its back and leapt onto its head.

'I'm not going to let you eat my husband!' Logan yelled as he smashed the axe down, fear and rage behind every blow. The axe's blade caught one of the glittering, faceted eyes, which erupted in a sickly green ichor. The thing skidded to a halt.

Got your attention now, don't I?

The thing stood stock-still, and Logan waited, his heart in his chest.

Then it shook its whole body. Logan planted his feet, pushing down, but it wasn't enough. The thrashing head sent him sprawling onto the sand, the axe flying from his hands. He rolled over, sand blinding him. The thing squealed, and Logan threw himself aside as a pointed foot came down where he had been lying. Again and again the thing tried to skewer him.

Logan panted, half blind, every inch of his body aching from the fall. A glint of metal caught his attention. His axe. If he was going to die, it wasn't going to be empty-handed, at least. He lunged for it, twisting to avoid another attack, and wrapped his hands around the axe. The cool weight of the weapon comforted him.

As the leg came down again, Logan swung, striking and sending a chunk of the creature spinning away. The beast screeched and rolled away from him. Logan pulled himself to his feet. 'And there's more where that came from!'

The beast lumbered momentarily away from him. The colours on its carapace brightened and swirled faster.

'I said, it's me you want!' He waved his arms.

Its head turned towards him.

'That's right. Me. I put out your eye. Let me put out the rest of them for you, too!'

Logan almost didn't see it until it struck. It caught him in the shoulder, piercing deep into the muscle. He let out a cry as sharpened chitin dug into his flesh. The creature pulled him into the air, holding him as blood flowed down his chest.

Logan's vision blurred, but not enough to obscure the sight of the mandibles opening before him. He struggled weakly, but the motion only succeeded in tearing his own muscles. The grotesque insectoid's face closed in, filling his vision. He fumbled, reaching for something, anything, he could use to save himself. His hand clutched at Morigen's knife.

The throw was clumsy, missing most of the eye, embedding itself in the bottom. A flash of violet light flared up from the wound and the beast reared. It flung him aside, cast him off like a child discards a toy. Logan hit the ground hard, slamming into a rock that jutted out of the beach with a loud crack.

Probably my ribs.

He lay back, black spots clouding his vision. His shoulder had gone numb, while his chest burned with a bright pain. He clung to the feeling as if it were a raft in a stormy sea. Pain meant he was alive. As long as he held onto that agony, he was still alive.

His eyelids drooped.

Was it enough? Had he done his bit? There were still the spellcasters, and the remains of the skeleton army. The countess was cunning. He couldn't see her losing to a bug. Perhaps he'd done enough, and he could close his eyes for a few minutes.

Just a few minutes.

'*There is a man from down Strangers Hollow . . . and they call him a legend, a hero… and I'll tell you why . . .*'

The song cut through the darkness, brighter than pain. It filtered through his senses, rushing through his body, lifting his heart.

Pie.

'*He's seven feet tall, hair like thunder . . . carries an axe that's twelve feet high…*'

The corner of his mouth twitched. *Seven feet? Bloody bards. Catchy tune, though.*

'*He's Logan, Logan the Bear!*'

Logan pulled himself to his feet as the beast turned its attention to Pie.

While it was occupied, Logan ran.

A drumming behind him competed with the song. He glanced over his shoulder and saw Bones racing towards him, Pie on its back. The horse skidded to a stop, and Logan pulled himself awkwardly onto its back with one hand, wrapping his arms around his husband.

'What are you doing here?' He pressed himself against Pie, drawing strength from his presence.

Pie didn't break song but reached across and tapped the knot tattoo on Logan's bicep. *You could have trusted me. We could have dealt with this together. That's what marriage means.*

Logan put his hand over Pie's fingers. 'Together, then.'

'You want me?' he yelled over his shoulder at the beast. 'Come and get me. I'm Logan the Legend, bitch!'

He put his heels to Bones, wind streaming though his hair, Pie's voice loud in his ears. The thing lumbered after them. Ahead, the unicorns stood in a semi-circle at the narrowest part of the beach. The portal, wider than any he'd seen before, large enough to swallow a beast. Logan caught sight of Gary and Seraphina holding each other at Freddy's side.

Maybe Pie had been onto something after all.

The thing was still coming.

'Come on! Take a swing at me. I hurt you. You want to hurt me back, right?' In the background, Pie's voice faltered slightly, and Logan felt the missed note in his heart. *Just believe in me a bit longer, then we can go home.* It was so close now Logan could see the oozing remains of its eye.

Logan backed towards the portal, taunting it. He had to piss it off more. He'd had a lifetime of pissing people off, surely he could manage to annoy this thing?

He made a dive for one of the legs and pulled himself up the segmented joint. The black chitin was hard and smooth beneath his fingers, and his injured shoulder meant one arm was largely useless. But Logan clung on with three limbs and four decades of stubbornness.

The creature rocked, threatening to shake him off. At first, he thought the action was a deliberate attempt to dislodge him, but the thing spasmed again and this time he heard the crunch of rock. Logan gritted his teeth and pulled himself up, until he could clamber back on the carapace.

Behind the creature, the spellcasters had split into three groups. Two flanked the creature, throwing rocks and fire at it. The third group, behind, were working the seawater the way they had when the *Avenging Arrow* rescued them in the Bay of Sighs. A wall of water knocked into the creature's rear, and it fell forwards. The remains of the countess's skeletal army raced forwards, grabbing, pushing, pulling whatever they could to move the thing towards the portal.

The creature screeched and shook, but it was losing ground. Gary called out to the unicorns as they paced forwards, pushing the portal with them. Logan crawled across the carapace as the thing was dragged towards its doom. His arm was drenched in blood, his fingers cold and numb. But Pie's voice sustained him.

He made it to the thing's head as it dug its legs in at the edge of the portal.

'You've lost. Give up.' He reached down for the knife. Around him, the spellcasters joined in with the chorus, splashing his name around the beach. Pie was right: he hated it. A grin broke out on his battered face.

Logan grabbed the knife and stood up. *Time to go.*

He moved to jump down as the creature tottered at the edge of the portal. One more jump. One more push. He shoved the knife in to his belt and leapt.

The creature twisted its head.

Mandibles wrapped around his legs.

It gave one last scream, and toppled into the portal, dragging Logan with it.

Chapter Twenty-Nine

Logan floated.

Unlike the unicorn farm, this place had nothing physical, no grass, no sky. No up or down. The air was purplish, like a bruise, fading to black and then brightening to a sickly yellow colour. The beast floated nearby, legs spasming, mandibles clacking. It was dying here, and it knew it.

Logan knew it too.

His body grew cold, and he could barely feel his fingers or toes. His heartbeat slowed, his breathing shallow. He wasn't afraid, though. The pain faded too here, and the growing darkness embraced him. He thought he could smell the scents of his childhood – wild garlic, mud, woodsmoke. His mother's musky odour as she chopped wood behind the house.

It wasn't right.

He knew that. He knew he was giving up on so much on the other side of the portal. But he couldn't fight this.

Death wasn't a monster. Death was an embrace.

Logan closed his eyes.

Something bit his hand.

He looked down to see a skull gripping his hand with its teeth. Slowly, he turned his head and saw a chain of bones stretching back toward the portal of shimmering light.

Something scurried along the bone chain. A hand, walking like a crab on its fingers. It waved at him. Logan waved back, dazed. The skull's grip on his fingers tightened and the bone chain constricted, pulling him towards the light. Logan didn't fight it as he was pulled along. He was too exhausted to fight anymore.

With a hard thud, he was dropped unceremoniously onto the sand, the sun blinding him. Someone dropped down next to him, blocking out the harsh light. Logan reached up to caress the face.

'Pie.'

'You stupid fucking idiot!' Pie yelled, spilling tears over Logan's face. 'That wasn't the plan! That wasn't ever the plan.' The last word was swallowed up in a sob and he threw himself at Logan.

'Makes for a good story, though, right?' Logan grinned. Gods, even that hurt.

'Come on, Al darling, your husband needs a bit of patching up. Don't get in the way now.'

Pie's weight shifted off him, and other hands touched him, calling for supplies. Logan looked up at the countess.

'We did it.' His voice came out even rougher than normal, as if he'd been gargling with the sand.

'Never had any doubts.' She pulled Pie close to her, patting his back as he sobbed against her shoulder.

'Am I dying?' Logan asked quietly.

She shook her head. 'I shouldn't think so. Looks like just a flesh wound. Al darling's just being overdramatic.' She gave him a wink. 'Bards.'

'Bards.' Logan barked a laugh and immediately regretted it. 'Did everyone make it?'

'No,' Adella said. Her voice was cold as seawater, pain washing through it like waves.

Logan forced himself to sit up, earning glares from the pair of spellcasters who were trying to deal with his wounds. Adella approached, a body in her arms. She laid King Ervin reverently down on the sand.

'The king is dead.' She passed her hand over his face, closing his eyes.

'I suspect he died months ago,' the countess said softly. 'The man named Ervin never came back from falling off the ship. That thing was keeping his body going. A corpse moving through magic. Blasphemy, really. The dead belong to the Dark Mother. Well, the sudden loss of the monarch is going to cause all sorts of issues.'

Logan didn't care. Didn't give a damn about who ruled what, as long as he was free to take Pie and go home. There was something else to take care of, though.

'What about those things, from the Chalice?'

The countess shook her head. 'They melted away when the portal closed.'

'Dammit.' He clenched his fist. Hot tears burned at his eyes. 'Dammit.'

'It's all right, Logan.' Ophelia appeared in front of him. She gave him a sad smile. 'You tried. That's what matters to me. I forgive you, for everything.' She turned to the countess. 'I'd like to go now, please.'

'There must be something,' Logan said. It couldn't end like this. Ophelia deserved so much better. He couldn't take her forgiveness and give her failure. 'There must be something you can do.'

The countess stroked her chin. 'There is something. Perhaps. It's risky, and Ophelia may not want to go through with it for a number of reasons.' She eased herself free of Pie, who dropped down onto the sand next to Logan. Logan reached for his husband's hand, their fingers entwining.

'What?' Ophelia asked. The mixture of hope and fear on her face echoed in Logan's heart.

'A body dies when the spirit leaves it,' the countess explained. 'But spirit can sometimes be called back, for a body to live again. Perhaps it does not need to be the same spirit.' She pointed at the body of Ervin.

'Take over the king's body?' Ophelia's mouth dropped open.

'I won't allow it,' Adella hissed, rushing toward the countess.

The countess patted Adella's shoulder calmly. 'My dear, the man you knew and loved is dead. You can't change that.'

She glared at the countess. 'You can, though. You can pull *his* spirit back, like you did hers.'

'And drag him away from his loved ones? After he's been reunited again?' The countess shook her head. 'Grief crushed King Ervin's heart once. Twisted and turned him into a shell of who he was. He's found peace now. Would you pull him back from that? I didn't think you so selfish.'

'You can't know.' Adella brushed a hand through the king's hair.

'She does, though,' Logan replied, thinking of the little skeleton outside Krensten. 'And if Ophelia goes through with this, she's going to need help. Someone she can trust. Someone who can help her carry out the role and restore Ervin's legacy and the kingdom to what it once was. Someone to end the killing and the fear. You didn't fall in love with the man for that, did you?'

Adella shook her head. She wiped away her tears. 'No, I didn't.' She turned to Ophelia. 'You should do it. The kingdom needs you.'

The countess took a step towards Ophelia. 'It's got to be your choice. Living in a body that isn't yours, I can't imagine how hard that will be. But I believe you are strong enough, if you want it.'

'How long do I have to decide?' Ophelia asked.

'Not long. The longer we leave it, the more the body will start to decay, and then it won't be useable.'

Ophelia closed her eyes. Her lips moved slightly, maybe talking through her options to herself. Maybe praying.

'I'll . . . I'll do it.'

The countess smiled. 'Good. Right. Someone fetch me a stick, something to draw with.' Hurriedly, she busied herself making a circle on the sand around the king's body.

Logan turned his attention away. The bleeding in his shoulder had been stemmed, and someone else had strapped up his cracked ribs. He felt like shit, stepped-on shit, but he was alive.

Logan sat on the sand and let everyone else move around. He was too tired to move. Too afraid that anything he did would set off some other disaster. So, he sat and watched Ophelia. Slowly, she nodded at the countess, stepping into the body of King Ervin. For a moment, they all held their breath. Nothing happened.

Then, suddenly, Ervin jerked, and sat up. He opened eyes that were now green. Adella held out a hand and helped the king to stand. As Ophelia glanced around in her new form, heads bowed respectfully to their new monarch.

Ophelia swayed a little, stumbling here and there, but by the time they reached Logan, they managed a comfortable walk. A fist smacked Logan in the jaw.

'Huh. Not nearly as satisfying as I thought it would be. Well, take care, Logan the Bear.'

'You too . . . *Your Grace*.'

'I could get used to that.' Ophelia smiled.

'You'd better,' Adella said as the rest of the Black Company approached. 'And quickly.'

Ophelia nodded, and left Logan alone.

He hoped Ophelia would be happy now.

'We can go home now,' he said to Pie.

'I wouldn't recommend that just yet!' Gary called.

Logan looked up as Gary walked over. Seraphina held his hand and as they approached, she placed a kiss on his cheek. Logan swore, and Gary stopped, a hurt look on his face. 'What?'

'Two weeks of cleaning out the goats,' Logan muttered, and Pie laughed.

'See, I told you. Always trust a bard in matters of the heart.'

Logan rolled his eyes, then turned back to Gary. 'What do you mean, I shouldn't go home yet?'

Gary rubbed the back of his neck. 'It's a long way to your home, from what Al said, and you've been hurt pretty badly. Why not come and stay with me and Freddy for a while, until you're healed up?'

Logan looked up at Pie. 'What do you think?'

Pie gave him a grin. 'A few days' rest would do us both good, I think.'

'You just want to write songs about unicorns.'

'That too.'

'Sounds like a plan then, lad,' Logan said. He turned to the countess. 'I take it you won't be joining us.'

She shuddered. 'Of course not. Horrid place. I guess this is goodbye, then, Logan the Legend. I won't say it's been a pleasure, but it has definitely had its moments.'

Pie stood up and she wrapped him in a tight hug. 'Take care, Al darling. And promise me you'll bring your husband to dinner sometime.'

'Wouldn't miss it for the world,' he replied. He whispered something in her ear, and she grinned.

She mounted her bone steed and set off down the beach, Bones trotting along after her.

'Do you think she'll be all right?' Pie asked.

'I don't think there's a force in the world that could stop that woman,' Logan replied. 'Unless she wanted it to. What were you two whispering about?'

Pie grinned and tapped his nose. 'You'll find out.'

'Not sure I like that,' Logan muttered. 'Not sure I like that at all.'

Williams came ashore to meet Erin in person, and as she walked across the beach, she picked up the discarded axe.

'I think things will change for spellcasters now,' Logan said. He drew in Seraphina, Williams and Erin, and explained what had happened to Ophelia. 'I'm entrusting you with this knowledge. It cannot get out among the general population. If it got out that the king was no longer himself, it could put everything in jeopardy.'

'We'll keep her secret safe,' Williams replied. 'As long as she does right by us.'

'Spellcasters saved everyone from that thing. Pie will make sure that truth gets out. Ophelia can use it as an excuse to rescind the ban on magic.'

Pie nodded. 'They'll be singing it from every tavern.'

Williams sniffed and offered Logan the axe. 'Guess I won't be needing this, then.'

He met her eye. 'Are you sure?'

'Try not to drop it next time,' she said with a shrug. She took Erin's hand, and they walked back to the boat.

The rest of the day was for the dead. The countess had walked the skeletons back to their graves, and they'd tucked themselves back up in the ground, but the people of Mywin still lay where they'd fallen on the beach.

The people of Rekmin drifted back from hiding and out onto the sand to help. A sanitised version of events was passed around – King Ervin had been investigating the disappearance of the people of Mywin, as had Captain Williams's crew. They'd worked together to put down the creature that had committed the atrocity.

Seraphina did her best to identify each body, and their names were noted down in a book before the body was wrapped up in a shroud. Gary held her hand the entire time, and Logan was glad she wasn't doing it alone, as the task was clearly taking a toll on her.

She stopped at the body of a man. 'Oh, I don't know this one.'

'I do.' Pie knelt down and brushed a hand over the face, closing eyes that matched his own. 'His name is Matteo Montague.'

Logan put a hand on his husband's shoulder. 'I'm sorry, Pie.'

Pie stared at the body a moment longer, then stood up and rested his head against Logan's shoulder. 'It's fine. Honestly. I grieved for Matty already. That's not him.' But the hitch in his voice said otherwise.

A large grave was dug by the spellcasters on the cliffs. Ophelia in Ervin's body declared a monument would be erected to honour the people who had been sacrificed by evil, so their story would not be forgotten. The king gave a simple eulogy, commending the dead to their chosen gods.

Ophelia was settling naturally into the role already.

As the bodies were gently laid in their final resting place, Pie sang. His voice clear and strong, even as the tears streaked down his cheeks. He sang of loss and longing, of grief and love, of the passing of something beautiful, lost forever from the world. Of long-gone unicorns.

Logan hated that song.

The portal opened, and Logan's heart leapt at the sight of their cottage ahead. He turned back and put his hand on Gary's shoulder.

'Thanks, lad. Don't be a stranger, you hear? You come and visit us, any time you like.'

Pie threw his arms around the young man. 'We mean it. Especially keep us updated on matters of the heart.' He jerked his head towards Seraphina, who was grooming one of the unicorns a little way away.

Gary blushed vividly, and Logan extracted his husband. Staying at the farm had been a great idea, and he felt refreshed and revitalised. He still sported the sling on his arm, but a few days of sitting around in the warm sunshine and then a few steps through the portal was a far better option than making the journey back on foot.

He stepped through and paused. Something was wrong.

Without waiting for Pie, he hurried down the path towards the pigpen. The gate was open, the pen empty. Logan put a hand on the wall.

'Oh, Bacon!'

'I guess someone spotted we weren't at home and decided to help themselves,' Pie said. The front door to the cottage hung half on its hinges where someone had kicked it in.

Logan swore. 'When I catch whoever it was . . .'

Pie shook his head. 'It doesn't matter, love. We can replace everything. We'll start again; we'll get another pig.'

Logan hung his head sadly, gazing at the empty pen. 'Not the same.'

'We were never going to actually eat him, were we?' Pie asked with a laugh. He put a hand on Logan's chest. 'Home's here, love. It's you and me.'

He wandered down the path and let out a shout. Logan lifted his head slowly. Pie emerged, leading one of the goats by the horn.

'Was this one Bastard, or Other Bastard?' he called.

Logan sighed. Of course, out of everything, it was a goat that had survived.

'There's something else for you down there.' Pie grinned and pushed him down the path. Logan rolled his eyes but didn't resist. He turned the corner to the goat shed and let out a laugh at the sight.

'Bones!'

The skeletal horse regarded him with empty eye sockets, then stepped forward and rubbed its skull against his arm. Tucked between a couple of vertebrae was a piece of paper. Logan broke the ling's seal, and the word CHARTER was written across it in large black letters.

'I told the countess how fond you were of that horse,' Pie said. 'We arranged to have him sent to you, along with an official note permitting you to keep him, on certain grounds of course . . .'

Logan read further along, his eyes scanning the parchment. 'I'm to be officially named Logan the Legend and knighted as a hero of the kingdom. I never asked for any of this, Pie.'

'No one ever asks to be a hero, love. They don't name themselves. They rise up.' He kissed Logan's cheek. 'And no one ever rose up quite like you.'

Bones pushed its head against Logan's arm. He grinned and gave the skull a scratch. 'Thank you.'

Pie pushed the goat into the stall and closed the gate. He held out a hand to Logan. 'Come on, let's go in. We can start the rebuild tomorrow.'

Logan nodded and took his hand. 'We'll have plenty of time. I don't plan on going further than the inn for a long time.'

'Sounds good to me. Just you and me.' He paused in the doorway and kissed Logan. 'I love you.'

'I love you, too.' Logan kissed him back and pushed his husband inside.

Home. They were finally home.

THE END

Acknowledgements:

I'm so thankful to so many people who have stuck by me during the creation of this book. My wonderful partner and son, thank you for putting up with all the stress and drama of writing, then publishing a book. I'm sorry and it will happen again.

My beloved PitSquirrels – Beck, Liv, Janet, Amelia, Kim, Ariana, Noreen – who were there from the start when this was just a fun distraction from Pitchwars.

My amazing CP, LM Sagas, and my beta readers Erin and Miranda, thank you for helping to shape the book into something cohesive. Maria Tureaud, who gave me so much help with the query and opening, and Simeon from Rogue Mentors, who helped with advice on querying. Erin Fulmer for coming up with that title.

Cass, Pie's biggest fan and a massive support on this journey. I'm so happy we're travelling together.

My incredible agent Becca Podos, who was the first person in publishing to believe in *Bard* and has always had my back at every stage. My wonderful editor, Tash Qureshi who took the manuscript and made it great with her vision. The talented cover artist Mia Carnevale and designer Lydia Blagden who put together the absolutely beautiful cover.

And my online friends who have been an absolute rock for me in the emotional roller coaster of publishing – Liana, Bethany, CJ, Kal, Ollie, Miriam, Birdie, Chloe, Dominique and Aubrey. I love you all so much.

And finally, Tab's friend, who did nothing at all.

Acknowledgements

WANT MORE?

If you enjoyed this and would like to find out about similar books we publish, we'd love you to join our online Sci-Fi, Fantasy and Horror community, Hodderscape.

Visit hodderscape.co.uk for exclusive content from our authors, news, competitions and general musings, and feel free to comment, contribute or just keep an eye on what we are up to.

See you there!

@HODDERSCAPE HODDERSCAPE.CO.UK